LOST LOVE SONGS

Ingrid Persaud's debut novel, *Love After Love*, won the Costa First Novel award, the Author's Club First Book Award and the Indie Book Award for Fiction. Other prizes include the BBC National Short Story Award and the Commonwealth Short Story Prize. She was born in Trinidad and lives in London.

Further praise for *Lost Love Songs*:

'The women's relationships with Boysie make for a fascinating story, and Persaud creates a memorable supporting cast of characters who drink, gossip and betray one another . . . Persaud's characters linger long after the final pages of this epic, sometimes harrowing, tale.' *Observer*

'Doris, Mana Lala, Popo and Rosie . . . we will never forget them; women who in trying and ultimately failing to shape the man end up shaping themselves.' Marlon James

'Persaud writes in an Indian Trinidadian vernacular that feels sharp, vivid and true, and the story alternates between the women, each adding a new piece to the emerging picture . . . the women Persaud gives voice to tell a compelling story.' Shahidha Bari, *Guardian*, 'Book of the Day'

'One of the chief delights [. . .] is the Trinidad dialect of the characters: its rhythms and musicality [. . .] A strong sense of place and social dynamics are a forte of the novel.' *Irish Times*

'The merry-go-round narrative generates genuine shock while making us question how far we're ever the main characters of our lives.' *Mail on Sunday*

'What we are seeing here is a talented writer getting into her stride. Like *Love After Love*, her voices are credible; their language is right and you can hear their lyricism in your head as you read.' *Trinidad Guardian*

---

by the same author
LOVE AFTER LOVE

LOST LOVE SONGS

INGRID PERSAUD

faber

First published in 2024
by Faber & Faber Limited
The Bindery, 51 Hatton Garden
London EC1N 8HN

This paperback edition published in 2025

Typeset by Sam Matthews
Printed and bound by CPI Group (UK) Ltd, Croydon, CR0 4YY

A CIP record for this book
is available from the British Library

ISBN 978-0-571-38651-2

Printed and bound in the UK on FSC® certified paper in line with our continuing
commitment to ethical business practices, sustainability and the environment.
For further information see faber.co.uk/environmental-policy

Our authorised representative in the EU for product safety is
Easy Access System Europe, Mustamäe tee 50, 10621 Tallinn, Estonia
gpsr.requests@easproject.com

2 4 6 8 10 9 7 5 3 1

For my parents,
Lucy and John Steward

PART ONE

THE TRINIDAD MONITOR

PORT OF SPAIN, TRINIDAD, B.W.I.
FRIDAY, 23 AUGUST 1957

The End of Boysie
By Gerrard Max Davidson
Staff Reporter

KNOWING THE END was coming, John Boysie Singh (the Rajah), who once controlled illegal activities in Port of Spain and in the Gulf of Paria, said, 'I have lived. I have seen things and I have done things. Now I must go, but I am innocent of this crime. I always tried to help people and that is how I got a great deal of my troubles. That is what has me here now.'

He asked to go first but on 20 August 1957 was made to wait an hour until eight o'clock after Boland Ramkissoon's body was cut down and laid aside. A Catholic priest, Father Tiernan, who asked for his name not to be reported, walked him to the gallows. Wearing prison-issue white cotton pyjamas, the Rajah met death chanting, 'My Jesus mercy, my Jesus mercy, my Jesus mercy.' As prescribed, the hangman was paid $77 per man for his duties.

A Gregorio Brothers van took the body from the gaol to the General Hospital and then to the St James cemetery where Boysie was laid to rest in a crude, white pine, unpainted coffin, his name written on top in chalk. None of his close relatives, seen visiting the condemned man in the days leading up to the hanging, were present at the graveside.

3

ROSIE

While the shop ain't busy I told myself, Rosie girl, drink a cup of coffee-tea and check the papers. Nobody's coming for a shot of rum this hour and on the dry goods side it's always one-one person throughout the day. Aye, aye, I ain't sit down good when I spotted the wretch. Man dead and he's still making front page. And look at that. Boysie playing innocent down to the end. Exactly who that badjohn think he fooling? At least now he's in the ground we might get an ease from seeing him all the time. Something else will take over the news. Every night the Lord's seen me on my knees begging that boy doesn't fill the gap he's left. They say goat don't make sheep. Well, this is one time I hope they're wrong, yes.

A sudden hard rain made me put down the papers. Two schoolchildren, a girl about seven and a boy child a little younger, rushed to shelter under the shop awning. The way she held on to the boy I could tell she was a good big sister. I called to them.

Come inside and don't get wet. You see how the sun still shining? Rain go pass now for now.

They came and stood by the door. I smiled.

Come in. Come in. I don't bite.

The girl pulled her brother where they were safe from the pelting rain.

You know that when sun shining and rain falling, monkey does be marrying. Either that or the devil and he wife fighting.

Poor children looked at me like I was about to gobble them up.

A good five minutes hadn't passed and rain stopped just so. The two bolted. I watched them speed off, holding hands tight tight. Steam rose from the hot pitch, releasing a sickly sweet smell that made me feel slightly nauseous. Then something happened. Maybe it was the pitch smell or the little boy and girl holding hands or just reading the death notice. Could be all three. Suddenly I realised what had been bothering my head. I was thinking of Boysie.

What's that game children play? The one with two circles holding hands and singing in turns. Oh, yes,

> *In a fine castle,*
> *Do you hear, my sissie-o?*
> *In a fine castle,*
> *Do you hear, my sissie-o?*

Without missing a beat, the second circle would reply.

> *Ours is the prettiest,*
> *Do you hear, my sissie-o?*
> *Ours is the prettiest,*
> *Do you hear, my sissie-o?*

What song did we throw back? Ah yes,

> *We want one of them,*
> *Do you hear, my sissie-o?*
> *We want one of them,*
> *Do you hear, my sissie-o?*

From the side, under a laden guava tree, a boy, had to be less than ten, was watching us playing in the road. Our eyes made four. Without words he knew that we coolie orphans, holding hands while singing louder and louder, had room for other unclaimed children.

Which of us do you want?
Do you hear, my sissie-o?

I broke hands mid-song so he could join my circle. He came forward slowly and gave me his hand. That little hand squeezed mine just a bit tighter than the others. I squeezed back.

Which of us do you want?
Do you hear, my sissie-o?

A scared boy, out on the road by he-self, nobody looking to see what he was doing, that barefoot, raggedy child grew into John Boysie Singh, the Rajah. How that happened?

POPO

I raised my head and my sleepy gaze followed the line of interlocking black hairs that trailed up his belly.

Boysie, you hear somebody outside?

He sucked his teeth in a long steupse.

No.

You think Dave reach back?

Less the talking, nah. He's in some carnival fete, two drink in he head. It's Ash Wednesday before you seeing that ugly face.

While he's there talking he flipped me over and sat on my face. Shoved his laar straight down my gullet.

This will shut you up.

I stopped breathing just in time. He kept ramming until I gagged. Put a shilling on my mattress and all man come the same way. So long as they don't rough me up where it shows, I ain't vexed. Otherwise, they're interfering with my livelihood. When he's ready Boysie's hand can be like a hammer. I tired warn him. Do your do but leave my face alone. And best not to mark up my leg or my hand either. A little licks every now and then. Fair enough. Back, backside, stomach, tot-tots is all right. Dave does go crazy if a mark showing and I didn't tell him so he could charge extra. Them times I does run or else it's more licks on top of what I done take.

Boysie shifted and jooked me from behind. Forget all the

long talk. In that position he's finishing in two-twos. Of course
I ah-ahed and ooh-oohed as if this jook sweet like sugar cane.
My noise gets him going. Shame he can't finish looking at me.

Afterwards, eyes half open, he tugged the chadar to cover up,
and propped himself on the crocus bag pillows, stuffed thick
and firm with dried coconut husk.

Aye, Popo, bring your sona a cup of water, nah.

You ain't no sweetheart. Get your own water. And where my
money?

By now he should know I ain't making joke but he can't help
himself.

Money, poi poi? What for?

Boysie, doux-doux, a little freeness now and then is all right.
But ain't Dave warn you to pay or don't show your face here?

He skinned he teeth. Soon as he leaves I best clean up this room,
yes. Them dirty wares belong in a bucket ready to wash by the
standpipe.

Ain't I is your man? Last night when I bring rum and roti
you did well glad to see me.

I watched him cut eye.

You think Dave will say, oh, as you bring thing for Popo, take
one on the house?

Dave Leach is an asshole, old neemakharam. Why I must pay
for milk when it's my cow?

I buss out laughing.

Oh gosh, don't carry on so nah, man.

You is my woman. Story done.

Boysie saying I is he own when two of we know that by the time
he leave and reach the road he done forget me. Until that laar
needs a warm hole I might as well not exist. I played like I was
vex vex.

Look at my crosses. Dave saying it's he cow and you here
bawling is your cow.

He pawed at me until I offered his greedy mouth my tot-tots.
He had a dry suckle half-hour ago. It doesn't matter. Each time
he latches on it's as if he never got breast before. Can't seem to
help he-self. I gave him a minute or two on each side then gently
tugged to get away.

It's my dood all you man drinking and I ain't have a farthing
to show for it.

He grabbed and suckled hard then kissed me like he was leaving
Trinidad.

That Leach and the whole maakaachood gang he's posing
up with can wait right there. You see me? I ain't paying a red
penny.

Aare! Get Dave vexed. Next thing he'll buss your head.

Boysie looked like he'd sucked lime. I poked he chest.

And what about me, eh? Dave might let you get away with
thing but who getting your share of the licks? Me. Put a little
something in my hand let we keep everybody sweet, nah.

Hard ears, I said no. Now, stop harassing me and bring a cup of water fast before you feel my hand.

Boysie doesn't give a shit about how much ruction he's bringing on my head. In fact, it's the direct opposite. He over love a fight. Feel he's a big badjohn. I must ask him how much years he have. Can't be more than a year or two above me so, what, twenty-two, twenty-three. And that right there is the problem. Young and strong. Older fellas don't carry on so. They understand not to cause commess. I treat them nice; they pay and crawl back where they come from until the next time. Boysie thinks giving me sweet eye and bringing a little food does spring open my legs for free.

I wanted to wash myself and sweep this place. But he's only play asking for water and pushing me with he foot. Joke or no joke, I fell off the mattress and landed on my bottom. Lucky thing this house leepayed just the other day. Say what you want, I does make sure every few months this hut's leepayed good and proper. A regular, nice Indian fella, at least thirties, he does help me. Together we mix cow dung with white mud from the river, throw in some water and use that to plaster the walls and ground, smoothing it with a cloth.

Suddenly an elbow jooked my side.

Popo, for the last time, move your blasted korheellary foot and bring my water. You're getting lazy like the rest of them girls.

Oh, so I lazy now? I wasn't lazy for you last night, though? And which rest of them girls you're talking about? Them does bother with you when your pocket empty? Damn poohar, yes.

I pulled myself off the floor and took my cool time zipping my dress. What he go do me? I felt a hand rubbing my leg before he yanked me and I fell on top him. He watched me straight in my eye then kissed me hard. I ain't go lie. That look does tingle even a hard-back woman like me.

The sun was sweeping a gentle light under the door and throwing tiny circles on the walls.

> Instead of bothering me for water make tracks nah, man. You're lucky I let you stay the night. Go now before anybody see and tell Dave you left morning time and I ain't even charge for an hour.

Boysie stretched like a stray cat.

> Bring the water and I go leave you in peace.

> All right, but put on your clothes. I ain't want no fight breaking out. See me here? I ain't ready to sit down in no hospital or worse yet, a funeral home.

I picked up an empty bucket and eased the door open to a glowing orange sky. By the roadside was a standpipe. Filled to the top and that bucket is nuff clean water for the whole day. As I turned to walk back I heard my name called.

> Popo. Popo. What happen? You're deaf or what?

My stomach dropped and my skin felt instantly cold. Only one person says my name like it's dog they're shooing. When that voice says jump, I only ever open my mouth to ask, how high? And don't think I'm the only one 'fraid him. Dave is the kind of fella you're never sure will hug you up or cuff you down. All depends on he mood. And watch nah, he's a proper boss man in

Port of Spain. When it comes to running girls, gambling, protection money, that kindna thing, whole parts of the city locked down tight in he hand.

What you have for me?

Aye, boss, things slow.

Carnival Tuesday morning with all them Yankees and Limeys in town and you ain't have work? What happen?

Ease me up, nah, boss. This evening I go have something for you. For sure for sure. You see me toting water. Soon as I bathe I'm hitting the road.

Dave put he two hands on he hips like a market woman.

All these years together and this is how you're treating me?

I ain't lying, boss. Today will have plenty work.

I was talking loud loud, hoping please, Ram Sita Ram, Boysie had managed to slip out. If he hadn't by now he would be stuck. They'll see him clear. My hut doesn't have a window he could jump out of to make tracks through the bush. Leave by the door now and Dave's bound to spot him.

So wait nah, you telling me it didn't have fares last night? Nobody ain't even see you by the gap. You wasn't with that waste-of-time coolie Boysie Singh?

Me? You done tell me to run Boysie if he come looking for freeness. I know what's what.

His bloodshot eyes bored into mine.

Popo, you know what he's after?

Well, yeah.

No, chupidee. Boysie looking to run you. That's why he ain't paying. It's to disrespect me and groom you for he stable.

I steupsed.

Boysie can't run nothing. I'm yours, boss. You know I'm always here.

Dave lit a Lucky Strike. Instinct made me step back before I became his ashtray.

Don't come crying to me later because I done say what I have to say. And if I ever find that blasted coolie boy taking money from my pocket, so help me Jesus, I go kill him. And when I done with he, it's your backside I'm coming for.

Boss don't be so, nah. I'm going down the road just now.

He knocked my shoulder hard as he passed. One kick and the bottom half of my door was hanging from the hinge. That's pure spite. Now how that getting fixed? It's Dave self I would normally ask for help with trouble like that.

You're damn lucky he ain't here or was me and you today.

I didn't realise I'd been holding my breath until I exhaled. Where Boysie's gone, I ain't know and I ain't care. Behind my back I balled my fists to steady the shaking. Suddenly we heard shouting from the back.

Hold him! Boysie running away. Hold him!

Dave's eyes beamed pure rage as he landed one hard cuff on the left side of my face. I staggered from the blow but it was the look of raw anger that had me more frightened. With one speed they took off into the tall razor grass. I told myself, girl, stay and they go kill you dead. Run, they go still kill you. But they'll have to snatch you first. I ran.

MANA LALA

Back in the day when we were still teens, things were good good between me and Boysie. Early mornings, when the place was still making dark, we would hide in the bush behind the house and do thing. During the day he was forever stealing away from the docks to find me. Anywhere people couldn't see we was good enough. A day we made seven rounds. Seven. And since we started I don't think we've missed a day. Nobody can call him a soft man.

I knew Boysie from when he used to pitch marbles with my brothers and them. All the boys went Newton school. Now we're coupled up my family's making out like he was a badjohn from ever since. True he ain't 'fraid a fight but he have cause. Port of Spain Indians scarce. If we don't stand up for we-selves no back-up there to help.

But my dotish family went looking for another match for me. As if I would ever, ever, take a next man. I'm never leaving him. Of course I can't say what in he mind. Over the years we were separated only to end back as one. I know what Boysie's passed through. Just thinking about it makes my eye water. He talked things with me that he ain't tell another living soul.

We're the same age so he must have had only ten, most eleven years, when police picked him up on the Savannah for flying kite. The law say you can't do that but plenty other fellas were there same time. Yet how come police only threw little boy Boysie in a jail cell? Treated him like he was some big-time criminal. That was wickedness to the bone. And the judge didn't show an ounce of mercy. Six strokes with a tamarind rod for the child.

Six. Big men does shit they-self in pain from two-three strokes but they gave a small boy that punishment?

Boysie's clear that he ain't forget and he can't forgive. Me too. Makes my blood boil. And to think I would've seen him playing in the road and not realised how much he was passing through. Just the other day he squeezed my hand in the dark and said that if that first court sentence hadn't happened, he would've had a different life. The shame of that cut tail went deep into he bone marrow. Police like to play God. And it's not as if Boysie's family looked out for him. Mostly it was he alone so an easy mark for other people's wickedness.

During the time me and he were first going out police held him again. And for what? Some small-time sebby-lebby gambling that happens on practically every corner in town. How come nobody else got arrested? He landed another six of the best with a tamarind whip. That is how the law's supposed to operate? Unfair so? It grieved my heart. If I could have taken them lashes instead I would. For Boysie it was even more shame piled on top whatever he'd already suffered. I know because he hid from me for a good week. The skin was beginning to heal by the time I massaged fresh aloe jelly into the slashes. It still scarred.

Through all this hardship we talked wedding, how much children we go have, where we go live, we future then. Boysie had scrimped and saved. We could have married straight away but Boysie wanted a few dollars coming in steady steady before we did the shaadi and join as one. As he was good with fishing the savings turned into a boat instead of a house. *Perseverance* was he own, bought when he was barely out of short pants. I was so proud. And it wasn't no dotish boat either. Twenty-two-foot long and painted white with a thick navy-blue stripe down the sides. I 'fraid water so I haven't gone for a spin yet. Not Boysie. He swam like a fish and fished like a shark. All I wanted was to look after him good. An easy man to please. Give him the sea, a little gambling, and he's happy like pappy.

Once Ma accepted my heart wasn't budging from Boysie, she went with she fass self by Pundit Gosine checking if it was a good match. Well, if you ask, best be prepared for the answer. In our case the message was sour like green mango. Using the patra, Pundit Gosine predicted that if we went through with the shaadi I'd better ban my belly because real hardship was coming. The problem was Boysie's young soul. He had plenty more reincarnations before a comfortable earthly existence was possible. Pundit was right. Let Boysie stray a tups and police are there ready to throw him in jail before anyone else. He got catch doing a little pickpocketing. One look and the court sent him down for six months' hard labour. Six months. At least I never missed a visiting day and always walked with hot roti and takari. Boysie's doing back-breaking work in jail and nobody else checked on the boy. Why blood family so? Look like they done write him off.

That hard labour stretch left Boysie bony and with skin dark like baigan from being whole day in the hot sun. I begged him, please, poi poi, keep low from now. Police will clearly use any small excuse to harass he soul. For a good few months he boiled down like bhagee. After jostling at the docks he would land up by me. I used to hide food for whatever time he reached. Two of we would squish up in the hammock and talk and, well, the normal things you would expect. He liked nothing better than me squeezing he foot and pulling he toes until they each made a cracking noise. Foolish boy would laugh and say that my massages alone made him want to married to me.

But, according to Pundit Gosine, his karma was destined to

be cruel. What others do all the time and got away with, Boysie would do once and pay a heavy price. Sneaking into a cinema for the matinee happens regular regular. Boysie creeped in without a ticket. Instead of putting up he hand and saying, sorry boss, he let go he temper. Next thing you know the security guard got cuff down. How Boysie was to know this fella used to be police? The man went and well bad talk Boysie to all he police friend them and he was convicted before it reached court. Without looking up, the judge handed down twenty-one days' hard labour. One month hard labour inside is like six months outside. Every single minute of those days while he was punishing, I punished too.

Boysie reached back to me a skeleton. I begged him to be careful. Police big eyes boring on him and the next time he trip up it go be a long long stretch in jail. This was one prediction I prayed would never come true. But it did. The judge didn't blink while locking him up. But what really eat me inside was that this trouble had no business landing in a courtroom. So unfair to my Boysie.

A man had reported that Boysie knifed him. Boysie said, yes, it happened for true, except it was pure self-defence. Who you think the court believed? To add insult, this man is some pumpkin vine family that Boysie's father had helped plenty. Pa only dead recently but that is another story. Anyhow, this so-called family living quite-o quite-o in the bush near Chaguanas. Transport ain't easy from so far. Whenever he was in Port of Spain, the Singh family, out of the goodness of their heart, let him rest the night in their front gallery.

The ungrateful wretch stood up in court and said he had over a hundred dollars in a string bag tied around he waist and pushed inside he dhoti. Cash to buy a cow. In front the judge this fat muk threw some good tears about how he was there sleeping peaceful peaceful when he felt somebody cutting the string to thief the bag. As he was holding the string tight he hand get cut. One loud bawl and the thief ran. But he saw piece of the robber's face and brought police for Boysie.

On the stand Boysie reminded people that Luis Street is where he born and grow. This man was an unexpected visitor. That night he'd come home, rum buzzing in he head, and saw somebody hiding in a corner of the gallery. With a knife for protection, he crept quiet quiet to see what was really going on. The man sprung up ready to fight and, as he lashed out, he hand connected with Boysie's blade.

Only one of them should've been in that gallery and by rights that person should be able to protect he-self from thief-man. Well, the court had a different mind. It threw everything at my sweet Boysie. Me, he ma and he didi, the big sister, all of we heard when the judge passed sentence. I fainted and woke smelling Bay Rum on my skin. Security dragged he didi from the court. Like she went mad and screamed at the judge that they were out for Boysie and if he was an Englishman protecting he castle he wouldn't even be in court. That was too much. Think them things but have sense and don't say it to their face. Opening she trap cost she a month in jail.

Boysie landed four years' hard labour in the jail on Carrera Island, off the north-east tip of Trinidad, a place with rat big like cat running wild. The sea around there rough too, bad with waves tall like an upstairs house. All I know about there is when it make news. Big strong men reached Carrera and in months, braps, they've dropped down dead. Four whole years of not seeing my Boysie. By the time the Bay Rum revived me Boysie had been taken. I hadn't even said goodbye. Apparently he face had turned grey from shock.

Carrera made my Boysie suffer like nothing else in this world. Them prison guards must be reincarnations of Ravana. Had to be. We heard that if the guards so much as thought he'd given them a hard look they would throw him in solitary. A cup of water and one piece of stale bread and that was you for the day. My sona told me later that in the dark, alone except for cockroach and rats, the stench of shit filling your nose hole, he would talk to the walls and beg to live so we could be together again. Every punishment they gave he took like a man. He behaved so good they ended up sending him home early. I bet that pained the guards. Still, that judge thief three years and two months of my poi poi's best days. And mine.

Whole time my Boysie was making a jail I didn't so much as sneeze near another man. Not once. A Belmont fella used to buy from my market stall every week and refuse to take he change. That went on for months even though I told him that he was wasting time and money. Ma and me aunties them tried to tie me down. I might not be the prettiest girl in town but oh gosh. When I tell you they shoved me in front some ugly, country bookie fellas from far down south, places I've never even seen, like Fyzabad and Barrackpore. I told them straight. If they married me off to one of them obzokee men I will swallow 2 4-D. How I could possibly leave Boysie while he's suffering? Eh? We grow together. Nobody could come close to what we have. A few years in jail was nothing.

Boysie said it was time to married but before we could fix the shaadi my belly started swelling. A batcha was growing inside me. Oh Mother Lakshmi, I was happy. Every day I was carrying I did puja that the gods would grant me a son who was the print of he pa.

POPO

It's not two times I left Dave. Run away. Come back. Run away. Come back. Take licks. Come back. I mean to say, it's only he I had looking after me, keeping me safe. Dave could have any woman, yet I'm the one he does come by when life's a botheration. Plenty times he tell me we have something special, a link. Maybe in another life the two of we were married or even brother and sister. None of the other girls have that kind of bonding with him. None.

But something about this carnival Tuesday was different. The air smelt of trouble. Big trouble. I fingered the tabeej on a leather string that never leaves my neck. This bullet-shaped pendant is the only thing I have from when I was small and so far, please Lord, it's kept evil from killing me.

Dave had a mad, wild look in he red eyes that wasn't from smoking ganja. I'd seen this look before. Bharti's hand get break from the Diwali time Dave ordered she to work the docks and she refused. But that's nothing. A next girl, Seetha, well, Dave heard she was running clients on the side and pocketing the cash. He beat she so bad the poor girl went into hospital on a stretcher and left in a box.

I don't know if Boysie do something else that have Dave vex but me giving away a whole night free? He wouldn't forgive that. Not today. Deep in my guts I knew this was my last morning with Dave. Either I go dead, or somehow by hook and crook, leave Port of Spain. I had to think fast. If I wasn't coming back, who would take me in? I can't go by any of the girls. They would tell on me. Somewhere I have a brother but it's how to find him.

Even if I got back to the sugar estate who will want a whore, a randee, like me?

My last change I spent on bus fare to Luis Street, where Boysie's living. He'd carried me there before when he didn't want to trek up to me. Under a brick I found the spare key. To get a little freeness he used to say I could come anytime and stay. Well, lucky he because I'm here right now. Just let him try putting me out on the road. Boysie brought this trouble on my head so he'd better protect me now. But they might beat the shit out of he ass or kill him. If Dave take him out I wonder how long it's safe to stay here? Boysie's talked about a didi, a sister. That didi might come to claim the house. Hopefully that still gives me two-three days' shelter to come up with a plan.

The longer I waited without seeing Boysie, the more convinced I was that he had taken some good licks and was half dead, in a bush somewhere. I stood in the gallery checking the road. As it's carnival plenty people were up and down but no Boysie. Every now and then a truck passed, usually blasting King Radio's 'Tiger Tom Play Tiger Cat'. I bet that tune getting the Road March 1932 crown.

When I recognised Boysie's friend coming up the road I knew the news couldn't be good. Playing calm, I asked,

Aye, what happening?

You ain't hear?

I shook my head.

Your boss put a beating on Boysie bad bad. Talk about mash up. Them fellas carry him hospital.

Mash up like they go bandage him or mash up like he go dead?

Me ain't know. All I hear is that it was licks like peas.

The news whacked me in my chest. Now was the time and all I could do was pray I'd called it correct. Dave ain't changing. Why would he? He's happy happy with how we're living. One minute he's treating me good good, I'm the best, and he go fix me up in a nice house. Next minute it's blows in my tail for no good reason.

The best thing for me is to find myself by the hospital. Time to look after Boysie. Man need a nurse-wife, someone to make he feel cared for and special, like Christmas, Diwali and Eid reached same time.

Spare me bus fare to reach the hospital, nah.

His eyes narrowed, unsure if to ease me up.

Ain't you know me and Boysie in thing?

I don't want trouble on my head. You belongs to Dave.

Why I here then? I'm done with them maakaachood people. You'll get back your money.

Coins passed from his front pocket to my hand.

God go bless you.

Now, me and hospital don't mix. Times I've needed a patch-up, them nurse and doctor carried on as if they were seeing cock-roach. Once a cutlass lashed my leg and I got one long cut. Some drunk as usual. The white doctor stitched me up like he was closing a crocus bag. I'm there bleeding, pain burning me, and all he could say is, well, what you expect when leading such an ungodly life?

Casualty was ram-jammed. People like they waited until it was a holiday to take in sick. Vomit and piss were vamping up the place. Nonstop bawling and wailing hurting my ears. The quiet

ones looked like they think they go dead before anybody take
them on. Stay still for a second and latrine flies big like red beans
landing all on your face and hand. In the middle of this commess
a mad fella named Wheels was up and down acting like it's drive
he driving car. He does be all about dodging traffic, changing
gears, turning corners and mashing brakes between the benches
of people. I had to step out his way to find Boysie chook up in
a corner, only that wasn't the same man I'd had in my bed a few
hours earlier. From head to toe he was broken, bruised or bleeding as if stick plus knife had passed. I bent and tried holding him
but he pulled away. Even my soft soft touch hurt he skin.

Aare, what they do you, sona? I there worried for you. Soon
as I hear I rushed come. You know I wouldn't leave you to
manage by yourself. Don't worry, I'm here now. Stay close.
Let me deal with everything.

Boysie threw back he head and closed his eyes.

You is a good woman, Popo. I always say that.

He straightened and looked in my eye.

Leach don't know who he fucking with.

Don't study him.

Apparently Dave told Boysie he was asking for licks. This set of
bruises and them breaks was to teach him a lesson. Carnival or
no carnival, no Woodbrook coolie boy robbing him by taking
freeness off he girl. I smiled.

Dave warned me that you're only curry-favouring with me
so I go work for you. I tell him that is not how we does move.
He didn't like that at all at all.

Of course he go say that.

But Boysie, I can't believe you take licks for me. Nobody ever stand up for me so.

Boysie smiled in a way that made me feel before this moment he hadn't thought of himself as my saviour. He seemed to like the role.

A man have to do what he have to do.

From where I was sitting I bent forward and touched his feet.

You know I can't go back. If this is what he do you, think of the beating I go get. He wouldn't satisfy until my blood washing the road.

You don't have to go back.

I looked up.

You're sure about what you're saying?

How you mean? Stay by me.

I rested my hand gently in his.

I go look after you and keep the place good. I ain't 'fraid hard work. That's all I ever know.

One corner of Boysie's lips smiled. Long time I haven't had to do this poor-sweet-girl-need-saving chupidness. But hear nah man, it was working good.

*

The only reason we didn't spend the whole day in that confusion was because Boysie's cousin's neighbour was cleaning in the hospital and he spotted him in Casualty. When he saw the state of Boysie he went and begged a favour. The place was so busy all the doc managed was to give him tablets for the pain and fix one arm in a sling. We left with Boysie under heavy manners to go home and take bedrest for at least a week.

Rest never came. As we were walking out of Casualty who we go bounce up but a set of Boysie's family rushing in with his unconscious nephew. Boysie's didi looked in shock. She son ain't make more than fourteen, fifteen years and he was there looking half dead. Me ain't know these people and I suddenly realised what I must look like in the old dress I'd pulled on to go to the standpipe. To tell you the truth I didn't even have on bra and panty. He didi must be thinking, look at that nasty woman. How she could leave the house and ain't even pass a comb through she hair? Thank God I wasn't close enough or the smell of my rum mouth would confirm every bad thing that was passing through she mind.

Boysie got real vex when he found out who beat the nephew. It was Dave.

What? That neemakharam Leach do this? Nah. He go pay.

He forgot he broken arm one time. Another nephew piped up.

We was minding we own business, joking, watching carnival bands coming down the road. This gang started to carry on that we on their territory and have to move. We said this is the government road and we ain't going nowhere. They said Indians getting too up with they-self and is cane we should be cutting not liming in Port of Spain. Well, fight break out. It was plenty of them and only three of we.

Boysie shook his head.

Leach gone too far. Whatever happens now he bring it on he own head.

Boysie's was so mad vex he didn't even bother introducing me so I stop right there full of shame in front he family. Anyhow, they went in and we made tracks. I kept reminding him the arm can't take pressure. He could want to fight all he want, but one arm against two is plain dotishness. And this ain't nice to admit but watching him mash up I couldn't help feeling a tiny bit glad. It's not right to wish this on anybody but at least now he have an idea what it's like being Dave's punching bag.

We limped away from the hospital, Boysie leaning on me barely able to walk straight. Truth is Boysie's always in some fight or the other. Everybody knows not to cross him or it's licks. A time he came by me covered in mud, a cut above he eye but happy happy, skinning he teeth. I threw water on he skin while he told me how he took he blows but the other fella took plenty more. All because the man thief a few of Boysie's crab traps.

Now he was in the unusual position of receiving a cut ass good and proper. I was 'fraid for him and for me. If he dead today where I going to live, Mother Lakshmi? Tell me where.

Boysie, ain't the doctor said you probably cracked a rib and to take it easy? Forget Dave for now, nah.

Boysie groaned.

No way. He feeling something today today.

Rest out this week, nah.

Hush. All you woman can't understand these things.

I bit my tongue. Right now I ain't sure if I have a roof for a day, a week, a month. Best I leave him thinking chupidness. One more beating and Boysie would be dead but it was how to stop him.

Dave doesn't move without back-up. Two-three partners. How you go beat him today? Hold some strain and make a surprise attack. It wouldn't matter then if all you is ten and them have twenty.

No answer. With his good hand he wiped his forehead.

Boysie?

He grunted.

Hush. I'm thinking.

I could see he was craving action before nightfall.

Time longer than twine.

That's you. I can't left he thinking he's wiped me out. Nah. Not happening. He think he bad? Well, he ain't seen bad yet. Watch me. Even with one hand I go beat Leach. I just need a little help.

What a real gadaha, stubborn for so when he ready. In fact, that's all man.

Let me do puja. Ask Lord Shiva, Destroyer of All Evil, to fight with you.

He steupsed.

Don't bring no backward puja thing by me. George and short man, Edgar, is them I need today. Them two and me with Three Little Threes? We go do for them.

The way Boysie talks about Three Little Threes you would swear it's he partner. First time I saw it I couldn't understand what the fuss was about. It's a piece of hard wood, a poui stick. But he mustn't hear you calling it a stick. You have to give it the full name: Three Little Threes. And don't make joke about Three Little Threes unless you want to see him mad vexed. Apparently some Mother Gizzard worked obeah convincing Boysie she put a divine power in the wood that protects he and he alone.

An Indian like Boysie should've passed by Pundit Sharma to bless the stick rather than Mother Gizzard. But talking to Boysie over the months I realised that apart from Diwali celebrations he ain't know one fart about being Hindu. I'm sure he doesn't remember when last he went inside a mandir. Just like my parents, he ma and baap crossed the kala pani from India and born Boysie in Trinidad. But that is where the Indianness stop. On the outside he might look Indian, and a sharp one too. Cut Boysie open and inside he's black, like Dave. No joke. From a baby come up all he seemed to know is Port of Spain ways. I suppose he can't help it since Indian people scarcely living around there. He grow with black people. I tired warn him that not respecting the religion flowing through he blood will bring bad karma on he head. Let him carry on. Next reincarnation he'll come back a centipede. Or worse.

*

It took time but tookra tookra we made it to the house. Whole road I was holding him up but he didn't seem to notice me. I could tell he had pain.

Popo, get the key, nah.

You're serious about me living here, right?

How you mean?

I can't go back.

He waved his good hand.

Relax. Ain't I say you're staying here?

I know you go look after me good.

As he hobbled inside and flopped down on the bed I was glad he missed seeing my relief. Thank the Lord I have a place for now. It's small but plenty better than mines.

Let me light the chulha and boil water. You go feel better when I wipe you down.

Like I was minding a small child, I gently peeled off his torn merino vest and dirty short pants. He didn't like me feeling up the broken arm.

All right, all right, I wouldn't touch it. I done now. This merino can't wear again. It could make cleaning cloth. You have sweet soap to bathe?

Shelf by the back door.

Outside, I filled a clean bucket, half and half hot water and water from the pipe, picked up the piece of soap and came inside. One look and he shook his head.

Carry it back outside. I can bathe myself.

He limped to the back door and I thought he was going in behind the galvanise wall where it have pipe. But the pain catch him and he stood right there on the dirt, naked as he born.

Throw the water for me, nah.

I ended up wetting, soaping, and rinsing him. That man could talk. He never stopped prattling about Dave this, and Dave that, and what he's going to do to him. I listened while drying his back. Boysie needed handling or the next fight would be he last.

Let me tell you something, Boysie, and I learnt this the hard way. The worse licks I ever get, wasn't from the biggest badjohn.

His body stiffened.

I'm talking the worst-est licks by a mile.

I took a deep breath. Might as well tell him everything.

A time four fellas carry me in the middle of a cane field. Place pitch black. I tell them it's one at a time in the back seat. Them say nah, nah, nah. They want me to come out the car. I there thinking they see some picture with a girl sprawl out on a car bonnet and they wanted me to pose for them. No. They wanted me up the back passage. Well, you know that's not my speed. I say that's not what we talk 'bout but we go have a good time.

Why did I start this talk? Now I had to keep going.

I never saw the cuff coming. It was the small man that I did hardly bother with. When I tell you that lash hit hard. Knocked me out thandaa cold. Catch my ears. That's why I don't hear so good in my right ears. It's from he cuffing me.

I made like telling him this didn't still hurt. Besides, people think I deserve whatever pass me.

You might feel it was four of them and one of me so I was always getting a beating one way or another. Maybe. But it vex me that I didn't see that blow coming and save my ears.

Boysie remained looking like he was far away. He didn't say nothing but he patted the bed for me to sit down. I touched his hand.

Surprise Dave. Leave it alone and hit a day he ain't expecting trouble. You strong like two Tarzan. Wait and use all your strength.

He nodded.

You might have a point.

DORIS

As the Lord is my witness, I remember the first time I saw Boysie Singh. Some part of me knew this man was trouble. I'm not saying I thought he was a bad person. No, I watched him good. When he smiled his eyes smiled too. I wondered where life with him would take me. You see from the time I was small small people were saying, Doris ain't make for Toco, or, Toco ain't make for Doris. Either way I grew up marking time. My real life was waiting for me only I didn't know where exactly. Sometimes for no reason my foot itches and that can only mean one thing. I'm going on a long journey. It could be Arima or San Juan. Plenty Toco people worked in Port of Spain during the week and ran back on their day off. That kind of half and half thing wasn't for me. To leave Toco only for work was to put one foot, not even a whole foot, more like poking a big toe, elsewhere. Me? When you see I pack my bags it's to join in the big city life. Although I'd never visited, even then I felt in my belly that Port of Spain was where I'd end up. Of course I would do maid work. But watch me good: I'm not staying so. I'm going to be a somebody.

Even as I dreamt of living beyond Toco, Elena and Julia kept me bolted down here behind God's back. We sisters were tight. Nothing we don't do together. But they love Morne Cabrite village, Toco, like it's England's green and pleasant land. They'll take whatever work they find, marry a boy from around here, assuming they can find one that isn't blood family, push out at least four children, and bury in a plot at Cumana RC Church. Born, married, dead. So when people singled me out as not belonging here it was only this de Leon sister they were talk-ing about. If I left, rather, when I left, I would be making tracks alone.

So why me? Don't think I'm going to blush and pretend the house is mirrorless. When looks were sharing I rushed the line. Men like something to hold on to and that was me. Early o'clock my front and back filled out nice. The hair unfortunately wasn't always obedient. Little wiry. I plait it into two thick cane rows gathered in a neat low bun. We don't know exactly how we're mixed but the whole family's red. At some point a Spanish man and his black slave made a baby and maybe in time a French Creole passed in the mix. Yes, I was baked with a spoonful of French, half cup of Spanish, a dash of molasses and out I came, a light-skinned reds.

Being my colour definitely makes all the difference. No sense pretending otherwise. I knew I was always going to get more of everything life offered. Take my school friend Grace. The girl's face pretty but I'm sorry to say she's dark. When we walk down the road together fellas would say, look, night and day side by side. Nobody gave her the vibes to leave Toco and do something with her life.

Growing up I carried myself like I'd already married a rich rich man and was living in a big, brick house with a motor car parked up outside. You couldn't get higher than the school prin-cipal and our village plonked his wife on a pedestal. That was woman. My life's mission was to maco everything she did, her hair, her clothes, how she put on rouge. Now, don't get me wrong. Mammy's our rock. Everything we did was because of her. Except reading. Pappy handled books but everything else was Mammy.

The trouble is Mammy's so busy most of the time she looks like a frizzle fowl in her old dress, a comb sticking out of half-plaited hair. Not the headmaster's wife. She could be crossing the road to buy hops bread and currants roll and her face would have powder and the hair neat neat in a long plait. Mammy's happy to leave the house in any old thing with a rip or a buss zip held in place by two safety pins. The headmaster's wife's dress might be old but it would be clean, fitting, and un-holey. Years later when I learnt the meaning of elegant I thought it described that woman down to she big toe.

While I wanted to be like her there was something else I recognised even though I didn't understand it until recently. Put Mammy and the headmaster's wife in the same clothes, same everything and only one of them will carry herself like she's a queen. That her husband's running the only primary school for miles rather than working as a labourer was only part of that ease. It went deeper. Headmaster's wife didn't fret. It was as if she woke up and said, this one piece of life I have is going to be okay. Hard rain, burning sun, cool breeze, golden sunset, she took them all in her stride while the rest of us cussed and wrestled the bad times or went crazy with excitement when things were good. As a big woman I worked hard at looking the part of a woman in control but never, not for one second, did I trust I could manage whatever life threw at me. Even if it's my destiny to leave this village I remained terrified that no matter how far I ran, I could land back right in Toco wearing an old dress with a buss-up zip.

And if I think about it that's why Boysie and I fell for one another. We both had ambition to end up somewhere and the same doubt we'd never quite make it. What to say? It was meant to be.

MANA LALA

Our first fight was soon after the batcha was born. Boysie wanted he name Anthony. I ain't arguing. Whatever he wants is fine by me, especially since the Boysie that came back from Carrera has a real short fuse. Best to obey and keep the peace. Anthony Singh, we beta, has perfect tiny hands and feet and hairy like a monkey. He got that from my side of the family. I can't get over how this little batcha came from inside me.

Things soured because of Ma. She wanted the namkaran ceremony where the beta is named according to Hindu custom. I asked Boysie easy easy if he don't mind, please. I ain't care but let we keep Ma happy, nah.

What chupidness you want to do to my beta?

I kept my head down and spoke quietly.

It's Pundit Gosine saying prayers and giving the beta a rasi name which nobody supposed to know, much less use.

I don't want no ulloo pundit chanting dotishness on my child head.

He scratched his crotch.

Wait nah, that's not the same pundit that said something bad about my horoscope? And is he all you go bring to do prayers on my child? All you take me for a bobolee?

I whispered a small lie.

You're mixing up pundits. Please, Boysie, it'll keep everybody quiet.

37

A rough hand pushed up my chin.

I said, no.

Okay, okay. Don't worry. I go sort out Ma. Don't worry.

He grunted. I knew he was tired and me and all ain't sleep good since the batcha born. How something so small can have me up and down whole day and whole night? Anthony might be puny puny but when he put down a bawl you could hear him from down by the gap. Bawl, bawl, bawl. I don't think he's had more than a straight hour of sleep yet. When Boysie wasn't looking I aunchee Anthony according to how I see other people do. In a piece of brown paper I put onion skin, garlic skin, hot pepper, tied it good and passed the little pouch over Anthony. Even that didn't stop the constant bawling.

On top of everything, Ma won't stop digging in my tail for she namkaran.

You tell that badjohn father that I is the child nanee and I say we're doing the namkaran.

Ma, please. He mind done make up already.

Ask again.

Oh gosh, you know how he stop when he vex.

I see. So your beta must suffer to keep that poohar sweet? This is part of the child's growing-up. But all right, I done see what kind of mother you is.

All I could do was take Ma's bad mouth. Boysie was suffering from nerves. And it wasn't like I was okay either. My breasts them were paining me bad bad. Dood wasn't flowing as it should. She knew I was suffering and left me right there to fend for myself. I cut cabbage leaves from the back garden, put them in ice water and when they were thandaa cold I covered my tot-tots with them. Gradually I got a little ease. The only reason I even knew this remedy was from seeing Ma do it for my sisters and sister-in-law. My time now and she don't care. But then again she never cared. I was always the donkey who had to work hard. She didn't mind asking people how come I born so ugly when all my sisters were pretty pretty. All I get is endless talk that I ain't doing things right. First time I was bathing Anthony she snatched him saying I wasn't holding the batcha properly.

Poohar, you go break the child neck. He hardly born and it look like you're ready to kill him.

If I didn't love my beta how come he's getting hand whole day? Anthony loves hand. Once you're holding him he will stay quiet. Put him down for a second and it's, waah, waah, waah. While he's there crying Ma does be shouting.

Mana Lala! When last you feed the batcha? You can't hear he hungry?

I would give him a tot-tot even if he'd only finished suckling minutes ago. That didn't always shut him up which would make Ma grab Anthony and go off bouncing him. Just to shame me more the child would immediately stop fretting and fall fast asleep. Ma would hand him back.

Try not to wake him. See if you can at least do that.

I'm forever exhausted in a way I've never felt before. Everything hurts. I would give my two piece of gold jewellery to pull a long sleep. Of course, if Ma got she namkaran she would help out and not make everything into a quarrel.

As usual Boysie passed in the evening to see Anthony. I asked what happened that day as he was looking extra scruffy. He skinned he teeth. A partner paid him to put some good licks on a fella who owed money. With a few dollars in he pocket he'd spent the rest of the afternoon in a card game. I thought this was my chance while he was in a good mood and eating the roti and curry bodi I'd cooked.

Please, Boysie, poi. Let Ma do she Hindu rites, nah. It ain't changing nothing. A few prayers for the batcha to make sure he life good. That's all. I won't ask for nothing again. Please.

Warm food in he belly, and a big win playing whappee had him well relaxed. That, together with a quiet batcha cuddled in his arms and Boysie surprised me.

All right, all right. It look like I ain't go get no peace. Let nanee do whatsoever it is she want. But tell she for me that Anthony not changing to some foolish name. You hear me?

No, no, no, it won't change. Pundit will give him a sacred rasi name that's only for puja and thing.

Boysie wasn't bothering with me. I poked his side.

You and all must have a rasi name, Boysie. You remember it?

Nah. I don't think I ever had one.

You must do. Your pa was a big-time Sikh. He would've done namkaran for all he children.

He didn't answer. My rasi name is May.

*

If Ma was happy he'd boiled down, she certainly didn't bother to show it on she face. Without saying boo to me next morning she bathed, put on a good dress, the green one with flowers. She covered she head with a 'going out' voile orhni tucked into the thin belt made from the same green material and walked out the road.

Normally, it's forty days after the batcha's born that people do namkaran, which only left us a week to prepare. I was expecting Ma to bring plenty news from pundit. Instead, she reached home around lunchtime, passed me straight and went in she bed. Anthony was bawling and instead of the usual boof she called me in a sweet voice. Well, okay, maybe not sweet but it wasn't the vex voice either.

Bring the batcha and come.

She took Anthony into the bed and slowly massaged his precious pot belly then his little head. He calmed right down, cooing away.

I done cook. Take out a plate of food for you?

Normally she would bark, yes or no. Imagine my shock when she burst into tears.

Ma, what happen? Why you're crying?

Well, that made she bawl even harder.

The batcha.

Anthony good. Look how he telling you he like you rubbing him down.

I cooed back at the batcha. More wailing from Ma. For once Anthony was the quiet one.

Pundit say.

I waited.

Pundit say he didn't born good.

How you mean?

Using the good orhni she wiped she face.

Pundit take he birth date and everything. He looked in the patra and tell me Anthony ain't born with a good horoscope.

I looked at my perfect batcha, the little eyes smiling like Boysie's, the tiny hands, the little fingers.

He lie. Nothing wrong with my beta.

She blew her nose loud.

No, it's truth. But pundit say if we work fast fast we can correct the forecast.

What we have to do? Tell me.

Plenty things to collect. Sea water. All kind of things. I can't remember. He have to get all what he need and say prayers. And he want five dollars now.

But I ain't have that.

It's all right. I done ask to take my sou-sou hand this week.

You're sure, Ma?

She waved me away.

My grandson not starting life with a bad horoscope. You hear me? Nanee going to fix that.

Pundit got the five dollars and said all the prayers Anthony needed. By the time the forty days reached he declared the child was clear. I did my part by drinking karha, the spiced milk that cleansed from the inside out. On the morning I well bathe and oiled my skin from head to toe. Ma bathed Anthony and put him in brand-new clothes. He looked like a little prince.

During the puja, pundit made my didi mark the child with kohl around he eyes and in the middle of he forehead. Ma put a najar bracelet on all two of his tiny wrists. Each of these things, the kohl and the black-and-gold bead bracelets will stop people putting maljo on him. Suddenly, as if he'd just remembered, pundit asked me what happened to the navel string. I don't know why but he frightened me and I couldn't speak. Ma almost steupsed but caught she-self.

Mana Lala, you know it buried in the back by the chenette tree.

Good, good. When he's done this life the body is returned to the earth once it's been purified by fire of course. Good, good. You did the correct thing, nanee. He's grounded to the earth.

Something about this pundit I didn't too like. But the namkaran passed off good. Anthony was bawling down the house at the exact moment when my didi whispered in he batcha ears.

Your rasi name is Che.

I wasn't sure if I heard right.

Cha?

No, Che.

Pundit jumped in.

Give him a middle name like Chedee. Yes, Chedee is a very suitable name. But don't go round telling the marish and the parish. You don't want anybody using it against the batcha.

Ma pushed in she mouth.

Chedee is a nice name. I well like that.

I kept quiet. Boysie wasn't going to add no Chedee as the child's middle name. At least Anthony has had a name blessing like Hindus have been doing for thousands of years. That will protect him forever. Boysie's not the kind to get vex with me because of something that is protecting we batcha. If he does, well, I go take my licks and hush.

POPO

I could see that even talking was hurting. Ribs definitely broken.

Do something for me, nah.

Anything, Boysie, anything. What you want?

Go down the road by Gita's for a nip of rum. Tell she it's for me. And ask she to send for George to come by me now now.

George who?

Harper. George Harper who I does fish with.

The dark-skin fella with he eyebrows joined up in one? Ain't a night we drink beer with he?

He nodded.

What you want with he?

Better make George bring Edgar with him one time. And let Gita know I'm waiting. This is serious business.

I gently kissed his good shoulder.

What them two could do?

I trust George more than some of my own blood.

All right, you know what you doing. Anything else before I go?

Nah. Run do this first, boobool.

Gita's bar was jamming and I had to push to reach the counter. She watched me cut eye as she took twenty-five cents for the nip of rum. With Boysie's message she softened, said don't worry. She big son would fetch George now for now.

Back home Boysie was in a clean white merino and white short pants. He grinned.

You talk plenty sense.

About what? And why you get up? Rest nah man.

I go surprise the hooraar. Bring out the rat with cheese and chop off he tail.

Give that hand a two weeks and it go come back good. Then pick a day he ain't expecting trouble.

Two weeks? Nah, nah, nah. Once George and Edgar reach we heading out. Beat he ass.

But your hand?

He snorted like I was dotish. Anyhow, I gave my two cents so best hush my mouth. Go dead if he want. That hand can't beat a drum let alone Dave. I held the bottle while Boysie took a swig of rum and waited for his posse to reach.

So, what go happen to me if Dave advantage you? You study that?

Relax yourself. Nobody go throw you out.

News of the beating had done reach Edgar and George and they were heading to the hospital when Gita's son found them. They burst in hot and sweaty, ready to make mas.

Boysie man, give the word and we go burn down everything Dave Leach own. And we ain't sparing nobody. Woman, child, everybody getting licks today. All he people go find their ass is grass.

Fellas, we is one. But hold that talk. I revenging on what he do me. He and he alone must pay. When I finish nobody go even remember he name.

All three knocked back a shot of rum. George was eyeing the sling.

Aye, Boysie, I understand what you're saying but let me and Edgar settle with he. That hand looking like it need an ease.

Boysie ripped off the sling and the bandages pooled on the ground.

This is my day. I'm taking Dave Leach.

I watched them carrying on about what they go do. The three of them vex till it had them dotish. I wasn't hearing nothing that sounded like a proper plan. Edgar was saying how Dave always keep fellas close. I saw my chance.

Then take him at 66 Henry Street. He child mother living there. A time he tell me he does never bring business by that house, only family. If he's there things easy.

From their look I knew this was news. And then it hit me.

Edgar, Dave know your face?

I doubt.

Then you should be the one to go up to the gate. Ask for something. Say he father know your father. Anything.

The men were well paying attention now.

Get Dave to come outside on the road to talk. Then the two
of all you could jump him. What you think?

Boysie's whole face was glowing.

My patni. All you see how much sense she have?

I almost blushed. Patni. He'd just called me wife.

What if it ain't have a good hiding place?

Boysie threw he head back in the chair like he thinking.
Gradually a grin stretched from ear to ear.

It's carnival, fellas, and I go dress up. He wouldn't know it's
me. George, you should look different too. Maybe like you
now come from playing mas.

Boysie sent me in the press to find clothes for them to use. I had to
smile to myself. Carnival Tuesday and you could say these three
hitting the road in their very own mas band. Boysie dressed like
he had plenty age. Edgar was in tear-up, old clothes and George
had paint on he face and clothes. What if it went wrong? As they
were leaving I tried to memorise Boysie's face. Supposing that
was the last time I saw him? I would have to run somewhere far
far deep south like Moruga or even Mayaro.

*

Well oupaaya! Talk about turn around. Boysie came back saying
Dave's done for good. I'm free. I couldn't take it all in but it's true.
According to Boysie they landed in Henry Street and scoped out
the house. It looked like Dave was alone relaxing he-self. Boysie,
as a beggar man, stooped down on the roadside minding he own

business. George was in a bush pretending too much feting had him burnt out. Edgar went up to the gate and called,

Inside! Inside!

Nobody appeared.

He carried on calling and making noise until Dave came to the gallery. Edgar begged for a little food, a few farthings. To get rid of what looked like an old man, Dave walked down the steps from the gallery and unlocked the gate. Well, that was the biggest mistake he ever made. Soon as he was on the road George jumped him. Boysie flung off the old sheet he was wearing and the three of them well beat Dave. And here's the part that nobody will believe. Edgar said that never mind the hand break, it was Boysie and Three Little Threes that landed the hardest blows. He beat the man and would not stop. George shook his head. He thought the stick was almost moving by itself. Later we got news that Dave was in Port of Spain General Hospital. Doctors ain't sure he go make it.

MANA LALA

After all the commess that everybody must only call the batcha Anthony, and only Anthony, not even Tony for short, and never breathe the rasi name, Che, it was Boysie he-self who started calling we beta something completely different. He's small small. People would say, aye, look at that chunkee batcha or, look at the little choonksing. Boysie turned chunkee and choonksing to Chunksee. If we're not careful he will grow big and people will still be calling him Chunksee.

Everybody loves Chunksee. He's nice too bad. I feel I could eat him up he so sweet. If you tickle the belly he face does buss into a wide no-teeth grin. And I'm not saying that because he's my batcha. We're settled by Ma but Boysie finds he tail here every single day. Only way he won't see Chunksee is when he's at sea, fishing. Once his feet on land nobody else can get a love-up. The child might be our beta but he squeezes and kisses the batcha like he alone make child. I don't even try to take Chunksee out he hands except to feed. Boysie's totally in love with Chunksee. Even my brothers them boiled down like bhagee admitting the man is a devoted pa. While they no longer have a problem with Boysie the funny thing is I do. Tookra tookra, from the time Chunksee make about three months, I've noticed Boysie's changed towards me. He'll reach and pass me straight like I'm invisible. I joked that my father isn't a glass maker. Made no difference. He only sees Chunksee. Of course the batcha need plenty love-up but what about me? I'm not people too?

Worse than that, he goes out of his way to make sure my skin and he skin don't meet. An accidental brush when handling the batcha is our only contact. Otherwise? Nothing. He doesn't sit near me or even hold my hand little bit. That is not how Boysie before Chunksee would operate. I was big big, ready to drop, and he was still wanting to do thing. If he could get a piece every day he would take it. I don't understand this and of course I can't say nothing. My extra weight throw off. He knows I keep myself only for him. I'm not like them girls who does answer back, or forever bawling they want this and that. Day or night I'm always right here, quiet, waiting.

Never one to miss a chance to make me look bad, Ma asked Boysie loud loud,

Aare bai, why you don't stop the night by we? Your batcha and your woman right here.

I concentrated on the ground. Boysie laughed a kind of embarrassed, ha ha, hee hee.

Next time. These days I over busy.

All right, but come and stay a week by we instead of hustling up and down.

For true.

Ma was well enjoying she-self. I made an excuse and went in the kitchen. From a block of ice I broke off enough to fill an enamel cup and began crunching. Just because I didn't fight back was no reason for people to make me feel small small. I thought Boysie would take me from here, protect me. Somebody probably swept over my feet because it look like I will never get married. Maybe Boysie's already taken with a next girl and she's making batcha for him. I wanted to curl up on my mattress and forget all of them, even Chunksee. Always hanging

off my tot-tots. I can't get no peace. I finished the ice and got
another piece.

*

Boysie reached by me with he hand in a sling. At first he laughed
and said he'd been in a fight and beat the other fella real bad.
I got frightened one time. This could bring police on he head
again.

Ha, you well believe me.

I looked at him hard.

Well, that's what you said.

No girl. I was busy packing some fish in ice and the boom
from the sail give me one hard lash. I can't tell you the pain I
had.

Oh gosh. Don't trouble it. Anything you want doing I could
do. It break?

Doctor ain't sure but they want me to rest it little bit.

But Boysie doesn't know what rest means. With both parents
passed before Chunksee was born, it's not like he has plenty
family around. Plus we done know all the police, white and
black, ain't take to he Indian face. Boysie's got to do whatever
to make a dollar. Me ain't blaming him for running small illegal
betting here and there. It's only a little whe-whe or cards, usually all fours. That ain't interfering with nobody. It means he's
not with me and the batcha as much, sometimes for a whole
week. At least it's work and not stray women he's busy chasing.

POPO

I hardly slept. My head was spinning from how fast life was changing. No Dave, and I'm sharing Boysie's roof. I'll figure it out. Right now he ain't have the strength of a newborn batcha. But remembering past fights and how things does work round here, Dave's partners will either come revenging or get police to do the work for them. Instinct from years of fending for myself made me rush to wrap back on Boysie's sling.

Leave it off. It humbugging me.

Trust me. Just wear it. Anybody come asking if you was the one in a fight yesterday all you do is point to the sling.

Suppose they don't believe me?

Don't worry. Leave that with me. I'm here now.

He steupsed but accepted the arm being bandaged and tied up. And lucky thing I did that, yes. A few hours ain't pass good and police was in the yard. They carted Boysie off to the station ready to charge him. Dave's partners had all pointed at Boysie. I smiled as the police jeep drove off.

Soon after, I was back at the hospital looking for the doctor from yesterday. I put down one bawl.

Doctor, help me please. Police hold Boysie. They say he beat a man and nearly kill him. Ain't you-self put he hand in a sling? He could ever trouble anybody? I ain't know why police out for he.

This was one of the good white doctors and he wasn't happy at all at all. Right then and there he wrote a letter. Me can't read too good but it looked important and even had a stamp at the bottom of the page.

> Carry this to the police superintendent and explain my patient could never have done what they claim. That is my professional medical opinion and if they don't believe me I will stand in up in a court of law and tell the judge myself.

Out of respect I knelt to kiss his feet but he pulled away.

> Nonsense. Only doing my job. Some of these chaps are far too quick to make an arrest. Well, I'm not having it.

That letter was the magic key. It unlocked Boysie's cell and the two of we went home happy happy. As we were walking Boysie rubbed up on me.

> How much times I tell you to come live by me but like you choose the best time. You real saved me there.

*

Two days later news reached us. David Leach dead.

Town only talking about Boysie killing Dave. As the story made the rounds it got crazy for so until you would think Boysie was some kindna obeah lord with a magic stick. If only they'd seen him while recovering. He was real mash up. And hear nah man, this badjohn people 'fraid so much couldn't remain by he-self for five minutes. If I so much as stay in the yard too long a sad little voice will cry, Popo, where you? A two-year-old batcha would manage better than this killing machine.

Since I can't be far from this muk I started clearing and cleaning from a side. Plenty old things chook up everywhere.

Boysie, I'm clearing out whatever's on top the press. You stay in the bed. I will show you things and you say what you want doing with them.

First, some doolar.

Oh gosh, man, you just get hug up. Lie down and stay quiet.

He showed me his poor-me-one face. I gave him a quick kiss. Once near my tot-tots he suckles as if he's feeding on dood.

Nothing there.

I still love it.

After he'd had a few minutes suckling from all two I pulled down my top.

Enough for now.

His eyes pleaded and I could see stiffness in he shorts.

Later.

I stood on a chair to reach on top the press. The rubbish that came tumbling down: old bottle, gazette paper, a cracked mirror, some pamphlets. Talk about hoarding chupidness.

All this have to throw away.

But I might need old gazette paper.

So much?

Maybe.

Sorry, but half going in the rubbish. And I have to take the rubbish out before dark or else they say whatever wealth you have will go quick quick.

I went back up and reached for whatever was still hiding. My hand touched a cold handle.

You're keeping a piece of iron up here?

Aye, careful. That's Pa's sword.

I go get cut?

Nah, the blade in a leather casing. Hold the handle.

I eased it down. Kara hoi! I never see a big-ass weapon so. You could chop off a man head with this.

Boysie, why this sword throw away under rubbish?

Well, I ain't using it. I have Three Little Threes.

I gently pulled the long, curved blade out to meet the sun. Easily three foot. Light caught it and dazzled my eyes.

You see you? You only playing you is a badjohn. A real rangotaso would carry this round he waist. From the time people see you coming they would shit their pants.

Boysie smiled and held his fists like he's some big boxer.

I have these two. That's enough.

I nearly choked laughing. He can be such a chupidee, a real ulloo when he ready.

The handle is supposed to be a chicken head?

Boysie steupsed hard.

Aye, chicken? That's a hawk. Look at the red stone eyes. They does call this a kirpan.

Well, chicken or hawk I know that two swish swash and it will chop up a man fine fine.

I sat on the bed next to Boysie, the sword across our laps.

Come nah, man, tell me how you get this.

First, put the kirpan back in the case.

Like you 'fraid I might use it?

Stop making joke and put it back nah.

All right, talk your talk.

Boysie adjusted the cushion behind his head, opened his mouth and the whole kheesa flew out. He could tell stories for a living.

When I was small, didi didn't want me near it so she hide it away. The mark buss a couple years ago and then only because she thought it was dangerous with she small children around.

This kirpan came with Boysie's Sikh baap direct from the Punjab. Most of the people I knew on the estate came from Bihar, or, like my parents, Uttar Pradesh. Anyhow, Boysie's baap was an army man. I was well enjoying this. Maybe as I don't have family I like to know about other people family. In India, everything was going good good until one day he and some sawatee, might even be a prince, got in a big fight, over what we don't know. Probably, was money or a woman. Bottom line is Boysie's baap killed the sahib. He had to get his gaand out of the Punjab fast fast or he was a dead man. Well, he was so 'fraid that he didn't just leave the Punjab, he crossed the kala pani from Calcutta on the *Avon* reaching Trinidad mid-March 1901. Being Sikh they had to let him on the ship with his kirpan, the same kirpan that may have chopped the sawatee.

Boysie remembered his baap regularly polishing the kirpan and saying prayers in front it. When the man was dying he gathered up the children and made them swear that as soon as he'd turned to ash they would throw away the kirpan. Not one of them could be trusted to do the prayers and the shining and whatever else he used to do. Before it brought evil they should throw it in the sea, bury it in the ground, anything, so long as they got rid of it. Well, the man passed and none of them bothered with what he said. Didi kept it and eventually it passed to Boysie. Neither of them shined the blade nor did prayers like their baap used to do. I stroked the leather casing.

If this was mines I would put it out for everybody to see. How hard is it to shine the thing and say two prayers now and then?

Me do puja for the kirpan? Nah. That's for them barracks country people.

So instead you're walking around with a big stick?

The obeah power in my stick more strong than all them Ganesh and Hanuman all you Indian busy worshipping. To besides, if you cut somebody with a knife police ready to throw you in jail one time. Trust me, I know. But hit a man with a piece of wood and them don't mind so much.

I'd said enough for today but if Boysie doesn't start using this kirpan soon he's more dotish than I thought. This was an unforgettable kheesa, the kind of story to pass to your children and their children and their children's children.

DORIS

My school went to standard five so at twelve I left. That was the age my brothers and sisters all found work planting the land or fishing. Since at home we had this unspoken understanding that my face wasn't made for Toco, Mammy kept me back with her. Whatever she did I was right there learning. When she went to clean people's house, I was under her foot. When she was cooking or baking I watched and learnt. Home she taught us all sewing on the small Singer that she bought in instalments from a Syrian man who used to come around on a bicycle selling mainly cloth. It's one thing to know your life outside Toco is waiting on you but it's figuring out how to reach it. I can see myself as a seamstress making fancy dresses for big people in town.

Leaving didn't happen just so. For a year I was a live-in maid in Arima for some white people called the Marshalls. From overhearing talk between the husband and wife it was clear the house wasn't to her liking. She cried about being taken from her father's estate in some place called the Home Counties and made to live in this 'bloody hot place in the middle of nowhere'. As I understood it she was angling for a return to England or at least a mansion in Port of Spain. As government big chief in the east here, hubby couldn't move. Plus he'd bought land and was trying to plant it up. His habit of saying 'stiff upper lip, old girl' used to drive the wife crazy.

Having four bad children didn't help. And I mean bad. Three boys and a girl. Talk about spoilt. I never knew people could have so much and still want more. Which five-year-old girl child has her own bedroom lined with dollies and forever getting more when it wasn't even a birthday or Christmas? Mistress put her in pretty pretty dresses like the child was a dolly too. I don't think she wore the same dress to church more than twice. And the little madam was one cry cry baby. I only had to gently ask her to move for me to sweep where she was playing and she would run bawling to Mistress. Of course I would get a hard boof for upsetting the princess.

Cry cry baby was one thing. Them three boy children were another. I grew up with boys so I know rough play. But these children had no respect. Oh gosh, man. Answering back, pinching me, ordering me to clean up food they'd deliberately thrown on the floor then daring me to tell Mistress on them. Don't start me on the dirty clothes. I was forever at the scrubbing board trying to reduce that mountain.

Most nights I'd drop down on my mattress exhausted. It was right behind the kitchen, screened off with a curtain. I ain't go lie. While working for the Marshalls I cried plenty. At the time I thought it was because they worked me like a mule, which they did. But it was more than that. First time living away from home, only seeing family once for the month, that was hard. Later I toughened up.

Each trip to Toco ended with me begging Mammy to let me stay and look for another work. She wasn't happy with me at all at all. To her mind that is normally how white people children stop. They paid my wages, gave me a little food and a roof. What more I wanted? Anybody beating me? No. Cussing me? No. Interfering with me? No. She made sense. If I wanted another job, I would have to find it myself. Market on a Friday was where I got the low-down on what was going on. I opened my ears and waited.

It didn't happen as I expected. I was walking to the shop for blue soap when I bounced up a girl I knew, Nadia. She was carrying a small grip and her eyes were red red. Even though me and she ain't no big set of friends, I stopped. The stupid girl's gone and got herself pregnant for the mister of the house. In her dotish head she thought he would set her up in a house and mind her and the child. She didn't dare tell the mistress. That would have been licks. To besides, people would say Nadia had brought it on she own head.

Before Nadia had time to think through a plan the mistress had knocked this morning, quiet quiet, and given her fifteen minutes to pack and leave. No cussing, no licks. Nadia said the woman didn't even raise her voice which made it even worse. I looked at her good. Nadia was showing, only a little, but there was definitely a belly sticking out of that skinny body. As she was leaving she asked the mistress how she knew who the father was. The woman gave her one cut eye and said it had to be somebody the guard dogs knew because they'd never barked once. Mister stayed inside, hiding. He never even said goodbye.

Nothing I could do for Nadia but wish her well. I said that when the baby comes things will be better. Talking out of my behind. How I would know if a baby turns things around? She rushed to catch a train and, think what you want, I forgot about buying blue soap and headed to Nadia's former place of employment. In two-twos I was out of the Marshalls and in with the Warners. God was definitely shining His light on me that blessed morning.

I took in front before in front took me and told the mistress I know my place and I'm not the kind to interfere with nobody man and they'd better be respectful too. Mistress wasn't taking any more chances. My room had a lock.

Moving from the Marshalls to the Warners caused real commess between the two mistresses them. Only they don't quarrel like us. Apparently Mrs Marshall and her friends no longer invited Mrs Warner to play bridge. For the time I was with the Warners the two ladies never made peace.

In those early years what really opened my eyes was how much people might have and still be unhappy. Take the Mister. Big job, big house, wife, child, everything a man could want he had and then some. Yet as soon as the clock hit five that same man started on the rum and didn't stop until he dropped asleep. Every single day, Sundays included, that was his routine. Up Toco we have a fella named Mop who does do the same thing except he's not waking up next morning and holding down a big job. If Mop feeling like fishing that day then good. He gone. Otherwise he's cooling himself outside Pam's Restaurant and Bar.

With only one child in the house, a quiet boy, head always in a book, I could do the job with one hand. Mistress could see I was little fidgety.

Doris, you mentioned you could bake.

Yes, Mistress. My mother learn me to bake.

It's not learn me. It's teach me. My mother taught me to bake.

I took a deep breath and spoke slowly.

My mother teach me to bake. I could bake bread. Any kind of bread.

Not quite right. Say, my mother taught me to bake because she already did it. Past tense. And you can bake so say, I can bake bread not I could bake.

I can bake bread.

I'm sorry for going on like this. I taught in a school before I was married.

She bent down and pulled loaf tins from a cupboard.

I don't want you to sound like the natives. Now, shall we make a start on some fresh bread?

From that day on we baked together twice a week. And it was easier with her kerosene stove rather than the dirt oven we had home in the backyard. Within months I went from bread to pastry. Mistress taught me how to make her fancy pies and tarts which was one more thing I could boast about if I moved on. I hadn't reached the point of wanting to leave them for something better when Mistress announced that they were leaving me. Mister's father had died suddenly. They were returning to take over the family business in York. I never asked but if they had offered to carry me with them I would have packed before you could say God Save the King.

They were good people, the Warners. Well, Mistress was good. I suppose Mister had learnt his lesson because he never tried anything with me. And I'm much better-looking than Nadia. I wondered if he saw the baby before leaving Trinidad for good. Mistress found me a position. Best of all they left me speaking so proper that if you only heard my voice, I could pass for rich, high brown. True talk.

I settled in with a French Creole family, the Bernards, in the heart of Port of Spain. These were rich rich people with a much bigger house and a four-door Chevrolet parked in the garage. And the best part? They were Catholics too. I told them up front. I have to be falling-down sick before I will skip mass. That alone made them treat me differently. Of course the true reason they treated me better, and paid me more than the going wage, was because I could be trusted to speak nice nice in front their white friends.

Doris wasn't made for Toco and Toco wasn't made for Doris. I suppose if Mammy had a crystal ball and knew about me and Boysie she might very well have kept me locked up. But that's life. What for you ain't going to pass you. Life had finally begun.

POPO

Boysie never knew and I ain't go say nothing now. Dave and I were close in a funny way. Outside it might look strange that I catch feelings for a man that worked me to the bone on the streets. But he treated me good too. It's he who noticed me by the roadside and bought me food. Looked out for me. And while he would beat me stink nobody else better feel they could lash me. In he own way he was, well, loving. And who else wanted me? After all these years we trusted one another. Then again, I'm not dotish enough to think it's me alone he kept safe in he back pocket.

Since man can't run blood to head and laar same time, Dave could easily have whispered the secret to a next woman he was jooking. This is a race. Who reach first keeping everything. Best I hurry. I didn't want to wake Boysie in case he catch a vaps and wants to come along. Worse still, he wakes up and finds me before I'm ready to be found. These are early days and I need to secure a roof. I whispered inside he ear.

Boysie, poi, sona, Boysie.

He stirred.

I'm just going to get my two-three piece of clothes and thing.

His eyelids raised a tups.

Go later and I'll come with you.

I good.

Dave partners might be there.

Nah. Relax yourself. It's Sunday. I go run down and come back now for now.

The eyes opened a little more.

Place still dark.

Nobody can see me.

He pulled me close and tongued my mouth.

Come back quick.

Either this man getting bazodee over me or he could well act. Maybe it's happy he's happy to have a woman minding him, washing he clothes, cooking hot roti morning time and making sure the place clean.

Whole road I prayed my secret had remained just that. Dave was mixed up in all kind of commess. He worried a day might come when he'd have to digs off the island in a rush, maybe to family in Grenada. This was passage money and a little something to help get started. I caught him burying it in the back by me. That money stayed in the ground and it never once crossed my mind to touch it because Dave would have hunted me down and made me suffer plenty before killing me.

My little place looked like I'd left it, the bottom half of the split door smashed and hanging down. Inside was cool and dark. I wasn't surprised to find thief had done gone through and taken the little I had. At least they had the decency to leave my two-three dress. As for my cook pot, tawah, enamel plates and cups, bucket, a cologne, slippers, I ain't seeing them in a hurry. Suppose the thief was coming back? I best do this thing fast fast.

In the dawn light, between house and latrine, my four-foot tall tulsi tree stood healthy and untroubled. A tulsi tree brings the household good fortune. Time to test if that Hindu custom is true. With only my two hands I started flinging dirt away. Lucky thing it was middle of the rainy season or the ground would've been hard like concrete.

I dug and dug and dug. My knees pressed into the rocky earth and I felt tiny stones sticking to raw skin. I broke a fingernail. I should've brought a shovel. Nah. I couldn't throw a shovel at this secret. My bruised hands worked fast fast like a dog searching for a long-buried chicken bone. I was in the roots and feeling around. Nothing. Only thing to do was go deeper. I had to be quick. Who else Dave might've told? The baby mother? And what about one of them yes-man partners he kept chook up near? But then again it was only me and he who put this in the ground and it's me who thought of marking the spot by planting the tulsi.

I was up to my elbows in mud and dirt when my fingertips touched cloth. As I pulled it out the force landed me bradaps on my back. The outer crocus cloth crumbled. Inside was a bulging pillowcase exactly as I'd prayed. No time to count but this looked like the whole two thousand dollars that went in the ground. Boysie or no Boysie, it's now my time, yes. I've taken enough licks. This money is what Dave had creamed off from the gambling business and made from my back. If he could hide up this amount imagine what he was making the rest of the time. Well it's going to work for me now so I ain't have to take another john so long as God spare life.

MANA LALA

Boysie reached early this morning and told me to pack a bag for the batcha.

Okay, I'll change one time.

You ain't going nowhere. Me and Chunksee hitting the road.

Why? Where?

We going for my didi to see him.

Why I can't go? Me and your big sister ain't have no quarrel.

No. I'm going by myself.

I blinked back tears.

What go happen when Chunksee want to lie down and sleep?

Put he in a bed or hold him. That ain't no problem.

Put him in a bed and next thing the batcha roll and fall down.

Boysie let go a long steupse.

You think I'm poohar?

I ain't saying you is an ulloo. It's just that you turn your back for a minute and anything could happen. Best that people come here to look for Chunksee.

Oh, so I can't take my beta to see he family?

Don't raise your voice so, nah. People go hear.

I look like I care? You can't stop me doing what I want with my own flesh and blood.

Boysie, that's not what I was saying at all at all.

Better not be. Look at that face. That's a little Boysie.

While we there quarrelling rain had started to come down heavy. All Boysie could do was cool he-self until it passed. Funny thing but before the Carrera jail time Boysie never used to shout at me. Other people yes, but never me.

I know he loves Chunksee more than anyone in this world. I know. While the batcha's so small I like to know exactly where he is and who have him. He might be hungry or need changing. Why would Boysie want to do them things when he could well carry me with him? And he say he going by didi. I hope my beta ain't ending up in some rum shop or gambling den. When I mentioned that Boysie got vex again.

You think I will carry Chunksee anywhere so?

I'm only asking a question.

You feel you alone know how to care for he.

I is he mother.

And I is he father.

Boysie pushed his head out the window. Rain had stopped as abruptly as it had started. He was holding the batcha. All I wanted to do was snatch Chunksee and lock the door.

Pack the bag quick. We go take a taxi down the road. In half-hour beta go be inside again.

I didn't move. It looked like he would walk away without milk, diaper, everything. I sighed and made up a parcel.

Don't keep him out after the place making dark. You hearing me? He will catch dew.

Boysie didn't even bother to say thanks cat or thanks dog. I kissed Chunksee.

My sona beta. Come back soon to your mama.

If I showed him that I ain't here to cause trouble maybe tookra tookra he will take me with him when he's showing off the batcha. Anyhow, this won't last. Boysie ain't changing diaper whole day. I think this going by didi has something to do with a secret Boysie told me and I don't think he's told another soul. His ma had dropped down dead a few months before Chunksee was born. Boysie felt she spirit came back to earth inside beta. I think he wants to see if he ma will try and send any kind of sign to didi. But then again I don't know if that was just talk he was talking. I mean to say, this is the same Boysie who didn't want pundit to do the namkaran but he believes he mother reincarnated as Chunksee. Talk about a pick-and-choose Hindu. I made a joke and said maybe it's he father that reincarnated in Chunksee. He got so vex for a second I thought he would box me. At least now I know not to call Bhagrang Singh's name again.

Boysie walked away with Chunksee and left me by myself. I burst into tears. Ma saw everything and didn't say boo. Apparently this is not she business. I hope I'm not losing my man and no way I'm losing my batcha too.

POPO

Of course, I knew life wouldn't stay sweet sweet. We'd hardly settled when things went crazy. Saturday morning and Boysie left whistling happy as pappy. Me ain't bother. I say he must be gone to check on somebody who owe him money. Aye aye, lunchtime reach and I see him opening the gate, only he wasn't alone. Somebody batcha hanging on to he neck and a bag I don't recognise over he shoulder. Just as I'd suspected. The neemakharam have child.

Chunksee, this is your Popo Tanty.

The child didn't want to see no Popo Tanty. He squished up the little face and hid in Boysie's neck. He leaned forwards for me to take the baby. I stepped back.

Who batcha you thief?

He pretended not to hear.

What happen Chunksee? Eh, sona beta? Whole road you there good good. Go by Popo Tanty, nah.

That made the batcha cling tighter. Boysie looked at me.

Ain't you told me you wanted a child but you can't make? Well, I bring one for you. Ain't Chunksee?

That was a hard slap.

I tried to take the batcha and he let go a bawl for the whole street to hear. Me and crying don't mix. And I had only said I don't think I can get pregnant easily but that didn't mean I wasn't

71

trying. Like he ain't bothered with we having batcha because a woman done make child for he.

Boysie was busy kissing the sweet cheeks. I swallowed whatever I was feeling and gently rubbed Chunksee's little back.

Hello.

Boysie smiled.

As he small small so we call him Chunksee.

I fixed my face not to cuss or cry.

I named him Anthony. Anthony Singh. When he get big that is what they go call him.

I smoothed his soft hair.

Hello Anthony Singh, Chunksee. Come by me for a love-up, nah. Come for doolar.

Nothing doing. The batcha gripped on to his baap's merino vest. I took the bag off Boysie's shoulder. Diapers, vests, socks, a piece of cloth that must be the baby blanket, two nipples, powder, coconut oil and a bottle of Bay Rum were all crammed inside.

Why you bring so much thing? Like he staying the night or what?

Boysie grinned.

Well yeah. I bring Chunksee for you to mind. He go stay here. Ain't my son is your son too, poi?

I focused on the bag.

Popo, we ain't making we own.

Tears were right on the edge of tumbling out my eyes. I blinked them away and cleared my throat.

Boysie, you gone mad? Who is this child's mother? And which part of your brain think I want to mind some other woman batcha?

I began clearing the table of the few dirty cups that were there.

I didn't say nothing to you but Mother Gizzard gave me thing to take. I could be pregnant this month, next month. For all I know I done have a batcha starting.

Then good. Chunksee will be a big brother.

No. The child can come and go but he ain't living here. Besides, he mother won't let you. Who is the child mother?

We're starting as a family today.

And if I say no?

He looked at the batcha with a love I ain't seen before.

Up to you but this is my son. If you don't want batcha, Chunksee's ma will be over happy to come here by me.

What you saying?

He laughed in a sick way.

You have brains. Work it out.

Boysie turned away from me and started bouncing the child and cooing in the little ears. I looked at the two of them hugging up and felt thandaa to my bones, like somebody put me inside an ice factory. Boysie's whole face was different when he played with Chunksee. Everything about him softened, was gentler, lighter. This little thing might be the only one Boysie truly cares for. I could mind Chunksee or what? The neemakharam had me exactly where he wanted.

I keep asking you who is the mother.

You won't know she. Mana Lala. Me ain't with she again. Don't worry, you ain't getting horn.

That's because you're busy horning me with plenty other woman.

He didn't answer. I took deep breaths. All this is a reminder never to trust a man. Any man. Ever. Let the batcha stay little bit. This might done itself when baap here gets fed up with a batcha wailing and shitting all the time. He-self might hand back Chunksee to his mai. I pulled open the bottom drawer of the press, pushed things round and began packing Chunksee's things inside.

MANA LALA

Just as I suspected. Boysie's moved a woman in and not any ole woman. It's a low-down whore, a randee he picked up off the street named Popo. If he ain't careful it's a set of nastiness she go give him. We back to doing thing now and then so he go pass it to me. Randee. How he could go from me to that? I kept myself for he and he alone all these years, waiting like an ass. Who was the one visiting jail, carrying food? When he came out last time, head hot wanting a batcha bad bad, every last one of my family told me to leave him. Instead, I gave the man a sweet sona beta. And this is my thanks? Leave me for a dirty stinking randee from the gutter? People say she ain't nothing to look at. Two thin foot and face like a long mango. Now I know that when he takes Chunksee it's Popo who minding him. If Boysie thinks she can look after Chunksee he'd better think again. Just because I don't push up myself, or talk nonstop, people take me for a cunumunu. Well, when it come to my batcha, I'll stand up for myself.

I told Ma what was what and stood back expecting she would call a panchayat with the family. She refused point blank.

But why, Ma? This ain't serious enough for we to talk about?

How we go stand up to Boysie? He's the child father. And since he kill that badjohn fella, Dave, nobody crossing he.

Ma sighed.

Believe what you want, Mana Lala, but more than one person tell me to my face that Boysie done kill other people. Don't

play like you ain't hear that talk. You think I want that kind
of commess in my house? No thank you.

But Ma, is your flesh and blood he's exposing to that randee.

Look, all of we tired warn you to stay away from that bai.
I tell you. Your brothers tell you. Your sisters tell you. But
you so own way you went and make batcha for he. Always
had to be different. Well, what to do? Now take what
come.

I was fuming but I couldn't answer back. It's she house I'm
living in.

Your brothers them trying to make a living. Them is good
boys. I ain't want them mixed up in trouble with Boysie.

Ma went in the bedroom. I followed.

Why you there behind me? I come to get the posey.

She took the full posey to the back of the house and threw the
piss in the bush.

So you ain't going to say nothing to Boysie?

Me? How much time I must tell you that is your business. I
staying far.

What I suppose to do, then? Eh? He ain't go listen to me.

Well if you done know that then keep your trap shut. Next
thing he get vex and take Chunksee for good.

Ma making sense but I can't stay quiet. What he should do is
have me and Chunksee live with he rather than some blasted
diseased randee. I walked to the side of the house where the

block of ice was stored in a covered oil drum and chipped off a small block with the ice pick. Ma watched me hard.

So early you chewing ice?

Yeah. Nothing wrong with that.

I never see somebody love ice so. But then again you was funny from small. I don't know what to say to you again. You never learn to do nothing good. Nothing. And now you bring worries with this man. I fed up, yes.

I wanted to say I know that already. How much times I have to hear how it good for me and how useless and worthless and ugly I am? No point begging for understanding when she done write me off years now. I put on my old rubber boots and went in the back garden where we plant things to sell. Sweet peppers and ochro looked ready to pick.

*

When Boysie next came for Chunksee I had dhal, rice and curry chicken bubbling in the iron pot waiting. Normally meat is only on Sundays but a lady in the market had fowl selling cheap. Boysie licked he enamel plate clean.

So, where you and the batcha going today?

He swallowed.

How you mean?

You going by your didi?

He grunted.

Where?

Mana Lala, he with me wherever I is, all right.

You're not carrying him near Popo?

Boysie let go a loud belch. He might be dressing better these days and looking happy happy but he still ain't have manners.

Food was good. Your hand getting sweeter.

If you parking him up somewhere then best leave him here. He'd be more comfortable.

Boysie laughed and a stink fart escaped.

Like you drink rum?

He pushed the plate away and stood up.

Give me he bag quick. And don't forget the little toy car. The red one. He over love that car.

I looked at the ground. Nothing I say will stop Boysie doing exactly as he pleases including taking my batcha by that randee today. Same time Ma came in hugging up Chunksee. A quick kiss on his sweet cheek was all I could manage. I wanted to cuff down Boysie. How he could do this to me? How?

Tell Ma bye bye. See you when I see you. Tomorrow or the day after.

While I cleaned and washed wares I tried to make sense of this. Who ever heard of taking a batcha all the time so from he mother? He doesn't need a pa now. That's later, when Chunksee's all ten, eleven years. A child belongs with the mother when he's small. We're talking wrong and right. For now my head had a pain and my heart was running a hundred yards race. I could kill that randee and all Ma can say is to bide my time. Bide my time when he's giving my beta to she?

Ma warned that with Boysie's hot blood it's best not to provoke him. He could burn down we house or make fire on we market garden. Boysie and he friends feel them is the baddest badjohn in the whole of Trinidad. I slumped into the hammock with a cup of ice. The pieces were too big and hurt my teeth. I liked that.

POPO

If anybody had said to me a year ago that Dave would be dead, his Town Boys gang scattered, and me and Boysie Singh living good good together, I would've laughed in their face. I'm learning fast. Unlike Dave, Boysie ain't no hard man. He might feel he's a big thing inside these few Woodbrook streets where they treat him as king, especially since he finished off Dave. Ask in town proper and it's, Boysie who? That lil coolie boy? He does thief from other fishermen. I hear he even thief crab pots from he own cousin. All he like to do is gamble. That is the talk.

People ain't 'fraid like they used to 'fraid Dave. The only reason people don't cross Boysie just so is because he will use Three Little Threes first and ask questions later. But he have looks and plenty sweet talk for the ladies. If Boysie passed anywhere within touching distance and didn't give me a little feel-up I would think he's coming down with something. The other night he reached home skinning he teeth so wide I thought maybe he was coming directly from a next woman's bed. Instead he wrapped his hands around my waist.

Popo girl, I was walking home and all I'm thinking is to reach home quick. You know why? Because you here.

Well hard-back me melted a little. I rubbed his head and teased him about being the big new man around town, the new Dave. He liked that talk too bad.

You have the respect already. Thing is you must turn that respect into money. Do that and black, white, dog, cat, nobody will be able to boss you around. They'll be begging you.

But Popo, where I finding money to start up a betting shop? The little bit of money I make with my gambling on the street plus the fishing don't come to much. Taking a loan from them sharks ain't worth it. I go be paying back till the grave.

Then find it somewhere else. A man like you should be controlling the whappee. That made Dave a good heap of change.

He nodded.

Give people around here a chance and they will gamble morning, noon and night. We should give them a good betting shop.

Oh gosh, babes. That is the thing self.

I stopped the head massage and plonked myself in the hammock so we faced one another.

Boysie, since you take me in my life change. You and me come as one. We even have Chunksee here half the time.

Exactly.

I'm not saying I want the shaadi because you is my man.

Same for me, poi. You already like my wife.

A hand smoothed over my chest, felt the shape of my tot-tots, and gripped one tight. I smiled.

Careful. One side go jealous the next.

Tell that other one to have patience. I'm coming to give it a
love-up soon as I finish feeling up this side.

With unexpected force he pushed my face into the wall and did
me rough from behind. I felt his energy. We could have it all.

Later, lying together quiet in the bed, I let him suckle and
snuggle up. He drifted into sleep with my nipple still inside his
mouth. I don't need to make a baby. He is my baby. Plus I have
to mind that boy child he does bring home.

Boysie woke less than half-hour later. I smiled and reminded
him about the betting-shop talk.

And Boysie, you-self know whatever put in making back
tenfold.

You see me here? I ain't have two farthings to rub together.

Nothing?

Nothing.

I took a deep breath.

Maybe you and me could start together.

But how?

I have cash.

He laughed. I waited. When he realised I was still watching him
quiet quiet the laughing stopped.

Where you getting money from?

I looked him dead in he eye.

A man leave it for me. I can't say more or I'll have to hand it
back.

How much?

Enough to buy a little place. Start off small and build, tookra tookra.

Boysie's face twisted all how.

How much?

Two thousand.

Boysie bolted out the bed, eyes opened big big. He got so excited I thought he might take in with a heart attack.

How much? Two thousand? Popo, you have that kind of money and you sit down here and ain't say nothing?

I didn't say I have it. But I can get it.

Boysie's mouth was open like he's catching flies. He walked around in a circle.

I could more than buy a place with that.

Aye, we. We could buy a place.

He leaned over and buss a kiss on my mouth.

Of course it go be yours and mines together. Everything I have is yours. You know that.

Well, that was news to me.

Look Boysie, let we do this properly.

Boysie nodded.

You and me go do this as if we married, pati and patni. But it's a loan. I ain't looking to jook out your eye. As the business come good you pay back with a little something extra. In your own time, tookra tookra.

He cracked his fingers one by one. Pop, pop, pop. I continued.

As far as town go it's Boysie's casa alone. They don't have to know we is partners and it's my money. In fact, they mustn't know it's my cash. What you think?

Boysie was skinning he teeth like it was Christmas.

That could work.

I smiled.

Yeah, man. We is a team.

Within days Boysie was bussing style telling everybody that he could buy a place. That ain't bother me. What I don't like is that he can see people scorning me and he doesn't correct them. They're thinking he take this poor randee and minding she. Home alone he's always taking up for me but nobody hearing that. It's all right. My money's out there looking for profit not love.

A few properties were good but they didn't work out. One had a problem with the licence. A next one the man changed the price. I liked Prince Street, number fifty-nine. It's a low house, long long that could divide into three. The front piece we could rent out, the back piece we could make into a gambling shop and we could live in the middle. The good thing is that we would be living right by the action. I wish I could be inside the casa, checking on things and keeping the business oiled. Shame no woman can step foot in them places. At least this way I'm close enough to see the traffic going in and out. My guts tell me this go make we king and queen around here.

DORIS

I liked working and living in Port of Spain long before I met Boysie. Definitely plenty more was happening in the capital. And I used to think that Arima was bustling. Well, don't talk about Toco. Up there they have no clue what's going on right here in Trinidad. Shiny motor cars are taking over from horse and donkey. Big stores like Hoadley's and Glendinning's are sprouting in town. If you have the money you can buy anything you want.

My people, the Bernards, are important. Sunday mass can't start without them taking up the front pew with their name on it. Nine children, all coming and going except the last three who are still small and under the nanny's care. They treat me like family. The days can be long because they're always entertaining but that is just how they operate. I have no worries. Behind the big house is a two-room cottage that is mines and mines alone. I'm not sure 'mines' is correct but I 'fraid to ask.

Being part of all the Port of Spain hustle is a new kind of freedom. Mistress Bernard is not one to nit-pick if I take my time to walk back from the market. They know I work hard and will always do extra without hinting that overtime might be due. Your girl know that give and take in life is the best way. My wages are decent. Toco gets something come month end. Every once in a while I buy a little two yards of cotton dress cloth from the Syrian man selling house to house, goods on the back of his autocycle. And I put away something under the mattress.

*

85

Two nights this week I've had the same dream. Town was flooded. Me and the Bernards were in a big boat motoring through Port of Spain streets. Morocoys by the hundreds were swimming up and down. Now, to have such a strange dream not once but twice must mean something. Friday market I asked a whe-whe fella to take my bet. He grinned,

Morocoy? You even know how to place a bet?

Ain't that is what you here for?

He laughed.

A nice thing like you. I feel you go come lucky.

I better be.

He pulled out a copy book. In the front was a picture of a Chinee man with numbers on his body and pictures with numbers all around him like he's a god.

Reds, watch me. If you dream morocoy then you should play twenty-five.

Aye, watch your mouth. My mother and father didn't put 'reds' nowhere on my birth certificate.

All right. Don't get on so.

I gave him a pretend cut eye and smiled.

Okay, so play twenty-five for me.

Wait, you could also play eleven as the partner and fourteen as the spirit partner.

Hush with all that stupidness. I look like I have money to waste?

That's nothing. If you was a proper betting person you would check the last number that draw. That was a five and you would make your calculations on the one-sixteenth chart.

I ain't have time for all that. Fifty cents on twenty-five and done with that.

He wrote down my bet, took the coins and told me to look for him all lunchtime so.

Boysie go buss the mark any time after twelve o'clock.

Boysie who?

Where you from that you ain't know Boysie Singh?

Now I shot him a proper cut eye.

I don't make it my business to know all you betting man them.

He skinned he teeth.

Well, if your number comes up that's who go be paying out.

He turned to go.

Wait, so where the mark's bussing?

Nah, nah, nah. I tell you and you run call police. Next thing I lock up in jail.

I rolled my eyes.

Go along. I'll look for you in half-hour.

I walked around the market with my list. Tonight they have guests from England so I need two chickens. Mother Gizzard in the far corner of the market has the best fowl. Only trouble is I 'fraid she too bad. I mean I 'fraid her too bad. People say she's an obeah woman. We have one up Toco. If she don't like your face she will turn you into a corbeau just for spite. But whatever Mother Gizzard's feeding them fowl or funny prayers she saying, it's doing the job. Sweetest plump chicken in the whole market.

Bracing myself, I headed to her section. Along the way I bounced up other maids and people I knew from Arima side. I spotted Mother Gizzard sitting on a peerha next to a wire pen with must be three chickens. Normally she has plenty so I stopped the ole talk and went straight by her. As I got to the stall my eye caught a group of men gathering right behind her. The Indian fella who took my bet was in the huddle waiting.

You come to buy chicken or watch, man?

I jumped.

Sorry. Morning. Two chicken, please. Good size. And you could fix it up for me?

Kill and pluck?

Yes, please.

You know that's extra. And give me a little time. Me grandson is the one who does do the cleaning and plucking but he gone walk about. He coming back just now.

No rush.

You want to choose?

I saw the men were now crowding in a tight circle around some-one but I couldn't see who.

Choose for me, nah.

Suddenly the men were shouting, some were clapping one other on the back, others throwing down pieces of paper. Mother Gizzard was saying something I couldn't quite hear.

That is all? Miss, that is all?

All? Yes. Thanks.

I looked at her properly.

That is whe-whe over there?

She nodded.

I placed my first bet today. I wonder if my number called?

As the circle of men fell apart I waved to my boy. He saw me, whispered something to a man next to him and began walking towards me. I was already planning how to spend my winnings.

So, how much I win, eh?

I caught myself. That was not proper English. At least it happened out here where people don't know better.

He shook his head.

Not today. Sorry. Them morocoy swim right pass and gone their way. Now, if you did dream horse, or nineteen, all now so you would be collecting.

Well, it served me right for betting when the law and church are clear. It's illegal and a sin. I should never have done it.

Anyhow, check me if you want to bet again. I does be all about here.

Me bet again and waste my money? I don't think so.

I turned to Mother Gizzard.

Let me make a rounds of the market and come back.

She moved her chin just enough to signal she'd heard and agreed. Definitely not one to use up energy by saying yes cat or no dog.

I picked up a few things. Pigeon peas were selling cheap cheap and the family love my stew peas with a little potato. I wanted watermelon but the man I usually buy from wasn't there. It was time to collect my plucked chickens and head up the road. Chatting away to Mother Gizzard was the bet maker and another Indian fella in white shorts and merino. I ignored them and smiled at Mother Gizzard. She handed me a brown paper parcel. I almost got a half smile.

Next time you passing come tell me how it cook.

Before I could say anything the Indian in the merino rushed in.

Mother Gizzard, you always talk truth. The thing is whether this reds here can cook your chicken good.

I took a step back to take in the fella properly.

Excuse me? I hear right? Who you think you is? Eh?

He grinned and I noticed his perfectly formed lips.

I know Mother Gizzard chicken sweet but I don't know your cooking.

The smile widened.

But I have a feeling you're good in the kitchen. And you know what they say about woman who good in the kitchen.

My face was heating up and I didn't know what to say except,

Move out my way.

He straightened up.

Oh gosh, I ain't mean to trouble you. We just talking.

Mother Gizzard play boxed his ears.

Boysie Singh, behave yourself and stop troubling my customers.

Okay, okay.

He turned.

I'm sorry miss. Miss, what's your name?

He real boldface, yes.

That is for me to know and you to find out.

Oh, I will find out. Trust me. I will find out.

And just so, he turned and walked off at a pace with my bet maker rushing to keep up. Boysie Singh. Ha! He'd better keep them pretty lips far from me. Damn boldface man.

MANA LALA

Mana Lala, stop crunching ice. Oh gosh, man. Whole day is this cricks, cricks, cricks of you grinding. Making my skin crawl.

I bit down on the piece already in my mouth as quietly as I could manage. It sounded even louder than before.

I'm still hearing you. Stop.

Sorry, Ma.

Look, stay in the yard when you're eating ice. Damn thing driving me mad.

I went outside. My cup of ice was done anyway and I wanted more. Don't ask me why I prefer ice to even ice cream. Nothing feels as good. Ma will have to cool she-self, yes. If I have any regret it's that I only picked up eating ice when my belly was big.

I spotted Boysie coming down the road and rushed inside to straighten my dress and pass a comb through my hair. By the time I reached outside again he was already playing with Chunksee. He said hello in my general direction but didn't look at me.

You taking Chunksee today?

Yeah, he's spending it with me and Popo Tanty.

Why?

Well, she living by me. Of course he go be with she.

My stomach dropped. I heard myself talking but it was like I was watching myself from beyond my body. Popo ain't new to me but oh gosh, man. He real throwing it in my face. Boysie won't be happy until I'm less than nothing. I held my hand out for Chunksee.

He need changing before you go.

Boysie followed me inside. I laid the batcha on the bed and pulled off his short pants. Until I saw the drops of water fall on his belly I didn't even know I was crying.

How you could do me that?

Do what?

We was supposed to do the shaadi. Chunksee is we beta.

He laughed the way he does when he wants me to know I'm poohar and he's smart. I couldn't help myself.

Why you pick she? Is we have a child together. We've been together so long.

More laughing in my face. His scorn's enough to make me boil down like bhagee. I don't get a say. Might as well crawl away quiet.

Relax yourself, Mana Lala. What do you? And Popo have plenty that you ain't know about.

Tears wet my cheeks. I was so vex, frustrated but I had to be careful. His mood was still good.

Please Boysie, this ain't fair.

Don't please Boysie me. It's your fault I don't want to stay here.

Me? What I do?

You there letting your mother make all kind of puja and rasi name and one set of foolishness on my beta head. All you too poohar. I ain't letting all you bring up my beta with that backwardness.

The namkaran was the only thing. We ain't do nothing else. Please Boysie.

All you so should've stayed cutting cane.

He picked up a fresh clean Chunksee. I reached to give them a hug and he elbowed me away. I tried again.

Girl, move. Move.

With one hand covering my face he pushed me back so hard I thought my eyes were going inside my head. I tried to peel he hand off, but a sharp kick to my shin made me bawl. Ma came running.

Boysie! Mana Lala! What happening?

She was between us. Chunksee started bawling. I was bawling. Boysie shouted at me.

That's the kind of mother you is? Upsetting the batcha.

I held Ma's arm.

He carrying my beta by that randee to mind.

Now Ma started crying.

Boysie, we ain't do you nothing. Leave Chunksee with he mother and nanee, nah. You and Mana Lala must patch up.

All you together since small. Why you carrying on so?

I don't even know if he heard what Ma said as he was busy rubbing the batcha's back and shushing him. I held out my hands, but Boysie marched off. Ma must have known I would run after them because she gripped my wrist and whispered,

Let he go. Vex that man more and I don't know what he will do. Don't worry. Chunksee will come back. No one can keep a beta from he mother.

I bawled and bawled. It took all my strength to stand there and watch as they turned the corner and disappeared. Ma and everybody in the family had been right. Boysie couldn't care less about me.

I went to the ice box and with one mighty stab of the ice pick hacked off a large chunk. This time I wasn't going to chip it into smaller pieces. Under the tamarind tree in the back, I cleared a place. It was far enough that no one could see me from the house and more better yet, Ma wouldn't hear to quarrel about my crunching. Slumped against the tree, I bit into solid ice long after my jaws and teeth were screaming in pain. But I didn't care. Each chomp of solid, teeth-breaking ice brought a tiny instance of relief. Over and over I vowed that when he brought back Chunksee I would stay quiet. I don't want to give him any excuse to stay away because I quarrelled or cussed him. He has to remember how things used to be.

Sounds of Ma talking reached my ears. My big brother had dropped in, probably checking what Ma had cooked. Making no attempt to keep their voices low, they well talked my business. Even though it was nothing new it still hurt the way they carried on like I was an ulloo for staying with Boysie. They couldn't understand why I was so dotish running after a man like he. Now I have Boysie's child that was it for me. Ma said she 'fraid Boysie. My brother agreed. We were stuck with him and he was bound to bring suffering to this house. Ma should make it clear this mess is my making and to put up and shut up.

All that hate for my Boysie, the man I chose. As I listened I felt I was dissolving like the ice block. None of this would have happened if that randee didn't skin open she legs to get in with Boysie. It's she to blame and I go do for she. Just wait. She think I'm chupid and ugly? Wait till I fix she.

I was so upset about everything I ignored the pain that had started in my jaw. Gradually it ramped up and up and by night time I couldn't rest, fuss it was hurting. I walked up and down chewing cloves. Every morning and evening of life I've cleaned my teeth with a datwan so toothache was new to me. Even Chunksee has a small datwan I made from a hibiscus stalk. Ma glanced inside my mouth but she ain't see nothing.

It's all that ice you does be eating. It ain't good for your mouth.

Well something happened because this is real torture.
Oh Lord.

By morning I was ready to do anything to stop the agony. Unfortunately the quack, Lalchand, doesn't open Sundays for nobody. Neighbour sent over some clove oil. That was supposed to be better than chewing cloves. It didn't touch the pain.

How I got through the day and night I ain't know. Worse than making baby. Lalchand yanked out one of me back teeth. He couldn't understand how it cracked down the side so. I didn't explain. No point because I'm not giving up my ice.

POPO

Look at you, Popo girl. Imagine, you have a betting shop. Well, the marish and the parish might call it Boysie's casa. So long as he remember who's the real boss, I don't mind what people think. True when we started out he tried to pull a fast one. We were buying this place and Boysie wanted me to believe that the lawyer could only put one name on the deed. He feel I chupid or what? I ain't have schooling but no way I was handing over all my money, because it's my money now, and have nothing to show for it. I went myself with Boysie to the lawyer and told him if he ain't know how to put two names on a deed then we go find a next lawyer to fix up. I look poohar? No, sir. Boysie grinned at the lawyer.

You see how she sharp?

He slipped a hand around my waist.

That is why I love this woman. She does keep me on my toes.

He should know better. That mamaguy is for chupid young girls. Boysie gambles too much and I need insurance in case he loss away. If it's not a card game he's there flying kite and betting on that. And with the whe-whe I've heard that instead of remaining banker the ulloo's stepped aside and let George do it so he could bet. Against he own house. That is so extra dotish I don't know what to say. I ain't show no vex face because that will only end with the two of we cussing and carrying on.

I waited. While squeezing he foot in the bed I said,

Please, poi, darling, it's your business. You must be large and in charge. Always stay banker. People must 'fraid you. Who go respect a man who losing money in he own casa?

Well, I suppose last week I did lose a few dollars. But I go win it back.

Boysie, you could win big every single day if you stop betting. We know the house always wins in the end.

Yeah but nothing sweet like a game of whappee.

I rubbed between he leg, my fingertips brushing wrinkled balls.

What? Sweeter than this?

He smiled.

Keep smart and you'll be king of Port of Spain. Then you'll know what feeling good is about. Imagine living in a big house and you behind the wheel of a fancy motor car. That will feel like winning a hundred, no a thousand, whappee games.

My boy skin he teeth, happy happy. Time to make the next move. I straddled him and whispered,

From what coming in, I feel we could start a second betting shop. What you think?

Second? Nah, nah, nah. This one alone have me tired. You ain't know how much I does have to do when the day come.

Get help. That way you'll able to cross between places making sure nobody ain't thiefing we.

I ain't know, Popo. What we have is good enough. And we living right by the casa.

This man needs patience I don't have, yes. I went deep inside, dug out a smile, and slowly started grinding down on him.

People will turn when you're passing and say, yes, don't make trouble for Boysie, you hear. He's the boss man of Port of Spain now.

Hearing boss man and Boysie in the same breath made his laar stiffen inside me.

I can't manage without you.

I lowered my head towards him expecting a kiss. Instead he bit my lip, then my neck, and slowly licked my face. In seconds we were on the floor, my arse raised high. He yanked my hair while shoving himself inside me. I hope the bruises around my neck don't turn black and blue.

MANA LALA

Once rain's not falling, I wash clothes on a Monday and press on a Tuesday. That's been me from since I can't remember. Even when the others were living home it was I who washed. Pressing passed to me when my big sister married and went to live near the Croisee. Well, I can't expect Ma to help with the arthritis in she hand. Today I was taking a five from the jooking board when it hit me. Why I didn't think of that before? If Boysie brought he clothes for me to wash then he ain't have a choice but to come by we more often. I'll see him and he wouldn't have reason to take Chunksee. It's no hardship for me to wash two-three extra piece of clothes. And I want to give this ease.

From the state of Boysie's clothes I don't think that whore he's minding knows about blue soap much more owns a block of starch. He's a man like he white shorts and a white merino. It come almost like a uniform. The randee's probably not bleaching the whites in sunshine or remembering to add a cube of blue with the final rinse water.

I told Boysie I don't mind if he wanted me to fix up his dirty clothes.

Nah, don't worry. That's all right.

I kept quiet. Next time he came for Chunksee I took a white merino I'd washed and held it next to his.

Which one more better?

Boysie thinks he's looking good. Well, let him see truth and decide which woman should be in charge.

I ain't want people saying Chunksee's pa looking like nobody does do for he.

He gathered up Chunksee's bag and off they went with the batcha hardly noticing me.

Truth is washing is hard work. Both palms have a slash of red soreness from the wire handle of the buckets. The standpipe's only a five minutes down the road but it's the amount of times I'm up and down, up and down, toting water. Of course if Boysie was around he might give a hand. He friend Tinsingh has a girl living not too far from we and she does boast how Tinsingh patched up the roof or Tinsingh dug a drain for them. Proper hard work. Why the father of my batcha can't be a little like that?

Boysie and Chunksee reached back that evening toting a bag of dirty clothes for me. Inside were all whites. I cuddled my beta tight tight.

Once it ain't rain, pass for these clothes day after tomorrow.
And you could stay one time and eat.

He nodded and went straight through calling hello to Ma. She said something but didn't come out she room. The only reason he does come inside the house this hour is for the plate of food I leave covered down in the kitchen. I wonder if Popo could cook? Today is one of his favourites: rice, dhal and curry seim, beans that I picked fresh from the back.

*

I scrubbed and scrubbed them clothes till my shoulder was breaking. Once they've taken some good sun I scrubbed them again, rinsed and hung them on the line to dry making sure I didn't hang them upside down. As it is I have enough bad luck.

By three o'clock the clothes were dry dry. I wanted to press same time but aare baap rey, all my shoulder, my neck, my back were killing me. Tomorrow I will starch the short pants them properly and press everything. Lifting that heavy hot hot iron does give me a pain all down one side. And talk about heat. As if the sun ain't hot enough, it's heat from the coal pot and iron. I wrapped the handle in plenty cloth yet still managed to take on a burn or two. But it's for my Boysie. Aside from Chunksee nobody in the world matters more.

I folded the clothes and wrapped them up neat neat in brown paper. When he saw the parcel of clothes he buss a grin and squeezed my waist.

But Mana Lala, you're better than the Chinee laundry.

That was all the thanks I needed.

From that day, and for years to come, me alone did Boysie's washing and pressing. At least he kept one foot here. He can be sure I care how he looks. Better than Popo letting him walk the road in dingy clothes. I told him anything else he wants doing just ask. This is he home too. It doesn't matter what time, day or night, if Boysie reach hungry I will get up and make two fresh roti for him. Bet she doesn't treat him so. All she good for is one thing. That might be fine for a while, but don't tell me he plans to keep she. Surely he have more sense than that.

Boysie should do the right thing by the beta and me. I might not push up myself like them other women but I'll remain long after they fly away. People like Popo only there to take what they can get. Turn around twice and you ain't seeing them. Boysie was my first love and he'll be my last. Even with all that's happened I'm here biding my time. One day we will live together as a family, me, Boysie, Chunksee and the rest of the children we make. He loves having a son so much I'm sure he'll want a next one with me as soon as he get over this maakaachood randee. I shouldn't cuss so stink. Patience. What goes around comes around.

POPO

Tookra tookra the whe-whe schools are bringing in the cash, especially the one in Laventille. Boysie's a natural businessman. He over love money. Our odds of twenty-nine to one are chopping the competition off at the knees. That was my doing but I let Boysie feel he had come up with it. Last thing I want is he thinking I'm pushing myself up in what is man business. If he would stop throwing a hand in whappee or playing whe-whe and losing to he own casa, I could relax myself. I want us to have a few clubs going steady and then maybe we could take over other businesses. I'm ready for anything that looks like it might bring in a few more dollars.

And I've noticed how much more respect Boysie's getting these days. We can't go nowhere without people coming up and saying hello or wanting to shake he hand. I suppose they know his star's rising and looking to see what he can do for them. Maybe they 'fraid him. His side hustle in beatings for cash and that temper bad enough to even frighten jumbie.

*

Now you see this minding child thing? That have me real vex. I have nothing against Chunksee but I am not he mai. Up to now I ain't see she. From what I hear she have she two hand, two foot so could well look after the bai. By rights a batcha should stay with he own mother. Of course, I don't show bad face but he's a handful. I have one eye on how each club's doing and the other on Chunksee running up and down the place. Don't get me wrong. He's a good bai. I just don't want to mind child. And when he's here it's plenty extra work washing, cooking, cleaning plus it does cost me. Me and Kalliecharan, who does walk the road selling fresh cow's dood, come good partners as I'm buying dood all the time. I keep spare nip bottles and a cough syrup bottle clean and covered down. Feeding time I fill one of them with Kalliecharan's dood, push a nipple on top the bottle, and give Chunksee. Mind you, he should be drinking from a cup by now. Must be the mai keeping him back.

This morning the batcha looked weakee weakee so I took him in my lap to feed like when he was little. Boysie looked at us with so much tenderness I thought he was ready to marry me on the spot.

You is a natural mother, yes.

He kissed Chunksee's toes, looked up and planted one on my forehead.

You know I love you, Popo.

I ain't falling for no sweet talk, but it's nice to see Boysie smiling with real joy on he face. And if I tell him Chunksee learn something new? Oh Lord. You would swear no child ever did that before. I never see a man this bazodee over he beta.

So later that day when the bai said something that made me laugh I called Boysie. He came out gruff gruff.

What you want? I was now placing a bet.

Chunksee have something to tell you.

He face soften one time. I picked up the bai.

Tell Pa what you just tell Popo Tanty.

He smiled and hid in my shoulder. I gently pushed him to look at Boysie.

Look Pa come to hear you. Say it for Pa, nah, beta.

That just came out. Forget Chunksee's new word. I called him beta. He ain't no beta of mine. I'd better watch myself.

Chunksee, Pa waiting. I'll play horsey with you after if you tell Pa.

The little face brightened up at the mention of me on all fours and he on my back pretending I'm a horse he's riding.

Maa, kaa, chood.

Boysie's face dropped.

What, beta?

Maakaachood. Maakaachood. Maakaachood.

Now you couldn't miss what he said. I never saw the slap coming.

You teaching my child to cuss nasty?

I was too stunned to answer. Boysie grabbed the bai from my arms and hugged him tight. He held the little chin and looked Chunksee in he eye.

Beta, you mustn't say that word again. Ever. You hear me? That is a bad bad word and Pa will get vex if he hear you say that again. You understand?

Chunksee nodded.

You sure you understand? Never, never let me hear you say that again or Pa will give you licks.

I looked Boysie in he eye.

Carry Chunksee by Mana Lala.

Boysie's mouth dropped open.

What?

Carry your beta back by he mother. I ain't minding no child that I didn't make. You want to put hand on me? Well, find another muk to do for you.

He steupsed.

Hear nah, man, what going on?

What happen to your hearing? I said I'm not minding your beta. End of story.

All this because I tap your face? It wasn't even hard. You get plenty harder than that before. And you had no right teaching the batcha to cuss.

Well, that didn't help he cause.

It wasn't me learn him that. And it was just a joke.

I picked up Chunksee's bag and began throwing his things inside.

Here. Now take your beta back by he mother where he belongs.

Boysie grabbed the bag and rested it on the table.

I mean it, Boysie. And if you don't want to do that then give me back my money and I will go my way.

He went out to the latrine. I don't care if he fall in there. I made tea and gave Chunksee a ball to roll around. Boysie went from the latrine to the shower outside. I went in the gallery while he changed. When I next saw him he had the bag on he shoulder.

Chunksee, come by Pa.

Boysie dropped the bai, came back, went in the bed like he take in sick and stayed for two days. He wouldn't talk, eat, nothing. I had to get George to go Laventille and Tinsingh took care of Prince Street. Neither of them I trust but it's not like I had a choice. Boysie carried on like all he family dead. Day three I touched his shoulder.

All right. Go. Bring back Chunksee.

He turned around.

You're sure?

Don't lash me. You hear?

He pulled me close and pushed his tongue in my mouth. I kissed him back without really kissing him and hoped he didn't spot the difference.

MANA LALA

To my mind if Popo did never push she-self on the scene, all now so me and Boysie would be together. I can't help wishing bad on she. In the next life I hope she's a big ugly latrine fly. True. I want that. She's stopping a mother, father and child being a family. I've heard people in the market talk about using oils to cure all kind of suffering. Apparently the chicken lady, Mother Gizzard, can work that kind of obeah magic. Asking a stranger to help with something so private wasn't easy. Mother Gizzard, though, was up front.

So let me hear you correct. You want to get back your man or you want something happen to the woman he take up with?

Well, both.

She fanned with a piece of cardboard torn from a box.

I doesn't put curse on people. That's not what my grandmothers them teach me. Curse somebody and you're as likely to find the trouble land on you. But getting your man back? I could help you there.

He will come back if she move along she way.

You're sure about that? All you didn't have any problems before this woman come on the scene?

I didn't answer.

What about a tonic to make him want you?

Like what?

Plenty things you could do. I have a powerful spell but it need you to do your part.

Like what?

Go every day for a month and dip in the sea nine times before the sun shines on the water. Then you walk home, wash off and put on fresh clothes. Comb your hair. Make yourself nice. After, drink a spoon of my tonic. While you're doing that I'll be saying special prayers. The wisdom of my grandmother's mother, working through me, will bring him back to you.

So I take something for she to go away? That don't sound right.

No, you drink the tonic and the man will forget about she. Only you he will want.

I have to think about that. I was hoping for something to give him or to give she. I don't like how I is the one taking medicine for them.

Well, most of the tonics I make is for the person coming to me rather than to give another body. You think about it. In the meantime I go pray for you. My prayers come free. Tell me anytime if you want the tonic.

Thanks. I thought you would at least have an oil or something to give him.

Best you find Papa Dooboo. He have oil for everything.

Where he does be?

Up in the bush. Petit Valley.

How I reaching there?

She laughed.

I'm only making joke. You don't have to go so far. He does sell coconut in the market. Go over so. But don't forget what I tell you. Sea bath every day for a month. Fix up and I go put some strong prayers on your head. I ain't been wrong yet.

I braced myself and went looking for this coconut man. Soon as I told him what I wanted he was over glad to help. From a jumbled-up set of bottles he pulled out a small clear one filled with a green oil.

This is the thing self. It ain't cheap but people does thank me. The outside woman will shrivel away. In no time you'll have your man back. You're lucky to get a bottle. I didn't think I had more. As I make it does sell out.

What I do with this?

Two-three drops in the lady food and wait. Mark my words. She will leave all you in peace. This little bottle is enough to do the curse nine times. Nine times, you hear? No more than that.

So I just drop it in the food? She wouldn't taste nothing?

Nah. It don't taste.

And I ain't have to say anything when I'm putting it in?

No. Papa Dooboo done say all the prayers my child. Everything corked up in the bottle. You just make she eat it.

Nothing else?

No sister. But take it now because I ain't know when I'm making more.

I paid Papa Dooboo and hid it in my purse. Soon Popo getting some real good food.

DORIS

I didn't know his name until a few months ago and now almost every time I leave the house I'm tripping over Boysie. I make market? He's there. Cinema? He's there. Leaving mass? He's hanging around on the main road. Today was the best. I nearly didn't recognise him because I was busy studying a fella in church who's been making sweet eye at me. Nice-looking, tall, always in a soft pants, starched white shirt, blue tie and shoes shining till you can see your face in them. He checks where I'm sitting and gets in the pew right behind me. His hand grips my back rest so if I move even an inch we touch. Sometimes he moves his hand and we make more contact before he takes it away again.

We normally talk as much as is decent after mass. I don't want people putting two and two together and coming up with fourteen. He's in the police, doing well for himself. I feel he's looking to settle down. At least if I allowed him to walk me home, and that is a big if, nothing will happen to me. A police escort. Not bad but I'm still checking all that Port of Spain's offering.

Anyhow, I sat down in my usual pew towards the back with the other maids and ordinary folk. Mass was nearly starting. Suddenly I heard shuffling behind me. I didn't need to look. The smell of perspiration mingled with Lux sweet soap and 4711 eau de cologne was as recognisable as Mr Police's own face.

We all stood to sing as the procession of acolytes and priest floated up the central aisle. But somebody was trying to find a seat in my pew. What happen? They can't wait little bit? I heard a loud whisper,

Dress round, dress round, let me get a place.

Instead of taking a seat at the end of the pew he was shoving and pushing until he was standing next to me like I was expecting him. I kept my eyes in front, minding my own business. Behind Mr Police was singing heartily to the Lord drowning out the rest of us. I felt the shirt of this new fella next to me. By instinct I shifted. The sleeve followed and an elbow chooked me. Who in Jesus's name is bothering me while mass going on? He whispered,

You ain't have a good morning for me?

That voice. Boysie Singh. I turned and gave him the nastiest cut eye I could manage.

What you doing here? You even Catholic?

The Bible say we are all God's children.

He grinned while the priest asked the congregation to sit. As I settled myself Mr Police leaned forward and whispered to the back of my head,

This man bothering you?

I shook my head and put a finger to my lips for him to shut up. One crazy next to me and one with tabanca behind. This was all I needed. Before mass done the congregation will be talking my business.

Boysie didn't know the first thing about a Catholic service. Time to kneel, he was still standing. We'd finished making the sign of the cross and he was now trying to copy what we'd done. It was my turn to chook him to stop. But worse was to come. Communion time and sure enough Boysie was moving to join the line. Imagine that. An Indian who ain't even baptised. As discreetly as I could I held him back and hissed,

Joke is joke but you can't take Holy Communion unless you've been baptised and confirmed in the Church.

Mr Police touched my shoulder.

Come sit behind here. It have place.

I shook my head.

I'm all right, thanks.

No, really. Take communion and then sit in my pew. I'll make place.

One thing I can't stand is a man trying to control me and he ain't even my man.

I'm good.

I hurried to get my communion with Mr Police up in my tail. At least Boysie listened to me and showed respect for the body and blood of Christ our Lord and Saviour. But I didn't want Mr Police pushing up big and brave to protect me.

Back at my pew I had a real shock. Boysie was kneeling, eyes closed and praying. Not no pretend prayer. My return didn't seem to register. He was concentrating real hard and stayed on his knees until the priest called for us to stand. Slowly he opened his eyes. All the schoolboy chupidness had vanished. Mass continued with Boysie seemingly in another world.

When church was over he left without saying boo. Mr Police walked me out and while he yakked all kind of foolishness about how this yellow dress take me good I scanned the churchyard for that so-and-so Indian. No Boysie Singh in sight. I didn't know what to think. He definitely came to church for me. Man had pushed his way in to sit by me, brushed my arm, flirted. It made no sense that he hadn't remained to talk. I wanted to give him a well-deserved piece of my mind. Damn foolishness. So where was he? Meanwhile Mr Police like he forgot he was off duty.

Doris, you know that man who pushed in the pew?

Not really. I've seen him a few times in the market.

That is Boysie Singh. Every police in Port of Spain know 'bout he. Trust me, he ain't no good.

What he do so?

I can't say certain things in the churchyard but I'm telling you he is not the kind of man you want to associate with. You're too good for he.

I could see perspiration beads forming on his forehead. Then he made his move and asked outright,

Doris, I was thinking we should take in a club next Friday.

I should be rushing to say yes. This is a decent, God-fearing man who clearly worships every inch of me.

My mistress might need me to work late. They're always having this one and that one for dinner.

So when you'll know?

Wednesday?

I will pass by you to find out.

You know where I'm living? And you can't pass just so just so.

Like you forget I'm a police officer.

I forced a smile. Yes, I'll go to the club but he can wait until Wednesday to know. Meanwhile, where the hell was Boysie Singh?

POPO

Not every woman would put up like me. Who he think he fooling? I know the maakaachood running Dave's girls and busy sampling the goods. Some days I swear Boysie's turning into Dave, yes. As if any of them women could jook like me. And Boysie best remember it's my money jumping up that he'll have to pay back with interest.

Home my life would be so much easier if Chunksee could just put on some size. I think that is why he's such a sickly bai. Miss Constance from over the road swears there's nothing like tea with condensed milk. A cup every night and he little body will strengthen. Morning time he's still drinking Kalliecharan's fresh dood. I've stopped the night dood and giving him the tea instead. But try getting him to eat a piece of roti and some takari and you could be waiting whole day. Boysie say he see Mana Lala making a game with each spoonful. I give him a cut eye. If that's what Boysie wants then take the batcha back by Mana Lala. Nothing wrong with that. I look like I want to play and feed same time?

Imagine, I'm accustomed to knocking about all over when I want. These days I can't even go latrine alone because Chunksee will be outside waiting. Fed up hearing me complain, Miss Constance picked lime bud and told me to try that as a tea for him. She's a nice lady and one of the few that don't show me bad face like they're better than me. If I have to run to the parlour to buy biscuit or rice she will keep Chunksee, no problem.

And where is Chunksee's baap? Boysie's always out doing something. But give Jack he jacket. Once he's home, he does give the beta plenty doolar. Here and there I get an ease from

minding the batcha when Boysie takes Chunksee by Mana Lala.
I'm the one to ask if he doesn't think the child should see his real
mai. Mana Lala must be love Boysie bad because whatever he
tell she about Chunksee being by me she seems to have taken as
Lord Vishnu talking. Anyhow, I ain't getting in them business. I
have my own skin to worry about.

It crossed my mind that Chunksee with me not because
Boysie can't do without he beta. I've been wondering if he's
smart enough to plan that as I'm busy minding child I will leave
him and the business alone? Let's say that wasn't the case it's how
things are turning out. I decided to test what really going on. A
morning I waited till he'd finished breakfast and was about to go
open up the place.

Boysie, how much money Laventille take yesterday? And
Prince Street? Which place doing better you think?

I ain't know off hand. It mark down somewhere.

I used to have every number and now I ain't know nothing.

Don't hurt your head. Things good.

Doux-doux, I know things good but as all we money
jumping up in these betting shops I does worry.

He kissed me hard.

Don't study the shops. That under control.

I pulled his tongue in for a next kiss, long and slow. He got
excited one time and put my hand on the hard place in he
shorts. I pulled away.

Behave yourself. The child right there.

Boysie stood up and I straightened myself.

From today I think you should bring the cash box home for
me to count.

But me and Tinsingh find a place to hide up everything.

You think that more safe than me watching it? I could act as
watchman.

Boysie chewed he bottom lip.

I don't know.

Well, I know, honey. It's the best thing. Start from today. I
could save you time and go Laventille myself around four
o'clock?

Nah, nah, nah.

So, you'll bring the cash?

He sighed like he alone holding up the whole world.

I'll see if I have time.

Good. And any problems I will come and help. We is a team,
poi. You and me. Pati and patni.

I think he got the message loud and clear. It's dotish he feel I
dotish?

MANA LALA

My day started quiet, sweeping ash from the open stove, the chulha. Once clean I put in fresh dry wood and lit it. The phooknee to blow and get the fire going was missing and without that this fire won't catch properly. I found it nearby but not in the place it should have been. All my bones tired the morning. Why people can't rest things back where they find them? I put a pot of water to boil for tea and while that was hotting up I swept the steps and gallery with a new cocoyea broom. A man from the coconut estate going up Cocorite side was selling these brooms made from coconut palms and I bought two so inside and outside won't mix.

The oil I bought in the market has been troubling me. I ain't figure out how it reaching Popo's food. And I don't want nothing bad bad to happen. If she could just go along she way and leave Boysie that would be enough. Now that Boysie's betting coming big he needs a woman he can trust. Popo came from the road. Let him turn for a minute and she might well thief out everything and vanish. Watch and see. I did mention that if he want to hide anything leave it my side. I didn't add so Popo won't know. Boysie can trust that I'll see and not see, hear and not hear and never ever talk he business. That is what you're supposed to do for your man.

Where we live is thick bush going all up the hill, land where nobody goes. Boysie has free run to do as he please. I doubt Popo knows about his side thing burning cars for insurance. Trinidad's small, so if police looking they bound to find a missing car that same day or within the week. People need the vehicle to stay missing long enough for a pay-out in their hand. Tuesday Boysie drove up in a white car.

Where you get that?

You like it?

I nodded.

Austin 12.

I nodded again even though I can't name one motor car from the next.

Just now you go see a fire coming from the bush up so. Anybody ask, you ain't see me since weekend. You understand?

Yeah. You remember where we boundary there?

You think I'm poohar? I go burn it far from all you.

I know how this does go so I waited. The car took its good time to burn. By evening police were all over the land. Next day police came again asking if we saw a white Austin 12 around the village and who was driving it.

Me ain't see nothing. What happen?

It look like thief stole the car then burnt it. These gentlemen with me from Sun Insurance. It's a complete write-off?

The men nodded. Ma had been watching from the window. She marched outside wanting to know why they were by she gate.

Morning Tanty. We're just checking if you see anything yesterday. Somebody burn down a car in the plot next to yours. You was home?

Me ain't see nothing and all you better move from in front my house fast fast. I done have cataract in all two of my eye. Yesterday smoke was all in my nose and the fire brigade ain't study we. But all you reach today. I have a good mind to go to the papers. Any time something happen in this village police does come harassing my tail.

Fast fast the police left. Ma well good for she-self, oui. Them ain't coming here anytime soon.

*

Gradually, more things Boysie wanted to remain hush-hush he did by me. And them times of course Boysie, Chunksee and me got to be as a family. While me and the bai in the back, Boysie will be in the gallery. Somebody will reach and, although I know not to show my face, Boysie will still shout for me to stay inside. It's a friend passing. They talk and I does play like my ears clogged up with wax.

A time Boysie reached and told me he worried. Apparently since yesterday the batcha had refused to eat what Popo gave him. I don't blame the little one. In no time I made his favourite, curry pumpkin and roti. Chunksee sat on the peerha and ate what I fed him good good. If Popo used to feed him like this people will name him Fat Boy in no time.

Even if Popo's food half as tasty I bet she doesn't have my patience. For Chunksee to clean he plate I made each mouthful into a motor car. I broke piece of roti, used it to scoop some pumpkin, and vroom, vroom, vroom, the food car went into the garage that is beta's sweet little mouth. You do that if it's your beta who needs to eat.

While I was busy driving car to feed Chunksee, I heard Boysie saying something about a fire job that was way bigger than what he normally takes on. He was telling the man to stop offering foolish money to a big man.

What the jail is this? Boysie, you're digging out my eye.

Who digging out who eye here? You want me to burn down a whole nightclub for a thousand dollars? Nah.

Eight hundred is what Patiram charging.

Well, give Patiram the work. But it go be you to catch when he burn down the place with people inside. He careless for so.

It's a square thousand.

I made some noise so they wouldn't think I was listening. Vroom, vroom, vroom, vvvvvvvvrrrroooooooomm.

Nah, nah, nah. Go with Patiram. But make sure he stay sober. Once he drink rum he mouth don't stop running. Before you collect a cent from the insurance, police would've done locked you up. That's not how I does operate.

Eleven hundred and that is giving you a bigger share than I getting out of the job.

You feel this coolie born yesterday? Crystal Palace insured for big money. Ask around. When I do a job, I do it clean. No trace. And I never once run my mouth. What I know I taking to the grave.

The quiet between the two men was filled with my beta laughing and begging for car, car, car. I heard a chair grate on the floor-boards as the man got up.

All right partner, how much we talking?

Two thousand. Take it or leave it. Either way I easy.

I missed what was said. It must have been good because they bussed out laughing and Boysie offered the man one for the road.

By month end Crystal Palace nightclub was razed to the ground. Unfortunately, the watchman was sick that night and nobody else saw a thing. I heard police on the radiogram appealing for witnesses to come forward. Good luck with that.

POPO

Last Friday Boysie got waylaid in Laventille because of some problem with the roof leaking and he sent a message asking me to drop off the bai. I knew Mana Lala's expecting Chunksee for the weekend especially as Sunday is he birthday. Boysie agreed she could do she celebrations Saturday, the day before he birthday. Nobody invited me. Not that I wanted to go party. But seeing as I does look after she beta you would think she'd include me. Never mind. Let she stop so. No hardship for me to carry the bai and he jahaji bundle. Funny thing, though, it was the first time we met.

Before I even reached the house she was running to grab Chunksee.

Boysie couldn't make so I bring him for you.

She was busy kissing the bai and hugging him tight tight.

All right, see you next week, Chunksee. Behave good for your mai. Enjoy the birthday.

Mana Lala like she 'fraid me. With head down she asked me to come inside. Rasmalai just make.

Thanks. You know how long me ain't taste a good rasmalai?

She took me round to the back. Chunksee ran off.

Sit down in the hammock, nah.

All right.

I dropped down in the hammock they had made by stringing up two joined crocus bags. As I waited for the rasmalai I could hear Boysie in my head. The other day he was complaining I'd put on size. Only a few pounds. Not like I'm fat. Anyhow, he ain't my boss. I will eat how much rasmalai I want.

She brought a glass bowl with three big balls of paneer floating in the thick sweet milk and crushed nuts on top. I took a mouthful.

But this real good. Just the right amount of sweet. Hear me talking like I could even make thing.

Mana Lala gave a little smile, just as shy as I thought she would be.

Only me eating? All you have there is a cup of ice.

I good.

Reminding me of Diwali. My mother used to save up milk and sugar to make this. But that was long time.

We does make it then too.

Chunksee was running all over the place. He came with one speed and held on to he mai's leg.

Slow down beta. You will fall.

Nanee going to eat me.

Mana Lala scooped up the boy.

Don't study that. She's only playing.

Same time the lady I took to be nanee parted the thin curtain over the back door and wagged she finger at the bai.

Chunksee, your mai can't save you. I'm going to eat you with a hot roti now now now. Coming.

Chunksee held on to Mana Lala's neck tight tight.

I'm putting you down Chunksee. Ma, stop frightening the child.

He ran off with nanee pretending to gobble him up. Mana Lala asked me if I had a ma still living. I licked the spoon and fingered the tabeej around my neck. This is all I have of family and I don't take it off for nothing or nobody. Something unexpected was happening in this moment and it had me confuffled. One minute I was just eating a little rasmalai, swinging in the hammock, Mana Lala sitting on an old wooden peerha. Next thing I was remembering my family. I never bother with them. I looked at Mana Lala. Me and she are sharing Chunksee and look how she ain't showing me no jealous bad face. How a quiet nice girl like she got mixed up with a hard man like Boysie I ain't know.

To tell you the truth it's years now I ain't see any family. More than ten years, I think.

She looked at me with soft, quiet eyes and crunched ice. I kept going.

Thirteen children my mother had. Not all lived. I was the second to last. Ran away when I made twelve years.

Her gentle voice asked how I managed.

You do what you have to do. We was over poor. Mai took me out of school to cut cane. Whole day cutting cane. Picking up cane. Cutting cane. Picking up cane. I used to reach home dirty from head to toe, bathe with a piece of blue soap, eat a little roti and takari and drop asleep ready to get up five o'clock for work again.

Cutting cane is real hard work for true.

Chunksee raced past and into the house. Nanee was walking behind.

Excuse. We're looking for marbles to play pitch.

Mana Lala waited for them to pass.

So, where you ran away from?

South.

I pulled myself up.

Let me go, yes. I didn't plan to stop long.

Come anytime you want.

I called out for the bai.

Chunksee, I gone.

I looked Mana Lala in she eye direct.

You mustn't worry. He don't give no trouble.

Lie. Having him whole day means I can't go nowhere or do nothing without him hanging from my dress. I heard a loud crunch as Mana Lala cracked a piece of ice. We both bussed out laughing.

You well like ice.

Her mouth was full, so she nodded.

I cracked my teeth and all.

The other day I tell Boysie let the bai stay by Mana Lala for at least half the time. He laughed. You know that laugh he have like he crazy?

Straight away her eyes looked frightened. She swallowed hard.

And what he say?

I shook my head.

He said maybe but we both know that is he sona beta.

Mana Lala adjusted her orhni still looking down.

It's my sona beta too.

What I go say? Up to me the child would live here with he mai and nanee. But Chunksee is the one living being on this earth that Boysie loves body, heart, and soul. I could give him my life and he still wouldn't feel as much as he does for this little man.

Before I left she gave me a container with more rasmalai and told me not to share. It's for me alone to enjoy. I'm surprised but I really take to she.

MANA LALA

Part of me hates every bone in that randee Popo's body and half of me is wondering if Boysie ain't deserve some of that bad feeling too. But then she came by the house. Something about actually seeing she made me afraid to say anything or do anything because I couldn't trust myself. I thought of the green oil. If I was ever going to use it I'd better do it now. It wouldn't kill she. I'm just moving she away from my family.

Fresh rasmalai with nuts on top soaked in four drops of the green oil. He said the dose was two but I might not get a next chance. She was well glad for the sweet and gobbled up a bowlful. While she chatted away I watched for any sign of poisoning. This ain't worth making a jail. Who would Boysie bring to mind Chunksee then?

From the way Popo talked you would think that the two of we were good good friend. That had me confused. How could I like a woman who is living with the man I should be with? As she talked more and more about she family bacchanal it finally hit me. I am a nothing. In she head I must be so much of a nothing that she done rule me out as ever getting back Boysie. I asked if she wanted to carry home some rasmalai. What she took had six drops of the green oil. That should be enough for the magic to work.

What really helped me keep nice face to Popo was my secret. I ain't see blood two, going on three months. A brother or sister for Chunksee and, oil or no oil, that's it for Popo. Boysie must realise we need to be together as a family. He'll do the right thing.

*

The beta had been all right when Popo dropped him but next day he was clinging. All he wanted was doolar, hug up. His skin was hot. I bathed him in thandaa water to cool him down and force out the heat. Boysie came by and wasn't happy. One look and he was ready to carry Chunksee for a bush bath.

No, Boysie. Don't mix beta in thing so. If you want I will find a pundit to jharay he.

Boysie rolled his eyes.

You and your country bookie dotishness. What jharay go do?

Although he was saying what I expected his voice didn't sound vex. I touched his shoulder.

Sometimes I does wonder if you even Indian. Your ma never had you jharay when you was little?

Ma didn't have time for me. She had cow to mind.

Let we get Chunksee jharay. It can't cause nothing bad.

I picked Chunksee off the ground.

It's two-three Sanskrit chants. Pundit will tie the bad spirit in a little bundle and burn it. Done.

As usual when Boysie's mind fixed, he won't budge.

Nah, forget pundit. Bush bath is the thing.

Chunksee was wriggling to go back on his pa. Boysie kissed his cheek.

Beta, I'm carrying you by a lady named Mother Gizzard. She go know what to do.

*

We weren't alone in looking for Mother Gizzard. Chunksee
found a little girl to play with in the group of us waiting and was
running around, no cough or fever. By the time Mother Gizzard
called we inside he didn't look sick at all at all. If anything, me
and Boysie looked like we needed a tonic. I wasn't sure Mother
Gizzard remembered me and I wasn't about to remind she. It
didn't matter because she and Boysie knew one another good
good. She asked him about Three Little Threes.

How the stick? You're keeping it good?

Yeah. Nobody have a stick like that. Powerful. I normally
have it with me but I didn't walk with it today. We come
about the bai.

Meantime I was there trying to keep Chunksee from touching
the bottles and dried plants that lined the walls and were chook
up everywhere. As fast as I took one he went for something else.
I slapped him, a light tap really.

Chunksee, behave.

Boysie gave me one cut eye and grabbed the batcha. Mother
Gizzard was quick to say it was all right.

Never mind. Children like to touch.

The look she gave said she remembered me.

Now, what a nice couple like all you come for? Tell me your
troubles.

Boysie looked at me and huffed.

Tell the lady.

I was feeling shame that a stranger glimpsed how Boysie does treat me. Plus, how I could say the batcha's sick when right now he looked happy like pappy? As I hesitated Boysie pushed in.

You will never guess but up until we reach here the bai was coughing coughing and he skin was hot. And he don't like to eat. He's not strong.

How much years he have?

I was going to answer but Boysie gave me a look that said hush your mouth.

He born April 1931, so he make three tomorrow.

Good, good. Now bring this little monkey close, let me look at him.

Stand up, Chunksee.

Beta only have to hear his pa say something once and he obeys, same as me.

Mother Gizzard held Chunksee's hand and gently pulled him close.

Where's hurting?

He pointed to his dusty foot in rubber slippers.

My big toe.

We all buss out laughing. I told Mother Gizzard that nothing was wrong with he toe.

By now she had Chunksee in she lap and was bouncing him up and down and tickling him. While he there laughing away she was running she hands over he leg, belly, back. She pull down the bottom of he eye, looked at the tongue, felt up the neck.

What's he name again?

We both rushed to say Chunksee like we were in primary school trying to curry favour with the teacher.

All right, Chunksee, go by your father.

Chunksee did a dive into Boysie's arms for a love-up.

Oh ho, daddy's spoil child.

She looked at me.

All you make a nice couple. Now, this child want fattening. Anything he want to eat, any time he want to eat, full him up. When he get fever again, boil what I give you. Leave it to cool and soak he skin in with it. For big people I does tell them to drink it but he too small. Even I find it bitter in my throat.

In a basin she mixed leaf, grass and oils from different bottles. This is my beta so I asked what is what quietly in case I upset Boysie.

I'm giving you fever grass and one we does call jackass bitters and a little shining bush.

When was time to go Boysie asked how much. Mother Gizzard dazzled with a gold-teeth smile.

Whatever all you could manage, I good with that. I is a poor woman and I ain't doing this work to get rich.

Then she looked at me with a soft face.

I want to recommend a tonic for you. Come back and see me any time.

Boysie left the batcha by me whole week. It was real good not having to pack Chunksee's bag and watch him leave. How I go help the beta to get better when that will cause him to live Prince Street? And I hadn't heard anything about Popo leaving so the so-and-so oil ain't work. Maybe it does take more time.

POPO

Helmet passed by Prince Street looking for Boysie. I was stooped down washing wares.

Boysie don't be home all now. You-self should know that.

Yeah, but I take a chance as it still early. Like he don't sleep here or what?

I didn't bother to answer. Helmet chewed on a strip of bamboo sticking out the side of he mouth.

If it was me living with a sweet woman like you I would be home all the time.

Helmet, he's not here and whatever it is I can't help you.

Don't raise your voice. I'm only talking. Nothing's wrong with making conversation.

He inched closer in front me.

Where the little bai?

I didn't look up.

Go. Boysie probably playing whappee. Best to check down Fort George.

Instead of leaving, Helmet came close close. I looked up and my eye was in line with he hand feeling up a bulging crotch.

I never see a man like card so. When Boysie's playing whappee night and day come the same to that man. I like me card game. But he? He have it bad.

Helmet was like a wall blocking me in.

You're still working on the side?

I suddenly felt a tiredness from my little toe to the hair on my head, the kind of tiredness that sleep for a month can't touch.

What happen, Popo? Like you forget me?

Normally, I have an answer for everything. Today all I could manage was asking him to please leave. He laughed.

Me, leave? You really think I don't know where Boysie is? He with a woman. I see him with she last night. And if it's not she it go be a next one tonight again.

I stood up and forced we eyes to make four. The man was actually licking he lips.

Relax yourself. He ain't coming home now. Look after me and I go give you a little change to hold. Boysie don't have to know.

Look, Helmet with your big ugly head, I don't do them thing again. I have one man.

Well, I'm telling you point blank. He's dropping horn on your ass so you might as well go back to doing what you do best.

That was enough.

Cattle horn never too heavy to carry. Now, leave my yard right now or I go tell Boysie how you tried a thing on me.

He doubled over laughing a hollow laugh.

Oh luss. Don't do that. He might give you away to be my
dulahin.

I spat on the ground.

Your wife? You looked in the mirror recently? Man, haul
your ugly ass. You're spinning top in mud.

He wagged a finger in my face.

Once a whore, always a whore. Don't worry, I go come find
you again.

I was ready to cuff him down but I thought it best not to make
trouble. I opened the gate and stood while he took he cool
time to walk off slow slow. Helmet think he bussing style on
me? Maakaachood. I hope he steps in a pothole and breaks he
obzokee big foot.

That morning the cocoyea broom got some good use. I
swept that yard from a side whacking the thick bundle of coconut stems on the ground. Vexness was rising from the pit of
my belly and gripping my throat. Of course I know Boysie's
running down woman all over the place. I didn't need that
nasty gadaha, donkey, coming in my yard to insult me so. I'm
looking after everything. Yes, he's managing things much better than a year ago but people don't realise everything would
fall down braps if I leave. Boysie doesn't show respect. Unless
he running two-three woman he ain't feel he name man. Well,
it's time he stepped up and treated me correct.

MANA LALA

It's been three months going on four. Once I see the charmine, Raksha, and she's sure the baby growing correct, I'll run tell Boysie. He'll be overjoyed for Chunksee to get a brother. Or sister. And that is Popo done and we as one family. The oil was a waste of time. Now, me giving Boysie another son? That is real magic. Having strong men to look after me in my old age will make me heart rest easy. Daughter is yours only until she married. After that she ain't have time to see 'bout you when you take in sick.

I was restless whole Sunday knowing I have to wait until tomorrow to see Raksha. Thankfully my friend Radha came with she little girl child. I was glad for the company. She used to live near we and since she moved I don't really have anybody to talk to. We had baby same time. Our two turning five this year but she daughter well force ripe. Soon as they reached she grabbed Chunksee's hand and announced that they're playing house. Hands on hips like a big woman, she complained about how much cooking and cleaning it have and don't talk about the amount of clothes to wash. We belly laughed. Children does listen to everything yes. I asked what she cooking.

Dhal.

That's all?

Rice.

I stifled a laugh and gave them an old cup, a wooden spoon, a small handful of rice and a little yellow dhal. She gave me back a sweet sweet smile.

Now, what takari you're cooking?

Chunksee yelled out,

Damaadol choka.

I turned to the girl child.

You have damaadol?

She shook her head.

Come Chunksee. We making market.

Two of them went in the back, picked some green damaadol and showed us.

Nice. Now, when you're buying from an Indian you can say damaadol. But if you're buying from a Creole, what you must ask for?

The little girl shook she shoulders. Chunksee shouted.

Tomatoes.

Good bai.

And another thing I want you to remember is you mustn't pick the damaadol, or anything really, after six.

Why?

All the plants and trees them does be sleeping. How you would like it if people bother you when you're sleeping? Same for the tree.

Chunksee was filling a cup with water.

Give me ice.

How I teach you to ask?

Give me ice, please.

As I stood up a sharp pain took me in my side and my lower belly. I eased back down.

Oh Lord.

Radha stood over me.

What happen?

Ouch. Oh gosh. A pain taking me sharp sharp.

You want anything?

Get the ice for Chunksee nah and break off a piece for me to suck.

The children ran off into the yard to set up their kitchen. If we're lucky that will keep them busy. Meanwhile I crunched ice and tried to ignore the cramps.

So tell me your news, Radha.

You're sure? You look like you in pain.

Don't worry. It'll pass.

Ouch, ouch, ouch. The stabbing pains were coming quicker now. As she was talking my head started to feel light light. The ground was spinning.

More ice.

I tried to stand but my knees refused to hold me up. Radha rushed to stop me falling.

Sit back down.

I looked at she face. Panic.

Mana Lala, you're bleeding.

I looked down and my dress had a dark patch.

Must be a heavy monthly.

I turned around and that's when I saw the back of my dress and the chair had red.

Oh Lord, what happening? No. No.

The children them rushed in at the same time wanting I ain't know what. Radha shooed them back out.

Go and play. Tanty not feeling so well.

Chunksee stood staring at me.

It's all right, beta. Let me rest for a minute. Play with your friend.

He ran off and Radha helped me to the latrine. By now I was biting my hand so no one would hear my screams. My baby. I was losing my baby. I was sure. No. This couldn't be happening. I'm at least three months gone. Why? My panty was soaked with blood and the belly cramps were worse than any I'd ever felt. Why I'm punishing like this? What I do to deserve this? And all the while I was bawling I never made a sound. If I let out this noise Chunksee will frighten bad.

Don't ask me how but I managed to wash off and pack a clean cloth in my panty for the blood. It was like a river coming down. I was doing everything quiet but I couldn't see good through the tears. Radha came in my room with a cup of black tea.

Drink, nah.

I shook my head and tried to sit up. I just couldn't.

You stay there. Lie down.

I mumbled for ice please.

Mana Lala, tell me. Where your mother gone?

She by she cousin spending holidays.

So you alone here? You want me to get anybody for you? I never see anybody get bad monthlies so.

Only then did I realise, but of course, Radha didn't understand my world was sinking. And suddenly I was vexed.

Monthlies? You think this is monthlies? I just lost my baby, you poohar.

Shock was all over she face and she stepped back. I wasn't done.

You dotish chupidee. It gone. My baby gone.

I buried my face in a pillow to stifle the noise and bawled and bawled and bawled. Radha left me right there. I had no right talking so. And she's my friend. Why I gone and do that on top of everything? A few minutes and plenty tears later I called out for she. Lucky thing she is a good soul, yes.

For the rest of that day I stayed in my bed. Without bothering me Radha cooked food and kept the children away. After all this time I nearly gave Boysie a brother or sister for Chunksee. Popo can't do that. Thank goodness I ain't tell a soul, especially Boysie. He would have cussed me for losing it. Maybe I did something wrong. I don't know. Why me, eh? Why? So much girl does make baby them ain't even want. I wanted this batcha bad bad.

How you feeling? I brought the ice you wanted.

The cramps less.

You're still bleeding?

Yeah. I sorry I called you all kind of thing. I didn't mean it.

Girl, relax yourself. I feel we should call the charmine.

Don't bother. I know I ain't making batcha now.

The bag of tears burst again. She pulled me into a hug.

All right, all right. God's saying the batcha wasn't to be. Something wasn't right with it.

I bit down hard on the ice and a thick block cracked in my mouth. A side tooth cried in pain. The splinters swirling around my tongue were cold comfort. Radha squeezed my hand.

You wanted a next child with Boysie? I mean he living with a woman. And Chunksee already up and down as it is.

I had to be careful what I said. Even if people laugh and talk to my face I know what they think of Boysie. Town want people to believe that he's a big-time criminal. True, he does do things I'd prefer he didn't. But people should really be pointing at Popo. She's the real devil. Have him like an ulloo. Without she Boysie would never do half what he's doing. All the beating up people, the pimping, the insurance scams. She's the one pushing. It's only money she love. He was doing good good with the little fishing and small betting. But she came and turned everything topsy turvy.

Where the children?

They're good. I give them food. I bathe them. Don't hurt your head.

At least we have one batcha. I've told Chunksee over and over since he small. I am your ma. Popo is only a tanty. He must grow knowing in he bones that nobody else in the world loves him like me, he real mother.

POPO

Once Boysie gone morning time, he ain't coming back till all five, six when hunger take him. Imagine my surprise when it was hardly twelve o'clock good and Boysie marched through the door. Chunksee was on the floor pitching marbles.

Sona beta, go and play outside little bit. In fact go next door by Teresa Tanty.

Give Jack he jacket, Chunksee's a good child. Tell him something once and he will do it.

Soon as Boysie was sure the bai had reached next door he pushed me in the bedroom and began unbuckling he brown leather belt. I got confused one time. What I do wrong now? But the belt stayed on the shorts. He carefully pulled down his sliders.

Look.

He yanked me closer. I pushed him back.

Stop shoving me. You ain't make me so don't feel you could knock me about just so just so.

Do fast and come. You can't see nothing from there.

Green pus. I knew straight away. Don't ask me why but I started to laugh.

Maakaachood randee. Stop that.

Well, it good for you.

It's you give me this.

Me? February make five years we living as pati and patni. I've never so much as looked at another man since I come by you. Not me. I ain't taking the blame for this.

How I know you ain't working your old tricks when I out the house?

When? My foot tied down minding your beta.

I ain't know. You could've sent the bai by neighbour. How much man you used to do in a day? Eh?

Nah. Stop unfairing me so.

Unfairing you? Look what I have.

God punishing you for all them girl you does be horning me with. You know how much people pass here just to throw spite in my face? Oh, they see Boysie with so-and-so. Or, Popo girl, Boysie still living here? He does be by so-and-so all the time. I really thought you and he done.

What I do is my business.

I went right up in he face.

Well, it's my business now until that stop. And while we talking let me ask you something. Who is Doris?

What?

Don't play your ears ain't working. Doris. Town say you're fucking a reds named Doris. Big fat backside and tots-tots falling out she dress.

Shut your mouth. Doris is a good woman.

Oh, so is Doris you does be with? Well, you best go show she your laar.

Leave she out of this. It's you give me this.

Me? Well, how come nothing ain't happen to me? Eh? Answer me that.

How I know nothing ain't happen to you?

I don't have any nastiness and if I get any I would know exactly who give me. You, neemakharam.

No, you're the double-crossing traitor.

He huffed and got a piece of cloth, wiped the tip of his thing, and tried to clean his sliders. I expected at least a lash or a cuff. Nothing happened. Boysie had enough worries to bother giving me licks. I bit down on my teeth to stop from saying all what I had on my mind. Boysie looked up at me.

Well, poohar, tell me what to do. It can't be the first time you see this.

I watched him cut eye.

So what going on with you and this Doris?

He pulled up his pants and fixed he-self.

None of your damn business. And I don't want to hear she name in your mouth again.

I couldn't hold back. Fight started. I gave as good as I got. Cuff, cuss, belt. I broke a chair on he head. Neighbours reached and parted the two of we but we remained shouting. Teresa Tanty managed to calm we down by pointing to Chunksee in the yard bawling.

Boysie, Popo, stop this, nah. Look the child crying. Stop. Sort out all your commess in private. Upsetting him. And the whole road hearing your business.

Boysie watched me.

It's you make Chunksee cry. This ain't done.

Well carry him for this Doris to mind. See if she want to mind a next woman child.

He backed away and went for Chunksee. Two of them left. Later I did a little Lakshmi puja for protection. If Boysie comes looking for a fight again one of we will have to dead.

MANA LALA

I made Radha promise not to tell anybody about me losing the baby. By the time Ma came back from she cousin I had stopped breaking down every five minutes. Even if I told her she wouldn't be a comfort. I bet she would say it's a good thing and why I ever wanted a next batcha for Boysie in the first place. I did go by Raksha, the charmine, and she looked after me. She was sure that I'd get pregnant again soon and it will go right through no problem. If I ever have a girl I will name it after she. I prayed she won't open she mouth and tell people my business.

I'd barely got over that when I had another problem down there. This time I was too frightened to show Raksha. Don't ask me why but I took taxi to where this other healer's living. From the road I could hear her voice calling,

Here chicky, chicky, chicky. Here chicky, chicky, chicky.

At the back of the old board house she was throwing feed for the fowl them.

Morning. I say let me come see you.

She waved and smiled as if I was expected. Mother Gizzard has one of them face that have age but it's anywhere from forty to sixty.

Come, come, I well glad to see you. Remind me your name. Come inside.

While making fresh mint tea, she started up.

Whatever it is people tell me I does keep right in these four walls. When the Lord ready for me, I taking it all to the grave. Ask anybody. I'm not a woman to talk people business behind them back.

I lowered my head.

Let me ask you something. Ain't you is a Hindu?

I nodded.

I born here.

Yes, but you ever eat cascadoux?

I had to laugh.

I could curry cascadoux fish good good so it don't matter where I go. I deading right here.

You and me both.

She poured tea.

You have a pundit?

This ain't for pundit ears.

I promise you it ain't have nothing you could tell me that I ain't hear a hundred times.

I looked at the roof, at the wall, my lap. A deep breath and I let it tumble out. She face didn't change once.

Must be a week ago I spotted something funny-looking in my panty and it frightened me bad. I ain't feeling sick. The only thing is this green, yellow oozing now and then. And Boysie is the only one does interfere with me.

She made me lie down on a mattress and checked me over good
and proper.

> If you only with one man then I sorry to say but he pass this
> to you. It does come from a man sexing a woman with the
> disease. He oozing too?

> I don't know.

Mother Gizzard scratched she head.

> Sickness does work different on man and woman and from
> one body to a next body. He mightn't even know he have it.
> But when it come it's one set of pain.

> What to do?

> I ain't go lie. This won't go just so just so. And I don't take
> people money if I can't help.

Well now my heart dropped.

> You can't fix me?

Mother Gizzard let out a big sigh.

> We could try. I know two-three remedies. And I'll pray hard
> for you. But it does take a time.

> And if I take the cure and Boysie doesn't, what go happen?

> He must take it too or else you bound to get it back. Once
> you're sexing a man with it, trouble in your tail.

I scratched my head. Refuse Boysie? I want to kill that randee.
Bringing nasty sickness on all of we. I dressed while Mother
Gizzard searched around in a set of little bottles.

It right here somewhere.

What?

A red powder in a clear bottle.

Two of we searched.

This?

She smiled.

That is the thing self.

You want me to take that?

Hold your horses little bit. This real powerful. If you take it straight from the bottle is dead you go dead and then police will come for me.

She pointed to the peerha.

Sit down while I make up a tonic for you.

A few minutes later she was holding up a small bottle filled with a dark brown liquid.

Now listen to me good and do all what I say. You're listening?

I nodded.

Right. This will burn. No two ways about it. One teaspoon three times a day and the burning you feel is the remedy taking all the poison from your body. All that pus and thing will burn from the inside. And finish the bottle. Don't come back by me crying it ain't working and the thing half full.

She handed me the bottle.

Now, the next part. This disease don't like heat so give your body plenty heat. I want you to hot up water, soak a cloth in the water and put the cloth on your privates. Keep soaking the cloth so it take on the heat. And take it as boiling hot as you can manage. Do that morning and evening. You understand what I'm telling you?

Yeah.

Tell me what you go do.

I will drink the red medicine three times a day and put heat down there.

Correct.

She sat down.

Now this is the hard part and I ain't know how you're going to do it. Boysie must get treatment too. All I can think is that soon it will start to bother him and he will be begging for a cure.

Me? I can't tell Boysie what to do. And I ain't telling him 'bout this. He might think I gone with some other man.

Mother Gizzard sighed.

And let me tell you, the man cure is worse than the woman cure. By far.

My body twitched all by itself. Boysie doesn't like to take medicine, period. No way he's taking a tonic that will pain him.

The disease have to burn out of the man's privates. Woman only drink the medicine.

She pointed to my red bottle.

That have to rub on he privates and get all up inside. And the hot water must go inside too.

I looked at the red bottle and I didn't know what to do.

If they ask I will do it for a man. Otherwise I does send them by a man healer. Let he deal with that confusion.

Not Papa Dooboo?

We both buss out laughing.

Mother Gizzard of course didn't have a price. I gave a few dollars which was more than I could afford and left with my bottle and a reminder to take the heat. Shame she couldn't give me something to lift my spirit. I can't wait to get home and chip up some ice.

*

Whole road coming back from Mother Gizzard I was studying how to get Boysie to take the cure. He ain't have to know I'm taking it too or maybe I have to tell him. So long as he understand it's Popo who brought this on we.

Later that day Helmet came with Boysie. I pulled Boysie to one side.

Any another fella they call Helmet?

No.

Hmm.

I left it there and walked off to chip up some ice.

The men did whatever they had to do. I stayed inside near a window and eyed Helmet packing crates of beer into the jitney.

Just before they left Boysie came inside.

Why you asked me if it have more than one Helmet?

I looked out at the yard.

Oh, well Chunksee knows a Helmet Uncle that does come to the house. I didn't know if this was he.

Chunksee wouldn't know this fella here.

Yeah. Probably a next man.

I studying who that could be.

Leave it, nah. Just some friend Popo have.

Boysie left without another word. Serves she right.

POPO

I was checking Chunksee's head for lice when boss man breezed in. Me ain't see him for two nights straight. I knew better than to ask a question. If I asked he would always throw it in my face that we ain't married, this is he house, and if I don't like it I could always leave. Like I have a next place to go.

The bai ran to he baap and Boysie lifted him high and swung him round and round.

You getting too big for lift up.

More! More!

The bai wrapped he legs around Boysie's waist like he was never letting go.

You bring sweeties?

Boysie pushed the child away slightly so their foreheads rubbed.

Sweeties for you? Oh gosh, I clean forgot.

Chunksee looked about to cry. Boysie hugged the bai tight.

You think Pa forget?

Chunksee giggled.

Where them?

Guess.

Your pants pocket.

No.

Well, where then?

He tried to put the bai down but Chunksee's locked legs remained around Boysie, refusing to stand up. I let go a steupse.

Get down and give your baap a chance. He now reach home.

Chunksee had some story about snake on the ground and he frightened.

Snake? Really? What colour?

It green, Popo Tanty.

Boysie gave Chunksee a squeeze.

Them green snakes don't do you nothing. But if you see one with red, black and white stripes that is a bad snake they call coral. Stay far. Could kill you dead.

The bai was looking more scared now. Boysie was still going on.

And then they have one that light brown with a dark brown kindna pattern. That's the bushmaster. Worst yet.

Carry on with this talk and the bai go can't sleep. You want that?

Boysie glared at me. I got up and tried to prise him away. Time he was in the bed.

Come, stop this chupidness now. Change clothes and tea. Sweeties tomorrow.

Boysie gently pulled the bai off him. Children understand and Chunksee knew play was done. He stood up properly on his own feet. As I turned to go in the kitchen Boysie's left hook connected with my jaw. I heard Chunksee scream and run. For a few seconds I was too stunned to even feel the pain, then, have mercy it burned as if my jaw had cracked. Boysie's eyes bored down on me. Despite bells ringing in my ears I heard a low steady voice:

Next time you come between me and my beta I go kill you.

He turned and in a completely different, now tender voice called,

Chunksee, where you, beta? Don't frighten. Chunksee?

While he went to he beta I leaned out the window and spat out the blood that had filled my mouth. I stayed there paralysed. Even though it was late I soon heard the gate open and shut. I supposed Boysie was taking Chunksee and spending the night by Mana Lala. If she's ghachoo enough to take he in then more fool she.

Once I had washed my face and rinsed my mouth I could see the blow wasn't so bad. Amazing that no teeth break. My lip buss. That is a week before the swelling will ease. I should have gone in my bed one time. Instead, I went with my buss lip and head, jaw, everything hurting, and sat in the small small gallery. Plenty stars were out. Don't know why that surprised me. I looked at the way the stars were jammed up, filling the sky and asked God what I do to deserve this. Somehow I'd fooled myself that Boysie was different. Not true. He's the same as every last one of them man that ever lash me. More than anything else I was vexed with myself. How a woman like me who hustle all them years get catch so? How? I should know to handle Boysie. I should know to stay quiet when he come home and behaving off-key. This buss lip that's swelling by the minute is a reminder: Popo girl, watch your step.

I fell asleep in the gallery and sometime in the middle of the night Boysie came back without the bai. I woke up ready in case a next rounds of licks was about to start. But he was done fighting. Boysie's always the same. Once he's finished playing badjohn he does turn soft soft. He helped me up and two of we went in the bed. I pretended to instantly fall back asleep. He whispered that I should know better than to get him vex. If I didn't interfere when he was playing with Chunksee I would never have gotten cuff down.

You understand it's your fault? You make me hit you.

I didn't say boo.

Popo, you mustn't get me vex. You bring this on yourself. The last thing I want to do is lash you. Now, tell me you won't do it again.

Right then I hated myself. After all I passed through I ended up with a man who beat me for no good reason.

Yes, Boysie.

Yes, Boysie what?

I won't make you hit me again.

Good girl. Good.

He crawled on top me, pawing and kissing. Easier to give him what he craved. He pulled off my top and straight away locked on to a nipple, suckling my milk-less tot-tots like a hungry batcha. He didn't even push he fat laar inside me. Five minutes of suckling hard and the man was snoring.

I must give comfort like he's a baby? He have that all wrong. If Boysie only knew my heart he would get up and leave before I slit he throat with that same sword he's keeping on top the press.

DORIS

An evening on the town with Mr Police and, true talk, it was sweet too bad. The man's a solid bet. None of this here today, gone tomorrow, at all at all. We went Ling Nam on Charlotte Street, a place I'd heard so much about. While we were inspecting the menu he nudged up quiet quiet,

I bring plenty money, Doris. Order anything you want.

Talk about a gentleman. You only had to watch him, dressed neat neat with the shirt buttoned up to the top to know he go be a family man. Will be a family man. No horn. Doris wasn't made for Toco. Was Doris made for Mr Police? I was tempted for sure. We could save up, buy a piece of land and in time build we own house. Build our own house. I could see myself settling down with four, five children. Anyhow, best not to count egg in fowl bottom. When we were little, me and my sisters used to play house and pretend we had up to fifteen children. Gosh we were dotish. I miss them more than I care to admit.

We held hands walking home talking and laughing. So why didn't I kiss the man properly by my gate? I said it was because people might see. That's ole talk. The place was dark and we could easily have stepped behind a bush. Men like Mr Police, you must watch them carefully. We'd already been holding hands. Put my tongue in his mouth and it's the same as opening my legs. Deal sealed. I know the type. And if I don't, I'm a good for nothing cock teaser. As if they're entitled. Trust me. I kiss Mr Police and in days he'll be asking the priest to read banns announcing our engagement.

*

Mistress well tease me though.

The tall handsome young man is in love with you, Doris.

My face burned.

Oh to be young and in love. I remember when Mr Bernard
wooed me.

I put on a smile and braced myself to hear this story. Again. For
the hundredth time. She brain going. No, it's her brain's going.
Whatever, she not all there.

My father had a stud farm. Racehorses. I've told you this
before, haven't I?

Maybe. I don't remember clear, clearly. Tell me again, please.

I love how careful you are to speak properly. My friends are
so jealous I have you. Some maids, well, you almost need a
translator to understand them.

She wiped her hands and sat down. Here we go.

We still have the farm, of course. My brother and his wife
took over when Daddy died, God rest his soul.

I made the sign of the cross.

Anyway, this man would come to look at the horses. One day
he came when Daddy wasn't there. He wanted to try a new
horse he heard Daddy had bought. I said the horse was wild
but would he listen to a girl? Oh no. He saddled up and took
her for a ride. That horse tossed him off and he broke his arm
and leg. I felt terrible I'd not stopped him. I went to see him

out of guilt. Didn't fancy him. He's quite a bit older, as you know. Anyway, I took him a tart which he liked. But what he really loved was the thick custard. Said it took all the pain away to have my custard. So, I went back the following week with another tart and a bowl of custard. I swear he married me for my custard. He would say, Margaret, your custard's even better than my grandma's and hers is exceptional. To this day I can make him smile by serving custard.

Your custard is the business.

She sighed.

But don't be getting married and having babies too soon. You need to help me with my little ones.

Yes, Mistress. I ain't leaving. I'm not leaving all you anytime soon. No stress about that.

So what about the young man who walked you home? He seems keen.

Yeah, but I'm not a hundred per cent sure about him. He's a good man. In church every Sunday.

Mistress nodded.

Yes, I've seen him.

But I'm not feeling it.

Mistress got up.

Feelings come second. If he can provide and is a solid man, I don't see how you can refuse him. Now, I need you to finish making lunch and remember the sheets need changing today.

Yes, Mistress.

I went on with my work, Mr Police still on my mind. When later that same afternoon the gardener came looking to tell me a man was by the gate asking for me I told myself, like he ain't wasting time. I smoothed down my hair and tidied myself before heading to the side gate used by servants and, well, most people who aren't white. It's a good thing my heart's strong yes because it wasn't Mr Police waiting to see me.

POPO

Town say nowhere good like Boysie's clubs to take a bet, down a shot of rum and ole talk with your partners them. Fellas playing whappee steady and we there taking five cents on every bet up to a dollar. Between a dollar to ten dollars we're creaming a cool ten cents a bet. After that is twenty-five cents. Clink, clink, clink, clink, clink.

Every now and then my ears will pick up that Cecil or Tinsingh acted as banker so that muk could loss away we money. If I didn't name woman I could be in there running things better than Boysie, Cecil, Tinsingh and George put together. I'm watching good. The second I suspect thiefing it go be me and them.

If I could only get Boysie to think smart this business could look after we for life. My head studying what we should do next. Give me two more years and Port of Spain won't know what hit them. From nothing to king and queen of Port of Spain. Patience is my middle name. The funny thing is I bet he thinks he's a smart man and I'm poohar for handing over my money. Well, we go see who land up the bigger poohar.

Right now I have a new worries. The government gone and changed up their mind about gambling. Come next month the law is gambling clubs will be legal once they're licensed. We don't have none so I sent Boysie by the government office. He came back with he two hand swinging.

You get the paper?

He steupsed.

Bring some cold cold water, thandaa water, for me fast.

I put ice in a big cup of water and handed him.

So doux-doux, what happen? You went where I tell you? The
office near the Red House?

All he wanted was to dhakolay water down he throat. Glob,
glob, glob.

I asked a question. You get the licence?

He drained the cup and gestured for more.

We ain't need licence. We go manage without.

How you mean?

Girl, I reach and first thing the guard man say is I can't come
inside wearing a merino. I must have on a shirt. I tell him,
well buy a shirt for me nah. He start to carry on that it have
a way to dress when you're coming to a government office. I
say, look, I done reach. Let me do my business and next time
I go put on a shirt just for he.

Boysie crunched the ice.

Well, dress and go back.

You mad or what? I ain't going back there. I talk nice nice to
the man and he still ain't let me in. Well, I get so vex I cuff he
down. Somebody sent for police so I had to digs out of there
fast fast.

I hoped my face was staying sweet because inside I was burning
vex. A simple thing and this ulloo can't do it. Too much false
pride. Now I have to undo this commess.

Leave it with me, Boysie. From what I hear you pay for the licence then carry it by the police for them to write it down in a book and stamp it. It's the police them that does give out a paper for we to nail up on the wall inside to prove we legal.

All right.

I know a police. Let me ask a question.

In Dave's time he used to keep the police sweet with freeness. Every once in a while I passed in the rush. Not that I had a choice. Now let we see if they will return the favour.

Across from Woodbrook Police Station I waited in the shade under a tree. From there I could see every man coming in and out. Constable Maxwell or Constable Ross were my targets. I waited, I waited, I waited, till I was fed up waiting. The only person I could see to ask a question was the guard in front.

Pssst.

He ain't take me on.

Pssst. Mister Guard Man.

He looked up and we eyes made four. My smile got him off that fat backside.

I was watching you. Why you standing up there so long? Eh? A sweet dulahin like you.

Aye, I say like you ain't going to talk to me. I'm looking for Constable Maxwell, a tall Creole fella or the other one, thin like bamboo. Constable Ross, I think he name.

Look at my crosses. I well thought it's me you come to see.

I put on a sad face.

> I glad to see you but I come for my father. He seeing worries and I need an ease up. Them two police had dealings with him. You think you could call them for me? I can't go inside in case people say I'm interfering with the case.

> So, what I getting?

> Aare. What kind of question is that?

> Them fellas busy busy. You ain't seeing them just so.

I bent my head and touched his arm.

> Please help me. Pa too old to make a jail.

The guard man looked left; he looked right.

> Come, but don't make it look like you're following me.

He walked around behind the police station and into the bush. I steupsed. Why all man so? When I reached where he was hiding, the pants already unzipped and one ugly laar like a little finger poking out.

> Do me fast.

> I ain't sucking that.

> Well, use your hand then. Hurry up.

It didn't take long.

> Oh God father, you're good.

He straightened and told me to go back under the tree.

> I go tell them an Indian whore here to give them thing.

I steupsed and walked off. He better do for me now or I will bite
off that puny piece of laar he have there.

Must be a whole half-hour later Constable Maxwell eventually showed he face and called me to one side in front the station. This town small, yes. He done know about we club. The
officers were deciding how best to handle Boysie.

From what I hear all you busy day and night. Every last
badjohn seems to pass through 59 Prince Street.

Well, officer, that's a good thing. Now you know where to
find certain people you might be looking for.

He laughed. I continued making my case.

You know Boysie don't let fighting and thing happen in he
place. No matter who you is. If it's trouble you're making he
letting you have it. Soon as he bring out he big stick, fellas
know to behave right away.

I like a little whappee myself now and then. And I really hear
that he's keeping the place good.

Port of Spain know Boysie's temper's hot like pepper sauce so
he club don't make trouble. He ain't 'fraid to throw your ass
out with two cuff and a kick.

Constable Maxwell nodded.

I know, I know. And what about you? You're still doing a
little business on the side?

Nah, nah, nah. I home. Nah, all that stop.

He gave me a wink.

If you say so, Madame Popo. If you say so.

He face turned serious.

But I can't do nothing about the fact that Boysie's running an illegal gambling establishment. That ain't me say so. That is the law. He should go and get a licence.

He can't do that. Some trouble with a man in the licensing office.

I took a deep breath.

I'm asking if you could pass on a Friday to say a friendly hello. Check nothing wrong with the place. What you think?

Every Friday?

I nodded and he smiled.

That could work. My sergeant will have to come too.

Yeah, man. Of course. So, I could tell Boysie you'll pass this Friday?

You could do that.

He half turned to go then glanced back.

It's only a little five dollars for me. Sarge is ten.

Thank you, officer. You real helping me out. I know you was always a decent man. I so glad to see you.

All right, Madame Popo. We go fix up this licence thing. Later.

Suddenly I thought of Helmet. He'd said something about once a whore, always a whore. Look how he ended up in the right.

*

The police them became regulars. Fridays they collected enve-
lopes. On top of that they expected drinks on the house. But
the main thing is we're legally open and the place busy busy. I
got a girl to help. She ain't too bright but she's willing. I told her,
head down and keep the place clean. She don't have to talk to
no man and if anybody bother she is me they'll deal with. But
like I said, she ain't no kerosene lamp. Today she came telling
me somebody was asking for Boysie. They wanted to know if he
does still charge thirty-five dollars to beat up a man. First I'm
hearing about this.

Tell me what he say exactly?

The girl bit her lips.

He say beginning of the year Mr Boysie charged him thirty-
five to rough up a man but he want Boysie to go back in the
man tail this week.

And you're sure sure it's Boysie and not Baje or one of them
he was looking for?

No. He asked for Mr Boysie. What to tell him? I could bring
him for you?

Don't bring nobody. Tell him to pass back. Boysie's there after
four.

Well, I thought I was making Boysie into a new man and look at
this. Beating up people for cash like some gutter fighter. How he
expect we to lift up if he's breaking people hand and foot?

Around four o'clock I sat on the step and waited. Boysie eventually reached looking all how.

Aare. I thought you was checking on Laventille and coming back?

I bounce up two partner I used to fish with and we end up taking a sea bath.

He could see my face swell up vex.

Something happen?

I let go a long steupse.

A man reach for you today. He coming back just now.

What name?

Me ain't know but he coming because you is the man to see to beat up people. I hear you have rates depending on what you do.

Boysie sat down on the middle of the three steps right near me and threw off he rubber slippers.

You're listening?

He remained quiet.

Boysie, how we go better we-self if you there carrying on like you're born and living on the roadside? Eh?

Nothing.

Aye? Sea water lock off your ears?

Still nothing. Boysie got up, looking more vexed than me, and went inside. I heard pots clanking extra loud.

Popo, where my food?

How you mean?

I ain't see nothing.

It have a plate covered down with rice and takari.

I waited already knowing what was coming next. He came outside.

That stale food is all it have? What happen? You ain't cook since this morning?

No.

A whole next quarrel started about how I lazy and one set of chupidness. He cussed and carried on and then I asked him again. What about the beatings for money? Not once did he answer me. Not once. But he's there going on and on about the food. Let him keep doing that and see how far in jail they throw him. Ulloo. Why he stop so? All he good for is to gamble and fight, fight and gamble. It's my money jumping up with this man so I ain't backing down. If it's cuss we have to cuss all the time then that's how it go be until he change.

DORIS

Boysie Singh was outside the Bernards' house dressed up like he's getting married. White shirt starched stiff, pants crease razor-sharp, papayo. I could see my face in them shoes they're so shiny. Pomade slicked down his hair neat neat and that face was well creamed. I didn't know he had money for nice clothes so. He looked good enough to eat. Like Mistress's custard.

I was going to check on my club and I tell myself, let me pass and check how you doing.

You own a club?

Two. Small, but I'm getting a big club. It need a little fixing but once that done it go be the most-est popular club in the whole of Trinidad. Trust me. People will be coming from all over, Arima, San Fernando, Curepe.

He grinned.

Even Toco. People will leave quite up there to fete in my club.

Where're the clubs you have now?

Woodbrook and Laventille. Steady money. Doing nice nice. Anyhow, I only passing to say hello.

Before I could catch myself he was gone.

Two days later he in front my house again. Your boy ain't ask me out. It was the week after that he finally made a move.

So, I want to carry you to the area I'm thinking of setting up my next club. You have time off Saturday?

I had promised Mr Police the Saturday but he's had a turn already. Let him wait. I played it cool.

I can't say if I'm working Saturday or not.

His smile made me realise any game I played, he knew already.

Decide. You're working or you're coming out with me?

I licked my lips slowly.

I might want to stay home and read my Bible.

Well, I'm happy to read it with you.

Or we could go to your place?

For a split second he looked worried.

Nah, not this Saturday. A next time. Place need a good clean. You know how bachelor does live.

Typical man. All you don't know how to keep nothing.

He looked away.

It's not that.

I didn't say anything. His words came out slowly and carefully.

I really like you and I don't want to lie. It have a girl living by me.

Well, look trouble.

I knew something serious was going on. You living with a woman and checking me? Look, Boysie, haul your tail from here right now.

It's nothing.

She's living by you and it's nothing? Don't lie.

Watch me, I wouldn't married she if she was the last woman on earth. To be honest I feel sorry for she. Poor, no family, so I take she in. We don't even sleep in the same bed.

I took a deep breath and turned to go.

Please, Doris. It's not what you think. She leaving soon as she find a place. A few weeks and she gone.

My heart was racing in a way it never felt when Mr Police called for me by the side gate. I watched Boysie straight and we eyes made four.

Don't come here again while that woman in your house. You hear me? I don't care who she is. When she move out we might talk. Might.

Boysie made the sign of the cross.

She will vanish just now like she was never there.

I rolled my eyes and shook my head. As if a woman can disappear like a magic trick.

POPO

Boysie didn't come home for two days and really that was the best thing that could've happened for both of we. At first I wanted to pack up Chunksee and dump him by Mana Lala. But I looked at him, quietly building something with old matchboxes. The bai ain't do me nothing. I don't know when or how but I have feelings for this child. He's always giving hug up. He ain't harden like some children and he don't answer back. Lord know why he ain't give me a child. Maybe Chunksee is the one I'm supposed to mother.

That love for Chunksee didn't stretch to he baap. Them two days waiting gave me time to think. Horning me. I pray I ain't get he nastiness. And I hope it make he thing quail up and drop off. Cheating on me one way makes me sure he's shafting me in my pocket too. All money in and out I make a mark in my copy book. From what I seeing it ain't adding up. If things as good as Boysie's boasting, then how come when the week done I ain't seeing more cash? Good week, bad week it's roughly the same amount we ending up with. Either Boysie's gambling plenty or them fellas busy fingering what don't belong to them. Oh, and what about the money from running the girls them? That is a whole side of the club takings I ain't seeing.

What I want to know is where the money. Asking Boysie ain't no help. That man wouldn't know a straight answer if it knocked him down in the road. A little recognition in the community and he head done swell up big big. You see me? I ain't no ulloo. Problem is I can't go inside to check exactly how things running. But I have eyes. Diggers I knew from way back and when he was looking for work I made Boysie take him on. I trust him. Let's see if he finds anything or turns neemakharam and next thing I know Boysie's looking to kill me dead.

Like the gods them looked down and said, Popo, we know from small you had things hard. We go help you out lil bit. Within weeks Diggers had mined gold. Boysie found cheap beer and needed an extra hand to do loading and packing. For whatever reason none of the normal crew were around. Diggers got the work. Up and down, Diggers stayed with Boysie. Guess where Boysie and the man selling the beer met? And guess who brought out a paper bag with the money for he to pay? I would never have believed it. Never, never, never. Boysie using that dopey muk Mana Lala and making she house he headquarters. I watched Diggers in he eye.

You're sure sure?

Yes, it was Chunksee's mother. That is the girl. Like she know everything about what Mr Boysie have.

How you mean?

Well, she hand Mr Boysie a fat roll of notes and later he asked to see the bank book.

Bank book? What I hearing today?

I ain't asking you. I'm telling you. She take out a Barclay's Bank book she had hide up in she brassiere. Anyhow, she put she hand in that area and pulled out a bank book.

So that's where my money going. What else?

Diggers shook he head.

All I know is Mr Boysie was flashing money around like he name Father Christmas.

Ha. If he parading with money that must mean some of the whe-whe funds jumping up in there too.

My blood was boiling. Boysie think he outsmarting me? Nah. I work too hard for what I have. And Mana Lala? That's how she pay me back for looking after she bai all these years? And I never once show she bad face.

Diggers had made himself comfortable and was probably hoping for a plate of food.

You eat already? I have food from this morning. It ain't much.

Well, I wouldn't say no.

I sat down next to him while he chewed like a cow. Everything and everybody had me vex. If Boysie walked in right now I think I was bubbling with enough rage to beat him with he own stick till he begged for mercy.

As soon as he finished I sent Diggers on he way. Anger was giving me a headache. I kept telling myself to calm down and plan but the only plan I had was for the whole of Port of Spain to see me piss on Boysie.

MANA LALA

Mother Gizzard's medicine worked. Boysie ain't say nothing about having problems. But then again he ain't trouble me. I don't know if that mean he have it or he gone off me or he happy with whatever it is Popo does do for he. Mind you, if Popo gave him it she might be real sick. I don't hear much about she these days. Maybe the oil from Papa Dooboo working slow slow to drive the two of them apart. That would be good. Of course she may be holding on to Boysie with she own obeah spell. How much you want to bet he's eating rice she squatted over? Yeah, it's probably sweat rice that have him bazodee. But that ain't getting in the way of we having a serious talk. Thing is it real hard to find the man by he-self. Every time I want to say a word he glued to he partners Baje on one side and Firekong to the other. I might have to just tell him in front them. If he get shamed well he shamed.

So when he pulled up in the jitney all by he-self I couldn't let him go just so just so.

Aye, Mana Lala, that blue-and-white cool box you have? Let me borrow it nah.

Come inside for a minute.

He stood still like he was thinking what to do.

All right but I can't stay long. Them fellas waiting on me. We making a river lime.

Which part?

Up Caura side, where they're planning to put the dam.

I couldn't help my mouth swelling up.

Me ain't know nothing because you never carry me Caura in my life.

He kept quiet. Two of we stood facing one another. Will this man ever show a little love?

The cool box in the back?

It somewhere there. And Boysie, I have something to talk to you about.

He nodded.

Let me hear but do fast.

My chance finally and I didn't know where to start.

I didn't tell you because I was there blaming myself. Well I done with that. Popo bring she disease and now I have it. You give me. Happy now?

Saying this out loud to Boysie's face opened my throat.

Me give you disease? But I ain't have nothing.

You lie. But that's on you. If you ain't see nothing yet never mind. It go happen.

I wiped my forehead with my hand. Suddenly I was more tired than vex. I'm tired of always keeping everything locked away to please Boysie.

I never tell you but I lost a batcha. We could have had a next beta. Nearly four months along. It's only now I get to know most likely it was because I had the disease. Worst yet, it does make you barren. Popo never had big belly. Now I know why. You can do what you want but you see me? I can't take this. Mess up my whole life. I will go to my grave hating that woman for what she do me.

I stopped. In all my years I've never talked this way to Boysie. I was sure he would explode. Maybe now or later when he drink rum I'll get a beating. But he surprised me.

I didn't know all that. A batcha?

He put two hands on top he head.

What you go do?

Give me a chance. I'm thinking.

Well, don't take too long. Every day you're with she is trouble. I lost a batcha. You might lose what in your pants.

POPO

This one hard to swallow. I've been turning it over and over in my mind. I didn't have a home and he let me live by he. But I helped. I could've taken the money and run. I looked after everything. I mind a child that's not my own. I put up with the horning and the gambling. Don't know why I thought we would be partners in this. Working together. Instead he was thiefing. He probably even planned to go back with that muk Mana Lala. People will say I got what was coming because I knew the kind of man Boysie was from the start. Make your bed; lie in it. Sometimes I wish I wasn't a woman. I could tell him point blank what I know but all that maakaachood will do is laugh and act like I'm poohar. Nah, it's time to thief from the thief.

I did the only thing I could. I refused to do anything in the house. A set of wares smelling in the sink. Clothes piling up to wash. If I didn't have Chunksee I don't think I would have left my bed. Lunchtime and me and the bai were eating roti and Bluenose butter when Boysie decided to appear. Instead of a good afternoon he started ranting.

What happen, Popo? Like your hand break? It ain't look like this house clean for a month.

Nothing stopping you from taking up a broom.

What the ass wrong with you?

I gave him a stink cut eye.

You leave me alone, you hear.

While we were talking Chunksee tried to sneak away. I grabbed him and pushed he bottom right back down on the peerha.

How much time I have to tell you? Eat your food.

Don't shout at the bai like he big.

Boysie smoothed the bai's hair.

Beta, eat a little bit nah and then you could play.

I steupsed.

With the last mouthful Chunksee ran off to find the neighbour's children. I went in my bed only for that maakaachood to follow me.

Anybody come looking for me?

No.

You're sure?

Who you're expecting?

I was just wondering. Somebody say they see Helmet.

Well me ain't see he.

Oh, all right then. You're sure?

You ain't hear me the first time? Now, leave me alone.

*

Me and Chunksee took taxi. Boysie was probably in a card game and forgot the bai's supposed to go by he mother. When he's settled in a game of all fours or whappee, I ain't seeing him whole weekend until late Sunday or even Monday, hungry and smelling rank. Most times he's probably lost plenty money and dhakolay rum straight down he throat. And if he wins I'm sure he'll spin by Mana Lala house first to hide up cash he ain't want me to see.

Mana Lala rushed to hug up Chunksee. I asked for an excuse. Whole road coming I was holding in a hot piss. When I came back everyone was in the kitchen.

> Beta, like Popo Tanty ain't feeding you? You're looking extra small.

I couldn't believe she was talking dotish so.

> He getting good food every day.

Mana Lala didn't answer back. Chunksee ran off to find he nanee. He knows she will carry him to the corner parlour for penny sweeties.

The two of we sat down in the gallery, me drinking thandaa water to cool down and Mana Lala eating ice. I noticed she kept rubbing she belly. I asked why.

> Girl, I don't like to be one of them people always complaining about some pain or the other but I ain't feeling myself. That's the truth.

> What troubling you?

She pointed to where it was paining most.

> You see here by my navel? That's the spot.

I put down my cup.

> But Mana Lala, you-self must know that mean you gone and strain your nara.

I did well think that.

Lucky thing I know how to rub nara.

For true?

My friend Doll Baby teach me. When my neighbour Teresa pulled she nara the other day who you think fixed it? It was me. You ain't bound to go by no hototo doctor.

All right, let we go in my room.

Nah, you need to lie down flat on the ground. Bring a paal and spread it right here.

She called for Chunksee.

Beta, run get my paal and take a chadaar from the press.

Where, Ma?

The paal under the bed and the chadaar in the press.

I know he's not my child but I does be so proud when he behave nice like this helping he mai.

Chunksee spread the paal in a corner of the gallery. Mana Lala got the other things I needed: a reel of white thread, a small glass, a piece of candle and matches. I made she lie down and push away clothes from she chest and belly. I lay the chadaar over she legs so she wasn't exposed. With the thread I measured from nipple to navel on all two sides while chanting the prayers I'd learnt from small.

Plenty difference in the two.

I held up the thread.

One side so.

I moved my fingers along the thread a good few inches.

And one side so. You see how it more longer?

Now I knew what I was dealing with I began hauling the nara by massaging upwards towards the navel.

Ouch.

Sorry.

For truth, I was doing this because I wanted to help ease the pain. Yet as I kneaded she skin I could feel my vexness that she was helping Boysie against me. Still, I kneaded away. Whatever bad spirit was inside I would move it along. Once the skin felt soft I lit the candle and placed it on the navel. This part I knew she wouldn't like. I turned a glass over the candle. All she skin sucked towards the glass. As the flame went out I tugged the glass free from she belly.

Okay, Mana Lala?

Yes. It hurt but a good pain. What you going to do now?

Let me see how much nara I catch.

Two thread measurements again and thankfully the difference was way less than at the start.

I prefer when the two sides come the same. Here it still have nara to catch. We should do this again tomorrow.

She fixed she clothes.

Take a cup of hot hot tea. Any little wind nara you have, the tea go fix.

By the time she'd made the tea I'd tidied everything away.

I folded the paal and chadaar. They're on your bed. And I put the candle and matches on the table.

I've been thinking hard for days and I had a plan that could help me, Mana Lala and Chunksee. This seemed the correct time to test the waters. Even though we were alone I bent close to Mana Lala and lowered my voice.

I want to ask you something, but you must promise me it staying with two of we. Not even your mai. From my mouth to your ears and no further.

No problem.

I told her I knew Boysie was running business from her house and that she was keeping cash for him that I never saw. Instead of denying it like I thought she would, she said yes. That was the truth. As we talked things came out. Mana Lala was only doing what she must to keep Boysie from taking Chunksee. It wasn't that she wanted to see me get cheat. Plus, we both knew the feel of Boysie's hand and belt.

I ain't go lie, Popo. Under my mattress right now have a set of cash keeping for he.

How much so?

I think he say nearly two thousand.

My mouth dropped open.

Where he get that from?

A big all fours win the other day plus the clubs and whatever he get for small jobs. Insurance burning and thing.

I closed my mouth before flies went in.

Let me ask you something. You're never tempted to take a little bit for yourself and Chunksee?

She laughed.

You want Boysie to kill me?

But what if you could get away from Boysie and make a new home for you and Chunksee?

How you mean? I always live here.

This was the first time the words left my mouth. I took a deep breath and talking low I said we could take the money she was keeping, plus whatever I could get my hands on, and run away far far where Boysie can't catch we.

What you mean? That's the beta's father.

So, you're good staying here with Boysie telling you if and when you can see your own bai?

No. But what else I could do?

I had the feeling she wanted to say something. Instead she crunched ice and stayed quiet. Boysie have she real poohar.

Come with me.

Where? Go where? You living in Boysie house. Where I supposed to go?

You know Tobago? Near but far enough. Let we go there.

Mana Lala eyes opened big big.

Why Tobago?

She put down the cup. I watched as she sucked hard on a piece of ice so big it was sticking out she mouth. I explained how fellas working boats that go Tobago every week would take us. For a price they would keep their big mouths shut. Boysie would never even think to look at Trinidad's twin island.

Neither of we 'fraid hard work and people always need to eat. We could plant garden and sell.

I 'fraid, Popo. Anything go wrong is kill Boysie go kill we. Chunksee would grow without a mother. How I could do that to my beta?

That is why if we do this we have to go somewhere he will never look. Nobody will think to look Tobago. A fella once told me that the English even tried to sell off Tobago but nobody wanted to buy it. There better than any bush in Trinidad.

She bit down on a piece of ice so hard I thought she teeth might crack.

When you're thinking to make this move?

I took a deep breath.

A boat leaving in two days.

She scratched she head.

Nothing like this ever come to me before.

I told her I would leave now as I had to buy some things in town.

All after lunch she would see me and she could tell me then what she wanted to do.

But if you see Boysie before I come back?

She made as if zipping she mouth.

I ain't no neemakharam.

*

I was back by three. Mana Lala's face was carrying plenty worries. She was holding a Klim tin.

Two thousand in there. Take it before I change my mind.

It seemed right. I'm at least getting out what I put in. I hugged her tight and whispered.

You is my sister. We go do this together.

We talked more about who need to get pay off, where and when. I didn't want to take all the money but Mana Lala thought it best if I handle that side of things.

You there working side by side with Boysie running big club. You keep the money.

I laughed.

You ain't 'fraid I take the money and run away by myself?

Well, it crossed my mind.

She paused.

Give me something so I know you're coming back for me and Chunksee.

What? I ain't have nothing. You want the two piece of gold I have in my ears?

Mana Lala shook she head and pointed.

The tabeej you have round your neck.

Nah. I never take this off. This is the only-est thing I have from my family.

I pulled out my gold earrings.

Here, take this.

Mana Lala pushed it away.

The tabeej.

No, take the gold.

She face was set a way I'd never seen before. It was the tabeej or nothing. She exchanged it for the Klim tin. I felt naked as I born.

Don't worry. It safe. The minute you come back for we I'll put it on your neck myself.

I told her to only pack a small bag. By tomorrow night we're out of here.

MANA LALA

Instead of sleeping I stared at the roof beams. My fingers played with Popo's tabeej around my neck. That was the safest place for it. Whole night I tossed around wondering who will reach the house first, Boysie or Popo. Morning came and no Boysie. All I could do was sit down in the gallery in the spot with a clear view of the road. I crunched so much ice that I thought a next tooth breaking for sure.

Lunchtime reached and still no Boysie.

One o'clock.

Two o'clock.

Two thirty.

Three.

Ten past three.

I caught a glimpse of Boysie jumping out a route taxi and straight away ran to my bedroom and started to bawl. I didn't have to pretend. I was crying out of complete fear. Ma came running in.

What happen?

Oh god Ma, Boysie money gone! We get rob! Oh Lord, when this could've happened? He go think I lost it. Oh Ma, Boysie go kill me. He go take Chunksee for good. Oh God oh.

Hush. How much?

Two thousand.

What the ass you was thinking? Ulloo. You-self keeping that

kind of money in this house? That's asking for thief-man to
come. When last you see it?

Yesterday.

Ain't the press does be locked?

I burst into more tears now.

I forget was to lock it back yesterday. I wasn't feeling too
good and in the hustle for Popo to rub my nara I left the
thing open.

Ma bit she lip.

Don't cry. Don't cry. Let we think. Maybe you put it
somewhere else? Who went in your bedroom?

Only we, and, well, Popo.

Somebody sneak in here and take it.

Lord, how I telling Boysie I lost he money?

Boysie's voice boomed.

Afternoon! Chunksee! Chunksee!

I had no choice. Ma walked out with me. One look at my face
and Boysie panicked.

Where's Chunksee? He all right? Anything happened to him?

Ma answered.

Chunksee good good. Neighbour had prayers and she's
sharing sweeties so you know he in that. Just now he will
reach back.

Boysie eyed me funny.

I heard bawling.

Ma put she hand around my waist and begged Boysie to show mercy on this house. I couldn't help the fresh bawling.

Ma, make your daughter stop wailing and tell me what happen.

It took a few more seconds before I blurted out that the money was missing.

But how, Mana Lala? Nobody know you have that kindna cash.

I dried my eyes.

Yes. One person went in my room yesterday.

Who?

I took the tabeej out of my pocket and handed it to him.

The person dropped this.

POPO

Things have to do fast fast. I sent a message with one of them little boys to my friend working the Tobago boat to say I will pass later with something for he. I'm packing so it doesn't look like I'm gone. We need all the head start we can get. If I could do magic we would be in Tobago before Boysie even sniffed we gone.

He turned up while I was looking through my drawers and I had to pretend I was in the middle of searching for a piece of clothes. A wedding coming up. Cool as ever, Boysie was gaawaying an Indian tune, if you could call that singing, and talking about how this Christmas breeze calling for a good kite fight. I tried to act interested.

You're making mange for the kite?

Yeah. Pulling mange with fine glass to cut down them other kites.

He went outside while I quickly tidied up the clothes. A few minutes later I found him at the side of the house grinding what was a soda water bottle with a loorha on a big sill.

That is not my good loorha you're using? That's for grinding geera, methi and them thing. Ain't you have your own stone for pounding glass?

Yes but this one does get it like powder.

I steupsed.

That glass mash up enough.

Nah. It have to be plenty more fine.

Well, all right. You do your thing. I'm cleaning inside.

Boysie remained outside a good while. I suppose he was making sure the glass was small small. When he did come in he had a plate. He smiled, pointing to a piece of roti stuffed with aloo and bodi.

Let me feed my poi poi.

Well, it's now my mind get confuffled. He's been treating me bad for so long, hardly talking to me. Why change now? I was too frightened to refuse.

Don't bother yourself.

But I want to.

He sat next to me on the bed and laughed while he told me to open my mouth, roti coming. I'd barely swallowed when he was pushing another piece of roti in my mouth.

Eat your roti, poi.

My mouth was too stuffed to answer. I tried to smile. As soon as that mouthful was down he shoved more in. I nearly choked.

Too fast, Boysie.

He ain't bothered with me.

Stop. Let me chew me food good, nah.

Boysie was carrying on like it was one big joke feeding me fast fast. He looked real happy. Suddenly, I bit something crunchy. I spat it out in my hand.

Eat, poi.

No, wait.

I looked at what I'd spit out. Nothing strange.

I thought I chewed a stone.

He laughed.

Finish your food, poi.

The next mouthful was the same. This roti was like chewing fine fine stone or something.

Boysie, something in the roti.

Well you cook so you must know what in it.

He surprised me with an extra big mouthful. This time as I crunched something stabbed my tongue. I ran to the sink. Blood. Touch me then and I was probably as thandaa as ice. I rushed to the front door. Locked. No key. Boysie was sitting down skinning he teeth like nothing was happening.

What you do, Boysie? What you do?

The grin that stretched across he face and lit those dark eyes scared me more than any rage or hate I'd ever seen. I screamed,

Glass in the roti, you neemakharam.

Boysie laughed and slowly walked to me. I backed away.

Come Popo. Better belly buss than good food waste.

One hand grabbed my wrists and the other gripped my throat tight. I pushed but he was too strong.

Eat.

We eyes made four and terror went through my body.

You will eat every piece. I put a little extra spice just for you.

Still gripping my throat, he pushed me back on the bed and straddled my chest. Suddenly, I wanted my mai. I wanted to tell she that I loved she. I was going to die here in Prince Street without ever seeing she again. Mai, mai, mai.

PART TWO

ROSIE

I better chalk your foot, Boysie, it's so long me ain't see you. What going on?

Morning, Rosie. Like you paint up and thing. And you changed the name. Rose's Bar and General Goods Store. Sounding nice.

What I go say? I there trying a thing. But look at you running big club these days. They're calling you the whe-whe king.

Girl, I there fighting up. And how business? It's good you make the rum shop part more bigger and left the dry goods to the side. Rain or shine man always need a place to relax he-self.

Correct.

From what I hear you is the heart of the village. Ramkelawan's is the only other shop and that's a good pull from here.

If you say so.

I knew why he'd come because he'd already hit up the hardware and the little clothes shop down the road. Let me see what he's planning to put on me. Boysie pulled a stool close to the counter and settled he-self comfortable like the place really named Boysie's Bar and General Goods Store.

So Rosie, let we talk frankomen. You owe rent.

It was expected but I still felt my heart speed up one time. A deep breath and I reminded myself of the plan. Don't talk. Let him say what he came to say. Out came words about protecting we village from thief-man and bandit. While he's around nobody would dare trouble me or damage my shop because they know it's Boysie Singh they're answering to. And a woman by she-self with shop? That's extra protection. He would be sorry to hear how some hooligan interfered with me or that the shop burnt down. While he talked a big stick in he hand was marking time. Jeez-an-ages, it took all my willpower not to grab that stick and beat he ass.

> Don't worry, Rosie. We is friend from way back. I ain't here to dig out your eye. Let we work out something and month end I go collect. We good?

We were not. I watched him direct in he eye.

> I can't believe the Lord shine He light on me this Tuesday morning for you to come harass my soul. I need protection? From who exactly? All the years this shop here it never once had a problem.

I leaned in.

> The only commess is what you're bringing for me.

He rocked back and laughed wild wild like I buss a big joke. I gripped the counter and hissed,

> Not a red cent. I'm working too hard to give away money just so. Go trouble somebody else.

> Aye, Rosie, rest yourself. Thing must burn down with you inside over a little rent?

Boysie squeezed my hand so tight water sprang to my eyes.

None of this blasted rudeness, you hear. I'm talking to you. Rent collecting month end. Fix to suit.

I tried to pull away but he crushed my hand even harder. If he ain't careful he go break my finger.

Look at you with all your big club and still thiefing from a poor woman.

Thiefing? Since when charging rent is thiefing?

He let go my hand and skinned he teeth like two of we is long-time friends shooting the breeze.

Rosie, Rosie, Rosie.

Take my name out your mouth.

Oh gosh. Don't carry on so. Ain't you well used to like me.

I was young and chupid.

I watched him cut eye, fuming. Nothing I could do but pay this mother ass badjohn. Whole day my hand pained me.

*

Boysie Singh now is not the boy I knew all them moons ago. He'd bounced into the shop, same age as me, thirteen, fourteen, wanting twine for a kite, and dropped a sweet eye on me behind the counter. When he asked where I was from because he hadn't seen me before, I smiled, ready to see him back back and squirm like most people.

The coolie orphanage. Or the asylum. However you want to call it.

Instead of easing off he skinned he teeth and asked my name. The missionaries had found me this shop work with a child-less couple, Mr and Mrs Payne. Hot licks in my tail from them and again from the missionaries if I so much as looked at a boy. Lucky thing the shop was empty. I mumbled,

Rose Burnley.

He whispered back,

Indian with a name so?

I find you fass.

I like your long hair. Don't ever cut it.

Constantly checking nobody was coming, I whispered,

So, what they does call you?

Boysie. Boysie Singh. Actually, it's John Boysie Singh. I have an English name too.

Well, mind your own business, John Boysie Singh.

And that, as they say, was that. I nearly had age for passing out of the coolie orphanage and it looked like the Paynes would take me in permanently. They weren't able with the shop by they-self. Compared to the kind of hard work other girls had, this was paradise. My own room in the back and the old man too half dead to even think of interfering with me. I was grateful. Plenty stories went around of the man in the house bothering orphan-age girls. If you ended up with a swollen belly it was always because the girl was too fresh with she-self. Nobody ever asked the man what he wood was doing inside the maid half he age.

That same night I met Boysie I heard a noise soft soft outside my room. He had come for me. I climbed out that window so fast. We walked by the sea and squeezed up under a coconut tree. Cool breeze was blowing hard, the perfect excuse for a hug up.

Sweetness, how a pretty girl like you land up in the coolie orphanage? Where your mother and father?

I ain't know. Dead must be. I there from a baby.

No family ain't come look for you?

I bit my lip.

How come it's only coolie children in there?

I wasn't sure if I wanted to tell him everything just so. He elbowed my side.

You does always talk plenty?

I smiled.

You really don't know?

He shook his head and pushed a stray hair behind my ear.

The Orphan Asylum and Industrial School for Coolie Children is for children who lost their mother and father while they were crossing the kala pani from India. They reached Trinidad alone and the church took them in. Well, that's how it started, anyway.

I glanced sideways. Boysie was listening good.

Burnley was one of the people who started up the orphanage. A set of we carry he name. I don't know who picked Rose.

That's cause you're pretty and you smell nice.

The two of we sat listening to the wind swishing through the coconut branches. I'd said plenty. Quietly he took my hand and warmed it in his.

Rose, Rose, Rose.

I prefer Rosie.

MANA LALA

So he ran she from the house. What else Popo thought would happen? She wasn't so dotish as to think I would leave Boysie or take Chunksee away from he pa. She made me lose the batcha in my belly. And because of that thing she most likely passed to Boysie it look like I can't make another batcha. We never talked about how she made all of we sick. After that how she could even dream me and the beta would run away with she? I ever do anything, or say anything, that would make she feel Boysie's a problem? She was the problem. Six years I put up with she there carrying on like she is mistress and minding Chunksee. We know she can't make batcha. On top of all that madness she thought I would just hand over Boysie's money? Whatsoever belongs to Boysie will end up with we son. Thiefing from he is thiefing from Chunksee plain and simple. I mightn't look like much but small axe does cut down big tree same way.

When I next saw Boysie I held him in a talk. I wanted to know it's gone she gone.

Tell me again. What she do when you pulled out the tabeej? Must be a real shock.

Popo knew she get catch.

She ain't even try a small lie?

Nothing. Before I could tell she to go she was flinging clothes in a bag.

So where she now?

Me ain't know and me ain't care.

I jooked and jooked for more. Either he really didn't know or he's keeping me out of he business.

Aye, she left the place in a state? Let me fix up everything nice and clean for you. I'll stay a two days.

Man, don't hurt your head. I could sort myself out. You organise Chunksee.

I crunched my ice. Long steupse. All that Popo trouble and I'm not moving in? Maybe he needs a few more days to adjust.

Still, I can't complain. At least Boysie's by me plenty now. I'm doing he washing, pressing, cooking, and the child with me. That is family life. Who know all he business? Me. He's not thinking. The amount of time and hustling he could save staying in one place. But I best hush my mouth and don't vex him. He'll come round when he ready. Ain't true love keep patience?

DORIS

I was picked up in a motor car. A light blue Austin, if you please.

You thief this or what?

He grinned.

It's my partner's car.

He got out and opened the passenger door for me.

Don't hurt your head. I'm getting the exact one just now.

He got into the driver's seat and handed over a small white box.

And this ain't mine either. It's for you.

You didn't have to buy me anything.

Gift? On the first date? Nice. This could work. Inside was a small silver heart on a silver chain.

You like it?

It real pretty. Help me put it on nah, man.

Off we went to check out the Black Lion Bar, me posing in the front seat sporting a shiny new necklace.

We had a ball. We danced, we danced, we danced. Only when the band took a rest did we stop to eat. I ordered the expensive shrimps and watched to see if he would flinch. When the policeman had taken me out, I'd asked for steak. He ordered the cheapest thing on the menu. Boysie followed me with the shrimps. Now that is man.

All one in the morning we were now falling out of the bar. His arm around my waist felt warm and right. As we leaned on the car his hand slipped down to my bamsee and rested on my back.

Eh eh, none of that, star boy.

He pulled me close for a kiss. I closed my lips tight.

My hand have he own mind. I can't stop it.

More grabbing and pushing his face in my cleavage. Like he ears clogged up?

I said no.

Boysie pulled back and watched me hard.

So, what happen? Ain't we was dancing nice nice inside?

I had to spell it out.

Old-fashioned Catholic girls need a ring on the left hand. That alone unlocking these two knees.

He grinned.

You're sure? That's it?

I'm not playing. I don't believe in relations before marriage.

The evening ended without Boysie getting so much as a tongue in my mouth. I ain't care. He'll be back.

*

Before I could say Robinson Crusoe, Boysie was sweeping me off my feet again. Three weekends in a row we've gone somewhere fancy. He keeps trying a thing but I done made up my mind. Nothing like waiting for the goods to make a man hungry. I've made it clear that me and Boysie should not be sexing before marriage. That I sexed other people already is my business and mine alone.

After a couple months stepping out, I dropped a hint that he's seen all my nice clothes plus all the dancing had nearly broken up my one good shoe. I didn't have to talk that twice. As he said goodnight a roll of notes slipped into my palm. I pecked his neck, and he pulled me closer.

Boysie, you real like hugging up and holding hands.

You don't?

I like it.

You like hugging me up?

I whispered in his ear.

Nothing better.

He whispered back,

Stay by me and we go hug up whole night.

After.

You really going to make a big man like me wait? You know how much woman does be throwing they-self at me?

I straightened up.

Well, go. I ain't tying up your foot.

But I don't want them. I want you.

I opened the car door.

We'll see.

I walked to my room. Even if he finishes tonight with some whore, it's me who will be on his mind when he explodes.

ROSIE

People feel rum shop is easy money. Maybe, but it's me and me alone to catch. I'm not far from the Leper Asylum jetty so whole week up to late on Saturdays people does be passing through, in, out, in, out. Nothing happens in this village that I don't know 'bout. A time I knew who was making baby even before the child father. And the things I hear. Lord, Jesus, have mercy, I could fill the papers for a week.

Lou reached in the shop today same time as Diggers and he friend Boy Boy. Well, look trouble. Diggers over like Lou and she ain't business with he at all at all.

Rosie, give me a pound of sugar, two pound of rice, a tin of Klim and a tin of Milo. And while I'm here let me sit down with something cold. You have mauby?

It just make so it ain't cold cold but I could put a piece of ice.

That good.

Morning, Miss Lou. Morning, Rosie.

I said morning back. Lou barely nodded. Boy Boy asked for a mauby too.

What happening, Diggers? You're drinking or you're eating?

Girl, I ain't eat nothing for the morning. Give me a malt let me get back my strength. I go see what I want after.

Diggers looked like he was settling in.

So Lou, when last you take in a cinema? I feel me and you should see what showing.

Nah, nah, nah.

Oh gosh, why you getting on so?

You have hard ears?

I brought the drinks.

Look, me ain't going nowhere with you. Now, Boy Boy, if you had more age I might go with you.

Boy Boy put he whole face in that glass of mauby. Lou ain't play she wicked, yes. She turned to Diggers.

And you're working for that badjohn Boysie Singh? Worse yet.

What Boysie do you?

Me? I hear he mixed up in obeah. He does read people mind, you know. I'm telling you. He does know what you going to play so he can call a different mark. You there thinking it's an unlucky day and he busy pocketing your money.

Diggers took a swig of malt and belched. We all watched him hard. He steupsed. Boy Boy jooked him in his side.

Like you never hear manners maketh man?

What happen? All that mean is it gone down nice.

He looked at Lou.

If I tell you a real good piece of news that nobody know, you go go cinema with me?

Lou's quarter smile was all the encouragement he needed. He checked left and right. We huddled close.

Aye, you know why Boysie's racehorse them does win steady steady?

Now I steupsed.

Money. He has the best horses. That's all.

No, girl. He horse them have spirit help.

You lie.

But I'm telling you.

As Diggers gave the story, my mouth dropped open.

Boysie keeps eyes in the morgue and funeral parlour. Soon as a child pass they does send for he. They know he like the dead fresh.

What he want?

To cut out the heart.

I held my breath. Lou eye opened big big. Only then that I realised others in the shop were listening too. Everyone was waiting on Diggers.

All you know why he does dig out the heart?

Heads shook. We remained speechless.

He does take the heart and rub it up good good on the horse them foot. One time it was still beating when he ripped it out.

Diggers leaned back.

After rubbing the horse foot, he does talk in the horse ears. I ain't know what he does say but, papayo, after that the horse winning hands down.

Lou hugged she-self.

Oh Lord, oh. Taking a baby's heart while it's still beating? That mean he kill a child in cold blood. For a horse race? Oh gosh, man. Boysie Singh over wicked.

I watched Diggers good.

You finish mamaguying we?

He face looked real serious.

Oh ho, I lie? Well, let me tell you something. This is truth. I was in the jitney a night when he went by the morgue. Boysie came back with a parcel wrapped up tight tight in gazette paper. Blood soaking through. We went from the morgue direct to the stables. I know what I know.

Boy Boy gulped his mauby and slid the empty glass towards me.

I knew he was a badjohn but this is pure evil. He should hang.

A next man asked how come police ain't lock up Boysie yet. Diggers smiled.

You think them want their own children to land up in the morgue too? Boysie Singh powerful, yes. You can't just throw him in jail and hope for the best. He will do he black magic from behind bars.

A lady pushed up to the counter.

Rosie, I only reach for a little pitch oil and this is what I hearing? Old man Payne must be turning in he grave to know Boysie Singh does come here.

I try not to show bad face to customers but this one got me vex.

Old man Payne would be well glad the shop prospering. As for Boysie Singh? It's a free country. How I supposed to stop he from coming here?

She'd boiled down like bhagee. Thing is this lady never liked me and more so after Mr Payne passed. Poor man had too much sugar in the blood. Now that was a big funeral. Mrs Payne went less than two years later. She suffered. Blind, kidney stones, she couldn't walk good. Heart gave out with the pressure. A good set of people came for she wake.

Although Mrs Payne said she was leaving me the shop I still waited and worried. Some pumpkin vine family was bound to roll up and throw me out. They never did and the lawyer in Tunapuna, Mr Sharma, gave me a paper to say it's my house and land. Every single day I give thanks to them two old people. A girl like me was supposed to end up on the street catching my tail. Look at me with my own little shop. I ain't rich but I'm making a living. Well, I'm trying anyway.

*

That same afternoon, Diggers' story still resting on my chest, Boysie's badjohns, Firekong and Bumper, came for the rent. Month end and the shop was packed. Them didn't give one ass. Boldface boldface they barged in, knocking people. An old man nearly fall. Lucky thing he partner was right there or he would've break something. Damn hooligans.

Aye, Rosie, run the whisky. We thirsty. And bring some Crix biscuits and cheese one time.

I don't eat cheese.

All right. Open a tin of sardine for Firekong.

They can't just take the money and leave. Always calling for food and demanding whisky. What I can't stand is the way they enjoy starting a fight or mashing up something. Normally, I choose an easy life and give them the drink and whatever. Keep them quiet. Don't ask what got into me but I heard myself saying,

Sorry fellas, not today. Too much customers waiting.

Firekong pulled up he jersey just enough so I could glimpse the gun in he waistband.

What you say?

He looked around.

Like you forget who you dealing with?

I straightened my back and handed him the envelope.

Take it and go your way. Please.

In the middle of all this my long-time girlfriend from since orphanage days, Ethel Hamilton, everybody does call she Etty, stepped inside the shop toting she jahaji bundle. Bumper saw red. Etty is one of Boysie's girls. I fed up telling she to left that work but she's too 'fraidy 'fraidy. Seeing her tonight was unusual. Pay day's bound to be extra busy in the club. Bumper leaned he face right into she.

Who tell you you could leave the club? Boss know you're gone? And what in that bag?

Oh gosh, ease me up, nah. I'm not feeling good. I need a rest. Anyhow, enough girls working.

Bumper grabbed she.

You're going back Queen's Street right now.

She tried to yank free. Before I could get to him Bumper put one hard lash across she face. I screamed,

Leave the girl alone. She say she not feeling well.

Bumper, still gripping Etty by she blouse, turned on me.

You and all looking for licks?

He pulled Etty round towards the giant Firekong, and, with a pointed finger, jabbed me in the chest.

Don't interfere with what is not your concern or tonight self I'm coming for you.

I looked at Etty. She blinked slowly and carefully, eyes pleading with me to back off.

They marched she out the shop and I went back behind the bar. Those thugs are mad enough to burn down my shop in truth, yes. But I ain't done with them. Firekong have gun? Well, they don't know me. I nearly turned snake tonight. Roughing up Etty like that and in front everybody. I only held back because she asked me to. Just wait. I go do for them.

MANA LALA

Big family panchayat and after the talk plenty commess. All I know is my cousins dropped their mai by we like a sack of rice. Dumped and voosh they gone. Maybe I'm unfairing them but why we have to take she in when she big hard-back children could more than look after she? My mother's sister, Subhagya, my mausi, took to she bed a good couple years back. Tookra tookra she mind's going too. Poor Subhagya Mausi's only able to make a noise, behhhh, behhhh, like a goat. It's like caring for a batcha except this one's old and quailed up.

The only place we had to put she was the back room. At least plenty breeze always blowing that side of the house. Funny that Subhagya Mausi will spend out she days by we. Of nanee's thirteen children these two sisters carried on like cat and dog. Always in a quarrel. See how karma works? Subhagya Mausi was in need and only Ma opened she house. But don't tell Ma it's love she love she sister, even if it's Tobago love. As far as she's concerned its darshan, charity, that every good Hindu must do.

I'd only just settled Subhagya Mausi when I heard a vehicle pull up. It didn't sound like Boysie's jitney. Outside a man in a broke-up old car was by the gate asking for Boysie.

He ain't here. You check the clubs?

I went there first and a fella tell me to come here. You is Chunksee's mother?

Yeah.

Hearing his name Chunksee crawled out from under the table

in the gallery. He'd been making something with string and old tins.

Look at Boysie's son. Nice child. Take the father's looks.

I smiled. He waved at the batcha.

Aye boy, how much years you have?

Chunksee held on to my leg and hid behind me. I tried to pull him off.

Say seven. Nearly eight. Open your mouth when people talking to you.

Leave him. The boy shy.

Boysie does come and go. I can't say he movements today.

He nodded.

I could trouble you for some water?

I have to say the man's colouring didn't look healthy. I got him a cup of water and plain ice for me.

You come far?

Not too far. But I really need to find Boysie.

People always looking for Boysie.

He shook his head.

I ain't have a choice. Next week is court and we need to straighten out a few things.

My ears pricked up one time. First I was hearing about this.

What court you're talking 'bout?

It's me that take the charge but it concerning he jitney so they bound to call him.

What's your name?

Lester.

Like this Lester man was only waiting for a chance to talk. Apparently, he, Boysie and a next partner were coming up the road from Cedros. Place pitch black. Somehow the jitney hit a child and the little girl dead. Lester and my eyes made four.

I tell police it was me driving so they carried me in the station.

Boysie let you drive he jitney? He must real trust you. That's he pride and joy.

Lester sighed like the world ending.

We know that but police them ain't have to know.

I bit down hard on a piece of ice. It didn't crack. I tried again and a small end splintered off.

You're understanding me, Miss?

I ain't say nothing.

Times in life you help the boss man and other times he help you. Boysie fell asleep. Accident happened. Child dead. Now trial starting so me and the Rajah have to get certain things clear. He-self know I might make a jail.

All right. Yes.

Me ain't worried for myself. My back broad. But what about

my wife and the children them?

So you looking for big money? He mightn't have what you think he have.

I ain't here to dig out nobody eye.

Well, soon as I see Boysie I go make sure he know Lester passed looking for him.

I went back to Subhagya Mausi. She must be hungry. Time to feed she some of the rice, dhal and smoked herring choka I'd cooked. I had to mash it up fine fine and give she little bit little bit. Chunksee laughed because I played the car coming for she mouth same as I used to do when he was small. What to do? Maybe somewhere deep inside she's laughing. At least I hope she's not sad to be by we house.

I was still feeding Subhagya Mausi when I heard what was definitely the jitney's engine. Hungry, grumpy and tired, Boysie was back. I told him he had to wait let me feed my mausi.

But why you have to look after she? If your mother wanted she sister here so much ain't she should be doing the hard work?

I don't mind. Subhagya Mausi was always nice to me when I was small.

Anyhow, hurry up. My belly griping me.

While I was hotting up the food I mentioned that he'd missed Lester.

You fall asleep driving? You're paying him off?

Boysie grunted.

He asked for money?

Not as such but that's what he come for.

And he say I was driving?

Yeah. So you was at the wheel?

A man tired. Don't bother me.

*

Weeks passed and I ain't hear Lester name called or anything about a court case. When I asked, Boysie skinned up he teeth.

Oh that. Case dismissed.

For truth?

Like you ain't hear? Anyhow, you're here home. You ain't go know nothing.

You ain't tell me nothing.

Lester dead, girl. He went for an early-morning sea bath and like he heart give out just so. That was that. I promised to help the family. Burying the dead is real money.

That sounded too convenient and Boysie was a little too happy. Not my place to ask questions. Boysie must manage business however he sees fit.

DORIS

For our one-year anniversary as a couple Boysie gave me the identical heart pendant and chain I have in silver only this one was pure gold. The thing dazzled. When we stepped out that night in Copacabana, the new club on Don Donaldson Street, people turned around to watch. I played like I ain't notice them eyeing up the way this blue dress showed off my curves.

We had a ball. Music was sweet too bad and the place was jamming. I spotted a set of big shots in the crowd.

Boysie, you know those people over there?

Only by face.

Yes, the Worrells and the Whites. Oh, look by the bar. The Procopes.

How you know everybody so?

Well, I don't know them, know them. But some have been to dinner by we. And they're always making papers. A few in my church too.

I could see myself being friends with these nice people. Already we party at the same clubs. A few lucky breaks and who knows where Boysie could end up? He'll need me to smooth things over for him. Let me handle these kind of people. Yes, Boysie needs me to go up in the world.

That night when he dropped me home, he didn't have to do the usual begging for a little feel-up. It is one hundred and ten per cent clear that this man's bazodee for me. I compromised.

Gently holding his hand, I guided him up and down the outside of my bloomers.

You're wasting water down here.

I leaned in for a kiss.

I ain't made of stone. You're a good-looking man. Of course I want you bad.

Then let we go by me nah. I can't wait.

Buy the ring. Fix up for we, for us, to live good in a nice house. Every night it'll be your right to put more than your hand down there.

Boysie exhaled.

You well know how to torture a man, yes.

I done tell you how to get an ease.

I straightened my skirt and fixed my blouse.

Thanks for bringing me home safe and sound.

ROSIE

Orphanage life is all I've known, so fending for myself is what I do. Etty's problem was she had had a mother even if it was only for five years. When the woman dead she overseer father buried the child by we. Etty reached, pretty pretty, a mixed-up child with grey-brown eyes and brown hair in two long plaits. In a sea of dark eyes and black hair, I thought she was pretty as a dolly. But you see children? They ain't play they're cruel. Instead of loving the new toy they couldn't wait to mash it up for being too beautiful. In class the children would constantly pinch her hard. She made the mistake of telling Miss, which meant hair-pulling was added to the mix. Mud used to land on the back of she clothes regular.

First Christmas she was there we had a surprise. Looking back it must have been a good sugarcane crop because somebody was feeling rich. The orphanage got a donation of shoes for every last one of us. Big excitement in the place. The hall was cleared. A man with string measured each child's foot. Boxes upon boxes of shoes, white for girls and black for boys were piled high. I ain't go lie, it was my first shoes. Before I'd only ever had old rubber slippers. And even though the shoes were for outside, I hated these precious white things touching the dirty ground.

Come Christmas morning the shoes were getting their first outing. Etty woke and her shoes had somehow walked from under her bed and were soaking in a posey full of pee. Girls in the dormitory were cackling while she just stared at her spoilt shoes. I suppose she was in shock. If it was me I'd have been bawling. Not Etty. She sat like a block of ice with life slowly melting away. I got blue vex.

Every bit of my rage at being constantly reminded I was an unwanted piece of shit passed through me. I was only seven but I went at them older girls kicking and punching. Man, clothes tear, face get scratched, hand saw teeth marks. I knocked a girl and she fell long enough for me to stamp on she back. I gave licks for every blessed thing that ever vexed me. But me against three? They beat me up good and proper.

As punishment for starting the fight I spent Christmas Day locked in a chicken coop, no food or even a cup of water. But from that day the too pretty dolly and me have been best friends.

MANA LALA

Boysie was packing a thin cloth bag with whe-whe notes and books he'd been studying like he had to sit a test today.

What you dream last night?

Boysie, how much time I have to tell you? Once my eye open whatever I was dreaming does go clean from me.

Yes, but a time you remembered seeing a white horse bathing in the sea. I played nineteen for horse. Made some good change that day.

Truth is these days I can't forget my dreams. Always something to do with Popo. Last night she was walking in the road and a car was speeding coming. I shouted for she to jump in the drain but the girl remained in the way and get licked down. By the time I woke out of that nightmare my nightie was soaked with sweat. It takes eating a full cup of ice to calm myself.

So, you ain't remember nothing?

And then I thought, what the hell. Tell him.

I dreamt Popo. I've been dreaming she plenty plenty.

I knew I shouldn't say it.

Play sixteen for jamette.

She's long gone and he still won't choose me, take me to live with he, do the shaadi he promised ever since.

Boysie pulled paper and the little end of pencil he had in the bag and wrote down sixteen and then added a four. My blood turned to ice. I could ask a question or keep my mouth shut. I tried to stop myself but the words came out like somebody else was working my jaw up and down.

Four? Dead man?

He stopped flicking through the papers and looked at me.

What you expect? She gone and double-crossed me, the neemakharam. What I was supposed to do? Let she walk out with a sorry?

I picked up a notebook that had fallen to the ground. My hands were trembling.

Don't hurt your head. Nobody will ever find the body.

I will never be able to forget this. From his mouth to my ears. I was hearing and not hearing. Ma and Chunksee were in the back. Subhagya Mausi would have heard him but thankfully she can't understand the meaning of words like body, dead, Popo, dead, dream, dead, neemakharam, dead.

I said don't worry. Nothing will happen. To besides, who you think looking for she?

He fixed the bag across his body.

Oh, my partner, Dabiedatt, might pass today for the engine. You know the one covered down in the back? Anybody else ask about that engine you ain't know nothing. You hear?

I managed a nod but my head was dizzy. Popo is dead.

Make sure he give you the cash first. I know he long time.

One old thief. He done getting it for next to nothing. You think you could handle that?

He called for Chunksee, planted a big kiss on he cheek, got two kisses back, and was out the gate.

The rest of that day I moved like a haunted jumbie. While I sponged off Subhagya Mausi I watched for any sign that she'd heard what Boysie said. Normally I talk and laugh with she even though she can't talk back. Today I couldn't say boo. A pipe inside me was threatening to burst if I so much as said Popo's name out loud. She should have left us alone. That's all. Run away to Tobago. That was a good plan for she and she alone. Why was she still home when Boysie got back? For the first time I was jealous of Subhagya Mausi. If all my mind could come up with was a behhhh behhhh goat noise that would suit me fine. Can't think of any other sound I would prefer to make. I climbed into Subhagya Mausi's bed and two of we stayed there quiet, feeling the breeze, but only one of us can forget she sins.

*

Early afternoon the Dabiedatt fella reached for the engine. He handed over a hundred. I told him Boysie expected two.

Try leaving here with the engine and Boysie go come for you.

Without a word he put a next hundred in my hand.

It vexed me to think that Dabiedatt must have looked at me in my old clothes, bai clinging to my neck, and decided inside my head's empty. He could try a thing and pay less. Later when I thought about it again I realised Boysie probably thinks the same way. That's why he told me what he did Popo. A muk like me can't do a damn thing about it. And he will never know I had a hand in that killing. How I'm supposed to live with that?

DORIS

He wanted to walk on the beach at sunset. The low tide made it easy to distract myself by collecting pretty shells. I felt it in my waters. Boysie's proposing today self. Calm Doris, calm. Holding hands, we climbed boulders to a spot we could sit and catch the sky on fire.

Doris, something on my mind.

I held my breath. Please Jesus, the moment's perfect.

You like children?

Well, scripture states that we must go forth and multiply. I'm ready.

That's good to know because I have a son. A real sweet bai. Seven years. I named him Anthony. He small for he age and we does call him Chunksee. You must meet him.

What the jail is this? Me? Mind another woman's child?

You see, Chunksee does live between me and the mother. And so you know, me and she don't have nothing going on. That done long time.

The sunset's orange and red flames dulled to blues and greys. A flock of noisy pelicans flew past.

Why he can't stay by she all the time?

Boysie remained quiet. I pulled away and hugged myself tight.

What's she name? Her name?

Mana Lala. She's too backward to raise Chunksee alone.

Boysie circled me in his arms and kissed the side of my head.

I love you, Doris.

I didn't say it back. Not this time. After a few long seconds he added,

My place ain't set up for a family. This last year things have been real good. I'm looking to buy a big house. Actually, I know which house I want already. Let me carry you to see it, nah.

I didn't know what to say. Boysie is everything I want and I could make him into a better man for sure for sure. But taking on an outside child? That wasn't part of the plan.

Done the maid work. I'm making good money. You won't have to work again.

I listened, still locking my mouth shut. I'm really not sure about minding this Chunksee. What if he real rude and own way? I can't stand spoilt children. This could mash up now or we could vow till death do we part.

The sun was sinking behind the sea. He got up. I thought he was ready to leave. Instead he positioned himself in front me and got down on one knee. In his hand was a ring with a big maco rock.

Doris de Leon, you already know I love you with my whole heart. I want you to be my wife. Whatever I have is yours. Let we get married nah, girl.

Tears wet my cheeks as he held out the biggest rock I'd ever seen. Little child aside, this was exactly what I wanted.

Well, say something.

I smiled through my tears.

Yes. Yes, Boysie.

He slowly got off his knee.

I was catching cramp there, yes.

We kissed long and hard.

Now, when you're carrying me to see this house for we? For us, I mean.

*

I found Mistress in the living room. I went in and it was like seeing the room for the first time. My eyes took in the mahogany armchairs with white crochet antimacassars, plump velvet cushions and windows covered with frilly curtains. If Boysie buys a big house I'll have to choose my own living-room suite soon. And I ain't letting people come inside wearing shoes before they bring in dirt or mark up the furniture them. If that Chunksee's living with us he will have to play out in the yard otherwise next thing you know he break something or dirty up all my good good things. I glanced at my ring. In two-twos I'll make Boysie see that the best thing for the boy is to stay by the mother or get a full-time nanny. Me ain't able.

Mistress was expecting my news but for all the wrong reasons.

Me? Pregnant? No, Mistress. I don't do them things.

Oh good. So, you're handing in your notice?

Well, I want to help him as he's bringing up his business, Mistress.

And what business is that?

All kind of things.

Mistress shook her head.

Okay, but a word of advice, Doris. Anytime you can, put a little something away that he doesn't know about. You never know what will happen.

She looked out the window.

Mr Bernard said I could keep teaching after we married. Silly fool, I believed him. The second I became Mrs Bernard he changed his tune. Thought it looked improper that his wife worked. I had my own little school. Such a shame. But then our children started coming and, well, that was that.

I'll be busy. I have a house to fix up straight away.

I must say I didn't know marriage was important to you lot at all. I thought you just lived together.

I didn't know what to say to that. You lot? She knows I don't miss a Sunday mass unless I take in sick. Of course I'm having a church wedding. As always, it's one thing for the white people and another for the maid. Well, partner, she could stay right there and think that. For spite I wanted the biggest wedding Port of Spain has ever seen. Give me time and I'll have my own house, motor car and wear more gold bracelets and chains than Mistress ever dreamed of owning. Just watch me.

ROSIE

Every time I think about Etty my eye does jump. It have me frightened little bit because that is a sure sign bad news on its way. Since the time Bumper and Firekong dragged she back I ain't see she or get news. If by Sunday I ain't hear nothing I'm heading in town. We're talking about my first girl and still the best friend, lover, everything, I could ask for. I like to give she sweet talk that we go end up two old ladies together in we dotage. You think she taking me on? She says I'm too greedy to settle down quiet with only one woman or man. Maybe. But all foolishness aside, if I left the current crop of lovers it would be for Etty. People hop in and out your bed but few give love. I can count the people who have loved me for me on one hand. In fact I don't even need the whole hand.

Etty knew my secret snakeness and took it in she stride. My comfort and my rock. Funny how she ended up one of Boysie's girls when it was with him that I first had a hint of the snake power. Now he is a man didn't care for snake. But Trinidad's full of them. Mapepire, worm snake, common coral and false coral, doctor, horsewhip, parrot, red neck, and them is only the snakes that come to mind.

Me and he only ever met by the beach. A night rain began falling hard. All the crabs scattered in the sand holes. We got soaking wet. The only place we could dry out was by he.

Nah, that can't happen.

They say you must never ask a question if you 'fraid the answer. Still, I went through hard.

Why?

Silence.

Why, Boysie?

He sighed.

> My mother say I'll bring shame on we head if people know
> I'm with a coolie orphan.

Well, at least he talked he mind. I never saw the inside of their
house on Luis Street. Imagine, a pissing-tail crab catcher's family thought I was too low down to come inside their two-by-four
tapia house.

We sheltered in an empty fishing boat turned on its side and
fell asleep. Boysie woke suddenly bawling down the place. A
bad dream where we were doing it and as he burst inside me I
turned into a snake. What terrified him sounded strangely natural to me. I don't know why but from that day I knew me and
snake had something to do with one another. Soon as I'd saved
a few dollars, I did something that caused Boysie to run a fast
mile from me to Mana Lala. Coiled around my legs, across my
belly and up my back, was now tattooed a thick, hungry, pretty
cobra. From then things changed. Maybe I changed. I was done
being afraid of wanting more from this life.

Inking a snake on my skin felt like coming home in a way the
orphanage never had. Of course, I shouldn't like snakes. From a
serpent deceiving Eve come down, snakes have been doing bad.
But what about the fact that them snakes are why we're here on
earth? No snake, no Eve and Adam losing their innocence, no
children who grow and make more children, filling the world.

It's my snakeness that makes me hungry to mate plenty and

with endless different people. For saying what I want and taking it, I've been called all kindna names: beast, devil, monster,
whore. Normal women, good women, don't carry on so. Like I
care. Man them can't understand why I demand the same satisfaction they get from sexing. I would have been run out of most
villages but this place took me in. Maybe because I came here
from small. Equally, I don't shove it in people face. Whatever I'm
doing I try not to start any commess and confusion. If anything
the ladies are the ones sidling up to me quiet quiet asking how
they too can be a goddess under the coverlet.

Once I told a fella in my bed I liked to keep seven lovers all the
time. It's my ideal number. More than that and I forget who is
who. He was shocked. Man could do that, maybe. But a woman?
Nah. He little head shrivelled and never saw my punani again.
From then I learnt to keep quiet and just take what I needed.
Only a few, Etty being the first, have sweated with me joyfully
loving the snake on my skin and flowing in my blood. I live for
those moments of being wanted for all of me.

The depth of my snakeness came gradually. I was with a nice
Hindu man relaxing while he traced the cobra around my naked
body with his tongue. Later he looked at me hard in one eye at
a time.

Rose. Rosie. That don't suit you.

How you mean? A white man told me quiet that if I wasn't so
dark I would be pretty as an English rose.

Me ain't know about that. To me you is a perfect Saapin.

I sat up.

Well, that's a new one on me. You making this up?

You really never hear about Saapin?

No.

What kind of Indian you is, girl?

I ain't backward like you. I done baptised Anglican.

The Hindu laughed.

I backward? Oh ho, well, let me teach you something, poi.
A Saapin does look pretty pretty just like you. It's only when
you take in the tattoo you know it's she. Don't feel this tattoo's
just on your skin. It is your skin. And you have sisters all over
the world. I can't say how much but you ain't by yourself.

He held my face and smiled.

The tattoo ever come alive?

I shook my head.

It will. A time will come when this snake will be real and bite.
Once a person has your snake mark, their time's up.

I buss out laughing.

I will turn into a snake? A real snake?

He nodded.

If I had that kind of power you know how long I would've
lined up a good few men to taste snake poison?

You ain't thinking of me, though?

We both laughed.

Not you, sweetheart. Not you.

DORIS

Boysie shouldn't have to be told that engagement ring and wedding ring are two completely different things. This ring I'm wearing ain't unlocking my knees and for now he can forget about me, he and the little boy living together. Give Jack his jacket, he rented a decent place for me. I call it the wedding planning headquarters.

I've met the Chunksee. He's all right. Loves the father too bad. A little clingy, if you ask me. I made Boysie agree to a maid so between she during the week and the mother on weekends the child won't humbug me. Well, he'd better not be in my way because I have a hundred and one things to do.

Top of my list is Toco. This is news the family need to hear to their face. And call me old-fashioned but it's only right and proper that Boysie asks Papi for my hand.

Oh gosh, doux-doux, I don't have that kind of time. I'm trying to buy a next club, Sunrise, and it's plenty pressure.

Oh, so that's more important than meeting your in-laws-to-be?

He kissed my neck.

Don't say that nah, babes. In fact, I need you to come see this club.

Where?

Just down the road. Prince and Charlotte.

Clubs are your thing. Leave me to deal with the rest of life.

Anything to do with the house is my speed.

It's true. The club's a little rough for my lady.

He slipped a hand around my waist.

I really can't do Toco now. You go. Later down in the year we'll go again together.

Okay, but they'll want to know what kind of match I made and if you'll look after me good. You know what parents are like.

Watch me, before they even see me they'll know Boysie Singh is the best man, the only man, for Doris de Leon.

Boysie arranged for his driver to carry me Toco in his new Buick. Good thing it was only me, yes, because Boysie filled the trunk and back seat. One look and I swear Christmas reached early. If you see gifts: dresses, shoes, slippers, hair ribbons, a handbag for Mammy, purses for my sisters, shirts for the men, goat meat, beef, a big rice sack, a ten-pound bag of sugar, biscuits, a tin of coffee, sweeties for the children, rum and a carton of cigarettes for Papi alone plus more cigarettes for my uncles them.

The one road into Toco starts in Sangre Grande and for a mile or two the barber green's smooth. Don't let that fool you. In no time the road is all potholes, some wide enough for the whole car to drop inside. The last piece we took real slow or risked mashing up the Buick's suspension. Friends from school days, family walking home after working the land, all gave me a shout out. I enjoyed watching their eyes grow big big and mouths drop open at the sight of me in the front seat waving. I know for a fact some of them have never seen a Buick in their life. We passed the dry goods shop, still at the heart of the village. Today it looked small, paint peeling, the guttering hanging down. We beeped the horn in front a house. Aunty Allison in the gallery looked up from plaiting cousin Aisha's hair and dropped the comb in shock when she saw me. We shouted to one another. If they don't pass by later this afternoon, or morning at the latest, then my name ain't Doris. She and the rest of the village will want to maco good and proper.

I spotted my sister Elena as we pulled up in front my childhood home. The women helped take things inside while the men stood around admiring the fancy motor car and pounding the driver about the engine, how fast it does go and how much a new one like this does set you back. Mammy handed me fresh lime juice in one of the fancy glasses from the cabinet.

So long me ain't seen your face, child.

Why you put the juice in this glass?

But what's wrong? That's my good glass.

I want a normal glass. These are for visitors.

But you is a special visitor.

I squeezed her hand.

Don't treat me so. I need to know this is always home and I'm not a guest.

She kissed the top of my head.

All right, all right. Next time you'll drink from them old glass we does use. Happy now?

Yes, Mammy.

I shared out what was for the immediate family and my sisters organised when we were seeing which aunty or cousin to give them their gifts. Huddled up in the front room, my sisters already suspected why I'd come. One whispered a little too loudly,

So, you're marrying this Boysie Singh or what?

All eyes watched me. I took a deep breath and nodded. The engagement ring I'd hidden in my bag came out. If you hear them,

Oh God, oh. That thing real?

I never see a diamond big so. That must be come from away.

You fix the date?

How he propose? He kneeled down?

You're making baby? Don't lie to me.

Once they were clear that the ring was real, that he'd proposed properly and I wasn't already making baby, the party started. Papi opened a good bottle of rum he had put away and called the neighbours to take a drink. At last, he's finally marrying off one of his girl children. Amen. My sisters wanted to design their own bridesmaids' dresses. I couldn't keep up with the questions.

You're having a big wedding or keeping it small? Port of Spain or Toco? Or both? Have all two.

Only one family member's face set up like rain.

Mammy, what you think? I mean, Boysie's been very good to me.

Tap, tap, tap. Fingers stabbed the round mahogany coffee table that we'd had all my life.

Who, me? I ain't have nothing to say.

The place got quiet. She blurted out,

> Doris, how you could go and choose a man who never even get baptised? If he drop dead today he soul going straight to hell.

I'd prepared for this.

> Mammy, he ain't Catholic now but trust me. He'll die a Catholic. We read Bible together. We pray together. He and all want a church wedding.

> How you could marry a man that's not even Christian? Eh? Answer me that. This is the example you're setting your sisters and them?

> Mammy, please, trust me. He's going to join our church. The only reason he ain't do it already is because he's so busy with all the businesses and thing.

She snorted. Papi put his arm around my shoulders.

> Doris, it's a lot for your mother to take in. Left it so for now.

> Papi, I can't get married without a blessing from you and Mammy.

> You're happy?

> Yes.

> He does love and respect you?

> Yes.

> Well, child, as a father, I can't ask the Lord for more. Let we talk to Father Michael and see what we could fix up to get Boysie in the church.

MANA LALA

Chunksee came with a bag of sugar cake that Tanty Doris, Pa's new friend, gave him.

What kind of friend?

I want you to push me on the swing.

Boysie had made a tyre swing hanging from a branch of the old chenette tree.

Holding tight?

Push me high high.

Chunksee's growing up so sweet. We played a good while before I begged off tired. While we sat on the back steps drinking water I mentioned the new tanty again.

So, where Tanty Doris living?

I don't know.

You like she?

He shrugged.

She staying by all you or you went by she?

I don't know.

He ran back to the swing.
While he was eating lunch I tried again.

She fair? She have size or small like me?

Bigger than you.

She nice?

He nodded.

I hope she never give you licks.

He looked puzzled.

No. Only Pa can give me licks. He came in school and told
the headmaster even they can't give me licks or he will beat
their tail.

Good. Glad to hear that.

For the rest of the weekend I tried to pump out more about this
Tanty Doris and got only scraps. How many times Boysie will
break my heart so? Like he never going to choose me? Why I
not good enough? It's true I'd heard about some red woman but
I thought that was idleness. Boysie self should know better. Red
woman ain't easy. They does turn man head and then horn them
bad. At least she ain't moved in.

Chunksee, Popo clothes still in the press?

I don't know.

Tanty Doris have things keeping by Pa?

He shrugged.

When Boysie came later I was ready. Between crunches of ice
I mentioned the new tanty.

You didn't tell me a lady living by you.

What you talking 'bout?

Chunksee say some tanty made him sugar cake.

Oh, you mean Doris? She ain't living in my house.

She does look after Chunksee?

Sometimes. What wrong with that?

Well, I thought you would say something.

Well, now you know. Doris is a very decent, God-fearing lady. Real class.

I couldn't hear more. He handed over his empty glass and for a second I wanted to smash it in he face. Real class. Throwing that at me? So my face low down? I steadied myself while he walked away whistling.

A low behhhh behhhh reminded me I hadn't checked on Subhagya Mausi for a while. Poor thing. I pulled her higher up the pillow.

Don't worry, mausi. Mana Lala here now. You was wondering why nobody come to see you? Sorry, I was seeing Boysie off.

I settled down on the peerha and held her hand. It was bony, the skin creased like a balled-up piece of paper. To think this woman had mouth on she to well quarrel and now she can't ask for a cup of water. They say she probably can't hear but I does still chat away. And you must know if somebody's touching your skin. At least I like to think she feels she's safe with family.

Subhagya Mausi? Remember how I tell you I think Boysie take a red woman? It's truth. How he could finish Popo and in no time pick up with another girl? And all the while I here like a poohar. I ain't the mother of he one child? He wouldn't care if I dropped down dead tomorrow. That's the truth.

The tears I'd been holding in gushed out and nothing could stop them.

> He should've finished me instead of Popo and done the thing. If it wasn't for Chunksee I don't know what I would do.

This crying is becoming a habit around my old mausi. I feel if she could talk she would tell me it's okay. Do what I need to do. My hands covered my face while I bawled.

> I love him, Subhagya Mausi. I love that man with every ounce of my body. And he never take me. I'm never good enough. Don't know what I'm supposed to do.

I cried until I tired out myself.

> Don't take this the wrong way but sometimes I does wish I was like you. Nothing can bother you now.

I dried my eyes with the hem of my dress. This pain ain't stopping anytime soon.

ROSIE

Well horse dead, cow fat, and still no Etty. I thought it wouldn't hurt to pass by she. Plus I could use an ease from the work, day in, day out. Long time, my friend Pearl used to run a bar on Burke Street in town. On a Sunday she's more than glad for the little work in my shop and I can cool off. This was a rough week. I didn't get supplies of a good few basics like block cheese, sugar and of all things, peppercorns. A youth-man I carried to my bed two nights in a row had such a good time the dotish fella thinks he's in love with me. Now every evening he's propping up the bar, face like a long mango because I ain't have time for he. I need to get away from these crazy people, yes, even for a half-day.

I packed a food basket, slipped in a petit quart of rum and caught a taxi. Once I see black smoke belching from the electricity plant on Ariapita Estate I know we're near. I wonder if they'll ever bring current by we. I've heard big talk that one day the whole island will be covered. Put it this way. I'm not throwing away my kerosene lamp just yet.

Etty was well glad to see me. She's never had no big size and the weight she's lost making she look real maga.

What you doing to drop off so? It's a good thing I bring food. Like you stop eating or what?

Girl, I ain't know what happen but like I doesn't feel to eat these days. Food does rest in my belly heavy heavy.

Then once a week you must drink a Royal Extra Stout to give you strength.

We spread the food there in her poky room. I broke a piece of sweet bread and fed her. She took it and my fingers between her lips. That was all the encouragement I needed to pull her close. Clothes went flying and we drank from each other's mouths. My youth-man's hard and I scream with pleasure when he throws me about, pins me down with his strength. Etty's the opposite but the action's just as hot if not hotter. It certainly lasts longer. When a fella's done, even youth-man, they must rest before trying again. If they're able to go a second rounds, which is a big if.

Me and Etty? We started late morning and were still going strong when the place started to make dark. Once we stopped to eat, drink something, and it was right back in. I could suckle her breasts forever, inhale those sweet-sour armpits and catch the waves of water from between she legs as many times as they crashed on my face. She was begging and not really begging me to stop. As if you can ever come too much. No disrespect but man can't keep up with two bitches in heat. We called a halt to proceedings only because I had to find myself home.

I'd asked about Bumper but she brushed aside the talk and said everything was back to normal. Town was full full of Limeys wanting cheap punani so the club was making good money.

And when I tell you, Rosie, they does smell bad. Them British sailors like they 'fraid sweet soap.

Between making joke, eating, well mainly me eating, and rolling around in the bed together, we had the best day. My fingers softly brushed the stray hairs away from her eyes.

You had me worried when I didn't hear from you. Bumper carried on so bad in the shop and I couldn't stop him.

Etty looked away.

He's a chupidee. Bully. I keep away far far.

I was about to say what I thought of Bumper when she casually added,

And he warned me not to come by you again or is planass in my tail.

He mad or what. As if a nothing, nobody like he, could break up twenty-something years of love and friendship. Etty could see the rage in me bubbling.

Please, leave it alone.

Who he feel he is? He thinks he's Boysie?

Leave him alone. I don't want more confusion.

This is the thing about Etty that does get me vexed. Always hiding away even when she ain't doing nothing wrong. How me and she being friend have anything to do with Bumper? I pulled her close.

Come and live by me. Help me run the shop. Keep me from getting in trouble with youth-man them.

We both laughed and I pulled her in for a kiss.

I'm serious. I'll look after you.

She sighed.

Rosie, you're not thinking straight. After a month you go be fed up with me under your foot. And besides, one person never enough for you.

The sad part is she's probably right.

MANA LALA

At first I couldn't believe my ears.

Beta, you mean they're going to a wedding?

They're having a wedding.

Who?

I told you, Pa and Tanty Doris.

So Pa and Tanty Doris getting married?

Yes.

He tried to run off but I grabbed the edge of his vest. I didn't mean to rip it.

When? When is this wedding?

Now.

Next month? Next year?

He wriggled free.

Stop. I don't know nothing.

He ran off probably to find he nanee. She's always spoiling him.

Boysie was never into marrying. That's what he told me. Before I could run outside, the roti, the fried ochro and aloo, everything came right back up. I retched and retched until I didn't even have spit left in my mouth. Chunksee and Ma must be gone because I can't hear them. Subhagya Mausi was making soft behhhh noises. Nobody was going to help me clean this mess.

No matter what, I never expected Boysie would do me this. Marry a big bamsee red woman? How he can't see she is a nothing? What she have except she fair? I am the one that loves him come hell or high water. I am the one with devotion. Me, he should be marrying me. I is the mother of he one piece of child. And I don't need nothing official. We could get married under bamboo and done the thing. I stood up, my knees collapsed and the world went blank.

Don't ask how I went from collapsing to waking in my bed. I could feel my head was wet, soaked through with Bay Rum. Ma was wiping my forehead.

What happen to you, girl? We was by the front and all of a sudden I hear, bradaps. I thought Subhagya rolled off the bed but when I looked it was you on the ground. And like you vomit. Lucky thing neighbour was home. Two of we lifted you up.

My pressure must be come down low.

Well, stay quiet. Here, drink a malt.

No, just some ice to suck. Please.

Chunksee was by the foot of the bed looking frightened.

It's all right, beta. Nanee go play with you just now. Let your mai lie down little bit today.

I looked at Ma.

You hear Boysie getting married?

DORIS

I left Toco telling everybody to please God, keep June free. I wanted my wedding to be around the same time as Papi and Mammy's anniversary. Slowly Mammy's coming around and I could tell the June timing made her melt a little. Imagine my crosses when I reached back Woodbrook only for Boysie to tell me the date's set already: 27 July 1941.

> But how you come up with that? The whole of Toco's expecting a wedding come June.

> Well, tell them fast it's July now.

> And what if the priest only free in June to baptise you and do the wedding right after?

> I ain't bound to get baptise.

> Then how you plan to get married in church?

> Tell the priest I'll do it soon as I get an ease up. And you could tell him I does read my Bible regular. That's truth.

I was so vex I didn't trust myself to say boo. He can't decide to change the date all by he-self, himself. What madness catch Boysie? I'm only a bride once. He could see I was fuming and he still carried on talking.

> I was telling the boys that I'm getting married and Tinsingh jumped up and said he was thinking of getting married too. So I said, right, partner, let we double up and make one big wedding nah man. You and me marry the same day in

Rosary Church. Well, I never see Tinsingh happy so. He say the only time he was happier was when I made him manager of Sunrise.

My mouth opened like I was ready to catch flies.

Oh, now I understand. Mr Boysie Singh and Mr David Arno, known to the marish and parish as Tinsingh, got together, probably over a bottle of Vat 19, and decided that the two of them having a double wedding. You didn't think to ask me if I wanted to be part of that, eh?

I done give my word. Date fixed.

Well, why you don't marry Tinsingh and done with it? Yes, that is what you should do. Forget me. You and Tinsingh should hold hands and walk down the aisle.

Well, that got Boysie over vex. For a few seconds I thought he might raise a hand to me. I watched him straight in his eye.

Try it, nah. I promise that the day you lash me is the last day you lay eyes on me. Where I come from men don't get on so.

That cut him. I went in for more.

Don't mistake me for any of them low-class girls you're accustomed to. Who was the last one? Popo? Oh yes, I heard about how all you used to fight.

He stormed out like ten dragons. I steupsed. Boysie Singh better understand and understand fast. I ain't like all them dumb Indian girls he's kept under his thumb. He wants to marry a red woman? Let we see if he can handle it.

ROSIE

This month, after shoving the envelope of Boysie Tax in he pants pocket, he asked if I wanted American chewing gum and sweeties for the shop. A few boxes had landed in the back of the jitney. As I is he most favourite shopkeeper in Trinidad, I could get a good price.

Me? Next thing Yankee soldiers claim I thief from them.

He steupsed.

I ever bring trouble on your head?

All right. Bring what you have, let me see.

I turned to serve a little boy, Francis. He mother had sent him with she pink ration card for some flour and rice. Boysie held the child's shoulder.

Watch this lady good when she weighing out your goods. She pretty like coral snake and dangerous same way.

I ignored Boysie and marked the ration card. He mother owes for goods from last month but I'm not going to shame a small child by refusing him today. Some months I worry that the shop will go bust because I've given too much credit. Touch wood we're still limping along.

So how much cartons of gum you're giving me?

He rested them on the counter and I was about to turn away when I felt his rough hand squeeze my neck.

Stop with the backchat and just sell what I give you, all right.

He dug them long pointy nails into my flesh harder and released me. I caught my breath and in the same instant realised Francis was standing right there. Boysie turned to him.

Hurry up and go straight home. No dreevaying or your mother will put good licks on you.

*

Friday nights are always full. I expect that. But this is a Tuesday and I ain't had five minutes to rest my foot. Must be as it's the Christmas season. I can't complain. Puncheon and white rum selling and the ole talk sweet too bad. We had a new face among the regulars, a hot fella, dougla mix, came in with Boy Boy. In two-twos I found out he was staying the month while looking for a work. I'm not bigging up myself but the energy was there from the first time we eyes made four. It mightn't be tonight but before this weekend's done me and he going to enjoy one other. That's my plan anyway.

Whole evening the two of we were there making sweet eye on the side. I got distracted by an ole talk about Boysie setting up yet another whe-whe casa in James Hill. Somebody asked if it ain't already have big whe-whe up there. Boy Boy had the inside story from he cousin Vip who heard it from Winston who does drive taxi.

All you feel Boysie is a gadaha? You'll never guess what he went and do.

We, his audience, hushed.

Rosie, hit me a shot and I go give all you the story of what the Rajah do.

I slammed the drink down in front him.

Boysie tell the James Hill whe-whe man to leave. Well, the man looked at the boss like he mad. I mean to say, who does come just so and tell you to move because they want your business?

A next voice chooked in.

That is more than boldfaceness. You was there first.

Correct. Well, partner, Boysie went by the police and asked them to meet him at so-and-so place at so-and-so time. He would guarantee to show them a man running illegal gambling.

But wait. Ain't Boysie doing the same thing?

Yes, except he and the police have an understanding, if you know what I mean. But the superintendent giving them pressure to close down whe-whe. So they had to charge somebody. Better this fella than Boysie. Police happy, superintendent happy. Soon as they shut him down, Boysie moved in cool cool. Win, win.

Well I wasn't convinced.

That don't sound like Boysie. If Boysie wanted that patch he would lick down the man and put him hospital. Who wouldn't move after that?

But Boy Boy raised he hand in the air.

I'm only selling it as I buy it.

Fellas were nodding. One said the other day it had big ruction in

Hell's Yard down by Dry River. Somebody cheated in kite flying and they had to beg Boysie to spare the man's life. While serving beers I put in my two cents.

Coming back to the whe-whe. If that's how it happened then all right. But that idea ain't come from Boysie. He don't think so.

One of the old-timers took a drag on he Lucky Strike then touched my hand.

Rosie, you better believe that is Boysie through and through. Long time now I telling people but they ain't listening. That man made a pact with the devil he-self. He will do anything to get what he want. Sell he own flesh and blood if that's what Satan command.

He might well be right. Maybe all now so Boysie and the devil busy dancing. That's he business. I'm keeping myself quiet. I have drink to sell. Later that dougla fella and me could have a little fun.

DORIS

Boysie didn't follow me. I, Doris, who wasn't made for Toco, landed right back in the bush, tail between my legs. Maybe I didn't really know the man after all. I was sure sure that before you could say Robinson Crusoe he'd reach begging forgiveness. That didn't happen. Days drifted into long weeks with the yellow poui tree flowering twice. One more time and rainy season will be here with me still sitting down in Mammy and Papi's house. Talk about shame. I didn't go past the front gallery. People must be gloating or worse, pitying me. July edged closer. I didn't know if I was getting married or what was happening. I ain't go lie. Some days I never left the poky bedroom I'd once shared with my little sisters.

When I least expected it, Tinsingh reached with a message from Boysie. The double wedding was off. He wanted a small registry thing now and a big reception later when things were more settled. I asked how come my fiancé couldn't reach he-self and got some excuse about work tying up he time. His time.

But you're still getting married 27 July?

Tinsingh didn't know where to look.

Yes, and we're expecting you.

Well Boysie's picked the wrong woman for this commess. Dreams of my dress, five bridesmaids, the three-layer cake, pink and purple decorations, everything's gone. On top of that we don't even have a date settled? When I finish with that man he won't know what hit him.

The Rajah will want to know what you're saying.

Tell him I get vex till I turned dumb.

Tinsingh had barely left when Mammy rushed to put in she two cents. Her two cents. In my position she would have eaten humble pie. Papi overheard us talking and joined the argument.

Stay right here. When you're ready, you send word that you and he getting married. You're expecting so-and-so thing to happen and for you to get such-and-such. Otherwise nothing doing.

Mammy rolled she eye. I mean, rolled her eyes. Ah, shocks. What I bothering with all this fancy English for? Where it get me?

If you're staying you might as well help out the church bazaar. You can do the tamarind balls, toolum, sugar cakes, them kindna thing.

I watched to see if she was making joke. Not an ounce of mamaguy on that face.

All of that? It's only corbeau luck I have?

All right, you tell Father Michael you're too busy. By the way, that is the same Father Michael willing to baptise Boysie. But it's okay. You have more important things to do like sit down in the house whole day.

Fine.

The following Saturday I started in the kitchen all five in the morning. I made pretty pink and white sugar cakes, juicy tamarind balls rolled in sugar and I was starting on the toolum when Mammy rushed in. A big car had pulled up outside.

I'm not sure if Boysie's in the car.

I can't leave this. The sugar will burn.

Go. I will look after the toolum. Wash your face. Change that old dress quick.

The coward had sent Tinsingh and Cecil. Big and bad all over town but Rajah can't find himself here. I gave them a cold drink and settled down to see how we could done this bassa-bassa. Cecil acted as Boysie's chief mouthpiece.

See it from he point of view, Doris. Money spending left, right and centre. You buying nice clothes, gold bracelet, all kind of thing. Agreed?

My face alone told him I ain't agreeing to nothing so.

Then on top of that the wedding is getting out of hand. It's like buying a next club. You want to invite the whole of Toco and Port of Spain. All Rajah saying is cut back a little bit, nah. He making money, yes. But he ain't make back what he spent yet. Give the man a little ease up.

I took a deep breath and folded my arms.

All you looking at this one side. Talking about how much this and that costing. In life it's not what you know but who you know.

I paused.

I'm helping Boysie. The wedding is to introduce him to all kind of big people. They would never bother with a coolie boy like Boysie even if he has a few dollars in he pocket, his pocket. So when Boysie talk about the cost of the wedding what he's not understanding is that this is a business investment. But he's too cheap to see that.

Tinsingh jumped in quick.

Doris, you have it wrong. The Rajah ain't cheap. He does look after all of we like we is blood.

He tried to take my hand but ended up awkwardly hanging on to my wrist.

Give the man a chance, Doris.

Well, how come he ain't reach yet? I've been home a month and change.

Tinsingh shook his head.

You-self know he's full of pride. But he real missing you bad. Trust me on that one. He pulled two of we from work to bring you back.

I have pride too, you know.

Cecil laughed.

Two of all you is the same, yes. Stubborn for days. You know what they say? Two bo-rat can't live in the same hole.

I made it clear I wasn't going back with them. If Boysie wants me he'll have to come in person.

*

I had a plan. 27 July 1941 was in the papers. People are expecting me to marry that day and I'm getting married that day self. Who says it must be to Boysie? I'll show him. Watch me.

Donovan Wilson owns the Black Cat club plus a hotel in town and I think a next club in San Juan. From long time he's had a thing for me. Looks ain't everything but it doesn't hurt that he's tall and slim with a wicked twinkle in he eye, his eye. I asked if he wanted to come with me to a friend's wedding. Donovan ain't dotish.

What about Boysie?

What happen? Like you 'fraid him?

I don't have a problem but it's what he might do to you.

Do to me?

Watch yourself. Boysie's a crazy man. He don't like nothing better than a fight.

The day he raise a hand to me is the last day he'll use that hand.

Donovan cracked up laughing.

For a woman, you're full of big talk.

We had a few drinks, went dancing and next thing he tongue, his tongue, was down my throat. My escort to Tinsingh's wedding was set. He was so busy feeling up my breasts and bamsee that he would've agreed to anything. Besides, it was too good a chance for Donovan to show Boysie he ain't all that.

Tinsingh's wedding day, that should have been mine too, Donovan and I set off for Rosary Church. Two of we, us, were looking real sharp. Normally, I would respect the bride and leave white alone. Not this time. I had things to say beyond words. We drove up in Donovan's big Buick, me in a short, tight tight white dress and an imported white topee hat from a boutique on Frederick Street. My gloves were elbow-length, white velvet. My boy was in a smart blue suit and even his light blue suede driving gloves matched. If you didn't know better you would think we were getting married.

Cecil saw us first, took in the scene, and dusted it out of there. I expect he went to warn his lord and master that I was with Donovan. Not my problem. Early for the service, and as inside the church was making hot, we waited in the shade of a broad samman tree. Donovan knew everybody and soon we'd formed a nice group laughing and talking. Mathew, a church regular, came trotting over.

I see this white dress and when I looked hard I realised, but eh eh, that is Doris. How you going, girl? Long time no see. I find you're looking hot.

Boy, hush your mouth. I'm there fighting up. You ain't see me in a while because I was by my family in Toco.

But Doris, I find you well looking like a bride.

For true, Mathew?

While we chatted I kept half an eye open for Boysie. By now he must know I'm here, in a white dress, on the arm of a business rival. About fifteen minutes later, if that, a car screeched to a stop in the churchyard. Donovan leaned in,

Boysie.

Ha.

I edged closer to Donovan and slipped my arm through his.

He's walking over?

Yeah.

I turned around to see Boysie, looking so handsome in a new grey suit. Without a word he grabbed my arm, tucked it in his and we walked inside the church.

John Boysie Singh married Doris de Leon on 27 July 1941.

Ain't I said that would be my wedding day? And watch, a month later we had a wedding reception that lasted a week. A whole week. And the band I wanted? It played two nights. We had food like you've never seen and a bar that never ran dry. All that happened without a single moan or groan from Boysie. At least he's learnt what's best for him. And what's best? Me.

ROSIE

I jumped on the Route 2 tram to reach town. Etty knew I was coming and had insisted that I couldn't reach so close and not pass by the club to check she. Down Frederick Street I bought the little kerosene lamp I've been needing for weeks. The cost of things these days. Highway robbery. Nearly three dollars for one chupid lamp. Anyhow, it's not something I does buy often. Walking around I felt Port of Spain was buzzing. It real growing fast fast, yes. They go have to fix these roads because them ain't make for the amount of motor cars driving up and down these days. Add people hustling, bicycles and donkey carts weaving all in between traffic, and I remembered why I only land up here when needs must.

Of course unless it's work they're working, no woman dares put even a pinkie toe inside a club. At least not through the front door. Etty pulled me in by the back steps and into a box room at the top which the girls used for a smoke and to cool off between clients. If Boysie or any of he posse knew I was inside it would be mas in the place. And not just me will get burn. Etty would be in for a sound cut tail for sure. But when you're hot for a person all that doesn't come in your mind. It was enough to snatch a few minutes here and there as she was expected to be taking fares. Most of the evening I spent peeping through a hole in the wall macoing the goings-on below in the bar.

I watched Etty chatting up a Limey as if that pasty bamboo pole was the best-looking man on shore leave. He was knocking back the white rum like water. Before he got fall-over drunk Etty sealed the deal and they started up the stairs. That was where I lost eyes on them but she must have led him to a side room. I slumped back on the floor mat feeling funny in my chest and stomach. A long day walking around and then hanging out in this chook-up small room must be getting to me. No, that wasn't right. This was something else, something that I wasn't used to at all at all. I hated admitting to myself but pure jealousy was stirring through my body. Me, Rosie the Saapin, always running at least two lovers same time, was turning green that feet away Etty was giving that English sailor she sweetness. Well, look at that. Usually I'm the one giving the talk about not belonging to one person and one person alone. Don't shackle me down with possessiveness is what I tell anybody looking to tangle with me. Yet, for all that talk I was steaming vexed that Etty was doing the deed with some man when the girl was only making a living.

Until she was back in sight I needed distractions. I sat up and focused my eye to the peep hole. The scene was buzzing. Americans from the bases were out in force feeding the shiny new jukebox. That was smart man Boysie all over. He knew how to rake in those Yankee dollars by making them stay listening to tunes. Pining for home encouraged guzzling more beers, more rum, more whisky. Through the haze of cigar and cigarette smoke I saw fellas leaning on the bar, drinks in hand, laughing like whatever joke they'd just heard was the funniest thing ever. Over to one side a game of all fours was getting serious. A man leapt on he chair and, with a flourish, threw down the winning hand. The others cussed and shook their heads as they shoved a pile of coins and bills his way. One of he partners immediately called for a next card game to win back the money.

Suddenly the air itself changed. Men were turning around, doing a double-take, giving the nod, being less rowdy. Something was stirring just beyond my view. I heard him before I caught sight to confirm, yes, Mr Boysie Singh, the Rajah, had arrived. Give Jack he jacket, Port of Spain's gambling king knows how to keep he-self good. The face well clean-shaven and creamed up nice nice, hair greased down with pomade. That hat he had on looked just like the ones them rich white men does wear. And don't talk about the suit. Papayo, it was real sharp. The man had money to burn.

Boysie was hailing out regulars. As he got closer I heard,

Inspector Brown, what happening? Good to see you, man. Good to see you. That glass looking empty.

The inspector grinned and nodded.

I there, Boysie. You know I does like to pass and make sure nobody troubling you.

I saw Boysie reach inside he suit jacket and pull out a fat cigar and hand it to the police inspector.

Thanks for coming to my humble club.

Boysie shouted at the bartender,

Aye, Dragon, fix up Inspector Brown for me please. On the house, of course.

As he approached the all fours table the men stood and rushed to shake hands with the boss.

Who winning?

They laughed and pointed to the man who had earlier stood on his chair.

Bunty, you're thiefing these fellas' money?

Boss, you know me to thief? It's skills in their tail.

Boysie went back in the jacket pocket and handed the winner a cigar.

Take it easy, fellas. I might join you for a game later.

He continued around the room, a prince checking his subjects were still loyal. He stopped in front a short, round man nursing a beer.

Aye, Tallboy, long time no see. I does only read about you in the papers. You get through with the land you was trying to buy?

He slid into my vision. Men were greeting him a little too enthusiastically as if to say, remember I'm on your good side, Rajah.

As Dragon rushed to serve two beers and pour a next whisky, Boysie slid behind the bar. I saw him take a bunch of keys from he pants pocket and bend down. From my angle I couldn't see more but he was probably checking the liquor supply or maybe cash was locked up under the counter.

He straightened up and nodded at one of he gang. A man built like the jukebox ran over. Boysie whispered something and next thing the big hulk was firmly escorting a drunk American off the premises. And suddenly there was Etty again. She fixed the Limey on a bar stool, motioned for Dragon to take he order and began climbing the stairs towards me. I sprang to my feet, straightened my skirt and waited for the door to open. I'll lock she tight tight in my arms if only for two-three minutes.

MANA LALA

I'm learning what Subhagya Mausi likes to eat. Sweet potato and pumpkin are favourites. Ma said she can't taste the food. I don't feel so. She has understanding if we sit by the bed or hold she hand. I notice Ma's helping more with the daily sponge bath and cleaning when she make mess. When Mausi first came I kept Chunksee away from she room in case seeing the dying frightened him. The strangest thing but he is the one who is most natural, most accepting that is how she is. I don't even have to ask him to give she a kiss or a hug up.

Beta's keeping me going too. I waited for Boysie to tell me about the wedding. He never did. You know when he finally said something it was that he and Doris were already married. Such a badjohn, running Port of Spain and he only had the guts to tell me after he do he thing? Worst yet, I'm supposed to be happy for he and that reds? Eh? She could handle all what he does be doing? If she so God-fearing and big in the church then let me see how she go manage. Let she go in eyes closed. Popo must come up one day. And that Lester fella that had a heart attack? It's only me suspect? I give it a year and she'll be running back to Toco or whatever bush she came from. If she think it easy loving a man like Boysie then she in for a shock. I can handle it because I loved him from small. But she? Reds ain't lasting no time.

I told Subhagya Mausi that from what I hear it go be big wedding celebrations. Boysie acting like he's the Governor General throwing fete. Well fine but why drag me in their thing?

And you know what, Subhagya Mausi? They expect me to

come whole week, Saturday to Saturday, while they keep
up party celebrating this damn shaadi. And it's not me they
want. Nobody cares one ass about me. Boysie must have
Chunksee. So I have to take beta. He can't see I have feelings
too? Showing off he new bride to the marish and parish and
I should just be there skinning up my teeth? That man's heart
made out of ice, yes. He doesn't remember that we should've
married years and years ago when he was released from
Carrera?

I sent a message to say I can't make. Go ahead without me.
Quick sharp that afternoon a car pulled up in front the house.
He partner, Cecil, jumped out.

Mana Lala, how you keeping? You there good?

I'm holding up.

So, ehem, Boysie want Chunksee in the wedding party.

You ever hear people have party whole week so?

Well, that's them.

I let go one long steupse.

You can't come with Chunksee?

Why I must come? They take me for a nanny? I am he son
mother. No wedding changing that.

He sighed.

The boy have to be there so if you ain't coming maybe Ma
could bring him?

You think my old mother could take all that noise and set of

confusion? And who she go know there to sit down with?
Nah, that's not happening.

Cecil touched my shoulder.

Forget about all the showing off. Do it for Chunksee. You
don't want him there by he-self bouncing around.

I was glad at least he could see they were carrying on too much.
I nodded. Like there was ever a real choice.

*

Cecil collected us looking real dandy in new clothes and new
driving gloves. He brought shirt, pants, shoes and a little bowtie
for Chunksee. I'd already fixed him in he best clothes and me in
my one nice dress.

No, Rajah say to make sure he wear these. People go be
looking at the boy.

I searched. Not even a new handkerchief for me. Imagine, that's
how Boysie treat me.

Chunksee looked over handsome in the little bowtie. Cecil
chatted whole road about which big shots were expected. He
called a set of names like I would know who is who.

Mark my words. You see this wedding reception or party,
whatever you want to call it, this making papers. If you see
cars. A man tell me he count must be fifty-six already parked
up near Boysie. You ever hear more than that?

It was true. People like peas. Cecil pushed us through the crowd
to greet the new bride and groom. And there she was, the famous
Doris, in a tight tight dress showing off all she figure. Barely

decent. Open toe heels showed that she second toe longer than she big toe. I had to hide a smile. Woman with toes so does rule their husbands. He go get so much horn. No two ways about it. Poohar Boysie there acting like he's moved up in the world landing a fair-skinned wife. If Doris expects me to call she Mrs Boysie Singh, she go wait right there.

I've talked to myself plenty times. Best to hush and say nothing. Concentrate on Chunksee and try not to care. Once I'd survived meeting Doris and hearing them talking lovey dovey, calling one another my wife, my husband, I took Chunksee to the backyard where other children were playing. Nobody recognised me as the mother of Boysie's son. They probably thought I was the maid or the nanny and I could bet house and land that Boysie never corrected them.

From where we were settled I had a prime view of the goings-on. This Doris could well spend money. Nothing about the party was Boysie. Hundreds of pink and purple balloons, streamers and flowers decorated the house. Buddy and he orchestra was jamming. Real tops. Even I've heard of them. Doris took over the dance floor with some moves you wouldn't expect from a married woman. Good for Boysie. He go have he hands full with this one.

While the dancing was going on I took Chunksee to eat. Well, papayo, like they planned to feed the whole of Trinidad. Only Doris would show off with beef, chicken and pork jumping up on the barbecue and mountains of vegetable rice, macaroni pie, stew peas and salad. People could take and go back. I overheard a fella saying better he belly buss than good food waste.

But that wasn't all. The other side had Indian food jumping up. Curry chicken, curry goat, curry duck, channa and aloo, dhal, rice and roti were all laid out. I ain't shame. I saw George who works for Boysie and asked for foil to wrap up food for Ma and Subhagya Mausi.

Mana Lala, don't worry with no foil. Tell me what you want and I go get it ready in containers.

He leaned in.

I ain't forget. You was here long before the reds.

At least one person remembered the years I'd put in with Boysie through thin and thinner.

While we ate I looked around. Since when Boysie know all these people? And who were Doris's family? I crunched ice and watched the clock until it was reasonable for we to leave.

We survived and even though we had six nights more of this foolishness, I was sure the biggest, loudest evening must be over.

Well I thought wrong.

Next night was the same thing. I had on the dress I'd worn the night before to find a different set of big shots crowding up the place. Food and drink were giving away again. This time I walked with my own foil to pack away a little barbecue chicken and some fried rice. Ma really liked the fried rice. Madame Doris wanted everybody to know she's swimming in money so the open bar flowed with Scotch, Gilbey's Gin from America, champagne and endless bottles of ponche-de-crème. I'm not into the drink but it would've been criminal not to taste champagne. Wasn't for me. Little dry and sour.

It seemed like the whole of Port of Spain knew about the celebrations. I overheard talk that who ain't get invite stormed boldface boldface. They're lucky Boysie's heart big. His boys made sure the gate crashers got free beer and a plate of food. Not sure Doris would have been as nice to poor people.

And give Jim he jim boots. Boysie's posse came out looking sharp. I nearly didn't recognise half the fellas in their new
clothes and hair slicked down. No doubt they'll be back to their
old ways as soon as the party's done. A good few of them came
by and said hello to me and Chunksee.

In all the fancy celebrations I wasn't expecting trouble.
Unfortunately, trouble came. On the fourth night they had to
sort out some Limeys when they tried to thief Scotch. Cecil gave
me the score while driving us home earlier than usual.

> I mean to say, they ain't know the bride and groom from
> Adam and Eve. They drink free beer, eat free food, and on
> top of that is thief they thiefing so?

> Them Limeys causing too much trouble all over Port of
> Spain.

> You could say that again.

> So what happened to them?

Cecil laughed.

> The boys teach them how to behave when you go by people
> wedding.

> That mean some good licks passed. Well, they looked for that.

On the last evening of the celebrations, they had the band again
and Madame Doris performed like a randee, dancing up a storm.
I've seen enough to know that is one stuck-up woman. Feel she
better than everybody. Who would pay for the most expensive
band in the country to play two whole nights? She feel she married the king of England? Every single evening Madame had on
a different fancy dress. Them outfits looked like they came from

away as well. And the expense on food and drink. By the time they're done Trinidad won't have a chicken left to eat or a drop of rum to wet your whistle.

Boysie and Doris came to see Chunksee before they went on honeymoon. She mentioned, oh by the way, did I know that they had bought fifty-five cases of Scotch and every last bottle was empty? From eight cases of Gilbey's Gin from America, six cases of champagne and endless bottles of ponche-de-crème, not a drop remained. Guess how much beer bottles they'd gone through? Three thousand. I just stared at the floor and said something about how they treated everybody nice.

Doris touched me shoulder. I flinched.

How much you think the whole thing cost?

I can't count so high.

Well, it was a pretty penny, I can tell you that. Five thousand dollars, to be exact.

I looked at Boysie grinning like a chupidee. What a poohar. That red woman only using him for he money. But before anybody say Mana Lala's jealous I forced a smile. Besides, we know that what's sweet in goat mouth does be sour in the bambam.

ROSIE

Boysie passed for the rent. He was skinning he teeth and same time he pinched my arm hard when I handed him the shot of rum he wanted. People like they don't understand I ain't have a choice if he sit down by me. It still divided the rum shop down the middle. Half the village wanted to shake he hand and shamelessly curry favour. Teach, so old even he forget how much years he have, nodded at Boysie from his usual spot propping up the bar.

Rajah, I take my hat off to you. Plenty people once they come big shot them ain't know you. Not you. Town could say what they want I know the Rajah is a man keep he common touch.

Those who didn't want to suck off the Rajah stayed quiet, concentrating on their drinks. But Boysie's a smart man. This week, all people talking about is how he beat Nugget, we village boy, and nearly killed the fella. The only reason he's at my bar drinking is to deliver he side of the story.

As he was leaving he took out a set of money and flung it around the rum shop telling people to take and enjoy. Men went diving and scrambling for the coins scattered on the ground. Shame he ain't easing me up with the rent. Even as he was getting into the jitney fellas were still waving and calling, Rajah, Rajah, like he's the king.

Once he'd left people crowded round. Questions tumbled out.

Rosie, what Rajah tell you?

He sorry for Nugget or he lying?

But why they fall out in the first place?

Hands in prayer, I begged them to hold some strain.

Please, I'm begging. Don't cuss the messenger.

The way Boysie told the story I couldn't blame him alone for what happened. Whe-whe was going good and he was about to buss the mark. Everybody was waiting for him to call the day's number when somebody shouted, run, police, run, police coming. Every man jack scattered so fast that nobody get catch.

Boysie called a panchayat to find out how the police knew where and when the mark would buss. As he and the fellas thought about it they realised, but eh eh, the only body who should've been with them when the raid happened, and wasn't, was Nugget. They put two and two together and came up with Nugget as the Judas. Teach interrupted my flow.

Could be any reason why Nugget wasn't there.

You want the story or not?

Well, do fast nah, man.

Next morning, who reached by Boysie before he even drink tea? Nugget. When Boysie told me that I got frightened for the boy one time.

Heads around the crowded bar nodded.

Nugget had some story about how the doctor say he mother need a set of tablet and he hand empty. He was wondering if Boysie could spare a five dollars till pay day.

Teach piped up.

Nugget mother take in? How come I ain't hear that?

He partner nudged him.

Nothing wrong with she.

Teach shook he head.

Oh. Right.

Someone asked if Nugget mentioned anything about the police raid.

He ain't say boo about that. Anyhow Nugget got the five dollars.

I don't understand why.

Partner, me ain't know either. Eh eh, the very next morning Nugget reached back begging for another raise. Oh, the medicine for he mother was more expensive than he thought. Apparently Boysie said something like, we is family. Wait inside the club and he will come now for now with the money.

I looked around at the faces.

All you ready for this part?

Plenty steupsing and groans of hurry up.

Boysie locked all the gates, went inside the club, locked that door, and pulled out Three Little Threes. Blows for so. He well beat Nugget. The man passed out from the licks. Boysie say he threw ice water, woke him up, and beat he again. He beat him so long and so hard that one of he own men stopped him before Nugget dead. Boysie was cussing that he didn't care if he made a jail. Nobody should ever take he for a fool especially this pissing-tail little boy. Three fellas had to pin him down while half-dead Nugget went hospital.

Chan, one of the regulars pushed in he two cents.

Well me and the madame went hospital and the nurse them say they ain't sure he will ever walk good again. And I know that police questioned Nugget and he mouth was zipped shut.

I shook my head. Nugget was right. Normal law don't operate for Boysie. Too much police in he pocket. Why you think he took the time to sit down and give me chapter and verse about Nugget? That was to let me know exactly what he go do if I cross him. You see me? I work hard to get here. Let me keep my head down, do what the Rajah say, and hope I never feel Three Little Threes.

PART THREE

DORIS

The problem with organising a honeymoon is that my husband (I love saying that) has never taken a straight week off work. By the time the celebrations were done he was itching for the usual routine of work, work, work. But we need this honeymoon. Nothing big, it could even be a weekend. He agreed so long as we stayed close by, and he went to the clubs as needed. I took what I could get.

The thing that's bothering me is when I played hard to get before marriage it was to keep him keen. Seems my plan's back-fired. The wedding's come and gone, light's turned green, and he's acting like the ban's still in force. The first night as man and wife I put it down to bare tiredness and stress. But how to explain the second, third, twenty-third night together and still not even a finger has waved at my privates?

We moved into the house. I thought, amen, at last everything's in place. Well, I'm still waiting for us to christen the brand-new king-size bed. But patience. Maybe he didn't feel properly married until we celebrated with family, friends and the rest of the colony. That whole week he was on the dance floor bumping and grinding on me. People seeing us would think we're boopsing morning, noon and night. Truth is once the music stopped he done too. Let me see what excuse he'll think up on our honeymoon.

We settled on a week at a beach house in Staubles Bay. That was my first mistake. Being this close to town wasn't good for relaxing and romancing. Boysie was up and down, up and down like a yo-yo to the point where I hardly saw the man. If that was a honeymoon then better we'd stayed home. He didn't come in the bed a single night before I was asleep. Imagine a honeymoon without honey. I felt so shame. My husband's supposed to be this big sweet man. It must be something about me.

We packed up and were leaving Staubles Bay, the driver and Tinsingh in front and we in the back seat, when Boysie started complaining about who owed him money and who was thiefing. I wasn't really paying him no mind. He was in a bad mood and so was I. This morning, hurry hurry before we left, he'd been rubbing up on me, but couldn't get hard. I kissed his neck real loving.

Don't worry, honey. Plenty other things we can do.

He gave me a cut eye.

I ain't have no problem. This only happened with you.

Well, that was as shocking and painful as a scorpion bite. We've now started and already you're telling me your wood can't get hard because I'm not woman enough? Oh Jesus, Lord, Father, look at trouble. After delivering that blow to my soul I'd hoped he would stay quiet in the car. Not the Rajah. He tried picking a fight saying I only loved money and how I overspent on clothes and shoes for the wedding. I left the bait. He had pushed me to get more outfits. Best to let him talk and talk until his mouth's tired. If anybody had a right to be vex it was me after that insult in the bed. But Boysie just kept getting more and more vicious. Name a bad trait under the sun and apparently I had it coming and going.

Instead I gazed out my window at the flares of red and yellow poui in bloom across the Northern Range mountains when Boysie shouted for the driver to stop. As the car pulled over he shoved me hard.

Get out.

What happen? You're mad or what?

I said get out my car.

Stop this.

Move. Now.

No. You've lost your mind or what?

Get out or I will throw your blasted gold-digging ass in the gully. Indian people have a word for all you who always taking, taking and same time ready to stab you in the back.

He rammed my head into the car door.

Neemakharam. That's you-self. Maakaachood neemakharam.

Suddenly his hands were squeezing my neck tight tight. I couldn't scream or pull him off. Tinsingh and the driver rushed him. It took the two of them to make him stop.

Rajah, cool yourself. That's your wife. Cool yourself.

Cool myself? Ask why she married me? Eh? Ask she.

He was straining to get to me. By now I was bawling and all I could see out the corner of my eye was the long drop just a foot away from the open car door. Suppose he'd managed to throw me over the precipice?

Doris, why you married me? Eh? Why? Answer me that.

I don't know what you want from me, Boysie. What I do to make you treat me so? You could've killed me. This is our honeymoon.

Boysie screamed back,

> What you want me for? A coolie like me. Eh? You ain't want me. It's only money you're seeing.

> That's not true. Not true. I love you, Boysie.

He turned on Tinsingh.

> Move your hand.

Tinsingh wasn't taking any chances.

> Rajah, catch yourself nah, man. It's your wife.

He exchanged a look with the driver, then me.

> Doris, take a seat in the front, please. Don't worry yourself. This is just Tobago love.

Slowly, slowly I slid into the front seat. This isn't a taxi route or I swear I would've let them go along their way. My brand-new husband just tried to kill me. How that could happen?

Boysie didn't touch me for the rest of the drive. Instead he abused me by cussing and carrying on how I only married for money. I should have piped up that it wasn't for his bedroom performance. But I took the insults and didn't talk his business. Mass this evening I will take my troubles to the Lord. This marriage is going to need some good prayers.

MANA LALA

They sent to say Chunksee wasn't coming for the weekend. He had fever. Well, I put on my clothes and reached there in two-twos.

I found the batcha playing, looking healthy and Boysie absent.

I thought he sick?

Doris handed me a glass of cold water. She must have noticed I was perspiring from walking the piece of road to Rosalino Street in this hot sun.

He had roasting fever last night. I sapped him down with Limacol. Then about an hour ago it gone just so. I thought he should stay here in case it come back.

You should have sent for me. I is the mother.

So much else I wanted to say to she face. If my batcha's sick ain't he should be with me?

We didn't want to bother you.

Five minutes she on the scene and already feel she can look after Chunksee better than me? Madame Doris don't have no shame? She done take Boysie, who by rights is mine, and now she's after Chunksee too? Nah. That ain't happening. At least with Popo she didn't play mother.

So how he get fever just so? He was feeling sick before?

No. Yes. Well, we had a little incident last night.

What happened?

And with that the whole kheesa jumped out. Apparently the three of them were home busy reading Bible. I stopped she there. That didn't sound right.

Boysie? Reading Bible?

Well, I was doing the reading and he was listening and praying with me.

I hushed my mouth. Who she feel she fooling? Doris expect me to believe that she's turned Boysie around? So day is whe-whe and whappee and night is scripture reading? I let she talk, yes. I wanted to see how much more dotishness will come flying out that fat mouth.

We were reading Bible and all of a sudden Chunksee bawled out a man was by the window.

Seems Boysie grabbed Three Little Threes and ran outside to see who had frightened the child. Everywhere was locked up tight. After circling twice, Boysie came back inside. He well boofed Chunksee for lying. Doris threw in,

Chunksee doesn't like to upset his father.

She must have said that just to agitate my spirit. Instead, I reminded her that Chunksee and he pa have been close since he born.

Anyhow, Chunksee said the man he saw had on a white hat and a white jacket and pants. I told him it's a sin to lie and God will punish him. Plus he frightened us. I mean, when I heard that bawl I was sure sure bandits reach to rob we, rob us.

You mustn't tell a small boy that God will punish him. And he don't lie. Ever.

Hold some strain, let me finish.

I listened to how Boysie was well vexed and snatched away the spinning top Chunksee had been playing with and put it on a high shelf.

He give him back yet? That top is the batcha's favourite. He don't go nowhere without that in he pocket.

Yeah, man. He got it back after a few minutes. My husband's a big softie.

I didn't like how this story was going at all at all.

I went to use the bathroom.

She stopped and wiped sweat off her forehead.

Girl, as I turned around a man was standing in the corner wearing head-to-toe white. Well, I bolted out of there so fast, screaming for Boysie.

I couldn't believe what I was hearing. Boysie will never see spirit, jumbie, whatever, because me and he know to always have a match behind your ears for protection. How come soon as Doris reach this kindna thing happening? Mark my words, Doris and whatever that jumbie is reached here same time.

Well, Boysie went inside but he didn't see nobody, nothing. He ran for Cecil in the club. Between the two of them they searched from top to bottom. And with the barb-wire fence and the locked gates the man couldn't have escaped. Boysie started one quarrel about how me and Chunksee making up spirits. But I know what I saw.

I shook my head.

That don't sound good. Somebody dead and ain't pass over yet.

Cecil believed me. Same thing happened to him a few years ago.

But that wasn't the end. They got ready to sleep and as Boysie went to lock the door he saw the same man walking in the yard. Doris said he chased him cussing all kind of bad words but the man vanished.

And that is when Chunksee started crying with the fever.

Boysie saw the spirit? Where's he?

I shook my head. These people can carry on with whatever it is they're doing. My work in life is to keep Chunksee from all this madness. At least he should have a normal life without commess from the two of them. I had to get Chunksee out one time.

Boysie gone for Mother Gizzard. I wanted my priest to come but Boysie said this woman's real powerful. She better say some prayers on the house because evil in here.

I know Mother Gizzard. She real have powers but even so Chunksee should stay by me until all you sure the spirit's gone.

Chunksee's baptised?

No.

I thought once they start school all of them does get baptised?

I shrugged.

If he'd been brought into the church bad spirits wouldn't touch him.

It was only much later I found the words I should have used to put she in she place. She's a big-time Catholic. Why the spirit still took a turn in she tail?

Just then we heard the thick chain on the gate rattling. Boysie was leading Mother Gizzard. One step inside and the old lady said she needed to cleanse right through. Sometimes once is enough but she already sensed this house needed more.

All you see any lizards in the house?

Doris thought for a moment.

One or two.

Lizard is transportation for the spirit them. And all who living here must take a special tonic to drive away the spirit.

I pushed in one time.

You have something for Chunksee too? On top of everything it look like he had fever bad last night.

Yes but pass for it later. Boysie hustled me to reach and I didn't have time to make up anything except what is for he alone.

With that Mother Gizzard set about doing she thing. Me and Doris each had a part. Madame had to take the cocoyea broom and sweep in front Mother Gizzard as the old lady moved through the house saying prayers in the four corners of each room. My job was to pass candlelight over every opening. Under orders I also had to open every last cupboard, drawer, box, plus pass the light under the bed and all dark places. I took my candle and well macoed. I know Boysie's making good money these days and it's showing. If you see how much clothes and thing both of them have. And all the furnitures them smelling new. I never saw a bed make fancy so. I bet it's Madame wanting the place to look like a palace.

Mother Gizzard said she had done what she could and next week she would do the second cleanse so long as God spared life.

Boysie, by the time you done the tonic it go be time for the second spirit cleanse plus I will have a next bottle of tonic to give you.

Madame Doris turned up she nose.

I don't believe in tonic and obeah business.

Mother Gizzard nodded.

What you think medicine make with? The same herbs and thing I using them using too. Nobody forcing you but maybe take the tonic. Just in case.

We Catholics don't take them things.

The old lady stepped outside.

Boysie, come drop me home. Them chicken go be waiting for feed.

She turned to Doris.

Ask your priest to say prayers too. Take all the help you can get.

This was my chance.

Aye, Boysie, as the house ain't get the all-clear yet, ain't it's best Chunksee stays by me?

He twisted up he mouth.

What you think, Mother Gizzard?

I don't know about all you arrangement. The boy should be okay. Leave it and see.

As they were going Mother Gizzard held my hand and winked. She whispered in my ear,

I gave him the cure. Even if he ain't putting it on he thing it should still help to drink it.

For an old lady she well have tricks.

I left Chunksee playing, no fever, and in a house cleansed by Mother Gizzard. But in my own bed I couldn't sleep worrying in case an evil spirit was still there. Even Mother Gizzard had warned they don't always leave after one cleansing. Boysie won't like to hear it but that house needs a visit from Pundit Hanuman. I know he will say no backward Hindu foolishness in he house with man in dhoti talking funny. But I bet he will let the Catholic priest do their exorcism though. Anything to do with the white people religion must be good. Strange how Boysie take against he own people. All of we is Indian same way, from the same place. Once I managed to tell him that even if he doesn't feel Indian that is what everybody sees. Maybe I only thought about telling him and didn't actually say it. I do that a lot, think something but remain quiet.

Next morning I went to see how Chunksee had passed the night. Boysie opened the gate half naked, wearing only see-through sliders. He must have just got up. I looked at the ground shamed in case he saw the heat in my eyes. Until my last day on this earth I will love that man and want to eat him raw. People could say what they want about him, he is the best. This Doris ain't lasting. Just now he go get fed up with she holy, better-than-everybody ass.

As a joke I asked if he'd seen the man in white again. He shook he head.

No, but Chunksee had roasting fever again. Cry whole night. Beta only fall asleep around four o'clock this morning.

He should've let me take the batcha yesterday then none of this would've happened, but I knew better than to say anything so.

He saw the man again?

No. He was in a state feeling cold but he skin was on fire.

Boysie opened the front door for me to go through first.

Excuse but I getting dressed and thing. Go see Chunksee.

What we going to do about beta? He can't stay so.

Doris carrying him by Father Warren today. We'll deal with the priest first. If that don't work then we go think of a next plan. Right. I gone.

I went in to find a sleeping batcha. He best get away from this place now.

*

I stayed patient for two more nights while Chunksee had fever from the time the place started to make dark to just before dawn. Whatever prayers the priest put on he head ain't move the spirit.

I got Boysie's permission to carry Chunksee by the doctor in St James. He looked over Chunksee quick quick and decided it was a little infection that will clear up by itself. We didn't even leave with a prescription.

Boysie, it's the spirit. You big and strong. It can't do all you nothing. But Chunksee's there suffering. Send beta home by me nah, man. I could carry him to school and pick him back up same way. And in the night he go sleep right next to me. What you think?

He sighed.

Why we have spirit?

It was at the tip of my tongue to say something about Popo and maybe even Lester. I ain't resting easy about either of them. That definitely dented my heart. But Boysie like he ain't care.

Doris organised she prayer group in a novena. Nine days they're praying at six o'clock in the morning asking the Virgin Mary to heal Chunksee body and soul. The devil advantaging an innocent.

Since when Boysie know about novena and the Virgin Mary? Like he gone mad too or he forgot it's me he's talking to.

Chunksee came home with me. The only problem was he still had night fever. Tomorrow he's getting a good jharay from head to toe. Pundit Hanuman will tackle this once and for all.

ROSIE

She reached when the cock was beginning to crow, two hands full and two eyes dead, upset beyond upset. It was the same despair I'd seen in Etty that first motherless Christmas Day when she only shoes were soaking in a full posey. I took the bags and settled her in my bed.

Rest, I need to open the shop.

She mouth opened and closed without a word escaping.

It's all right. Hush. Plenty time for talk later. You're here now. And hear me good, you're safe.

My routine is mechanical. I open the doors, prop up the galvanise awning, sweep the ground, put out the chairs. Etty and whatever troubles she's facing flooded my mind. I almost didn't want to know because as soon as I have a name or names, it go be mas in this place.

When I couldn't put it off no more I made green tea for two of we, carried it inside and announced,

You don't have to tell me.

Letting she know she could keep quiet and not say boo unlocked a river of tears. Etty bawled down the place. All I could do was hold her tight tight. In between she told me enough. By the time she finished I was ready to make a jail for Bumper.

It's my fault. I should have defended myself.

How exactly you was going to do that, eh, Etty? He's six foot and change. You is what? A five-foot-two bag of bones.

She flipped between rage and despair, despair and rage.

Any of the girls could act as witness?

She looked at me surprised.

Witness? What you want with witness? You think anybody care what happened? So long as I'm able to work nobody give two shits. I ain't going back. Forget it.

All right, all right, but I still want to know if anybody see what happened.

She bit her lips.

I will find out, Etty.

She sighed and told the ground,

Two other fellas were in the room but I'm not sure who they were.

So let me get this straight. You refused a fare because the Limey was a violent drunk. He vomited all over you. Bumper ordered you to wipe down and take the fare because he was paying triple.

She nodded.

I opened the window to feel the cool morning breeze on my skin. After Etty refused the fare, Bumper had raped she in the back passage. Whoever the other two were they encouraged him to give it to she good. Bleeding and in pain, she snuck out when Bumper and the other two were busy drinking. The amount of trouble this girl's seen it's like she eat bread the devil he-self knead. Finding a taxi at that hour was a pure miracle. The Lord was watching, yes.

Soon as they realise I'm gone, my things gone, Bumper will come for me. He'll want everything back to normal before Boysie can ask a question.

Let him come. I'm waiting. Day or night. I hope Bumper's ready to meet he maker.

We didn't have long to wait.

That same night Bumper reached with he armed bodyguard, Firekong. Imagine that criminal, that rapist, walked boldface boldface into my packed rum shop with cutlass in he hand. He called for Etty, said if she left with him and didn't cause any more trouble he wouldn't have to tell Boysie she refused to work. I told him she was inside resting and had fired the work.

Let she come and tell me for she-self.

She don't have to tell you nothing. It's me telling you.

Listen, I fed up of you playing man.

He raised the cutlass.

Etty!

Well that was the wrong thing to do in Rose's Bar and General Goods Store. I had done a little preparation. Every last man in the rum shop pulled out a cutlass, a knife or a big stick, whatever they could bring.

Now, go from here and don't show your face again. This village ain't have time for you. Boysie want he rent? He can come or send somebody who don't feel he can rape and get away with it just so just so.

The two had no choice but to turn around and leave. We were rid of them for now but I was sure as God made Moses they're coming back. When Boysie finds out he go be hopping mad. I need a next plan.

DORIS

I know why my left hand's itching but it's not my fault I spend so much money. This house needs plenty things and it's best to spend the little extra and get quality that will last. We need a bigger dining table. Boysie's coming up in the world. People always dropping in and I have to start hosting properly. Weekends we should be entertaining business people and politicians. This Port of Spain scene ain't easy. You have to show you can throw a damn good party. And we're missing an opportunity not putting Chunksee in the Catholic primary school. He will make friends with the right sort of children there. Then I would join the parents association and be friends with the proper people. As it is they've put him in the Presbyterian school. That can't help the same way. Anyhow, I'm only the stepmother.

Leaving the house this morning to go shopping in town I nearly tripped and break my tail. Now, who would put this ugly plant in an old paint can right outside my newly painted gate? As I was rushing I left it there. Minutes to twelve I reached back home, and the plant was still in the same spot. Boysie was eating the macaroni pie, red beans and stewed pork I'd left on the stove.

Whose plant is this? Like somebody left it for we, for us.

He skinned his teeth with food still in his mouth.

You're too sweet. Correcting yourself to sound like white people.

Boysie slid a hand around my waist.

I could eat you.

Well you can always try. Now, this weed?

That's a tulsi plant.

I stood close so from seated his face was near my bosom. We still haven't had relations. This ain't right and it's getting on my nerves. Since small, men been watching me.

Put it in the ground. It's a small tree. Next time we're by my didi remind me to show you how it does look when it grow big.

Never seen it before.

That's because you is a Toco reds. Every Hindu home bound to have a tulsi tree for good luck. Keep it.

So why you ain't plant one before?

I don't bother with them things so.

I will plant it in the yard but we still don't know who left it.

He tried to get up from the table. My kiss stopped him. Mr Port of Spain Sweet Man and he ain't putting out for he own wife? I show my best side. He doesn't see me without powder, lipstick, my hair combed and clothes holding my figure nice, even if we're just home. But only in public will he pass a hand on my bottom. I get comments on my looks so I must be doing something right. And we cuddle, which helps. Maybe he can't do things with me because he's busy with a set of other women. You see me and horn? That ain't working. Even so, something might be wrong. Like he's embarrassed to be naked with me. That can't work. Besides, I want to get pregnant soon. While kissing all behind his ears and his neck, I asked him to go by the doctor.

Who, me? Waste money on them quacks?

He gently pushed me aside and took two small bottles from a cupboard.

What you have hiding up there?

I didn't want Chunksee to go with he fass self and find my medicine. Next thing you know the boy get poisoned.

Doctor Boysie swears that all he needs is this one bottle marked 'iron tonic' and a bottle of Ferrol Compound. That I recognised. Mammy uses that when her blood needs purifying. Both bottles looked brand new.

They're making you feel stronger?

Yeah. Plenty. But I have to take them more long before things come right.

You have to take them longer, not more long.

You and your fancy talk.

Listen, husband, people mustn't look at you and say corbeaux can't eat sponge cake.

Boysie laughed.

All right, doux-doux.

*

A month on Doctor Boysie's prescriptions ain't made an ounce of difference. I want to be patient. And Boysie could also rest himself more. He would work on the Lord's Day if I didn't put down my foot. Arguments usually ended with a long speech about the pressure he's feeling with the clubs, people thiefing, the whe-whe and whatever else happening. What about me? Yes, I could visit my sisters or a friend but I prefer being with my husband. And Boysie's crew around all the blessed time. He must be able to take time off for he-self, himself and for us as a married couple.

Anyhow, I don't want to put goat mouth but at least money from the clubs flowing like Caroni River in rainy season. Boysie keeps sending me to buy things. As his queen, he doesn't want me ever looking all how. I must have more going-out clothes. Right down the road from us is a tailor who does neat work. So far he's made two suits for Boysie and they fit nice too bad. I tried him for a dress, and it's okay, but I prefer my lady on Park Street. She understands my shape.

I think he's buying or already bought another place, the Dorset at 55 Queen Street. He told me one set of things about how good the place is. Why he feels I'm some stupid church lady? I know about the working girls and the liquor under the counter. We all need to make a dollar. If he's running girls it's because they need a job. If he didn't buy the whisky and gin from wherever, somebody else would get it. Better it's my Boysie lining he pockets, his pockets.

MANA LALA

I make a weakee bai, yes. Night after night he's there suffering. I thought with the jharaying, the novena-ing, keeping him by me and everything else, the fever would stop. At least I have him and no way he's leaving me until this sickness done. Boysie's here all the time checking on him. I have to say it's nice, just we, cosy, even if it's only for an hour.

Three whole months passed like this. In the day he was fine. Dressing him in the morning, greasing down his hair with coconut oil and making sure the parting's straight were the little things that made me the happiest woman in Trinidad. I didn't even feel to crunch ice.

And then it stopped. Just so. No more fever. We ain't know why it started or why it done. At least I never saw a jumbie-man in white walking in my house. Who knows what helped. He'd had enough tonics from Mother Gizzard and the doctor medicine. Priest, pundit, imam, everybody said prayers for him. To me Chunksee and the devil were doing battle and thanks be, Ma Lakshmi, evil was finally defeated. I'm still worried though. Hopefully these months of fever haven't affected his brain or stopped him growing.

The first fever-free week I was talking to Subhagya Mausi about how happy I was when in the telling I realised something. Soon as he's stronger, Boysie and Doris will want him back. They shouldn't have my batcha. It's their wickedness that brought out the spirits in the first place. Chunksee's safer with me. Boysie knows he can come here day or night and stay how long he want. It's not a bad arrangement. She can't talk but Subhagya Mausi has heard me plenty times and I'm sure she'd agree. I swear when Chunksee's not here even the early-morning dew doesn't smell as fresh. Whole day I breathe in a heaviness. Ma ain't much company with she hot foot, spending time by this one and that one. If it wasn't for Subhagya Mausi I would be talking to myself.

This afternoon I decided to make Chunksee's favourite, fried pholourie with a little coconut chutney on the side. If I give him a chance he will eat these split peas and flour balls morning, noon and night. While he was stuffing them, hot from the fire, I asked if it ain't nicer by me rather than with Pa and Tanty Doris. He head bobbed up and down.

So hear what we should do. When Pa ask if you're still getting fever in the night say yes. Okay?

He started to say something and sprayed food right in my face.

Swallow and then talk. How much times I have to tell you that?

He tried again.

But Ma, the fever gone.

Well go back by your Tanty Doris. Me ain't think she even know how to make pholourie.

I turned away. Lying is for he own good. Hands down he's better off with me. I left him alone in the kitchen to check on Subhagya Mausi. In seconds he came running.

I'll tell Pa I have fever.

Thank the Lord he see sense. I gave him a hug up.

Good beta. Now, Mausi wants to taste the pholourie too.
You'll help feed she?

*

A next month passed like this with Chunksee by me because of
his 'night fever'. And I warned him to make sure he's not smiling
up too much when Pa's here. It crossed my mind that when
Chunksee's 'sick' I'm most at ease. He's here and Boysie's in and
out the house. Of course I don't want Chunksee to actually have
fever but this play-sickness ain't hurting a soul.

Coming up to six months Boysie started to make noise how
the child looking okay even if the fever's still there. He's definitely
small for he age, though. A strong breeze could knock him down.
For me things real good and I've not set eyes on Madame Doris
once. Then, suddenly, Boysie changed he tune.

Mana Lala, Sunday I'm taking beta. Doris missing him bad.
She go be so happy he coming home.

Well that sent me panicking.

*

Boysie came as planned on Sunday and no way he could take
Chunksee anywhere. I'd bathed the batcha in hot hot water,
wrapped him up in plenty clothes, rubbed him down with
nearly half a tin of Thermogene, and sapped he head with Bay
Rum. I made it a little game.

Let me see what your sick face look like.

He put on a sad face.

Nah. That's sick?

This time the face twisted up like he confused.

Not a sick face. Wait a minute.

The new penny I held up was shining.

How much sweeties you will get in Miss Hilda's shop with this?

Well, now the face looked over happy.

If you put on a good sick face so your pa thinks you have fever, I'll give you the money.

The batcha was so good even I wondered for a minute if he had fever. Boysie left Chunksee to rest.

I really thought he was getting better. He looked so good the other day.

I shook my head.

The fever does come out of the blue and leave the same way. Tell Doris to say prayers.

ROSIE

Hard to believe but having just the one love under my foot, day in, day out, ain't so bad. It's actually nice to have a person around who has my back. She would understand if I went visiting another lady or gentleman. But it hasn't happened. My regulars are all busy with their own commess. One making baby. One have malaria. I ain't playing nursemaid for nobody. A next one having problems with he eldest so he's staying close to home. All good because end of the day I rely on me and me alone.

Etty has been slowly getting back her old self. Take the ice-truck man. It's a small thing but lately I ain't know what happen to he. Reaching any old time he feel. I does be there cussing and stressing myself. Not Etty. This morning she made me stay inside while she checked the ice man. Ten minutes later she came back with half off today's bill, a promise he will be more reliable and a new friend. I suppose you can't survive a whore house if you don't know how to talk to people.

Tinsingh, another Boysie lieutenant, did the next two rent collections. That was only for show. I'm sure the things we village passed through in that time were Bumper and Firekong's doing. Had to be. Chitram tied he goat in the pasture good good and went to work. Eh eh, evening when he passed back, goat gone. Mr Wilson came home to find somebody had stoned his glass window. Poor Myrtle's still in shock that anybody could wring the neck of every last chicken she was minding and leave them on the ground just so. But it was when the school caught fire I thought enough was enough. Lucky thing the caretaker was there to out it fast fast.

To my mind this was Bumper and Firekong working alone. If Boysie had had a hand the whole village would've burnt down my now. Best I find the Rajah first and let him know about these wutless fellas.

Meanwhile Etty's a natural in the rum shop. A little too good, if you ask me. I used to think I'm short-changing the customers leaving she in charge. Not so. They might even prefer she. I joined her laughing and chatting away to Boy Boy.

Aye aye, Boy Boy, that shirt and tie take you nice. You come straight from the Red House? How work in the courthouse treating you?

I there fighting up. I say let me sit down and relax myself because once I reach home and eat a plate of Granny's food I ain't coming back out. Anyhow, I was just going to tell Etty something.

He turned to her.

Guess who was in court today?

Before she could answer he partner shouted,

King of Port of Spain? I hear he like people to call him a land shark. Me ain't even know what that is.

Was he-self. How you know? And the Rajah's wife too. If you see how she dressed up like she from away with fancy hat and thing. And plenty plenty gold. You could see them have money.

Do fass nah, Boy Boy. What was the charge?

Police had he up for selling liquor without a licence.

I pushed in.

    I bet all he got was a fine.

    Hold your horses. It's my story.

We huddled closer, ready for the latest.

    Well, three police stepped in the witness stand, took the Bible and all three said the same thing. They went to the Dorset bar. Boysie offered them a drink. None of them tasted a drop.

Boy Boy tapped his nostril.

    Add to that the place was stinking of rum so, partner, they charged he tail. And they cleared out every last bottle lining the bar.

Etty laughed.

    How you mean they only smelt rum? Them same police always taking two-three free shots of whisky.

He nodded.

    Correct. Boysie's big-time lawyer was waiting for them. He pointed to the bottles and asked the police to take a taste. Well, if you hear the judge.

Boy Boy put on an accent like he just stepped off the boat from England.

    I find that highly improper.

I nearly peed myself laughing. Boy Boy continued.

    The lawyer begged and the judge said, proceed.

Boy Boy knocked back a shot.

So the judge make the police them taste it. Man, I wish I had
a camera. One sip and it was spit the officer spit right there in
the courtroom. The lawyer asked if he'd tasted whisky.

So what was in the bottle?

Tea. Every last bottle was full to the brim with tea. Well court
mash up. Man, you could see even the judge was trying not
to buss a laugh.

Well the whole bar was in uproar. Etty poured Boy Boy another
drink.

I could've tell all you them bottles was only for show.
Boysie ain't chupid. The liquor does be locked up
underneath the bar.

Front page of the papers next day was a picture of Boysie and he
wife, Doris, arm in arm, looking over happy. I must catch him
while that good mood lasts.

MANA LALA

Chunksee is an obedient child and although he didn't too care for the Thermogene smell he put up with it. And we had the advantage of knowing exactly when to expect Boysie on weekends. But during the week he could pass ten in the morning or ten in the night. I'm going to tell Boysie that same as before, the batcha's only ever sick when it's making dark. Daytime he's fine. He can go to school, play, everything, so don't think he's recovered just because he is running around in the afternoon.

As I was putting Chunksee to bed on Sunday night I gave him a tight hug up.

We well fool your pa today. You acted like a boss.

Ain't I looked real sick, Ma?

Good boy. But I was wondering what will happen if Pa come to look for you and you there fast asleep looking right as rain. You know what go happen then?

Chunksee's eyes opened big big.

He'll take you back to live with Tanty Doris and make she your only mammy. I don't know if they will even let you see me.

The batcha held my hand tight.

Don't let them carry me away from you.

I squeezed him hard.

I'll never let that happen, beta. But we might have to prepare just in case.

Like what?

I'll sap your head with a little Bay Rum when you're in the bed night time.

Oh geesh. That's stinky.

I know, beta, but it's only when we ain't see your pa before you go in the bed. I'll at least have to rub you down with Thermogene. Once your pa understands you're better off with me we'll stop.

He didn't look happy. I kissed the button of a nose.

You'll get a penny for sweeties.

For true?

On Saturdays, so long as you behave and don't tell nobody.

Every Saturday?

Every single Saturday.

I told Subhagya Mausi my plan. Don't ask how I know, I just do. She ain't good with this pretending the child sick and she especially don't like making Chunksee lie. That is not how to bring up the bai. But the loneliness without my batcha. Not seeing Boysie regular. I ain't able.

*

Chunksee was at school when Boysie passed a few days later. He shirt sleeve had a tear and he pants looked stained with blood. I rushed to help.

What happened? You all right?

I passed to take a quick bathe before I do my rounds this afternoon.

From the few piece of clothes he keeps here I handed him a pressed shirt and pants. When he had cleaned up I gave him a glass of cold water.

When this happened?

He let go one long steupse.

Girl, you believe I now done take my driving test and the man fail me?

No. Why?

How much years now I there driving up and down and he think he could come and tell me I ain't getting a licence today?

Boysie went down with he hand into the plate of dhal, rice and stew chicken I put in front him.

I do everything correct. You see me drive already.

Yes. I find you is a very good driver.

I do the parallel park. I hill start. I mash brakes for the emergency stop. No problem.

What wrong with that instructor? You supposed to pass.

He said I didn't make any hand signals so he's failing me.

But you ain't bound to make hand signal. That is why the car have indicator and thing.

He gave a grateful look. Of course I is the one who know him better than anybody. Including the wife.

So what you do?

I tell him, ease me up, nah. You know I is Boysie Singh? Rub my belly and I go scratch your back.

He sucked on the drumstick.

I hand the man a roll of notes. I didn't even count it. Had to be at least three hundred dollars. He said I still fail. I tell myself, this man real greedy in truth. But all right, I need the licence, so I went in my other pocket and took out a next set of cash.

He wanted more again?

Boysie finished chewing the gristle before continuing.

That poohar had the gumption to tell me no amount of money making he pass me today.

Oh my. That is not a nice person.

Girl, Mana Lala, I see red. I throw some good blows in he tail.

He deserved that, Boysie. Unfairing you bad so.

He sighed.

Anyhow, let me go up the road yes. Send a message if anything happen with Chunksee.

Yeah. But wait nah, the car in front. How you reach here?

I drive. Nobody can stop me. I is the Rajah.

He has a point. Nobody stopping the Rajah. It could be a driving licence or he son. If that is what he wants, he's getting it. I have no doubt that if he ever even suspected what I was doing he would take the batcha, ban me from ever seeing him, and put a beating on me that will make what happened to the man today look like a light tap.

DORIS

I was raised that if you're doing well you help the less fortunate. Boysie's business is booming, and I have a duty to my family. Forget duty, I want to help. My sisters, Elena and Julia, came to live with us. I was happy for the company but they hardly stay any time. Pretty, hardworking girls like them and still single? In two-twos we celebrated one marriage after another. Good Catholics, they started pushing out babies in a rush. Lucky them. I'm drinking tonic and keeping myself healthy. Me and Boysie have yet to do, well, to have, full relations. I've reached the point where I'm questioning if this is a marriage at all.

It would help if Boysie was home more. King of Port of Spain and everybody wants a piece of royalty. He's up and down Trinidad, and I mean as far south as Sainte Madeleine and Princes Town. All fours card tournaments which Boysie organises and then jumps in to play as well. Gambling like it's in his blood. Worse yet, he's been winning. How I can tell a man that's winning to stop? He will say I've gone mad.

My birthday's coming up and I told him I want a big party and we must invite all the Port of Spain big-ups. As a gift, Boysie will usually buy me gold, a pair of bracelets, a chain, earrings, something so. This year he begged me to go to the Guyanese jeweller and choose for myself. Elena and Julia came along for company.

Mr Mohansingh's shop is small small with one cabinet full of rings, necklaces and earrings taking most of the space. Soon as we reached he sent his son for refreshments and locked the door.

Ladies, all you can try on things in peace without them riff-raff bothering you. Now, something to drink? Eat? Anything.

My sisters lickrish for so. They ordered sponge cake and sweet-bread. Just because they done married is no reason to get fat. Wait until they get good horn. I'm watching my figure.

I flashed Mr Mohansingh a smile. I've been smiling a lot since his big son, the dentist, gave me two gold teeth. From then I've only been wearing gold to match my mouth.

We're keeping up my birthday and I'm wearing a long red and black dress. What you think will go with that?

He twisted he mouth, his mouth.

If it was me.

Mr Mohansingh watched me up and down.

And you say the dress have red? Plus, your skin light.

He folded his arms.

Rubies. Have to be. Simple but real class. Do one pattern for everything, earrings, ring, chain. But that is just me talking my mind. It's you wearing it.

Over the next hour and change I tried on everything he had with rubies. Sweet drinks and cake kept my sisters quiet although they toyed with cheaper jewellery. Sticking with gold and rubies it came down to two patterns. One was a lot more expensive than the other.

I don't know, Mr Mohansingh. My husband said to buy anything but same time I don't want to play the fool with money.

Don't dig no horrors. Rajah worships the ground you does walk on. Nothing is too much for he madame.

I don't know about that.

You mightn't know but he does be talking about you all the time. Everything is he wife. It's truth I'm talking.

I fingered both chains, slipped on one ring after another for the umpteenth time. Mr Mohansingh tried a different tack.

Forget the price. I'll give you a special deal. Which one you like more better?

I pointed to the pricier set. Both sisters cackled with laughter. They knew full well which I would choose. On a scrap of paper he tore from a copy book, Mr Mohansingh wrote some numbers, folded the paper, and put it in my hand. I liked what I saw.

That is very gentlemanly of you.

Take it. Go along. The Rajah's good for it.

That night I modelled it for Boysie. He looked real down but kissed my neck and whispered that I should've bought all two sets and done the thing.

Your husband can more than afford it.

This is what I don't understand. He does love me. We just don't seem to be able to turn all this kissing and cuddling into baby-making action. I don't like to complain but I'm too young for this. He interrupted my thoughts.

Sorry, Boysie, what?

Come rub me down, nah. Today was real rough. I lost big in
whe-whe.

He lay in my lap and I smoothed his hair.

What you want, doux-doux? Tell your wife.

He sucked my thumb and I understood.

Gently, I took him in the bathroom and sponged him off like
a baby. After drying and dressing him I put him under the sheet
and slipped in next to him. He grabbed my tot-tots, anxious for
comfort. Big man Boysie, Mr Badjohn, Rajah, Gambling King,
Land Shark, snuggled up like a newborn and suckled on my
milk-less breasts. In less than ten minutes he was in a deep sleep,
still latched on to me. Ever so gently I got him on to the pillow.
He never stopped snoring.

Boysie loves to play baby. I'd rather we make a baby. A big
man like he wants me to play he mother, his mother? I put up
with it because he likes it too bad. But it's not natural. I thought
I was marrying a real man.

MANA LALA

He came to take Chunksee for a drive somewhere. I can't say nothing direct only hope in my heart that he doesn't take beta with him when he's doing a job. He know better than that. Before they left he pulled me to one side.

Mana Lala, I have something to talk to you about. Sit down.

My heart was racing. Had to be something bad. Had to be.

In all these years I ain't give you a gift.

What chupidness you're talking Boysie? You always bringing thing for we and the little money every month does ease me up.

No, I'm making real money. Without them Yankees all over Trinidad I wouldn't have half the business I have these days.

I wanted to hold up my side of the conversation.

It's true. The base they have in Chaguaramas big, yes.

Yeah, but I bet you didn't know they have other naval bases. Plenty more.

Like where?

I does buy things from a base in Wallerfield out east. Aeroplanes does be taking off and landing there steady.

I didn't know about that one.

Them ain't telling we ordinary people nothing. Hear nah,

man, Yankees have base all about. Carlsen Field, Couva and even down south in Cedros.

For true? How them in England letting that happen here, I wonder.

Always some deal. I just glad the small man getting a little something out of it. And Doris real happy because they're looking at clearing bush up in Toco for a landing strip. They might put a base and all. Doris thinks it's high time poor Toco get something.

Doris this and Doris that. She's not even here and I have to put up with hearing that name.

Anyhow, the point is I wanted to tell you that as I'm making a little change these days I want to fix up this house.

Well, look at that. I knew deep down he'd never stopped loving me. The proof's right here.

You're sure, Boysie? I don't ask for nothing.

You ain't ask. I'm giving you this.

He went on talking about the Yankees and I held back my tears.

Doris doesn't like to hear about the Yankees. You and me can talk straight about anything and you don't get vex.

You know me, Boysie.

Only two things them Yankees want. To get drunk and screw woman, sometimes man. And you see my clubs? Ten times better than all the others in town.

You're talking truth.

Of course. Anyhow, let me make tracks. Hopefully Chunksee's getting he strength back. Lower down in the week I will send the boys and you can tell them how you want things. I'm doing this for you.

As soon as he left I rushed to give Ma and Subhagya Mausi the news. Ma twisted up she face and said she go be happy when she see it done. Later I went in the bed by Subhagya Mausi and had a little cry. He was supposed to marry me not she. Me. Marry me.

ROSIE

Boysie pulled up outside my shop and one of the young fellas in the back started offloading a set of boxes. I ran inside.

Etty, in the bedroom. Quick. Don't come out. You hear?

I went back out trying to act normal as ever.

Morning. What's all this, Boysie?

You get lucky today.

I looked inside a box.

Where these goods from?

Don't study that. I'm letting you have six box to sell. Pay me month end.

Excuse me, but who it have around here to buy all this?

Well you'd better find people. The boys will be round to collect as usual.

Ease me up, nah.

He laughed.

Rent is rent. I can't do nothing 'bout that.

I decided to test out what he knew about Etty and Bumper.

I'm in town this week. I will pass by your club to see my friend, Etty.

Well, if you see she tell she hello for me.

How you mean?

She gone somewhere. I know she ain't dotish enough to work another club. I'm surprised she ain't here.

I poured him a shot of rum. He knocked it back then burped up the fumes. I fanned away the sourness.

Manners.

You sound just like my wife. I can't burp or fart in peace round she.

I hit him a next drink.

Boysie, let we talk about Etty.

Oh? You know something?

She told me Bumper, well, Bumper did a bad thing. Really really bad. That's how she's ain't working these days.

Oh, so you know where she is and you ain't come tell me nothing?

I took a deep breath.

Bumper raped she. In the back passage. She'd refused a Limey.

Boysie let go one scandalous laugh.

What kind of chupidness you're talking? Bumper don't take woman.

You don't have to like woman to rape them.

He laughed again.

> Nah. Anything so I would know before Bumper have time to pull up he pants.

> Well, now you know.

> Etty tell you that?

I looked away and asked a different question.

> How come Bumper don't collect rent from me these days?

> Tinsingh buy a car so it more easy for he to make the rounds.

> So Bumper didn't ask not to come by me?

> I don't think so. I can't remember.

I nodded and the two of we were quiet. Best not to push this talk more today. But we ain't done at all at all. Boysie got up.

> I'm not saying you're lying but it's strange how nobody else give me that talk. Nobody. And I have eyes and ears all about.

> Yeah, well them eyes and ears probably frightened he do the same to them.

Boysie steupsed and turned to leave.

> Walk with me to the jitney.

I looked around the shop. Two fellas in the corner were pretending like them together alone. Boysie gripped my waist. Anybody passing would think we in something. That wasn't it at all. He was just making sure I went exactly where he wanted.

Still holding me he reached into the front seat of the jitney and took out Three Little Threes.

In the orphanage they ever beat all you with a poui stick?

I shook my head.

What they used? Leather strap?

I swallowed hard. Boysie skinned he teeth.

Remember Nugget?

Then just so he let go.

Tell Etty to find she-self back in the club. And I ain't want to hear nothing about Bumper again. You understand?

I nodded.

Go. You're keeping back customers.

DORIS

It's taken years and plenty buttering. Others would have given up. I didn't and that is why I'm a key member of the Circle. We are a group of Port of Spain church ladies who meet for lunch every Friday at Ricardo's in Woodbrook. Lunch is at noon for one hour followed by a discussion of what's been happening with our various charity cases. After that members are free to bring new cases for consideration by the Circle. It's only twelve of us but we have all been blessed and it's our Christian duty to give back to those less fortunate.

The husbands are suspicious. They should relax because we don't talk about them that much. Well, maybe a little. There was that time Gwendoline started to cry before we'd even finished our pumpkin soup. A close friend claimed that Gwendoline's shameless husband had been seen driving around with a young lady close close in the front seat of his motor car. Poor Gwendoline didn't know what to do. In the end she didn't have to lift a finger for him to stop all that foolishness. The ladies of the Circle went home and told their husbands. The stray dog had eleven men, including my Boysie, reminding him of his wedding vows. I guess that is why the men remain anxious each Friday when we have our luncheons.

I love the Circle. The few party invitations we have are all in some way connected to this group. It's breaking my spirit to think I might have to stop going to the Circle meetings. Last week, everybody was at the table settling in and the waitress came with a jug of water to fill the glasses. I was deep in a sweet talk when I felt a hand press my shoulder.

Is you, Doris? Oh my God. Look at you. What happen? Like you thief somebody husband you was working for? Well, you do better than me.

I didn't recognise the face straight away.

Gosh you're looking real nice, Doris.

Then I did. The last time I saw her she had a grip in she hand, her hand, after being chased by Mrs Warner for getting pregnant by Mr Warner.

I'm sorry. I don't think we've met.

Doris, it's me, Nadia. We used to do maid work Arima side.

The whole table was quiet, watching.

You must have me confused with somebody else.

It was a while back, yes, but you must remember me. I worked for the Warner family. The mister used to drink. It so good to see you.

I'm really sorry but you have me mixed up with some other person.

Doris?

Yes, that's my name but I don't know you or this Warner family.

Just then the owner, Ricardo himself, came to the table and greeted us. Thank the Lord. Nadia went off looking confused and I braved out the rest of the lunch. Nobody mentioned her again. At least she had the decency to let others serve us and we finished the luncheon in peace.

I told Boysie what happened. He didn't like that I was on the brink of tears.

Now Doris, listen to me good. You must go back next Friday.

But Boysie what if she come back in my tail with that talk?

She won't.

How you know? The bitch, excuse my language, enjoyed embarrassing me. She might even try to blackmail me. I wouldn't put it pass she, pass her.

Trust me, Doris. Go to your circle, square, whatever all you does call it. She will never bother you again. All right?

When Friday came Boysie himself dropped me Ricardo's. I had to promise to walk in, head high and enjoy my lunch.

It went well. I have to hand it to those ladies. They had the good grace not to mention what happened. Before I left I managed to ask one of the other waitresses about Nadia. They said she was gone. Some job paying twice as much came up in San Fernando and in two-twos she'd dusted it down south. I wonder how she heard about that work.

MANA LALA

I nearly get catch yes. Boysie passed this morning to take the batcha to school but my Ma told him we'd left already. In she mind he said he will be back tomorrow. Seven o'clock, kerosene lamp light, Chunksee in the bed and in the dark I heard Boysie's jitney pull up. Well, I rushed inside that bedroom so fast, threw Bay Rum on a cloth and wrapped the child's head as quietly as I could so he wouldn't wake. Of course he ain't have a fever. My hope was that Boysie wouldn't come too close.

Boysie bounced in looking sharp, hair slicked down with Brylcreem. Lord, the man does look good.

Like you're going out, Boysie?

I was hoping the beta ain't fall asleep yet.

He sleeping. You know the fever does come and go in the night. Leave him until the morning.

Well, I'll just give him a kiss. You could tell him I came.

Nothing I could do but let him into the bedroom. He stayed near the door looking at the batcha with a love on he face that nobody else in the world does get. I hope he hasn't given that big bamsee red woman this piece of he heart. I really should stop calling she that but it's hard. She is Mrs Boysie Singh. Imagine that.

I 'fraid to wake him.

Leave him, nah. Best let him sleep.

He kissed the outline of the batcha's little foot under the coverlet then closed the creaking door as softly as he could.

Instead of leaving straight away as I expected, he asked for a drink, a Scotch. It's he-self left the bottle for when he want liquor.

You ain't taking a drink with me?

I good.

He was in a funny mood. Whatever was wrong I'm over happy it was by me he came.

You all right, Boysie? You look like you have troubles.

He sipped the whisky and rocked back in the old chair. Still not talking. We settled into easy silence. I'm here whenever he ready. Minutes passed before he mouth opened.

You knew my pa?

That wasn't what I was expecting at all at all.

Little bit but I was small.

You know about the sword though?

You know something? I can't say you ever showed it to me. I think you said didi had it.

He nodded.

It's mines now.

He turned to face me.

I think the sword might be making the batcha sick.

How you mean?

I ain't know exactly. Pa used to do prayers and shine it up and thing. And he said we was to throw it away but we ain't bother with he. It under my mattress. You think the sword vex and taking it out on Chunksee?

I had to swallow a laugh.

Why the sword vex?

You're laughing? Pa said the sword had a calling for blood. I ain't give it any.

How you mean?

I prefer my Three Little Threes.

Oh. Yes.

Popo and Three Little Threes flashed through my mind. I kicked that thought away so fast. Boysie was saying something about Chunksee's fever being a warning.

The sword telling me it want blood. I ain't give none and it vex. It want revenge. Easier to take it out on the batcha than a hard-back man like me.

You're frightening me. Maybe your pa was right. Time to throw it way for truth.

I can't. Don't ask me why but I just can't. Something about me and the sword. We ain't done yet.

But if it coming for Chunksee then do something.

I don't know.

You know what I'm going to tell you?

No pundit. No puja. And I ain't want no jharay on my head.

Give it to me then. I will carry and get the thing blessed and make whatever offerings necessary. Just in case.

No, whatever going on is only concerning me and the sword. Any offerings it's me have to make them. Probably nothing to do with Chunksee. My mind was wandering all over the place.

My fingertips brushed he hand.

I don't take my eye off we beta. Don't worry your head.

We left the talk there. I need a plan. If he had only touched the batcha he would've known Chunksee's cool as ever. In no time we'd be back to the batcha staying weekends only. And nights like this, the middle of the week, Boysie's relaxing with me? Gone. It's too much to lose.

ROSIE

Rosie, do fast and run a soup there for me.

Too late. You-self know that Saturday soup does sell out fast fast. And I had your favourite.

Malcolm steupsed.

Cow heel soup? Don't tell me you didn't hide away a little bowl for your doux-doux?

Not a drop, Malcolm boy. I ain't even keep back for myself. The line was long before I even out the fire from under the pot.

Oh gosh, and my belly griping me bad.

I passed my hand through his thick black hair, the kind even women would kill for.

Crix and sardine or Crix and corn beef? Choose.

Whatever. I done see you're treating me bad.

Don't say that nah, man.

Inside the rum shop was making hot for so. Outside the ground dry dry. Grass brown. At least them crickets have been singing their heads off. If the old people are correct rain coming within six weeks. All I wanted was to lie down in the hammock and take a five. Instead, I opened a tin of sardines, mixed it with one good squeeze of lime, half an onion and a ripe tomato chopped up fine fine, a little chadon beni and slight pepper for season-ing. Crix biscuits on the side, two plates, two forks, and me and

Malcolm were ready to take lunch.

I didn't believe soup gone through.

Why I would say it ain't have if it have?

All right, just checking to see if you still like me.

I lowered my voice.

But you know that.

His hand brushed my face.

These days I ain't sure. Since that girl moved in it's like we done.

I took a cloth and wiped away a line of red ants marching across the table in single file.

It ain't easy.

But you always there making out you ain't for one person alone. And furthermore it's you-self tell me it ain't right to ask one body to be everything for you.

That's true. But she's different.

He cackled.

Rosie, you is something else, yes. God make you and break the mould.

I loaded a Crix with sardine and shoved the whole thing in he mouth. Peace for only a few seconds because he does eat fast.

So where's this woman that have your head tie up?

She gone up the road by Zena for a trim.

Malcolm's hand crept up my leg.

A quick thing?

Boy, behave yourself nah.

So you ain't miss me?

Look Malcolm, the place making too hot. I ain't want nobody touching my skin.

He went back to his plate.

Had a time you would be on top me because the place was making hot. This lady like she have you bazodee.

I looked down. A big woman like me and my face was burning.

Wait nah, you're blushing?

Hush your mouth. Now, what's happening with you these days? You're still with Boysie?

The Rajah giving the most work. Can't really say no.

His mouth was full.

Chew your food.

He paused before digging in with another Crix.

You hear my car get hit by police? It make papers.

I hear something so.

Girl, I there coming down the road cool cool, minding my own business. Next thing I know a police van, coming in the opposite direction, picked up one bad skid and crashed into my car. Mashed up the whole front. Thing is a write-off. And you won't believe who was in that police car.

Who?

Rajah and he right hand, a fella named Cecil. Nice man.
Worked for Rajah long time now. Crash break Cecil's neck
and bradaps he dead. On the spot. I see the body and all.

Have mercy. Sorry to hear that. He had family?

I don't really know the ins and outs but I hear Rajah's
organising big funeral and thing. It's one set of confusion
because people blaming he for the dead.

The ole talk was sweet too bad. Boysie's wife has extra reasons
to be vex. If this got in the papers she go shame plenty. Thing
is, she must know Boysie is Woodbrook's biggest ram goat. But
then again, love's funny. She wouldn't be the first to think that
if you loved a man plenty plenty he'd change to how you want.
Waste of time. The only body you can change is you, and even
that is pressure.

While we were shooting the breeze Etty appeared, hair shiny
and pretty. I introduced Malcolm and I could see she felt she
was interrupting something.

Don't run away. Sit down. Zena could real do hair, yes. And I
see you're finally wearing the earrings I buy for you.

Malcolm opened he eye big big.

Nice.

The little green stone dangling on the gold hook takes to she
colouring. Etty pulled up a stool.

Malcolm was just telling me about Cecil who worked for

Boysie. You know who I'm talking about?

She nodded.

Girl, he gone and dead.

Etty put she hand in front she mouth.

You lie. Cecil? Rajah can't manage without he.

Malcolm asked if Etty knew about two ladies in San Juan, Jag and May.

Yeah. He had them draped over him in the club. My blood didn't take to them. Fake to the bone. I hear they belonged to another gang.

Malcolm knocked back a shot.

I wouldn't mind doing sisters. One on my face and one taking my wood.

I pretended to slap him.

Aye, why all man so? Mind always in the gutter.

Excuse me, takes one to know one.

Go on with the story please.

Malcolm said the San Juan posse were mad vexed with Boysie. He was doing the girls for free. On top of that he was busy thiefing their whe-whe business. I shook my head.

Typical Boysie, taking whatever he feel to take and not caring two cents about other people.

Etty's eye twinkled.

What?

I'm just laughing to myself. All this talk about Boysie doing this woman and that woman. You know Boysie can't get it up? It's all a pappy show.

You lie.

But I'm telling you. That's what the girls does say. Of course it's hush-hush.

Malcolm put he hand in the air.

I don't know about that but give me a chance to finish my story please.

Malcolm went on. While Boysie was busy doing or not doing the sisters, the San Juan boys well pelted the house they were liming in with big stones. Mashed the place up good and proper. Somehow Boysie managed to sneak outside with Three Little Threes.

Etty nodded.

Yeah, he believes in that poui stick like it's a magic wand.

Anyhow, instead of running home and saying two prayers that he's still alive, the Rajah reached in the police station boldface boldface and reported the gang trying to kill him. You ever hear more than that? The police them had to help. One minute he's the gambling king they're itching to lock up and next thing they're bodyguarding him from another set of hooligans.

I had to laugh.

Boysie real smart, yes.

Cecil joined Boysie and the police. All of them gone chasing the gang. But the fellas must have spotted the police first.

Malcolm stopped for a swig.

In all this I was coming up the road cool, minding my own business, and I see a police van coming on one side and some fellas in the bush on my side. As the police driver put he foot down hard on the gas, the fellas tipped a barrel of oil on the road. Police van picked up a skid. It spin round like a top. Nothing I could do. It knocked away the whole front of my car. I still can't believe only Cecil dead. All of we was supposed to meet we maker that day.

Etty fetched a glass and I squeezed Malcolm's hand.

Must've been real frightening.

A drink to Cecil. Time longer than twine. The Rajah will get what's coming.

DORIS

I've cleaned enough big-shot houses to know how a place should look and our house is perfect. My new mahogany dining table's so shiny even God can see he face in it. I bought twelve matching tall mahogany chairs with burgundy upholstery plumping up the seat. Mistress took off the plastic covering on she chairs, her chairs, but I ain't taking that chance. Next thing somebody's stewed chicken fall and stain up my good good thing. Same with the couch and two armchairs. Hard plastic's staying on, oui.

So, I told myself, Doris, forget all the confusion going on. Cook some of the fancy things you learnt in service and throw a dinner party. In fact, throw a few dinner parties. Boysie was only too happy to be out of the doghouse.

Let we invite Tinsingh and he wife. And George. He could bring a girl if he want.

I shook my head.

Lime with them anytime. This is for important people. I'm thinking the Copacabana crowd like the Pillais, the Procopes, the Maynards, the Grells. They should be regulars by us. And nothing wrong with a few whites in the mix. English people will come just because they're fass with they-selves and want to see inside Boysie Singh's house. But it's all right. If they come they'll have to invite us back. I'll invite that nice couple, the O'Neills.

Yes, but my friends coming too.

If you want a lime for your friends them, that could happen any day of the week.

Do your thing.

Yes, but make sure you're here. And behave yourself.

How you mean?

I mean dress up, please, Boysie. Maybe propose a toast before we eat.

Boysie steupsed.

That ain't my kind of thing.

I steupsed.

All right, stay right there. See how far that get you.

He left grunting and muttering to himself, playing like he don't understand what you have to do to get ahead in life. Lucky thing he has me. And after the bobol with them two jamette sisters, and Cecil's passing, he should be kissing my feet for remaining here making him look respectable.

I studied my list of who's in and who's out. None of Boysie's partners will be invited. And as for the ones who can't even give away a smile in church, they will have to come crawling for an invitation when they realise they ain't make the grade. Must invite Father Hamel and Father Smith too. Oh, and I got the same man we had used for the wedding reception to write out invitations fancy fancy on thick white cards.

For the first dinner party I'd invited six couples thinking one will have other plans or drop out last minute. Only two accepted and they were from my Circle group. A little disappointing but

I chose three other families on my list. Two of the three couldn't make it. Including me and Boysie we're up to eight people. Really need twelve for a good crowd. Both priests accepted for which I will say an extra Hail Mary. As the date got closer and no one else accepted, from even my third list, I told Boysie to bring Tinsingh and his wife. So long as they don't open their mouth to talk gambling they can pass for respectable.

But this whole invitation business has me feeling a certain way. I mean we have money, more than most of them on my lists. I have colour. Every Sunday I'm in the right congregation and no one dares sit in my place in the third pew on the left-hand side. Had only a few turned us down I wouldn't have minded. But I was scraping to make up numbers. These people feel they're better than we? Better than us? Being rich don't seem to be enough. I had no idea people prejudice so. They must think their money better than ours.

MANA LALA

Boysie keeps bringing up this sword talk. I half encourage it
because he's so busy worrying about the sword he ain't looking
at the batcha too close. Once I say Chunksee ain't too good that's
enough. Today he reached excited about last night's dream.

I know how to make the fever go.

All right let me hear you, Doctor Boysie.

He grinned. In the dream Boysie and he pa were in India bathing in the Ganges. While they were throwing water on their skin
Pa told him the bai will get better once Boysie makes an offering
to the sword.

So, I tell Pa I ain't feel right fighting with that sword. Pa
throw more water and wash he-self. Then he said it have a
next way. A secret offering that's just as good. You know what
he said?

I shook my head.

If you can't give red blood then give red money. And give it
regular.

Red money? Like a five-dollar note? That's the only red
colour money we have.

Exactly what I was thinking. I don't dream Pa so. The dead
reach me for a reason. Pa came to fix the luck of he last
grandson.

349

Soon as Boysie woke up he'd pulled out the sword from under the bed. It shined up bright bright. He rested some five-dollar notes along the blade.

I talk to the sword and I tell it this red money is for it alone. I will never spend it.

The notes are in a bag next to the sword and both are now living on top the press.

It getting red money every Friday same time when I'm paying them workers. I real hope that will settle whatever spirit living in the sword.

Do what you have to do, yes. And don't expect the batcha to come healthy until the sword's happy.

Boysie nodded. This should be worth a good month.

*

In my heart I was convinced the worst was over and really the batcha's staying here with me. I began to slack off the nightly routine of Thermogene and Bay Rum smelling up the house. Imagine my state when Boysie came unexpectedly around eight o'clock, stinking of rum and calling loud loud for a hug up from he only batcha.

Mana Lala girl, I licked down every man jack in all fours. Every last one. And you know what else?

I pulled a cream orhni over my head so as not to catch dew.

What happen?

I took down that kiss-me-ass sword.

Boysie, quiet with the cussing nah. It making late.

He pressed a finger on he lips and continued talking just as loud as before.

I throw ten, fifteen, twenty five-dollar notes on the sword. I said, here, take your blood money and left my beta alone.

He slumped into a chair in the gallery.

I come to see my beta, my one and only. It ain't look like I go make a next one. Doris can't make child.

I didn't say a word.

Let me see if that kiss-me-ass, greedy sword still putting bad spirit on my beta.

Panic had been rising in me since Boysie screeched up in front the house. The tin of Thermogene and bottle of Bay Rum had stayed closed tonight.

Don't go inside nasty and sweaty. You want the beta to smell you so? Come bathe, eat something and relax yourself. Chunksee in the bed. He ain't going nowhere.

It's too cold to bathe now.

I go hot up some water and put in a bucket for you.

He suddenly yawned wide wide. I saw all he teeth and the back of he throat.

Let me relax myself in truth, yes. Two days straight I was playing cards.

I put a pot of water on the fire to boil. While Boysie cocked up he foot in the gallery, I sprinkled Bay Rum on Chunksee's sleeping head. He made a little noise but he's so accustomed to the smell it didn't wake him. Back in the kitchen I waited as the water rolled to a boil. I filled the hot-water bottle and soaked a small towel. An Indian tune he'd been humming now broke into gaawaying loud loud.

Tayto bani jai govind guna gaye re.

I went to the bedroom, pushed the hot-water bottle between Chunksee's jersey and skin. He woke straight away. I put a finger on my lips.

Stay quiet. Pa outside. I'm warming up your skin.

He didn't say a word as I quickly wiped him down with the hot cloth. I saw him pushing the hot-water bottle away.

Leave it there. You hear me?

I piled two thick blankets on top the boy.

Fall back asleep.

In the kitchen I poured the pot of hot water into a bucket, mixed in some tap water to cool it little bit, and toted the bucket outside.

Boysie, your water ready.

Coming. *Tayto bani jai govind guna gaye re.*

By the time Boysie eventually went in to the batcha his skin was warm and eyes shut. I don't think he was sleeping sound but Boysie couldn't tell. He was convinced the fever was there as usual and stormed out cussing the sword every which way he knew how. He ate, he drank, he cussed, he sang. Sometime during the early hours he lay down in a hammock and snored. I was drained. I curled up next to Chunksee and took a rest.

When I checked beta next morning he had two red, bumpy patches on he belly. Maybe it was a rash from something he ate. Were these burns from the hot-water bottle? I showed Boysie.

You well cuss the sword last night? Fine. Look how the sword gone and cuss you back.

But how he get that?

I ain't know. Chunksee didn't have this rash last night. He should go doctor.

Boysie nodded.

Keep him home from school and let we go. It have a new doctor in Belmont. They say if he can't cure you, prepare to meet your maker.

I went into Subhagya Mausi and explained I was stepping out for a little bit. Ma wasn't home either but the neighbour would check on she. It's hard to know if she understands anything. I got a behhhh and I swear it sounded sad, like she didn't want to be left alone.

I'll come back quick. Me and Boysie going Belmont with Chunksee. It's not far. You like this dress? I put too much kohl around my eyes?

She didn't make a sound which I took as a sign I was looking okay. Me and my two men stepped out together. It was our first family outing in I can't tell you how long.

The doctor was over glad to see Boysie and refused to charge a cent. The rash wasn't serious. It might be an allergic reaction to something the batcha ate. He had a tube of the cream and was about to rub it on Chunksee.

Let me do it.

Poor batcha. I gently smoothed the cream over the two angry red patches of skin. Hot-water bottles flickered across my mind. Yes, must have been something he ate.

Boysie dropped we home. As I walked inside my chest tightened and my belly ached. It might only have been a doctor visit but we did that as one family, me, Boysie and Chunksee. That is how it should be always. Why Doris had to come and spoil everything?

For the rest of week I kept the bai close. We put the cream on twice a day religiously. Until that red is gone gone he needs his Ma's loving care round the clock. He wanted to stay home but I told him he must learn he schoolwork. Me so didn't have a chance for education. Things will be different for my beta.

DORIS

People worthless, you hear. They might smile good to my face but once my back's turned the talk turns a green colour. It's jealous they're jealous that a woman like me moves about town in a chauffeur-driven car. I remind myself that people don't throw stone at mango tree that ain't bearing. What they want me to do? I can't drive. Leave the Buick home and take bus and tram? If it's not the chauffeur they gossip about it's how much gold I wear or the fact that I don't leave the house without stockings and gloves. Mrs Boysie Singh must keep standards. You just never know who might see you or what might happen. To me it doesn't matter whether I'm at a cocktail party or in Mount Lambert visiting my sisters. What I wear must never shame me or my husband.

And speaking of standards, our neighbours are a perfect example that having money is no guarantee people can behave in a civilised manner. Next door belongs to a doctor fella, a lovely gentleman. But the tenants? Lord, put a hand. Them English people carrying on a conversation in their living room and I'm hearing it quite in my bedroom. After lunch I like to take a five but it's yak yak yak like they ate parrot bottom for lunch. Boysie was upset for me.

Disturbing my wife? Them getting a piece of my mind today self.

Don't worry. I know you're busy.

Never too busy for my doux-doux, darling.

I wanted to say since my wedding night I've been waiting for you to have time for me. Instead I played nice.

> Thanks, Boysie. And talk to them easy. If they could please lower their voices, especially in the afternoon I would be grateful. This is a quiet, respectable neighbourhood. I'm not the only one taking a five.

For a week or so we didn't hear a peep. I thought nice. They got the message. Then the noise revved up again. Boysie went back over. He didn't use bad language. All he did was ask them to keep it low especially at times when I liked to sleep. It worked. We didn't hear boo for, must be, a month. But like they're missing a volume button in their gullet and before you know it the noise was happening again. Boysie said this was damn foolishness and sent for Doc.

People listen when Boysie speaks. Doc did. He was by we gate, our gate, calling hello that same day.

> Mr Boysie, Mistress Doris, good afternoon. How all you going?

We gave it to him straight. Parakeets make less noise than his tenants. The noise must stop now, today.

> Imagine, my wife can't rest in she own house. That is something I shouldn't have to bother you about.

Doc nodded in agreement.

> It's only out of respect for you, Doc, that I ain't do them nothing. Talk to them for me, please.

> I understand your position, Mr Boysie.

I is a reasonable man, Doc. But if them English people don't hush their mouth I will send for the boys. And you know what them boys go do? They go pelt the house with stones. You hear me? It go be raining stones on that house. Watch and see how crapaud go smoke their pipe.

No, Mr Boysie. It won't come to that.

All right, but if my Doris hear so much as a squeak out of them I'm sending in the boys. It go be raining stones.

This whole incident has me a little confused. The same man who tried to hurt me on our honeymoon, who ain't get inside my underwears yet, will go this far for my peace and quiet? What really going on? We're living in a big house with a dead bedroom and I want children. Marriage ain't easy, you hear.

Luckily them tenants went quiet or I'm sure Boysie was ready to make like Revelation 16 and have a great hail fall from heaven. He might actually have frightened them off for good. I find these days the place is always locked up tight tight. Sly like a mongoose I snuck through the thick sweet-lime hedge that separated the houses and peeped through where the curtains didn't meet. Dirty wares filled the kitchen sink. Cushions were dumped on the living-room floor. I couldn't see into the bedroom good but the high bathroom window only had a half-curtain. Tiptoeing on an old pail I pulled myself up to glimpse inside.

A scream hit my chest and knocked me backwards. Braps, I landed on the hard ground. Don't ask me how I managed to scramble back home. Boysie will never believe me. I know he won't. But I swear, Jesus, Mary and Joseph he was there. I saw him with my own two eye, two eyes. The jumbie-man was there. I'd know that white suit and white hat anywhere.

Later when I was taking a cup of tea, calming my nerves, I asked myself, Doris, whose jumbie is that following all you? It's moved with us from one house to the next. The ghost stopped me from taking an afternoon rest. Has to be a soul in purgatory. Lord, did Boysie take a life? For the first time I can't take my troubles to the priest. This must stay in the family.

ROSIE

All of we in shock. Boy Boy only kept up he twenty-third birthday must be a month ago. That is no age, no age at all. Only he and the grandmother lived in the house. They ain't released the body yet but from what we heard last night he collapsed right in front the land registry clerk. No warning, nothing. One minute he was talking good good and next minute he dropped down dead. We're still waiting to hear the cause of death. It wasn't like he was sickly or anything. How a young strapping man could be alive one minute and gone the next? How? No offence but like God got mixed up. Granny's the one due to be called yonder.

Etty and all real upset because Boy Boy used to like talking and laughing with she. He made her welcome in the village. She was also the first who raised concern that granny mightn't have money to bury the dead. I had to agree.

Time to pass round the hat. Boy Boy deserves a proper cedarwood coffin.

Good people living around here. They set up a rota of sitting with granny. Everybody took turns to cook and carry food. As more people found out I heard the same things over and over.

Boy Boy was never one to bad talk anybody behind their back.

He was my real riding partner. My horse.

And hear nah man, he always looked after he granny. Up and down with she. Taking time off work to carry she clinic.

Fuss he was a nice fella. Would give you he last dollar.

Always had a good morning in he mouth.

To think he was gone before he had time to find a love and make children. So much he will never know.

Come the day of the funeral we agreed Etty would stay in the shop while I went to Boy Boy's house to join the cortège. Riot will break out if the rum shop's closed.

Pulled by two white horses, the hearse stopped first at the dead home for the immediate family to say their goodbyes to the open coffin. We waited, gathered on the road ready to follow the cortège through the village on its way to the church. I saw granny kiss Boy Boy goodbye. If it wasn't for the ladies at both elbows she would've collapsed. Family came one by one to pay their respects and spray perfume on the body. A sleeping baby girl didn't even know she was passed over the coffin three times in case spirits came for her. Only then the procession, all of we in hat and Sunday best, began the slow march to lay Boy Boy to rest.

People lined the road, bowing as the cortège passed. Out of respect but also because nobody wanted spirits entering their home, doors and windows were shut as the white horses approached. I nodded to Etty standing outside the rum shop, our place closed up tight for a few minutes to honour a good soul taken way too soon.

I've thought about that moment must be a million times. If I knew that would be the last time I'd ever see Etty so much would have been different. I would have stared into her eyes hard so she'd know that no matter what happened, I would always do my best to keep she shoes dry.

DORIS

I slipped into a cream dress that skimmed my curves, white gloves to my elbows, and took myself shopping. Fogarty's is the best department store in town. And why not? A new hat or shoes will never waste. And their tea room is where you see all the big shots. Maybe not everyone wants to be best friends with Boysie. Fine, fine, fine, fine, fine, but I mustn't suffer too.

Soon as I walked into the tea room I recognised two groups of ladies, both with spare seats at their tables. Standing at the edge of the room I expected them to call me out to join them. It's a good thing my face doesn't show what I'm thinking. Not one of them had the decency to ask if I wanted company. To hide my shame I swallowed a cup of tea by myself while constantly checking my watch as if I was late for an appointment. Why people so? In the right light I could pass for white. I talk nice. My clothes are easily more expensive than anything they had on. What more they want from me?

That sent me in my bed early and I would have stayed the next day too but we had a family christening. My sister like she's pushing out her own six-a-side football team. Nearly all my childhood friends have babies too. Time to call a spade a spade. Me and Boysie coming up to five years. Five years. This is Boysie's fault. Yes, he has Chunksee but we're talking a single twelve-year-old. The way things are looking if I want my own bundle of joy I'd best look elsewhere.

All this was passing through my mind as I glanced at the blood in the toilet. Another month of disappointment. I took off the christening clothes and went right back in my bed. Boysie thought it was stomach cramps and got the maid to fix a hot-water bottle. Yes, that is thoughtful but I would prefer a real man massaging me. Like that will ever happen.

I was still under the coverlet the following morning when Boysie barged in.

> I'm going Chaguaramas to come back. A new shipment reach. Gin and whisky if I'm lucky. Soon as I come back let we buss a cinema lime, nah.

> Honey, go with your partners them. Me ain't able with cinema and thing today.

> No, Doris. Cramp can't make you lie down for two days. You're coming.

Same time the maid asked for an excuse. She wanted to know where to find silver polish. If she would just open her big eyes, she would see it's never moved from under the kitchen sink. I turned to Boysie.

> You have any idea what it's like to have a period? If men had periods all now so we done have a cure for this pain.

> Hush and ready yourself.

Boysie yanked off the coverlet.

> Get up.

That look. I wasn't sure what he would do next.

> I want you in the yellow dress with the matching shoes.

Even with my nightie on I felt naked.

> Boysie, let me rest.

No. If I say we're going cinema we're going cinema. You understand English?

I blinked back tears. Crying would only vex him more. I whispered,

What's showing?

Stormy Weather. Opening today self.

What's it about?

Me ain't know.

He grinned while pinching my cheek a little too hard.

Get up. The mattress need a rest from your big bamsee.

*

We went to De Luxe, the posh cinema. The Globe had it too but enough riff-raff does be there. After refusing to come out I was well glad he'd dragged me. From my failed attempts at dinner parties and being snubbed at tea, you'd think I'd married some beast. Nothing could be more different here. Ordinary people worship Boysie like he's royalty. This is why he's the Rajah. They came asking for a raise or thanking him for helping them out when they needed it. Some just looked at him proud. One hand is all you need to count the number of successful black and brown businessmen on the island. Off the top of my head the only one I can think of apart from Boysie is the fella with the Bonanza, Michael Maillard, but my brain is a sieve when it comes to names.

Well, *Stormy Weather* was a good film. First-rate singing and dancing. Wish I was like Lena Horne. Boysie loved loved

loved it. I think he's since been back must be at least three times. After multiple viewings at De Luxe he came home with a plan. From now on he's wearing the same suits as the star boy, Cab Calloway.

The thing with Boysie is that when he puts his mind to something, big or small, he does it heart and soul, a hundred and ten per cent. A month ain't passed good and Cab Calloway style suits in different colours were arriving steady. You should see how good he looked in the high-waist pants with turned-up hems held by matching braces. Jackets had a wide collar and were extra-long, reaching halfway down his leg. Boysie being Boysie, every suit had to pair with a matching shirt. The tailor even suggested buying shoes to match.

What you think, Doris? Get shoes in the suit colours?

If you want. You have the money. But I don't have shoes matching every dress.

Well, you're not a businessman hustling to make a dollar. If the white people had their way a little coolie boy like me would remain cutting cane. Them feel they're supposed to own everything. I have to come out looking extra sharp to get the respect I'm due.

I know, darling, I know. And I'm sure they feel their shops are better than your clubs. Get the matching shoes and show them who is man.

He laughed.

You is the best wife. You know that?

Chunksee bounced in same time. He's spending the weekend.

Aye beta, you like my new suit? You want one? Two of we could walk about looking like twins.

Chunksee's face lit up.

For true, Pa?

Yes, it's about time people start seeing you around. My beta.

But the boy's still in school. He don't need no suit.

I asked you?

That was all it took. Push any further and who knows what Boysie will do.

Mohansingh sold Boysie gold chains to wear with his suits. Three strands of different lengths flowed from his inside pocket with the last one so long he could almost trip on it. Dressed like that everyone knew he was the most powerful badjohn in Port of Spain. I teased Boysie that soon he'll have more gold than me. He shook his head. Seems I have so much bracelets and chains people think I own a gold mine.

MANA LALA

Boysie unloaded a set of furniture and car parts. Of course that's no problem. When he built over we little house he had the fellas fix up a good-sized shed in the back. Me ain't have nothing to keep there so he might as well use it. They carried what they had to carry and it looked like they were leaving straight away.

Going already? I thought as it's nearly twelve o'clock you go stay and eat something. Pot done cook.

Boysie waved.

Girl, I'm busy. Next time.

All right, then.

As he hurried towards the jitney I yelled after him.

Hold up a minute. I want to tell you something.

I caught up with him.

Chunksee's shoes getting too small for he. I have to go in town to get a bigger size. You have time to carry me?

He shook his head.

I could see if one of my partners could carry you.

Nah nah nah. It's all right. I was just thinking as you does be up and down I could've gone with you a day.

I look like I have time to buy shoe? Take taxi, nah.

So we ain't going out together anytime soon. If Chunksee asked him to go somewhere he would make time, though. The other day he even said that for Chunksee's sake five dollars a week is still going to the sword on the off chance it wants to start any commess. When the dead talk you must listen. But otherwise Boysie's only bothered with he-self.

All this was humbugging me when Chunksee jumped up asking for lunch.

Wait a minute and I will take out your food.

I gave the batcha dhal, rice and bhagee, set it on the table and reached for the pot salt. One good spoonful over the food was probably all he would manage. There was still the glass of water to drink. Another spoonful went in that easy. I stirred hard until it disappeared.

Chunksee, come beta. Time to eat.

From the first mouthful he complained the food tasted funny. I told him to finish he food or I would feed him like a little baby. It took a while but he cleaned the plate.

Don't forget your water.

He took a sip and spat it out.

It tastes like when you swallow sea water.

Water is water. Best to drink it down in one.

He stared at the glass.

Drink the water and you won't have to sweep the yard. You could play whole afternoon.

The face brightened one time and that water disappeared before you could say Robinson Crusoe.

Good bai.

Less than an hour later the batcha came looking for me. I was sitting with Subhagya Mausi hemming a dress.

Ma, my belly hurting me.

That's cause you went running about straight after eating. You don't know to let food settle?

It hurting.

I looked at him properly. Beta was ready to cry.

It real hurting, Ma.

Before I could do anything he let go a load of vomit all over me. Poor batcha was crying. More vomit came shooting out like a fountain on me. I stood up, unzipped my dress and stepped out of the mess. Lucky thing it didn't go on the bed or on Subhagya Mausi.

It's all right, beta. It's all right. Ma here. Give me one second to throw on a clean dress. It's all right. All right. Ma look after you.

I took him to the outside pipe in the back, got rid of his clothes and cleaned him down. He vomited twice again while I was getting rid of the old vomit. Even though he had nothing left in his stomach he kept retching and crying. I wrapped him in a towel and put him in the bed. My poor sweet batcha.

It's all right. Never mind. It's all right. You're going to be all right, beta.

I want Pa.

His voice was weak.

Pa not here, beta. I ain't know where he is.

I want Pa.

I'm here, honey child. I'll look after you.

My belly's still hurting.

It will stop just now.

You're sure?

Yes, beta.

Send a message for Pa to come.

Yes, I'll do that. You need to go by the doctor.

As if the gods were looking down on us, I heard the sound of Boysie's jitney pull into the yard. The man surely had a hundred and one things to do but he told me to dress and all three of we went back Belmont by the doctor.

The doctor checked Chunksee over head to toe, inch by inch. Boysie was worried.

Doc, this child is my eyeball, you hear. I can't take that he in pain.

And if I knew what was wrong I would tell you. Maybe something he ate didn't agree with him? I will give him medicine for the pain and to stop any more vomiting. Just let him rest.

While they talked I cuddled Chunksee and gently rubbed the little belly. The doctor smiled at me.

Give him the tablets and he'll be okay. Only thing I will say is he's small for his age.

He pulled the batcha's toe.

You're a lucky boy. I could see you is your ma and pa eyeball.

Doc again refused to take any money and said he expected Chunksee to be completely better by tomorrow.

Once he got us home Boysie said he had to leave. Doris was having some big dinner party and he had to get his tail back before she cussed him. I minded but not too much. After all, we'd enjoyed another family outing.

ROSIE

The sky looked set up to rain. Surprisingly not a drop fell as we followed the cortège to the church or during the service. Granny cried the whole time. After that eulogy there wasn't a dry eye in the church, me included. As we stepped outside to walk the piece of road to the cemetery the heavens opened good and proper. It seemed like God's way of washing our faces and distracting us from grief. We stood in the rain and sang hymns while earth was piled over the coffin. The spirits were given a last drop of rum and I threw a good handful of dirt on the casket. Most people stayed singing until the grave diggers had placed the wreaths on the mound.

I wanted to show my face at the wake but my wet dress was clingy and I didn't want to catch cold. To besides, Etty would be anxious to maco every detail. Aye, aye, imagine my surprise when I found Pearl serving behind the bar.

What you doing here, girl? Etty have you working?

Nobody was seeing to the bar.

How you mean? Since when you here?

Maybe two-ish.

But I leave Etty here good good.

I was hustling to the church and as I was passing a fella asked me how come the shop open and nobody there. I walked in. Your cash pan was skin open, empty and not a soul in the back. I say to myself you stepped out and get robbed so best I hold on. I ended up missing the whole funeral.

I real sorry. Go by the wake house now and pay your
respects.

I went in we room. Etty clothes hang up, make-up fling on the
dressing table, all exactly as it was this morning. I walked around
in the back calling for she. Pearl shook she head.

Etty gone and cash gone. Put two and two together.

I turned and screamed right in she face.

She don't have to thief nothing. You feel you better than she?
Eh? Answer me. You feel you better than she?

Pearl's mouth dropped open.

Right. This is the thanks I get? I should have left your kiss-
me-ass shop for bandits to take everything.

She marched off and I was left staring at the few customers in
the bar. No one said a word. I took a rag and wiped down the
counter while asking if anyone had seen Etty. No one had since
morning.

Whole afternoon into night I stared at the road waiting but
she didn't appear. Malcolm passed by and suggested going to
the police.

You think them care?

Somebody might've seen she. You don't know.

True.

Morning time, still no Etty. Instead of opening the shop I went
to the station. No damn use. The duty sergeant said Etty ain't

technically missing if it's only since yesterday she's gone. Wait another day.

Rumours were flying about the village, some probably spread by Pearl. Mostly people were saying I 'fraid the truth. The girl use me, thief from me, and first chance she get, she ups and gone. Even Malcolm reached with that talk.

You don't have to feel shame that she's an ungrateful thief. You ain't do nothing wrong.

I watched him cut eye.

It's you who don't get it. Etty would never do a thing like that.

I took a deep breath.

Am I the only one thinking Bumper had a hand in this? He was mad vex when the villagers turned in he tail. He take she. I know it in my bones.

Take she where? I'm up and down in the clubs and she ain't there. And Bumper looks cool as ever.

I'm telling the police Bumper take she.

Malcolm talked me down. I had zero proof that Bumper had been near the shop when she disappeared. Going to the police about Bumper will put Boysie in the frame. Now that would bring real big trouble on my head.

DORIS

I run a respectable household in a town where people love to maco your business. Four o'clock in the afternoon, two church ladies were with me in the living room taking tea and deep into Bible study. Boysie and his partners burst in straight from taking a sea bath. I was so shame. He's done this before. Soon as he saw we had guests he should have taken his wet, sandy gang round the back. But no. The Rajah will do what he wants, when he wants, even if it is an embarrassment to his wife. Never mind I'm trying to raise our station in society.

To make matters worse he'd brought an old lady and her two dirty overstuffed sacks and plonked her on my armchair. The stench was like the worst latrine. Bareback Boysie stood there dripping sea water on my good rug and explained how he had passed her this morning. On the way back home she was in the same spot, homeless, no family or friend. Big-heart Boysie got the fellas to pack she up, her up, and now she was mine. I could feel the heat in my cheeks.

> Boysie honey, we should talk about this in private. You see we have guests.

> But you does play big-time Catholic. What all you reading? Eh? Ain't the Bible say do unto others as you would have them do unto you? We could be on the street in we old age. Ain't we would want somebody to take we in?

Jesus's Sermon on the Mount. Caught by my own scriptures. I didn't know where to turn because Boysie was shaming me from all sides. The church ladies smiled and excused themselves. It was getting late. I could see they were suffering from the pong that Miss Rita, that's she name, her name, was giving off.

In our backyard is a small house like the one I lived in as a maid. Boysie was grinning when he insisted that was now the old woman's home. Of course that was the end of his involvement with Miss Rita. She had become my responsibility that I didn't want.

Miss Rita's living rent-free and taking three square meals a day. And don't think because she's old she only eats a little bit. That woman could put away a man-sized plate of food easy. Instead of counting the Lord's many blessings, I have to hear her wailing (that can't be singing) 'Abide With Me'. If she wasn't belting that one out I had to brace myself for 'Crown Him Lord of All'. Boysie doesn't give me a drop of sympathy. Singing brought the old lady a little happiness so I must put up and shut up. In my own house to boot. In fact he found the whole thing a big joke.

I could just about live with the loud hymn croaking but then Miss Rita interfered in my business. I came home from having my hair straightened and styled in two rolls with a centre parting so it's heart-shaped. It's not every day I get invited to lunch with a big-time French Creole family like the de Verteuils. But the good mood didn't survive walking into my living room. Miss Rita had taken it upon herself, with the help of the maid and yard boy, who should both know better, to rearrange the three-piece suite. My hands began shaking with rage.

Why?

The old witch, who only bathes when the maid drags her under the shower, came out swinging.

I do you a favour. A big favour. You had the furnitures them looking choke up choke up. I fixed it more better.

Miss Rita, it's my living room. Out there is your place. Move things around there but not in my house.

Well, her face set up like rain. She actually stamped she foot, her foot. I called the maid and told her to help the yard boy fix the place back how I had it for me please. Right now. Same time Boysie came in from the kitchen.

I didn't know you were home. You saw this nonsense?

Boysie skinned he teeth.

I find the way she do it looks better. Leave it so.

He might as well have slapped me in front everybody because that is what it felt like. I went and changed my clothes and left for lunch without saying boo to anybody.

From then on I avoided Miss Rita. Things were quieter for a few months. But every so often she tried a thing. A chair might be moved from dining room to living room, or she would bully the maid about not putting enough chadon beni in the stew beef. Nobody can accuse me of showing the lady bad mind. I bit my tongue and carried on. Boysie feels Miss Rita will break me? Maybe this would have finished that cunumunu, Mana Lala. It's not even denting Doris de Leon so he can put that in his pipe and smoke it.

ROSIE

Bumper banged the counter.

Run two beers. Make sure they're beastly cold.

He and Firekong were back rent collecting. That was Boysie showing me exactly what he thought. Well, if he doesn't want to help that is he business.

I find you well boldface coming here. Like you ain't understand what we said last time.

I think this village knows we can come and go anytime we damn well please. Boss man sent me.

I offered the envelope. He grabbed but I held on.

Where's Etty?

What you're asking me for?

Firekong grinned. I eyed them both.

You better watch your step. Boysie know 'bout you.

Bumper laughed hard.

Rajah tell me to make you shut your mouth. Spreading maliciousness. We look after we girls. It's all of we for she and she for all of we. One family.

I felt my snake hiss in my chest and wriggle in my feet. I shouted,

What you do with Etty?

He skinned he teeth at me.

You mad, yes. Let go the envelope and stop wasting my time.

Where she? I have to know.

We eyes made four. He leaned in and whispered,

Etty gone far far below and she ain't coming back.

After that the hiss of my snake drowned out everything. I don't know how the knife reached in my hand. I don't remember going for Bumper and I don't remember him turning the knife on me. But all that happened. Two weeks I've been on the ward in Port of Spain General, two weeks where in between the pain and confusion of ten stab wounds I faced the worst. Bumper has killed Etty and dumped she somewhere. He'd better accept I won't rest until he pays in full for that. In full.

DORIS

Mammy's birthday was coming up so I loaded the car with all kind of nice things and the driver took me to Toco for a long weekend. On the journey back to Port of Spain, I craned my neck for a first glimpse of the house. We have a huge, pretty pretty mauve bougainvillea growing on the fence that people use when giving directions. I've heard people walking past saying the directions they had were to take the turning after the house with the big mauve bougainvillea. I was looking and looking. But eh eh, I can't see the flowers. Only when the driver stopped by a bare fence did I realise my beautiful bougainvillea was completely gone, cut back to stumps. A cold sweat soaked me instantly. The yard boy ran to the car to take out my bags. I grabbed his hand.

What happened? My bougainvillea?

He bit his lip.

Miss Rita tell me to chop it down low low.

What? Why? Since when Miss Rita does give you orders?

She said how the plant had blight. It had to go or the blight would spread.

You ever see any blight on them flowers?

He didn't answer.

Look, leave my yard right now before I do something I regret. You hear me? Go home and don't ever let me catch you near my house again. Boysie will deal with you later.

I walked straight to Miss Rita's place, took a deep breath and as calmly as I could, asked why she'd interfered with my bougainvillea that had been growing for years, before I even moved in. As usual she was wrong and strong. The same blight story came out.

> Even if it had blight why you took it upon yourself to order it cut down? It's not your bougainvillea. It's not your house. It's not your yard. You could have waited until I came back and showed me the problem. If it had a problem. I've never saw a speck of blight. Not once.

Miss Rita came closer and watched me dead in my eye.

> You can't tell me nothing. The Rajah said I have rights. From now on I don't want you stepping inside my place. You hear me?

I felt a surge of heat burst out my chest and radiate to my stomach, legs and arms. In that moment I could have snapped her neck the way we used to kill yard fowls. Something had to be wrong with my ears. This stinking freeloader that Boysie bring to live in my house is telling me not to come near my own property? And he told her she has rights? I didn't hold back.

> What the ass wrong with you? You gone crazy or what? This is my kiss-me-ass house. Tenant? Tenant does pay rent. They does buy their own food. Rights? I will kick you and your rights so far you'll reach Tobago. You have no blasted rights to my house and land. This is all mine. Mine.

She was so close I inhaled her sour breath.

> If I say I have rights, I have rights.

> No, you old nasty toad.

> Who you calling toad?

Right, I'm calling my husband. I want you out of my house before the sun set.

I felt the blow connect with my nose. My hands went to my face and came back bloody.

No Toco red whore will ever talk to me so. You hear? Who you feel you is? You is nothing but a gold-digger. And that coolie husband belongs in jail. All you feel I don't know nothing? I know plenty.

I wanted to cuss from she mother come down, but I kept my dignity and walked back to the house barely seeing through my tears. I found the driver outside, told him to fetch Boysie immediately, and waited locked in my bedroom.

Boysie and he partners took their cool time to reach. He must have realised I meant it when I said this was the last straw. My nose didn't feel broken but that was only the grace of God protecting me.

There and then his fellas packed Miss Rita and drove her to the exact spot they'd picked her up eight months earlier. If Boysie brings another person to hurt my head I'll be the one packing. Just try me.

Maybe Boysie noticed my sour face because he bought us gold rings. His had a star and mine a crescent moon. I left it in the box and faked a smile.

You're too sweet.

Mohansingh has the matching chain and earrings. You want the set?

I shook my head.

You still upset about that crazy old bat? She's lucky I don't beat woman.

The honeymoon flashed through my mind. I took the ring out the box.

Pretty.

He grinned.

Buy the set and wear it to races with me Saturday. I want everybody to see my nice, fair-skin wife.

You know I'm not one for the horse racing.

But I want you to come. Please.

A please from Boysie's mouth is a big deal. I had to try. It was my wifely duty.

Races day I hit them with a real nice peach-and-black dress with long black gloves. It was fitted on top, buttons all the way down the front and a thin belt pulling in my waist. Why I should hide what God gave me? As I looked in the mirror to put on my new gold chain, earrings and ring I felt my old self coming back.

Doris, girl, you've still got it.

Boysie yelled from the bathroom,

What?

Never mind. I was talking to myself.

*

Queen's Park Savannah was jam-packed. Boysie's runners were busy taking bets although every last one stopped and practically bowed as he passed. People rushed to shake his hand or call out,

Rajah, Rajah.

King of Port of Spain, over here.

Check the suit. The Rajah looking like a star boy.

King, a little raise, nah.

He whispered that I must remind him to tell Chunksee something about the Rajah.

What?

When I dead he should put 'The Rajah' on my headstone. Better yet, put 'The Vagabond Rajah'. I prefer that. I hustled and worked hard for what I get and that is how I want people to remember me. Make sure Chunksee do that for me.

I squeezed his hand.

Hush your mouth. You have years and years to go still.

Business was calling so he took me to the stands, got me a cold coconut water and seated me next to some white people he knew through playing cards. Everything was going good good when people began shuffling to make place, shaking hands, cheek-kissing. I leaned forward to get a better look and went instantly cold. Mistress. Since when they like races? My heart was jumping in my chest. They sat feet away. I froze, not knowing if they'd seen me too. Before I could work out what to do my neighbour was touching my shoulder.

Doris, let me introduce you. Richard and Heather Bernard, this is Boysie Singh's wife. The famous Boysie Singh.

We all nodded politely and said hello like we were only now meeting. My neighbour, whose name had gone clean out of my head, was going on and on about Boysie.

Look through your binoculars. Look. That group over there. Can you see?

She pointed to a small crowd.

That's him. The locals positively adore the man. I hear he throws a carpet of silver coins and dollar bills throughout the grounds. So generous, don't you think?

The Bernards nodded and Mister, I mean, Richard, turned to talk betting odds with a man on his left. I faced forward and hoped they would talk among themselves which, thank the Lord, they did. Trapped, and without Boysie for protection, I didn't know what to do. During the next race, people shouting, eyes glued on the horses, I took a chance and rushed out the opposite end. Lucky thing I had on shoes I could walk fast in yes because I practically ran to where the Buick was parked. In the shade, the driver was pulling a five. I begged him send Boysie a message that I had a bad headache and my belly was griping me. It was an emergency and I really needed to go home. Without a special excuse Boysie will be hopping mad I didn't stay where he put me. It was either Boysie's temper or possible humiliation to my face. Hopefully the takings will be big and he won't care how long I'd stayed at the races.

As I peeled off my dress and put away my jewellery, it upset me to think what them white people probably said after I left. Look what the world's coming to when a maid can play mistress. Here I am with my big house, big car, driver to carry me all about, nice clothes, shoes and plenty gold. I had all this and they looked at me and thought, corbeaux can't eat sponge cake.

MANA LALA

I was cleaning the soot in the kerosene lamp shades while Boysie and Chunksee were in the yard, two heads deep inside the jitney's engine. He's turning fourteen, school-leaving time, and I have a feeling he will go into the mechanic trade. That's all he's interested in. Boysie gave him an old engine which he is forever taking apart and putting together again. Hours and hours he will be out there happy as pappy, covered head to toe in grease fixing this and that.

Every so often the breeze blew their words towards me. Most of it was nothing I cared about. Then suddenly I caught a piece of talk. Something Boysie was saying. If I heard right he was telling the batcha that Doris loves him and would like him to spend more time by them. I strained to hear more. It was hard to get it all without them noticing me. What reached my ears was frightening me. Chunksee was getting age and should follow he pa, understanding the gambling business because one day it's he who will be running everything.

He gone crazy or what? I don't know which piece of news sent my blood pressure up more. Say what you want, I've kept Chunksee from all Boysie's dealings. I might look poohar but I have eyes and ears. Now Boysie wants the batcha in the middle of all that gambling, fighting, thiefing and what have you? Not while I name mother. And as for that Doris. If she want boy child she should damn well make she own instead of trying to take mines.

While I was getting blue vex and ready to give Boysie a piece of my mind, Chunksee started up. Now I really couldn't believe what was going on. He said he wanted to work with Boysie and why did he have to stay in school a whole year more. He could leave now and learn everything from Pa. And Boysie was agreeing with him saying he never learnt much from book either. In the school of life Chunksee would learn what really mattered. I wanted to wring both their necks. But time longer than twine, yes. Before today done I will get my chance. Watch me.

I waited the rest of the afternoon liming with Subhagya Mausi. If she could talk she would wonder why Boysie's filling Chunksee's head with all that foolishness. That is the life he want for he one piece of child? Mausi's children ain't been the best but she made sure they all went to school and all of them doing well. In fact they're doing so well that they don't have time for their old mother. Their loss because she is no trouble. I could sit down and talk with she whole day. It's plenty less lonely since she moved in, that's for sure.

My big and small man came in for food around half past five. I stayed quiet, waiting to hear if they would say anything. Silence. Boysie asked me to pass the bottle of pepper sauce. I put it in front him on the table. Things already tense. Putting pepper sauce directly in a person's hand is asking for a quarrel to break out between them.

Your hand still sweet, Mana Lala.

I smiled even though I didn't mean to. He don't share nice words just so.

Nobody's roti does come out soft soft like yours.

My face burned.

Aye, you're blushing? A big woman like you? But you is the best cook round here.

I took the dirty wares to the sink, shame to be caught red-faced like a schoolgirl.

Well, I'm making a move. Chunksee spending the next few weeks by me. Just until the term done. Then it's holidays anyway.

He was talking to my back. I didn't turn around.

He should finish school by me, nah. He uniform and everything here already. Holidays he could come by you.

No. I want him with me when I'm doing my rounds. And he wants to.

I swung round.

Your pa talking truth? You want to go by he?

Chunksee looked at Boysie.

I asked a question. What happen to your mouth?

The batcha nodded.

Oh ho. All right.

Boysie pushed in.

Why you're carrying on so? It's no time at all. Beta old enough to know he mind.

That's what he want or what you want? The bai need an education or he go end up like we.

My heart was racing. I may have thought this before but the words never actually left my mouth. Boysie glared at me.

You drink puncheon or what? I said the boy coming by me. He don't have to go back to school for the term.

I heard the edge in he voice, sharp as that sword he does keep, and lowered my eyes.

Sorry, Boysie.

And I don't know about next term either.

He grunted then turned to Chunksee.

It's late already and some partners coming for a little cards. Stay tonight and tomorrow I will come for you after I collect Doris from church. That will give you time to pack and thing.

I could see Chunksee was itching to go now but he knew not to cross he pa.

Okay.

Good, beta. Tomorrow.

*

Cocoa tea in the morning is a must for Chunksee.

I put a small pot of water to hot up and grated the cocoa ball so the shavings fell directly in the water. It melted and thickened as I gently stirred. Time for a big spoon of sugar and a sprinkling of the white powder. Stir, stir, stir it up. All melted. Into batcha's favourite white enamel cup with the blue rim. I didn't need to check if he drank it all. Cocoa tea in the morning is a must, ever since he small.

*

The batcha wanted to pull out the engine. I reminded him Boysie was coming soon. Less than an hour and he should be here.

Help me shell some pigeon peas before you go.

Other boy children he age would've rolled their eye or talked back. Not Chunksee. He sat on the ground and began cracking the shells, tossing the peas in the bowls and throwing the skins on the gazette paper at the side. I watched the clock.

Twenty minutes later he left and came back with a small towel.

What's that for?

It making hot. I'm sweating.

Really?

I want some breeze.

He was fanning and looked cokey-eyed.

You're good, beta?

He shook he head.

I can't see.

He closed his eyes and his shoulders began twitching.

Chunksee, beta, what happening?

He was twitching more now, head slumped. I rushed to hold him before he fell back. His face looked like it was melting. Oh Lord, where was Boysie? Beta was having a fit. I panicked. What to do? Could I leave him for a minute and run get the neighbour? He might swallow he tongue. I tried to scream the word help but only a strange mumble came out. I tried again. The same. I took a deep breath and screamed as loud as I could,

Neighbour! Neighbour!

The gods brought people running from both sides. About six, seven people reached. Chunksee had stopped fitting but he was floppy like a dhalpuri. I heard someone ask if he was breathing and another say yes. A man took charge and said we're carrying him to hospital now now. I heard myself saying,

No. Boysie coming. We'll carry beta hospital together.

Mana Lala, you can't wait for Boysie. This child real sick. Somebody will tell Boysie to meet all you. Pundit Gosine carrying you in he car.

I could barely understand what was happening. People were saying move to give the child room. Somebody was fanning him. I heard voices talking. A hand touched my shoulder as I held Chunksee.

Don't worry. Just now.

They got the batcha in the car, his head on my lap. I managed to ask that somebody stay with Subhagya Mausi. Pundit Gosine put he foot down on the gas and didn't lift it up until we reached Port of Spain General. On the way Chunksee had another fit. He was sweating and groaning.

Hold the bai head.

I whispered,

Nearly there. Hold on, beta. Nearly there.

Pundit Gosine pulled up right where the ambulance does park, lifted Chunksee and rushed inside. I ran behind them.

One look at the child and they sent us straight to the nurse. She took Chunksee and asked us to wait outside. Someone was bawling and I was shocked to realise it was me.

That was the longest hour of my life.

When they called me in Chunksee's eyes were open. He looked weak. This doctor wasn't smiling like the one in Belmont. I sat on the edge of the bed and hugged the batcha.

Now, where was this child before he came to Casualty?

Home, doctor.

You told the nurse all he had this morning was a cup of hot cocoa. Correct?

Yes, doctor.

And he was only at the home?

I nodded. He sighed.

Well, he's lucky. He ingested an extremely toxic substance.

How you mean?

Rat poison. He was poisoned.

Tears streamed down my face and fell on Chunksee's hair.

You need to check around the house and make sure there are no poisons that are easy for people to get hold of. Even putting his hand on a bag with rat poison for example. Some might transfer to his hand and he puts his hand in his mouth. Think how easily this could happen if you are not careful?

Through blinding tears I nodded.

You could have lost him.

I wiped my face with my orhni and the inside of my elbow. I could have lost him. What if I'd insisted on waiting for Boysie so we could have another family outing? And where was he? That man still hadn't reached the hospital. Probably in an all fours game. I kissed the top of Chunksee's head. I could have lost him.

Part of me went quiet and still. The woman who left that hospital wasn't the one who went in. I could have lost him. And for what? Is Boysie worth this? I'm doing chupidness trying to keep what's already lost away.

PART FOUR

ROSIE

I don't deserve the friends I have, I really don't. The day of Boy Boy's funeral I'd cussed Pearl and behaved like a proper wajang when I couldn't find Etty. This is the same Pearl who heard I was in hospital and kept the shop going. Now I'm home getting my strength back I said I'd manage.

Hush your mouth. You ain't heal good yet.

But Pearl, ain't you done with this running shop business? I thought you wanted to take things easy?

It ain't my shop so the headache's not the same. To besides, I don't like sitting down home doing nothing. Best to keep busy. You know the devil love idleness.

But I owe you for all you gone and do. I was going to change the door where the wood was rotting. And the front needed painting. You do everything.

Don't study that. I had time.

One-one my regulars have been strolling in giving me news. I missed Fia's big prayer meeting. Forget the blessing. Nothing does taste good like that woman's prayers food. Dhalpuri roti, curry pumpkin, channa and aloo, curry mango, curry chicken and if you asked Fia quiet quiet, she'll show you where the curry duck's covered down in a pot. With Boy Boy's passing the village has banded together making sure granny's good and not missing clinic. A niece is moving in soon, thank God. I keep expecting to see Boy Boy walking past the shop in he white shirt-jack and dark pants. Oh, and like crime going up. Somebody thief Winston's taxi. Police ain't hold nobody but town say it's a group of Venezuelans who over here making commess. I say rounds them up and send they tail back to the Main.

Strange that in all the macoing Boysie's name ain't pass.

What about the Rajah or he lieutenants?

Heads around the bar nodded. Most avoided catching my eye.

Tell me. My back broad.

Teach cleared he throat.

Boysie ain't happy you attacked he man. He say that's like knifing he-self.

I waited.

Don't worry, Rosie.

Boysie ain't realise that if I'd planned for Bumper he was getting my special knife, Fang. And he still might.

So what else the big bad Rajah say? Might as well know.

The fellas got together and fixed up.

Fixed up what?

Teach steupsed.

Girl, don't worry. He came and put on a performance. Well cussed and carried on. Woman can't keep rum shop. How you're too tied-up with Etty.

I could see he was holding back.

And?

He mash up the shop door. He threw a flambeau in the road.

I got frightened one time.

He burn down anything? I ain't see nothing burnt.

Look, the shop in one piece. Just smoke blackened the front and we painted it over.

My heart was racing but I band my belly and asked if anything else happened.

I believe your rent gone up.

Pearl's hands on my shoulders gently guided me away from the counter.

Doc said don't stress yourself. Your pressure done high. Deal with Boysie when Boysie come.

*

Every day I feel a little better in myself and as it was a quiet Sunday I made Pearl take an early night. I stayed ole talking and serving the few customers who were liming. Nancoo from the next village was knocking back the rum steady.

What happen, Nancoo? Like the woman giving you pressure?

What woman? I is a confirmed bachelor. Fishing is the only woman I taking on these days.

I bent closer.

Your money nice but I think you're done for tonight.

Two half-open red eyes watched me.

Don't carry on so nah. I ain't ready to face them four walls.

He closed his eyes and swayed. I thought he might fall forward but suddenly the eyes opened big big.

Rosie, I strong like an ox. Ain't you know that?

I nodded.

But this thing have me mashed up.

What happen? I hear you was checking. What she name again?

Hush. That's for me to know and you to find out.

Ranita? Yes, that's she name.

He looked past me.

Things cool with she. It's the sea. When you're out there all kind of thing does happen. But not this. I wasn't expecting this.

My ears pricked up. Nancoo fished with Boysie. I've seen them leaving from Leper Asylum jetty.

It probably won't make news.

What?

I gathered the empty beer bottles and said goodnight as customers left to find their own homes.

Come, Rosie. I have a secret.

I faced him sideways so my ears was near he mouth. He whispered.

You like me? Say you like me, nah.

I steupsed.

I just come out of hospital and I have to put up with this chupidness? Look man, make tracks. I thought you had something important to tell me.

He looked like he'd lost he last friend in the whole world.

I have to tell somebody.

Go rest nah, man.

I know you'll believe me.

Listen, done the talk for tonight.

He grabbed my wrists.

Boysie killed and I helped.

Well, now he had my attention.

Shhhh. Bush have ears. Let me shut the shop.

It tumbled out. Yes he was drunk but I think it's truth he talk. He had no reason to confess otherwise. What I understand is that Nancoo was crew on Boysie's trip yesterday. Some fishermen were just cooling themselves in a boat off Waterloo village. Boysie pulled up. Both the crew and fishermen thought it was to take a laugh, maybe even beg for fish to carry home. Oh no. Boysie ordered Nancoo and the rest of the fellas to tie the fishermen to pieces of iron and throw them in the sea. He then personally started a fire that burnt their boat.

Rosie, you have to know I didn't want to tie them up. I didn't.

But disobey Boysie and he go kill you easy easy as if he killing a fly.

Who were the fishermen?

He paused.

You'll know them.

Nancoo started crying softly.

Mr Tate.

Our Mr Tate? With the bicycle selling fish? But he is Boysie's friend. I'm sure of that. And how come we ain't hear nothing?

People think he's still out fishing.

I poured two shots of rum.

But why? Tate had money?

Money? Them was liming. All Boysie get was the boat engine. And them wasn't going to put up no fight if Boysie had pointed a gun and told them to hand it over.

That is what he kill not one but two man for? An engine? I hear engines scarce but that is pure wickedness.

Nancoo's cheeks were wet with tears.

Mr Tate's voice is in my head. He begged, he begged, he begged. He wife in a wheelchair. He minding grandchildren. Boysie didn't have an ounce of mercy.

I wanted to know, and same time I didn't want to find out more. He gave me anyway.

Boysie laughed at poor Mr Tate. Imagine that. He laughed. Firekong was pointing gun at them the whole time. Boysie told them to say their prayers because they were about to meet God or Satan, one of the two.

Nancoo started fresh bawling.

Lord Jesus, forgive me.

I poured us both a next shot.

It have more.

What you mean more, Nancoo? My heart can't take more. You know Boysie have it in for me.

Tate's boat burning made big smoke. A Vene fisherman and he two boys stopped to see if anybody needed help. Why them do that?

I shook my head.

Don't tell me Boysie attacked them too.

He made us tie them up same way and throw them in the sea. They was still living.

Nancoo put he head on the counter and well bawl. I rubbed he back. Better out than in.

He should've used the gun rather than suffer the people.

Nancoo swiped he face on his dirty shirt.

Rosie, girl, I feel he enjoyed hearing them beg for life. You know what it is to have a grown man shitting he-self because he frightened? Nah, Boysie liked to make the torture last long. He mind must have disease. No normal human being go behave so. And from what I hear this ain't the first or even the twenty-first. He come like a pirate these days. All I know is this was my first and it will be the last one ever. I ain't going to sea with Boysie no matter what.

Telling this story had made the two of we hit the bottle. At some point I reached over and gently kissed his cheeks, his eyelids, the forehead. He grabbed me and we kissed through and through. It was like lighting a match. I bit his neck and he bawled out,

Not so hard.

I steupsed.

Fuck me hard or go home.

He stayed.

A few days later Nancoo was found dead. Snake bite poisoning. I had to help the fella. No way he could have lived with what he'd done on the *Marie Louise* and Boysie would never have let him walk away. Just how he went for Mr Tate, the Rajah's coming for me. My snakeness is the only protection I have.

MANA LALA

I think even Subhagya Mausi must find the house is missing Chunksee. Boysie's in and out as he please, hiding up whatever he's hiding in the shed. I can't ask a question because it's he money that fixed the house and built the shed. I'm trying to keep busy rather than hold him up in ole talk or put out food for him. He have wife and, from what I hear, second wife and third wife too. Imagine I ain't even make it as an outside wife with a number.

Mausi, you married when you had how much years? Fourteen? I don't know if you can understand how much I wish I didn't love that man. He's in my life but he don't want me. Some days I think it would have been easier if he'd just stopped coming here, didn't have nothing to do with me. He here and he not here same time. I know, I know. You does have to put up with me going on and on about how we belong together and should have married and had more children. It real hard to let go of that. I ain't love a next man and Boysie well know that. He knows. That's why he does take advantage. But Mausi, you think I could learn to un-love him? How else I go manage?

Subhagya Mausi's behhhh behhhh was soft as if to say hush. So it go.

We're lucky if two times in the month Chunksee comes to see we. Soon as he smelt the sea air in the fishing village, Cedros, that was it. He was gone. I wouldn't be surprised if he lived by the water forever. At least he looks happy. Boysie had him swimming like a fish almost as soon as the batcha could walk. The fellas working for Boysie all say the same thing. Chunksee is a natural. Give him any one of them thirty boats Boysie owns and Chunksee can fix the engine blindfolded. At least Boysie had enough sense not to throw the bai in the club scene. I don't know what I would've done if that had happened.

*

The other day me niece got married and I managed to pull Chunksee away from Cedros to go to the shaadi. They're from up Santa Cruz side. Boysie got invitation but he and Doris too big for a village wedding. Ma remained behind with Subhagya Mausi. She's wasting away. Thing is she can hold on like this for a long time. At least she's comfortable, no pain, and she's lived a long life. Ma can sleep good knowing she did she best by she sister. It's me that will miss Subhagya Mausi most. What will happen to me when I ain't have a soul to listen to my problems?

Chunksee chatted away in the taxi about fishing and Cedros. I'm glad just to see how he eyes bright bright.

Ma, them Cedros fishermen don't like to go past Soldier Point. They 'fraid the coastguard them.

You're talking like I know where Soldier Point is.

About seven miles from Icacos.

You think your ole ma know where that is? One of these days I'll see that part of Trinidad.

Well we is the only ones fishing way past Soldier Point.

The driver took the corner a little too fast.

Aye, slow down little bit. My heart can't take this speed.

The taxi driver looked in the rear-view mirror and grinned.

Sorry.

You'll know sorry if anything happen. This is Boysie Singh's son you have in the back seat.

Everything changed one time. I didn't have cause to say another word to him.

Anyhow, beta, you was telling me.

Well we trouble these days is right in Cedros. The people living down there love Pa. But you see the fishermen them? They jealous we bad.

What kind of trouble?

I don't really understand all what going on.

He chewed a nail.

Stop biting off your nail. You're hungry?

He laughed.

Well, you stop sucking ice then.

When last you see me sucking ice? If I could stop then you can leave your poor nails alone. Let them grow.

How come you stopped?

I had to think.

I ain't know. It started way back when you was in my belly. That I remember. And since Mausi living by we I just stopped. Maybe I'm too busy caring for she day and night.

He stuck a fingernail in he mouth and I play-slapped it out.

You were telling me about the trouble down Cedros.

People does be thiefing we fishing pots steady. We put them out and when we go back they're gone or empty empty.

All you know who doing that?

He shook he head.

You know if your pa catch them what go happen.

I should not have said that. Chunksee thinks the sun shines out of Boysie's backside.

That's true. It nearly had shooting over this the other day.

What happen? You were there?

Dhanraj, a nice fella, he tell Pa he saw a next boat pulling up Pa's pots. Pa see red one time. He and the fellas loaded gun and thing and jumped in a pirogue.

Oh my gosh. I hope you didn't go in boat.

Nah. Pa wouldn't let me. Wait for the story, nah. You keep jooking in.

I do like I was zipping my mouth shut.

They ain't find a single boat out there. When Pa reached back he had that look in he eye.

I tried to keep my face from saying yes, I know exactly what you mean.

I thought Pa was going to fight somebody. He and the whole gang went straight by Dadie's Dry Goods, right in the heart of Cedros. And Pa them walking with guns and well shouting and cussing. Pa warned the village that if he so much as catch anybody eyeball on he fishing pots he go shoot them. And when he done he go shoot their mother, their father, their children, their cousin, any and everybody he can find.

Oh jeez-an-ages. You heard him for yourself? I'm sure he was just saying that to frighten people.

You think so?

Yes. That's your pa making grand charge.

I don't know. He's talking about moving everything back up town side.

Well, I'll be glad for that.

But Cedros nice too bad. The air different down there. Everything clean. And if you see birds down there. They have these little brown-and-white ones up and down.

It not too quiet down there in all that bush?

I like it so.

He made to bite a nail. I pulled he hand away and planted a kiss. My beta. My one and only piece of child.

DORIS

Who is supposed to do what is clear clear. I look after the home and he has the business. Years I haven't stepped inside one of his clubs. Years. Now Boysie's asking for a hand. Some confusion over the licence or no licence of the Dorset club.

> Why you can't go? I've never been to a police station. People might think I've done something wrong.

> That is exactly why I want you to deal with this for me. You'll smooth things. In two-twos this will fix.

I steupsed and went back to plaiting my hair at the dressing table.

> I don't have time to go no police station.

He locked eyes with me in the mirror and I saw the precise second my husband changed from nice Boysie to honeymoon Boysie shoving me out the car. My back stiffened.

> No? Okay. All right. So, tell me something. You're happy to spend spend spend my money. But when I ask you to do me a little favour you can't help. Where you think the money does come from to keep you knocking about like a queen? Eh? You ain't do a day's work since we together.

He flung an envelope at me. I dodged and it fell on the dressing table knocking over my lipsticks.

> If you know what's good for you, you will go to the police station and sort this out before I reach back home.

Or what?

He bent close to my ear.

Or it's me and you today.

*

I looked through my wardrobe. The law is you can't go in any
official building without covered arms. My grey dress with the
high collar, fitted sleeves, waist nipped in and a skirt that flared
past my knee was the thing. Oh, and matching gloves. That
should keep the boys happy. But how Boysie talked to me rough
so ain't nice, isn't nice. What happen? Like I don't have feelings.
Anyhow, for the sake of peace I'll do my best.

I walked into Besson Street Police Station. Even in my
no-nonsense outfit the desk sergeant watched me up and down
like I was for sale. I swallowed and gave him a sweet eye.

Good morning, officer.

It's a good morning now. How can I help a lovely lady like
you?

I'm Mrs Boysie Singh and I need to see whoever is in charge
of club licences. You know who Boysie Singh is, right?

He laughed.

Papayo, well look at my crosses. Mrs Boysie Singh in my
station. Don't dig no horrors. Take a seat and I'll find
somebody to help you.

A good half-hour passed with me sitting on a hard bench like a
common criminal. I went back to the desk.

I'm still waiting.

For true?

Yes, for true.

I could tell he hadn't done a fart. This is the first and last time I'm getting involved in Boysie's daily business. Just then a serious-looking officer stopped by the desk. He looked down at the desk sergeant's notebook and back up at me.

You getting through?

Things changed one time. He took me to a small side room and began writing in a small pad. I showed him Boysie's letter.

You see, Officer—

He cut me off.

Sergeant Suerattan.

You see, Sergeant Suerattan, the police want to take away the licence from Dorset club at 55 Queen Street. Well how they could do that if we never had a licence in the first place?

I see the problem.

We can't quarrel about a licence we never had.

You're so right. I can't say I know how to sort this out without plenty headache.

While he was busy writing I don't know why but I relaxed for the first time since stepping inside the station.

You have trouble with these licences?

He looked up. I noticed his eyes carried the soft smile that had started on his lips. This one ain't mamaguying me.

Not too much. But your husband is one of the biggest club owners in the country. Anything he's involved in we hear about it.

I sighed.

People are jealous of Boysie.

Imagine my shock when he nodded in agreement.

Truth.

He lowered his voice and brought those eyes and lips closer.

Plenty people would be happy to see all your husband's clubs closed down. We're under pressure from the boss to close Dorset. But he's under he own pressure. I will explain that we can't close down what never opened. But Mr Singh should keep Dorset quiet.

Sergeant Suerattan, I will say a special prayer tonight thanking Jesus for bringing you into my life today. You've taken a weight off my shoulders. My husband will be so happy.

His eyes smiled again. My skin warmed when he spoke.

You look real familiar. By any chance your family from Morvant side?

Toco. And yes, I know all you think it's only bush up so.

Well now he was skinning he teeth, his teeth.

That is it. Toco. You know Pinky and Fish?

Fish, who don't like to wear shoes? And his sister Pinky? We grow up together.

Trinidad ain't play it small, yes. Sergeant Suerattan's cousin is their cousin by marriage which makes them pumpkin vine family. Through them he knew our village. Strange that we never bounced up.

Ask your Toco friends about Harry. Harry Suerattan. And you mind me asking what's your Christian name?

Doris. Up Toco side they know me as Doris de Leon.

Doris. Nice name. Strong.

I don't feel strong these days.

What the Lord say? This too shall pass. Remember that.

Oh, so you know your Bible?

How you mean? I'm a Church man. Presbyterian.

Catholic.

White people Church.

Nah, man. It's not like that. Come to a service and see for yourself.

He laughed.

I'm good with my little church, thank you very much.

I left feeling excited. Of course, I was happy to be able to tell Boysie not to worry about Dorset. But deep down I was remembering Sergeant Harry Suerattan's smiling eyes. I might need to become Boysie's right hand for everything to do with the police and licensing. He won't be able to carry on that I'm useless then. Kill two birds one time.

ROSIE

Slowly, slowly the stab wounds have healed. Only one got infected and took longer. Still, nothing a little Mercurochrome and aloes couldn't fix. I waited for Boysie to reach. He took his time and when he came it was with Three Little Threes spinning in he hand. I braced myself. People like Boysie can smell fear.

Aye Rosie, I hear you land up in Port of Spain General. What you was trying to do, girl? Pulling knife on a big man like Bumper. Like you was looking to get kill?

Your mouth don't have good morning in it? And thanks for asking if I'm better.

I done hear you up and about like nothing happened.

I had planned that when I saw Boysie I would say my piece calmly. One look from he and all that gone through. Something about the easy way he pulled up a stool at the counter like it's his living room vexed me too bad. He moaned about how much things cost these days, how people owe him money and he have bills too. I wanted to spit in he face. That is what I'm facing. He's taking my money because he can, because he's the law round here and nothing I can do about it. So he clubs getting competition from new places. That don't mean he must squeeze small people like me.

I know he's doing wickedness all over the place. Who stopping him? Answer me that. Before Nancoo had confirmed the robbing and killing, town was busy whispering that Boysie's running a thing he does call 'the chute'. When the fishing boats aren't catching fish they're busy carrying people between Trinidad and the Main. I could well believe that's true. Boysie will make a dollar out of any situation. If the fishing's slow then the boats need to be good for something else. Moving goods and people is a straight Boysie play. Only as Nancoo knew, instead of dropping people off in Vene, Boysie was taking them to meet their maker.

Look Boysie, I ain't long out of hospital. Christmas coming. Let that pass and in the new year we go look at the rent again. That's fair.

While I was talking he kept spinning Three Little Threes like it's a toy stick.

As it's you, but don't tell nobody that. You understand?

I nodded and whispered,

We have to talk about Bumper. He as much as tell me he kill Etty and hide the body where nobody will find it.

Boysie didn't say boo, all his attention remained on the damn stick.

You ain't going to say nothing?

He stopped spinning the stick. We eyes made four.

You stabbed a fella working for me, a man I trust. I doubt he actually said he killed Etty.

Well, no, but he said she's gone where I'll never see she again. I know what he meant.

You think you know.

I know.

I repeat, you think you know. Best behave yourself, little woman. Unless you have proof keep your trap shut or it go land you in more hot water. I don't want that for you.

Who the ass you calling little woman? You looking for a snake bite or what?

He watched me cut eye and I instantly regretted the snake talk.

If you have proof we go talk. Until then stop playing you're bad.

And if I have proof?

I will deal with Bumper. Etty was one of my girls.

If I bring proof, I want you to throw Bumper down the chute.

Boysie rocked back he head and laughed.

Oh ho, you believe that chupidness? The chute? Well, all right, bring proof and just for you I'll flush him down a chute.

I'm holding you to that, Boysie.

And remember, rent going up in the new year.

Where the hell I finding proof that Bumper killed Etty?

MANA LALA

Yes, I know he thinks I'm a chupidee and not good enough to married. But I am the mother and Boysie should listen. I couldn't do nothing when he took beta in the fishing business. All right, you name father first. But he ain't a big man yet. Why Boysie giving him hard work that nearly drown him? Live life how you want but when it's Chunksee he should show more sense. Anyhow, while beta was resting up by me this week I called Pundit Hanuman to do a little puja for good luck on the sea. And to cover all my bases I went by Mother Gizzard as well. She must be nearly a hundred and still going strong. I left with a six-point star pendant on a leather string which she wants Chunksee to always keep round he neck as protection. I felt a drop in my stomach when she handed it over. No one knows that a few years ago he needed protection from what he own mother nearly did. I look back and think I must have gone mad. Some things you take to your grave, yes.

And that poohar George Harper better stay far. I never liked a single bone in that man's body. He feel he big and bad? Wait until I see he face. Chunksee gave me the story and he ain't go lie. Boysie and George carried Chunksee fishing in the Gulf of Paria, some sweet spot Boysie's christened 'the hole'. Apparently it's up north side, near a place on the Main they call Güiria. Nobody goes there. According to Chunksee 'the hole' might be good fishing but the currents have real bad mind. One minute the sea will be good good like a pond. Next thing waves tall like an upstairs house flinging boats around like they're toys.

They divided into two boats. Chunksee was with George and

Boysie was by he-self. That didn't surprise me. Boysie always prefer doing thing by he-self. People only humbug him. I think Boysie has a magic mirror hide up. Every now and then he peeps in it and instead of seeing the face God gave him, he sees a giant, stronger than ten Tarzans. The problem is he forgets not everybody have that mirror. Beta is not Boysie. He had my batcha fishing in 'the hole' three days and three nights straight. What kind of madness is that? Chunksee said Pa kept bawling that sleep is for when they reached back home.

Beta's too obedient to say when he can't make. And George? He only know how to say yes to Boysie. Poor beta worked like a dog, fishing, fishing, fishing. And when they catch the fish it's not like they throw them in the boat and done with that. Fish had to be ice packed or they'll be stinking by the time they reached back to dry land. On top of that Chunksee was worried the Vene coastguard would catch them. I hear that once you name Trini it's a case of take your boat, lock you in jail, and if you don't starve or get killed inside, they might let you out after a year. Thank you Lord Vishnu that didn't happen.

Chunksee was happy that at least they caught plenty fish and filled all two boats. They started for home and that was when trouble started. The sea was making real waves whacking and lashing them. Dotish Pa was forcing them to sail through that craziness. In the middle of all this confusion batcha forgot to top up gas in the engine and just so, cootooks, clataks, the engine stopped. At least Boysie turned around and latched Chunksee's boat onto he one. While they were busy Chunksee was calling for George to help.

Ma, imagine I'm there trying to get the gas without falling in the sea and bawling for George to catch the rope. You know that big-ass man was crouched down crying and wouldn't move? I cuss him stink and he still wouldn't move.

Boy, I don't know how you managed. But what you mean you cuss him stink? Since when you know how to cuss?

Chunksee pretended he ain't hear what I said.

My boat was fulling up with a set of water. I had to tie the rope and bail water. George there bawling, we go dead, we go dead. I told him, yes, we go dead just now unless you get your ass up and put gas in the engine. Eventually he filled the tank.

Thank you, Mother Lakshmi.

Oh, but that wasn't the end.

No?

I suppose I can't blame him too much seeing as the place was pitch black.

Chunksee slumped back down in the hammock.

What George do?

Chunksee gave a half smile and I had to smile too.

Just now you looked the print of your pa.

Whenever I say something so he face lights up. I'll never really get away from Boysie, yes.

Don't ask me how but George wrapped the cord around the starter and that was it. The lever jammed. We couldn't go nowhere. Lucky thing I had a small engine for back-up.

Mother Lakshmi was watching over you.

Anyhow with the next engine we pushed through. I thought, it don't make sense for Pa to stay back. We will take we time and reach. So, he went on. Eh eh, you know the small engine gone and cut out on me too?

Oh gosh, no.

Yeah. I was so vexed. I ain't go lie. Ma, this time I really thought it's done we done. Water was filling up. I'm bailing. George was bailing but then he got tired and started back with the crying, we go dead, we go dead. I wanted to cuff him down good and proper.

I steupsed.

Boy, no one would've blamed you. I feel to give him two good cuff myself.

Anyhow, I left him there and after that I don't think he lifted a finger. I bailed and bailed and then I did the only thing left. I dropped anchor. Once we were little steady I went to see if I could unpick the cord from around the first engine.

I took his hand closest to mine and kissed the deep criss-cross gashes. I've rubbed aloes hoping it will take away them marks.

Later I will rub you down with coconut oil and put extra in them cut.

At least I know now that if I go blind I could feel my way through life. In the dark I had to get out them knots. And I got all, you know. I asked George to go take off the small engine so I could put back on this one. But like he loss away.

Wouldn't budge. Everything I had to do myself. I begged, I cussed, while he only bawling, we go dead, we go dead, that he can't make, and telling me to say my last prayers.

If it was me I might have strangled him by now.

Chunksee laughed.

You would never do that. You're too soft.

Stay there and feel so.

Now, let me tell you why you mustn't get vex with Pa. Just then I saw Pa's boat reached back. He said he's not going without me in tow. I told him I'm good now. But you know how he does get when he head hot. He made me tie my boat to his, cut my anchor loose, and it's so we reach.

He looked around for the cup of ice water he'd been drinking. I held it out for him.

Thanks. I ain't know how much hours it took to hit land but whole time I was there bailing water. George never emptied a single bucket. I think it was that last part, bailing water, that took my strength.

I smoothed my batcha's hair.

Just a couple more days and I'll be ready to go back to work.

Couple more days? More like a couple more weeks. You went through plenty. Now it's time for me to wait on you hand and foot.

All I could think is that Chunksee is a blessed child, too good for this nasty world and too good to be me and Boysie's beta.

He wants me to stay good with he pa but to me Boysie's crossed a line. This could easily have led to Chunksee coming back in a cold box. I can't let this kind of thing happen again. Ever.

DORIS

August hurricane season and the place is making real hot. The only cool is inside. Boysie's in Cedros mostly and frankly I'm glad for the peace. Don't seem we have too much to say to one another these days. I know the clubs going down and he's doing more of the fishing as well as buying and selling goods between here and Venezuela. Anyhow, that's his business. Bedroom dead as usual. Actually, that's not true. What was never alive can't die. Some days I wonder if I love my husband. I think so. But am I in love with Boysie? That has me scratching my head. Was I ever in love with Boysie? The way my parents still love each other or even the way Tinsingh's bride looked at him as she walked up the church aisle? That was never me. I worry the love we have is shrivelling up fast fast. I don't know what to do. I really don't. Marriage is for life. How I'm supposed to keep living this life? And what if Boysie kicks me out and refuses to look after me? I wouldn't put it past him to behave so.

In the middle of the afternoon, I was lying down studying all this when I heard a horn blowing outside and my name calling. I peeped out and couldn't believe my eyes. Fish from Toco. Have mercy, he still ain't have on shoes.

Doris de Leon or I should really call you Mrs Boysie Singh. I was passing this side and I tell myself, let me go and see my old darling doux-doux.

Watch your mouth with the old. I stopped having birthdays long time.

423

As I opened the front door fully there was a next shock. On the doorstep behind Fish was the Besson Street policeman. My cheeks burned.

I think you know Harry already.

I tried to sound like it didn't matter.

Yes. Hello, Sergeant.

I'm off duty. Just Harry.

Where your husband?

You've missed him. Gone fishing.

I put them in the nicest chairs and brought out the good rum and whisky. From the cabinet I took three fancy glasses.

Relax nah, man. Two beers and we go call that George.

I could always ask the maid to make something.

Nah nah nah. We good with the liquid refreshments.

The afternoon passed easy easy in one sweet ole talk. Toco news went through the usual of who got married, who still can't find husband, who take in sick, who dead, who gone away, who turned priest, who fighting over land. Strange how much a few hours' talking, connecting with my home people, lifted my spirits. For the first time in I can't say how long I felt I was in company with no judgement whatsoever. I say no judgement but the maid is a complete macommere. News that my family named Fish and his friend Harry visited is guaranteed to reach Boysie's ears the second he's on dry land. As long as that is all she can report I'm not worried.

How the maid will know that Harry's even nicer and better-looking than in my daydreams?

All you making a man want to go Toco now.

Calm yourself, Sergeant.

I kicked Fish and put fingers to my lips. He was about to say something but stopped himself as I nodded towards the kitchen. I almost laughed out loud to see his eyes open big big as it dawned on him what I was saying. A policeman Boysie didn't have in his pocket was in his home? That could cause plenty ruction.

Next week my car's in the mechanic for a tune-up. Give me a week or so and then we could take the whole family for a drive. Ask your stepson if he wants to come too, nah.

I could borrow my brother's car. Doris, you coming?

Well, yes, Harry, I could come, I suppose. Chunksee's doing his own thing but I will let him know. He likes Toco.

He grinned. The look we exchanged was clear. Chunksee wasn't going nowhere. Fish was enough chaperoning, thank you very much.

*

Two weeks later, on a Saturday morning, Harry pulled up in his brother's car alone. No Fish.

Harry, I can't be seen leaving my house with you just so just so.

Yes. Sorry. I didn't think.

It's all right. Pick up Fish and pass back for me. I'll wait.

With Fish in the front seat and me in the back we headed to Toco. Now that was a wonderful day. I don't know the exact moment I forgot myself and went bazodee for the policeman. Could it be how he held the door for me? Or was it that he made a point of walking on the outside so I was always protected? I loved the way he said my name, his laugh, the number of times he checked if I was all right. Whatever it was, by the time he and Fish dropped me home I was giddy. Manners demanded I invite them in to take one for the road even though Boysie's jitney was parked up outside.

Cuz, I ain't want to come in people house when it's making dark already. Give your husband my best. Next time.

With Fish there me and Harry couldn't say a word about meeting again. But I knew something had passed between us. I wasn't wrong. Two days later I heard a horn blow and a voice called my name. That sound was sweet too bad.

ROSIE

Bring proof, bring proof. He's seeing too much damn cinema. That is the problem. Taking me for Humphrey Bogart playing detective? Etty's gone from the face of the earth and he want all this tre le le and that tra la la when two of we know it's Bumper. She ain't hide away with no man. Even if he won't admit it to me he must feel in he guts I'm talking truth. And he didn't deny the chute. For all I know Boysie put Bumper to do the robbing and killing out in the Gulf of Paria.

I've questioned the village left, right and centre and not a soul saw Etty leave the shop. Who wasn't walking behind the cortège was watching the white horses pull the carriage. I have nightmares that that raping, murdering so-and-so slit Etty's throat and shoved she down the chute. One witness and Boysie will have to do something.

I kept up the pressure hoping a tiny clue would leak out until my regulars had to warn me, Rosie, girl, you're humbugging people. The village talk is that it's better walking the extra twenty minutes to drink in peace by Ramkelawan's. At least there a man didn't have to hear Bumper this and Bumper that all the flecking time. A man even told me to my face that he was so fed up listening to me that he felt like killing Bumper with he bare hands if that would shut me up. I said that could work.

I ain't any closer to proving a damn thing by staying in my crease. Time to try a new tactic. Diggers is still doing whatever day work Boysie shares out. I sent a message and about seven that evening he pulled up a stool at the bar. Diggers like he'd bathed extra. The hair was greased down and the parting straight like it

427

make with a knife. I never knew he owned a starched shirt and good soft pants with crease you could cut yourself on. My boy was looking real sharp for so.

But Diggers, you ain't tell me is date we having. Where we going? And I in old clothes.

He blushed. If I didn't know better I would say he was embarrassed.

I'm looking all right?

You never looked better. Is where you going?

That same red flush crossed he face again.

I buy a ring for Lou.

My mouth dropped open. Them two real fool we, yes. Quarrelling all the time when in truth it was love like dove. Damn Tobago love.

Congratulations, boy, I well glad for both of all you. I have some good Scotch in the back that I was saving.

He touched my hand.

Wait with that. I don't want goat mouth. When she say yes and things straight then we go take that drink.

Fair enough. She's expecting you'll propose? She ain't say nothing to me.

Kindna. She might.

I squeezed his arm.

You're ready to stop running down all kind of woman?

Yeah. This is it. I love Lou.

Then I wish you the best.

He raised his beer to that.

Anyhow, Rosie, you sent for me. What's the action?

It could wait. You have enough to think about.

Oh gosh, don't carry on so. Tell me nah.

I explained I wanted to look around Bumper's room. Diggers rapped his fingers on the counter as he thought.

Well, these days Boysie's more in the sea. Bumper does crew a good bit of the time. You might find something in his room in the Dorset. I ain't know.

But you have to tell me when the coast's clear.

We go work out something for an evening when he gone. Leave it with me. I go fix up.

MANA LALA

Even we pundit can't understand how she ain't dead yet. Subhagya Mausi's still holding on and we're doing our best for she. Last night while rubbing her down with Limacol I asked her what to do about Boysie. Anyhow you look it's pain. One pain is if me and he don't have nothing whatsoever to do with one another. I would miss him down to my bones. It ain't just two-three years we've been together. We're talking donkey years. Of course I could do the opposite and stay, hoping one day he'll appreciate what's right here. But that waiting mashing up my heart. Either which way, Boysie's bringing me grief.

And speak of the devil, he passed me heading to make market and slowed down the car. I thought he was offering me a drop but that would've been too nice. Instead he barked out the car window,

Mana Lala, do something for me nah, girl. I need cloth.

He shoved a roll of bills at me.

Fifteen yards of cotton, as black black as you can get. No dark blue posing as black. You understand? And drop it by Mr Evans. He's making uniforms for me and the boys.

The way he asked me while holding up traffic I could hardly say no. Best keep on he good side and swallow the steupse that was forming in my mouth.

Yeah, all right. I go go later. After market.

No. Go now. He wanted the cloth since Wednesday. Thanks.

You is my girl.

He feel calling me he girl is enough to get me to do anything? I only agreed to keep the peace. Once he was far I let go a long steupse and ducked into Khoury's. They had the thing self. At least I didn't have to go hunting all over the place. That would've vexed me more.

Mr Evans was really expecting the cloth. I don't know him good good but the few times we've bounced up he was full of chat. Anybody who say women does maco haven't spent a five minutes listening to him. Put it in the papers or tell Mr Evans, whichever is easier because he mouth will reach the same amount of people only faster.

Aye, Chunksee mother, long time me ain't see you. How you going?

He took the cloth.

This heavy thing you toting? Why Rajah make you bring that? Sit down, sit down. Take some breeze.

Mr Evans brought me a glass of water, thandaa cold.

Cool down. This place ain't play it making hot.

He ruffled the cloth between his fingers.

So, you know what Mr Boysie want doing with this black cloth?

No. I didn't get a chance. Something about uniforms?

He leaned closer.

Well girl, I have a story for you. But keep it to yourself. He won't like that I tell anybody, even you.

Mr Evans rocked back in he chair.

The Rajah sit down right where you there now, must be end of last week. He asked me when last I went cinema. I say, well, now and then I does take in a matinee. Anyhow, he wanted to know if I remember what Errol Flynn had on in *Sea Hawk*. You did see that?

Me? I does hardly go theatre.

Well, in *Sea Hawk* the star boy was in a kindna pirate outfit. Rajah want that exact costume for he-self and he crew. All of them want to look like Errol Flynn.

I rolled my eyes.

Pirate? What he know about pirate? Cinema gone to he head.

That's what he want. I'm supposed to make a black pants and black shirt for each man. And you know Boysie. It can't be all how. He want everything neat neat.

So why all of them dressing up? They go sweat bad in black.

That is what I'm saying. I measured Boysie plus he bring them ugly fellas he does have with him steady. What they name again? Help me.

I bet it was Firekong and Baje or Bumper.

Correct.

He didn't bring my son, though? If it's one thing that I ain't playing with is getting my son tangled up in any worthlessness he's doing on them boats.

Nah nah nah. I know Chunksee. He wasn't with them.

And where they going dressed up so? They're having pirate party?

Two of we buss out laughing.

You leave them alone in peace. Rajah and he friends want to look like them in Hollywood. And where you see things hard these days, I glad for the little work.

I went home and whole road my mind was tied up wondering about these pirate outfits. Boysie doesn't do thing just so just so. Always a reason. But in 1950 a big man like Boysie pretending he is Errol Flynn? Damn worthless. He can't be serious.

DORIS

I've been daydreaming about Sergeant Suerattan, Harry, Harry James Suerattan. Gosh he nice too bad. Such a gentle soul who can stand up for himself without carrying on bad or threatening people. And his smiling eyes. Maybe my husband's eyes once looked at me like that but they don't any more. He bought the cow then decided he didn't want milk after all. Look past Boysie's fancy suits and he's still carrying on like a small-time hustler and street fighter. I mean to say, a married man, a rich man, he should never have been caught in a house with those two San Juan jamettes. Look how Cecil end up dead because he went and trouble other people woman. I know it cost Boysie a pretty penny to keep them parts of the story out of the papers. But whether the marish and parish know is not my business. I know. I know every last detail. I wonder if he could get it up for them? That would make me so vex. Thing is, I should have had the gumption to leave his tail since the honeymoon.

He may not be threatening me these days but he loves to threaten others with that damn stick, Three Little Threes. Always proving he's the baddest man in town. Don't get me wrong. He's still winning fights but at a price. A quarrel broke out in the Dorset between Boysie and a Yankee from the Chaguaramas base. Now what is Boysie doing beating up his best customers? Come Friday they're spending free sheet on whisky and girls. And, jeez-an-ages, everybody knows the customer's always right. Not Boysie. He whipped the man's tail but the fella only went down after wringing Boysie's neck so hard he needed the doctor. Three weeks now Boysie's been parked up in a nursing home by

434

the Savannah. And when Boysie says he's in pain and can't move his neck you know it must be really bad. If only he would obey the doctors them he might get better quickly.

A few days ago he announced that he ain't taking more injections. I explained that the doctors only trying to give the muscles an ease so they could heal. When I tell you that man harden. He's carrying on like he has degrees and certificates. Like I don't have enough to do coming here every day to see his sour face. I gave it to him good. Take the medicine or stop wasting money on a private hospital. He didn't like that at all at all. I had to hear for the umpteenth time that it's he money and he will spend it as he damn well pleases.

On top of all that he whispered that forces in the nursing home were looking to kill him. Whatever happened to his neck may have interfered with he brain, his brain, turning him mad.

Some of the nurse them is straight jumbie. One is a La Diablesse.

Really? How you know?

I see she have one good foot and one cow hoof hiding under she long dress.

Well next time call out and the security guard will come.

I do that already and them say they ain't see nothing. But it's like the man in the white suit. Remember? I feel he behind this.

My stomach dropped.

You see him? White suit, white hat?

Boysie shook his head.

Not sure.

Well, make sure and tell me if you do, okay?

Visiting the nursing home is exhausting. Boysie wanted fruits. I bought a bunch of expensive grapes, the blue-black ones, and a few shiny red apples. The ward sister washed and arranged them in a bowl for me to give the sick.

Here, doux-doux.

His mouth swelled up big big.

What's that?

How you mean? You asked for fruits.

Grapes does work my belly. How long we married and you ain't know that?

I moved the bowl. Just in case.

Why you so, Boysie? This is the thanks I get?

Oh ho, I'm supposed to be grateful? It's my money that buy them. Mine.

Just then a nurse shuffled in carrying a chair.

Excuse, I borrowed the chair. Sorry.

Don't worry. I now reach.

I sat down and plastered a smile on my face I didn't feel. As the nurse was leaving Boysie turned on her.

Don't take my chair again, you hear? And what time the doctor passing? Whole day I here and all you ain't doing a damn thing for me.

But Mr Singh, I does be checking on you every hour.

Yeah, but you only jooking your head by the door in case I dead. What that doing for me? I'm here suffering.

Let me see if Sister knows what time doctor making he rounds.

She pulled the door almost closed. Silently I began counting, one, two, three, four, five, six. Unfortunately counting didn't work. Before I got to seven I let go.

Why you have to talk to the nurse so? Have some decency, nah. She's not Firekong or one of them badjohn working for you. This is a young girl doing a job.

I can talk to she any way I feel like. It's my money paying for this blasted nursing home.

Stop carrying on about your money, your money.

Well, it look like you need a reminder.

What's your problem?

My problem? My problem? Everybody busy spending my money and I'm holed up in here. I don't know what going on in the clubs or with the boats them. I'm sure thiefing happening left, right and centre.

You want me to check on things for you?

He grunted.

You? You know anything? The whores them have more business sense than you. Even Mana Lala know more than you.

Well, I couldn't help smiling.

> Really, Boysie? You don't think after all these years I ain't know a few things? To besides, I could always always get somebody to pass and check out the clubs them. You want a policeman to pass? I could arrange that for you.

He grunted and waved me away. I got up.

> Boysie, let me go please before I say something I regret. Tomorrow, God spare life, I'll see you.

> Yeah, go. Go and take them sour grapes and old apple with you. When I ask for fruits I want portugals, mango, watermelon, pawpaw, pomme-cythere, sapodilla. That is fruit. You hear me?

I never returned. Later that same day the doctor discharged him. They said Mr Singh refused the injections and threatened to kill the doctor. Now if I bounce up any of them in town I'll be so shame. But you think he cares? He's lucky I'm still here yes. Real lucky.

ROSIE

Morning, morning. You is Rosie?

The middle-aged Indian fella propped his bicycle against the side of the shop door.

Yes, morning. And you is who?

Lord, it making hot. Seepersad. Seepersad Naipaul.

He wiped the sweat from his forehead with a clean, white handkerchief.

Diggers asked me to drop a message for you as I was coming this side.

Well take a cold something, nah. You want a mauby?

Just ice water, thanks.

I let the man recover little bit then asked as casually as I could,

So what Diggers have to say for he-self? Since he and Lou get engaged the man scarce like gold.

He want you to collect your parcel today from the Dorset around two o'clock.

He frowned.

That make sense to you?

Yes, yes, all right, let me fix up. Give me the time there.

Ten past nine.

The man drained the glass like he was landing a shot.

Right. I gone. I'm interviewing some people down by the jetty. I heard the fishermen have some quarrel.

And thanks, Seepersad. Stop anytime you're passing.

It didn't matter that this was Friday, two weeks before Christmas. I locked the shop and took a taxi straight to town. Diggers was liming outside the Dorset. He sauntered over cool cool and casually led me round the back.

Bumper gone out but you still have to hurry up. You never know who might reach.

Don't ask me how he got the key but he opened Bumper's room, gently pushed me in and closed the door. There wasn't much to see, a single cot bed, a small chest of drawers, and a line strung across the room with clean and dirty clothes thrown over it. I started with the drawers. Chooked up in between clothes, tablets, Bay Rum and soft candle was a wad of Yankee dollars. As tempting as it was I didn't touch the money. I needed to find something that would shout out to the world that Bumper had a part in Etty disappearing. Three months on from Boy Boy's funeral most of me is sure she's dead and gone. Yet a tiny mad place in the pit of my belly hasn't stopped hoping.

From the drawers I moved to checking the clothes. Nothing. But the second I raised the mattress I found treasure. Papayo, if you see things underneath. It had cutlass, knife, pictures of Boysie cut out of the Gazette, an ice pick. And what's he doing with a lady's silver cross on a chain, a red lipstick, a dirty panty? Men things were also there and they weren't all his. Who was the real owner of a black wallet with the initials 'T.W.' stamped on the leather? As I searched further I found a knot of broken gold and silver chains, a good few thin bracelets, rings, and earrings most missing their twin. Slowly I fingered the knot asking myself if I was ready for this. My heart was racing. I knew I would find something and at that exact moment my whole life would change forever. As I sifted through the tangled ball I saw it: one side of the green stone earrings I had given Etty. My entire body went cold. It's one thing looking and quite another finding proof.

Rage blinded me. Wherever Boysie was today I was tracking down he backside. Proof? He ain't touching Bumper without proof? Well take this. But finding Boysie wasn't so easy. Diggers quite rightly said he part was done and dusted. If Boysie ever suspected him then he would be the next to disappear. He suggested Laventille but when I got there Boysie had done come and gone. Another fella said Boysie left to go fishing and we ain't seeing he for a good few days. A next one said, nah nah nah. He'd wanted to go fishing but the *Marie Louise* engine was giving trouble. He and Chunksee were in Cedros fixing it.

By this time the place was beginning to make dark and I decided to spend the night by Pearl. That woman is a saint. No notice but she opened she house to me. A cousin was there liming. I didn't plan to take over but my worries felt bigger than their talk about who was making a baby or a jail. The cousin sat up.

You're looking for Boysie Singh? All you had to do was ask. Boysie by he child's mother. You know Mana Lala?

I shook my head.

I'm not surprised. She real quiet. Boysie have big wife so you won't see Mana Lala with he.

How you know he there?

She living in the gap by we. I passed Boysie with he two foot cock up in the gallery not long ago. The way he was dhakolaying rum I think he go remain right there.

Pearl got she friend Gravy to give we a drop. Boysie was right there in Mana Lala's gallery draining a bottle of Old Oak. The three of we went up like a delegation and surprised him.

Aye, is you, Rosie? I ain't make you out. I'm so accustomed to seeing you in your shop I didn't realise it was you.

It took all my strength to explain the side of earring from Bumper's room. He stroked he chin.

We go come to what you was doing in Bumper's room but it look like you was right, Rosie. I go have to do something.

Yes, you damn well better do something.

He watched me cut eye and I immediately regretted my language.

All right, all right. Let me hear what he have to say for he-self.

Why? The Bible say an eye for an eye, a tooth for a tooth.

What you want?

The chute. Take him and throw him down the chute. I never want to see that man face ever again.

You know what you're asking?

Yes.

You're sure?

Yes.

He shrugged.

All right, Rosie. If that's what you want. I can't say that is what I would do myself but that is just me. You want the chute then all right. Be that on your head.

MANA LALA

I was there in the rocking chair listening to the radiogram and picking rice when one of the young boys who does help out Boysie came running up to the gate calling my name hard hard.

Aye, Shortie, hush your mouth, nah. I ain't living on the road.

Come now. You have to get he out.

What?

Shortie, hands on he waist, panting,

Rajah carrying on bad. They go beat he if he don't leave the club.

Hold up. I can't hear you good. Let me lower the radiogram. Who send you?

They turn on Rajah. I didn't know what to do. Rajah only ever do good for me. I ain't want to see nothing bad happen.

Who?

Fellas who working for Rajah, running things when he's not there.

Shortie, a youth-man pushing well past six foot, said I was the only-est person left to get Boysie away safely.

What happen to Doris? That's she husband.

Miss Doris? She run me. Watched me up and down like I is dirt. You should hear she. Boysie could be deading, she ain't stepping inside no club. And just so she slam the door in my face.

Of course, I expected nothing different from that ungrateful wretch. Anyhow, that mistake done make already. But Shortie self should know I can't walk inside a club just so just so with all of them drunkards and gamblers liming in there. People will think I'm whoring. Imagine if a neighbour saw me? Worst yet, think of the shame if I bounced up somebody I know inside the club. Now that would be commess. Must be serious bacchanal for this boy to come here.

Mana Lala, hustle, nah.

Hanuman, give me strength. The things I does do for this man.

All right. Two minutes.

I put on my going-out dress, covered my head good good with an orhni, and we headed for the tramcar into town.

*

They say it's best to take in front before in front take you. I lowered my head, adjusted my orhni and slid into the club. Hardly anybody was in this front part. Two bloodshot-eyed fellas were at a table, a nip of rum and a jug of water between them. A Yankee was sprawled out over two chairs pulling a sleep. Wax must be clogged he ears for he to sleep through the ruction that was coming from the room beyond. Above a calypso chorus with something about a ram goat baptism and a Brother Willie, two voices in particular were cussing and carrying on. I recognised Boysie's drunken slurs. Shortie nudged my side.

You hear?

I took a deep breath, pushed aside a curtain of red, white and blue plastic strips, and entered the smoky, half-empty room. Thankfully I had the orhni to cover my nose from the rank piss and sweat smells. Whatever I'd expected, it wasn't as ramshackle as this place. The only decoration was a picture of a white girl in a bikini hanging crooked from a nail. Yellowing paint was peeling off the walls. A broad, ugly fella was behind the bar facing off with Boysie who looked like he might fall off he stool any minute. I couldn't understand what was going on. That man supposed to be working for Boysie. What the jail was this?

I must say Boysie wasn't looking like the boss of anything in a dirty string vest that once upon a time was a shade of white and a nasty white-grey short pants with yellow stains by the crotch. Till the day my eyes close I will love him. But right now Boysie looked bloated, hair greasy and no razor blade had touched that face this week. I didn't need to smell his breath to know he was drunk as a lord. A voice behind me,

Aye, fellas, look a dulahin reach. You come to give we a little Indian dance?

Whistling and all kind of nasty words were suddenly falling through the air. I rushed to Boysie's side.

Time to go.

He pulled back, shocked to see me.

Mana Lala? What you doing here?

Come let we go.

He threw an arm around me.

Just now. I was telling this gadaha here to give me the

whe-whe takings for today. He said it ain't have none. That make him an ulloo.

He looked up at the badjohn behind the bar.

You ain't Indian so let me explain. Ulloo is like you. Somebody who over dotish. Ain't have no sense in their head.

Boysie tapped his head and turned back to me.

But Mana Lala, he don't look to me like he's a common, Port of Spain ulloo like you does find all about. If you ask me—

A loud, sour belch dropped right in my face.

—this is a neemakharam. A real chor thiefing my money.

I grabbed Boysie round the waist and pulled him up.

Enough. We're going home.

Behind me I could feel fellas getting closer. Comments were being thrown about how my face really looked under my orhni, that my leg had shape. Boysie, swaying, pointed a finger at the barman.

You chor, you want to play wrong and strong in my bar? With my money? Mine. You're looking to get lick down or what?

The badjohn turned to me.

Lady, carry this drunk home. He's putting off the customers.

I don't know why but I couldn't help myself.

What whe-whe money he talking about?

Stay out of man business. We ain't owe Boysie nothing. It's he who run up some serious debts in a card game. Now he want the bar money to go back and play again.

Boysie banged on the counter so hard I thought he might break it.

Where my kiss-me-ass money you neemakharam?

Boysie, please come. For Chunksee's sake.

I want my money now. I ain't leaving. Damn chor.

He bent down, grabbed Three Little Threes and started waving it about.

You want fight? Eh? You could fight me? Eh?

He lunged across the bar but the badjohn caught the stick. Before I could blink twice he had whacked Boysie hard with Three Little Threes. He own stick. I felt that for Boysie. Then the man leapt from behind the bar and put a few more lashes on Boysie who was bracing for the pain. I was screaming, trying to get between them and nearly get lash and all. Then something happened that I hadn't seen except the day he mother died. Boysie Singh dropped to he knees bawling like a batcha. The badjohn kicked him.

Go home before I change my mind and crack open your skull. And don't come back here. I'm running the club now.

DORIS

I know the maid sees everything, so I don't give her anything to maco. Taking a taxi into town is normal. No way she can know I change by Park Street and head for Harry's place. Lucky thing too we don't have a pattern. With his shifts forever changing it's impossible to say Doris has a man and she goes to see him on a Tuesday lunchtime and don't reach back home until all six o'clock when the place starting to make dark. Sometimes we don't even know more than a day in advance if we can meet. This week Wednesday afternoon and Friday morning were clear. Last week we linked up on the Monday and not again until Thursday around four. It would be nice to dress up sexy for Harry, but I can't risk drawing attention to myself. At least I do my hair, slip into my best undergarments, and spray plenty perfume all over.

Thing is, six months we've been seeing one other. No way Boysie doesn't know something. We go stay married but he do his do and I do mine. I don't find it so easy. The guilt eats at me. My only ease is that I don't matter to Boysie, not really. That's not to say he wouldn't kill me for the horn and with a policeman to boot. Well, I'm alive so what that says? With Boysie that can only mean I'm still useful to him. Maybe he even likes that I took up with a policeman. Now he has someone on the inside track. That would be Boysie all over. Using me to the last.

Then suddenly everything exploded like fireworks but not in a way I'd ever imagined. Without warning the police arrived bright and early and shut down the Sunrise and the Baltimore. They promised that those clubs will never again, until thy kingdom come, get another licence. You ever hear more? Why?

And how can they do that? It's not just we to catch, us to catch. Come Friday every last man and woman working in those two establishments have obligations and people depending on them. Where are they supposed to find work now? I asked Harry about the raids but he swears on the Bible he didn't know anything about it and why now. He'd better not be lying because I'm done with men and their lies.

*

Once the clubs closed that was most of our cash gone. And the savings I thought we had seem to have been gambled away. My sister Elena, God bless her, said I mustn't worry. Worst case I could sell my gold. I couldn't admit the gold's already jumping up as surety for a loan Boysie needed to buy a boat. Imagine my husband has let it come to this. Just five minutes ago other people were begging him for a raise. Now he's the one looking for money to keep body and soul together. This is all his fault. He should have been keeping people sweet so no one would want to shut him down. Look at Donovan. His clubs still going strong. I never hear a bad word about him. But Boysie's over dotish and greedy. Running down woman and gambling never ended well. And this damn fishing hardly paying for itself.

Elena insisted I pack a bag and spend a few days with her and the family. A noisy house full of laughter rather than my silent jail of a house was tonic for my mind. Even better would have been to move straight in with Harry. He loves me. Boysie's making me leave him. I tried to show him a little refinement, a way of doing things with class and the ways of God. Life could have been so different if he'd only eased up with the temper. Now, after what's happened I'm not sure how long we'll even have a roof. It's all crashing around us so fast my head's dizzy.

A few days turned into a few weeks. In Elena's care I got my strength back. But I had to go home sometime. I braced myself. Nothing I imagined was as bad as what hit me within hours of reaching home.

One of them front-pew Syrians pulled up by my gate calling for me. Now we ain't friendly except to say hello. But here she was talking about how she's in charge of decorating the church this Sunday and if I have any flowers in the garden to pick. Somebody told her I have plenty anthuriums growing.

> They mixed me up with somebody else. I don't have a single anthurium.

> Never mind. I'm just glad to see you're looking good. What happened the other night would have driven me to the madhouse.

I opened the gate and brought her inside one time before the whole street heard this the same time as me. The fences on both sides have ears and eyes to maco what is not their business.

> Come, come. You want some coconut water? A cup of tea?

> Girl, don't trouble yourself.

I gave her a cup of tea and sat opposite.

> What happened? I was by my sister and I ain't see Boysie yet.

> In that case I don't want to sound like I'm bringing news. He'll tell you.

I sighed.

> If it's about a woman I know already.

Oh, nothing so. It's one set of commess. I should shut my mouth.

I watched her hard.

Don't do me that. I am his wife, and I don't know a damn thing. Excuse my language. As a wife and a Christian sister you should want to tell me.

Piece-piece it came out. Boysie's been playing poker in the white people club and losing money upside down. The house added up all what he owed and it reached over fifty thousand dollars. My stomach dropped. We didn't have that kind of money in cash. What hurt my heart the most is that foolish Boysie is not a poker man. Whe-whe, all fours, whappee, that's Boysie's speed. He can't play poker. Them white fellas took a dumb lamb to slaughter. Dotish Boysie was probably grinning away thinking at long last he was liming with the big people. Meanwhile they roasted him alive. Now they're laughing all the way to the bank. I am not one to show people bad mind, but you see them French Creole and Syrians? None of them getting a red cent from me again. I will walk and buy my cloth and whatever else I need from anybody else. Not them. As for Boysie? This is the last straw. Me and he done, done, done.

MANA LALA

Boysie reached Friday afternoon and lay in the hammock like the world ending tomorrow. I'm not strong enough to ignore him when the man's so upset. I can help bring him back to his normal self. Lucky thing just this morning I picked fresh seim beans. Curried with aloo, and two hot sada roti on the side, I hoped it would lift he spirits. He pushed the food around for a while then handed me back the plate. All he wanted was to lie down in the hammock, eyes closed, although from the way he was breathing he ain't relaxed. No point in forcing people to tell you what's humbugging them. The kheesa will come out he mouth in good time.

As six o'clock reached sandflies started biting. I lit a cockset near the hammock.

You want anything?

Nah. I good.

You ain't have things to do? I know the clubs closed but you still have a few things going.

Slowly he eyes opened.

Give me a cocoa tea.

I had to look away. Since that day years ago I don't make cocoa tea if I can help it.

Put a shot of puncheon rum in it?

He nodded.

Correct.

Once he had his warm enamel cup I sat on a peerha close enough to rock the hammock. Tookra tookra, Boysie told me what had happened that very morning. He went with some government big people to see about two of he boats the Venes them have been holding nearly three whole years. Everything was calm and cool. He talked to them nice and asked back for he boats. Dollars or pounds, whichever you prefer, them is big boats that cost real money.

Sweating in suit and tie, the top Vene looked Boysie in he eye and had the boldfaceness to tell him that,

After careful consideration of the matter, we must inform you, Mr Singh, that the boats will not be returned.

Boysie thought he didn't hear right.

What you saying? Repeat that for me.

The boats were legally confiscated by Venezuela. They were found illegally fishing in our waters. This was not a first-time offence. The law is clear. We can and have confiscated both vessels, as is our legal right.

So where my boats them?

They're in the custody of the government of Venezuela.

Boysie got out the hammock.

I told the man, I'm asking you again. Where my boats? You know what he said?

I shook my head afraid to guess.

He said, what were previously your boats are now employed
by the Venezuelan national coastguard who patrol our
waters.

Boysie whistled.

I said, hold some strain. You making joke? You mean to tell
me that you take my boats and give them away like you is
Santa Claus? And you have so much bad mind that you gone
and give it to the same coastguard that run we down?

As Boysie gave it, them big shots were looking all about, anywhere so as not to catch he eye. He stared down the Vene official.

That's the same coastguard that does be terrorising poor
fishermen like me. Yes, once or twice we might stray to the
wrong side but it's by accident. You go punish we for that?

The Vene shook his head.

It's not one or two boats straying, Mr Singh. I think we have
established a persistent pattern of you breaking the law.
We've made our decision. In fact the boats are right now
being outfitted with the coastguard's colours and flag.

Boysie took a deep breath and asked the Vene official,

You're sure you want to do that?

Yes, of course. What do you mean?

Boysie paused and spoke slowly.

I'm asking you one more time. You're sure you want to do
that?

Quite sure.

Boysie laughed.

Well, all right then.

He walked out without another word.

Mana Lala, you hear me say I asked the man not once, but twice, if he's sure. Two times he looked me in my eye, bold as brass, and said yes, he's taking my boats and fixing them for the coastguard. He had he chance fair and square. From now on its war in their tail.

Hearing that had me frightened.

No, Boysie. They go shoot you if you try anything in the Gulf. They go shoot you dead.

But Boysie didn't seem to be hearing me. War with the Venes was the only thing on he mind.

PART FIVE

ROSIE

Malcolm stood in the middle of the rum shop.

> All you, whole evening the talk is about Boysie. But I would like to propose we fire one for he partner. To the late Philbert Peyson. Boy, I didn't even know that was your name until today. All of we called you Bumper. Well, yesterday, 20 April 1950, you made history. Aye, you, Bumper, Philbert, whatever you name, you make history as the first black man to reach inside Trinidad Yacht Club. Never mind you was dead and your skin wash away to make you pass for white. The first black man. Put that in your pipe and smoke it.

People buss out laughing and raised glasses and bottles to toast history. I was skinning my teeth too yet worried same time. Big news that have we in shock. Boysie and he gang get charged with Bumper's murder and all now they're sitting down in jail. Front page of the papers was a dead that's supposed to be Bumper, hand and foot tied up and the body strapped to a long piece of iron.

I'm shitting myself because police bound to come for me soon. First chance he gets Boysie will sell me down the Jordan. I can hear him telling them Rose Burnley wanted the man dead. Doesn't matter he didn't kill Bumper when I asked him. So, he took he cool time. He still only did it because of me. Boysie might even lie and say I put cash in he hand to do the job. Diggers and Pearl would never tell the police a word so it's down to Boysie. Meanwhile I'm serving customers like nothing's happened.

*

Diggers pulled in the rum shop later that evening. We eyes made four.

Rosie girl, better make it a whisky. Imagine if Boysie end up on the gallows?

Hearing that caused plenty glasses around the counter to raise and clink. A chorus started,

Boysie to the gallows. Boysie to the gallows.

A fella asked for a next beer and then somebody wanted a nip of rum. I was busy busy. In between serving drinks I took in the ole talk.

All you know the man who found the body is Miss Ella's cousin?

For true?

Yeah, he name Sanjiv. Apparently he was doing he work normal normal when he spot something in the water.

Papers calling this the case of the floating corpse.

Well, ain't that is how they say Boysie does kill when he out on the sea terrorising people? Kill and sink them with a piece of something heavy? Only this time they float.

Aye, Diggers, who else get charged?

Boysie and, let me see, Baje, Firekong, Durant, Paka Beyer, Frisco and Toto.

I grabbed Diggers before he left.

What really going on, Diggers? When Boysie was doing

he killing on the sea, we never hear anything about Vene contrabandistas or fishermen floating up. How Bumper reach so?

He shook he head. I lowered my voice.

I need a message to Boysie.

I could try.

Tell him I hope this ain't have nothing to do with Etty and what I said.

Why you bringing that up? Leave it. Police ain't coming for you now they have the big fish he-self.

You're sure?

Yes, man. Don't say nothing.

I hope he ain't planning to drop me in it later.

Diggers sighed.

All right, all right, let me see what I can find out.

And if you hear my name you'll run tell me, right?

Relax, that ain't happening.

MANA LALA

Boysie get charged. Murder. I don't know what it says about me that a piece of me believed it straight away. He could have killed Bumper easy. But I have Chunksee to study. Seeing he pa in court going to break the bai's heart. Whatever happens I have to stay strong for my one child. Pundit Hanuman better come do some prayers, yes.

As usual it's only Subhagya Mausi I can talk to and she's help-less like a newborn batcha. Still, something about being with she, holding she bony little hand, is a comfort to all two of we. Things clear up when we chat. This whole Bumper business reminded me about a next fella. Town say the man, Santos, wanted police to hold Boysie but they chased him. No proof. That vexed him too bad. I can't remember the exact amount but let we say a round thousand dollars. That went in Boysie's pocket to carry him from Trinidad to the Main quiet quiet because he ain't have no papers. Three-quarters of the way there Boysie stopped the boat and said, right, we reach the chute. Boysie pointed a gun to he head, took all the man gold and money and what have you, tied him to a heavy piece of iron, and threw him over the side.

Now, I'm not saying that Boysie wouldn't do something like that. But, if that is truth, how Santos reach back Trinidad? He story is that Boysie didn't strap him good. He lose the iron, swam like a fish and reached some mangrove where a boat found him. That hurt my head. Boysie was always a thief-man. But I never thought he'd drown a man in the sea for he money. I'm making extra puja as thanks that Chunksee ain't tangled up in that commess.

Long before this Bumper case I'd heard the fellas talking about chute this and chute that. But I'd no clue it was throwing people off the boat, people paying for safe passage. How I didn't put two and two together before? I remember hush-hush talk about Dalip. He got a girl from this village in trouble. Pretty girl named Alya. Anyhow, Dalip's father is a big pastor and he raised money from the congregation to send the bai Venezuela. Left Alya to raise she girl child alone. Well, Dalip's missing. Never made it to the friend on the Main. Talk is Boysie sent him down the chute.

Sometimes when I think of what might be going on I just want to grab Chunksee and go live somewhere far far. That's what Popo wanted. I'm not taking up for Boysie. Them days done. However, people does run they mouth and talk a set of foolishness when they're ready. Take the donkey story. Cousin Tewarie said he got it from a Cedros man who saw it with he own two eyes. Boysie went out a night with one passenger and a donkey. Four o'clock in the morning he reached back. Passenger gone. Donkey gone.

Well all right, the man like he donkey and carried it with him. What wrong with that, Tewarie?

My cousin was waiting for me to say just that.

Apparently Boysie does take a donkey to kill it, cut it up, and throw piece-piece in the water. Sharks love it. Boysie throws the passenger over. Meat is meat. One donkey cut up could cover a few trips so he doesn't need one every time.

And how he get the donkey to stay quiet on the boat?

Girl, it's obeah he working steady. Trust me. Obeah on the donkey and on the people. Ain't you is the one who tell me he and Mother Gizzard is friend? Well, she's an obeah witch.

> Stop right there. Mother Gizzard is a good woman. I will ask she if donkey have anything to do with she religion.

Tewarie wasn't ready to drop the talk without putting me in my place.

> Of course the other thing is he could just be cutting up people and throwing them in the water without any donkey bait.

> So now Boysie's killing left, right and centre? People jealous Boysie. Maybe your friend was watching how much money Boysie's getting for these trips and made up this chupidness about donkey to end Boysie's side thing.

I said it with more heart than I felt. It's too much to take on.

And then, aare, Mrs Rodriguez found me and all doubt about Boysie's passenger service was done, done, done. The lady reached bawling. I could see she was going mad, fuss she worried. Five children, the last one in diapers. She husband used to buy up things in Trinidad and sell on the Main. He usual boat was damaged so he paid passage for Boysie to carry him. Normally he would be back after, three weeks, a month at most. Nearly six months now and nobody ain't seen he face.

She didn't ask for nothing except my help to know what happened to she man. That lady's pain hit hard. I can't ask Boysie nothing. But I couldn't do nothing. Time for that overs. I took what I had in my purse and put it in she hand. She ain't have two cents to rub together but same time didn't want me to feel she'd come begging. She'd heard about the chute and it haunted her to think that maybe he died just so. What should she tell the children them?

And suddenly I realised something. This lady was asking me for help because I was as close to Boysie as she could get. What that made me? The shame I felt was punishing. From that day I started to do something that not even Subhagya Mausi knows about. Every Wednesday I go by Mrs Rodriguez with food and play with the children little bit. When I'm leaving I hide some change in she purse. It's from money Boysie asked me to hide away. One day he's bound to ask back for he cash and I don't know what I'll do. I tell myself it's from money she husband paid for his passage. The rest really belonged to Popo and she would be happy to see it help Mrs Rodriguez. Imagine I turned thief and taking from the biggest thief of all.

ROSIE

With Boysie in jail it's like people eat parrot bottom. Everybody's talking their Boysie story. Business brisk because of course they need two drinks in my bar to wet their vocal cords. From what's in the papers it looks like nearly every missing body is down to Boysie's hand. They're saying he might have killed plenty others including a Limey. A next one reported he cousin's missing and he will bet house and land that Boysie kidnapped the fella and threw him in the sea. Had to be.

The area around Leper Asylum jetty's crawling with all kind of people wanting news about what Boysie did out there. At some point they always end up in my rum shop. Even reporters have reached by me. The only one I welcomed was Diggers' friend, that nice man, Seepersad Naipaul. He came riding bicycle, sniffing for news. I told him what I'd heard about Boysie's pirate days. If he did end up writing about Boysie for the *Trinidad Guardian* column I missed it. From how he talked I think he took Boysie's nastiness personally. He'd let down all the Indians in Trinidad. That I could understand.

But Boysie's crew took any and everybody, irregardless. A dark-skinned fella in my shop last night whispered how he personally made enough money working for Boysie to buy a piece of land. On one raid they found seventeen thousand dollars. Boysie took he half and Baje shared the rest for everybody.

What about the crew of that boat?

He lowered he head.

466

Firekong gunned them down. About a dozen men. We had was to scramble for iron to sink all of them.

Sick. Why he feel he could boast about that? No shame. He better watch out because just now a snake coming to bite he backside.

*

Only Pearl and Diggers know that under all the hustling I'm living day to day waiting for the knock that lands me in a cell beside Boysie. I can't eat. I can't sleep good. Doc said I'm suffering with nerves. He gave me a tablet to take, one in the morning and one in the night, with something in my stomach. Them little white pills can't carry away my worries. Police could come for me now for now. Yes, it's been months since the arrests and the trial's about to start. But all it would take is a word from Boysie and boodoops badaps, I'm in the dock. It's reached the point where I don't care what he's going to do. The not knowing is the torture. I need to look Boysie in he eye. Only then I'll know where I stand with this Bumper business.

Unfortunately, when the trial finally started, the rest of Trinidad also wanted to see the Rajah. I've never seen excitement like this in town. Quarter past seven I reached the Red House hoping for a seat in the public gallery. I couldn't even get near the place. The streets around were jam-packed. I asked a man in the crush what time he got there.

Six o'clock and it done had this crowd. I ain't know if we getting in.

A woman in front turned around.

I find police should make we form a line coming back so. You know how much people come after me and push up in front?

That got me vex.

Don't let them do you that. Push back.

Me? Suppose one of them in Boysie gang? I 'fraid.

Nah. Don't 'fraid. You by the Red House. The court here.

Lady, I ain't taking no chance.

I had to cool myself under a samman tree in Woodford Square facing the Red House. Good thing I did that, yes. Some slow-coach people from the village came and chooked in. Everybody was talking and laughing but in a nervous nervous kindna way. We didn't know what to expect from this murder trial because nobody like Boysie had ever stood in the dock. I mean this is the Rajah, king of Port of Spain, rent collector, pirate, gambling lord, big-time pimp, ole thief, badjohn, stick fighter and that is just what I can reel off the top of my head. People say he get away so far because spirit protecting him. We go see if spirit can keep he neck from breaking.

By eight o'clock the whole of Woodford Square was full, full, full. Where I was had shade and people were edging in. I had to cuss a couple. He shoved in and dropped a basket while she plonked she bottom on my dress hem. Plus the place was smelling rank. Like sweet soap scarce.

A nuts man passed. Even though it was a little early the smell of the hot nuts had my mouth running water. Today was different, the kind where if you wanted to eat fresh roasted nuts at eight in the morning, then full your belly. I called out,

A pack of nuts here, please.

He tossed a fat brown paper cone at me.

You're doing good business today.

You could say that again. I'm only selling in the square. My partner them covering St Vincent Street, Knox Street, Hart Street. All about fulling up with people and they're buying nuts for so.

All them roads?

Yeah. And people still coming.

Not long after I heard shouting. Crowds were parting and police were blowing whistle hard. I got up, straining to see. It was a big black motor car. A man behind me said that was the judge pulling in.

How you know?

He steupsed.

You ain't know the judge car?

People were throwing questions in the air and whoever wanted caught them with an answer.

What's the judge name?

It's Mr Justice Kenneth Vincent Brown.

He fair?

What fair have to do with it? I say carry them to the gallows one time and save the Crown money.

A few times well the crowds thought Boysie had reached only to find it was lawyers and other court officials coming to work. I could taste the restlessness on my tongue.

And then it happened. Shouts then all I was hearing was Boysie's name calling.

Look Boysie there!

It's Boysie!

Rajah! Look me here. They can't do you nothing.

You is the Rajah! Don't worry.

Almost as many were bawling.

You go hang, Boysie!

You done kill too much!

Judgement Day reach for all you tail!

I was straining for a little look-see but too much people. Fellas climbed trees and acted as eyes for the rest of we.

Plenty police.

Yeah, but what else?

Police hiding him. Wait, that's not Boysie. That's one of the other men they charged. Hold on, hold on, I think Boysie coming up in the back.

What you seeing?

Hold some strain.

What happen? You cokey-eye? You can't see nothing?

Lady, if you feel you can see better then climb up nah, man.

That argument was hushed by another voice.

Boysie! Right, he here now. He have, one, two, three, four, yes, four police walking with him.

Forget the police. What's he looking like? He fat? He thin?

Man looking sharp like a razor blade. You can't tell he's coming from jail. Light blue suit and a blue shirt. Blue tie.

He wearing that long gold chain he used to pose with?

He have little size. And he hair comb neat neat.

I ain't seeing no gold chain. Look, look, he carrying a book in he hand.

A book? Boysie does read?

It's a Bible. Boysie going to court holding Bible. You ever see more?

He even Christian?

Yeah. I think so. He married in the Catholic Church.

You lie.

How much you want to bet?

Before you could say Robinson Crusoe he was inside the Red House and show done. Thousands of we left outside had no choice but to wait for news from inside the Central Criminal Court. Mid-July sun ain't easy and not a breeze was blowing. Even while sheltering under the tree I was perspiring. But the day no one ever thought could happen had started. Mr mighty Boysie Singh was in the court and if this trial went against him he was going to hang. Surely if I was going to face a charge police would have come for me by now?

MANA LALA

This is Trinidad all over. People for so. We're talking about men fighting for their lives. Have respect nah, man. Go to work. Mind your own business. Instead they're spread out liming with one set of food baskets and ice coolers. I felt more tension in the public gallery. Them newspaper people here just stirring up more commess. Every little thing that happens they're busy running out to write it up for the news.

I don't know how to feel. If Boysie ends up hanging it will be what he deserves for all the bad he do. But say what you want, he's been a good father from the start. Chunksee will grieve for a long time. Me? I'll only ever be as happy as my child.

The court usher saved seats so at least we can see what's going on. I was 'fraid to ask so Chunksee went over to Boysie's lawyers. We wanted to know how much days this trial will take. They and all clueless because seems Trinidad's never had a trial like this before. At least two weeks we're here and likely more.

Big legal words batted between the lawyers and the judge. I couldn't make out what was really going on. An old fella leaned over and asked we quiet quiet if we needed him to explain anything.

What happen? You is a bush lawyer?

He shook Chunksee's hand.

Toby's the name. I in court most days. I does come and hear the cases. But I could tell you something. In all my years I've never seen one like this. I done meet people from all Mayaro and Point Fortin who in town just for this.

I took in the small, obzokee man in a shirt straining to button and a pants hemline like he was expecting flood. I bet he ain't know one ass but I smiled sweet. Well more fool me. By the end of the trial we were chatting like family. He real know plenty.

The big man for the Crown they call the Solicitor-General was sweating like a hog. Every few minutes he stopped to mop he face. Whereas Boysie's suit made out of nice flowing gabardine the Solicitor-General had on thick wool. He acting like this is England. Plenty fancy words fell from he mouth and even with old man Toby putting in he two cents I could only make out half of what was going on.

As best I understand it, the Solicitor-General's side of the story was that Bumper, Philbert Peyson, was last seen in the flesh 14 April with Boysie, the four others charged, plus a boy we does call Loomat who ain't get charged. All of them left the Dorset in Boysie's jitney and went Cocorite. Boysie jumped out there to bring around he boat from the Leper Asylum jetty.

Mr Solicitor-General said Boysie reached back and between them they cuffed down Bumper, tied up he hand and foot, then latched him to a seven-foot piece of iron. Loomat stayed in the jitney while they went off with Bumper in the boat. Half-hour later they came back and headed to 55 Queen Street. The next part I'm sure is truth. He told the court that them fellas last the whole evening until all three in the morning drinking and whoring it up loud loud. Poor Chunksee. He face was getting longer and longer as the Solicitor-General talked he talk.

Beta, things now start. Hold up.

*

For Chunksee's sake I got up early, bathed and did puja. Incense filled the whole house.

Thanks, Ma.

I asked Mother Lakshmi to guide the lawyers them.

In court Boysie's side let go a real different story. Boysie went straight to Besson Street Police Station, called the police inspector one side and made a statement. Apparently he knew that Loomat and Durant had killed Bumper. Durant and Bumper both loved up on Loomat. All two were fighting to see who could get the bai. Well, I never heard thing so. But it got worse. Durant gave Bumper a roti laced with poison. Only when that didn't kill him that he got Loomat to mamaguy Bumper and take him to Point Cumana. Once Bumper reached there Loomat and Durant killed the man and threw him in the sea.

The Solicitor-General didn't say that Boysie's story was a fat lie. Plenty in that story could well be true. But he thought what really happened was that Boysie used Loomat as love bait to reel in Bumper to the spot where the gang of them did the murdering.

Setting people up to fight one another? Lying? Tricking? That's Boysie's speed. And weighing them down and throwing them in the sea? That is Boysie self. I tried to keep my face from showing anything.

Newspapers were cover-to-cover pictures from the trial, with a big one of Boysie alone looking like a movie star. Chunksee read piece that said Boysie was the best-dressed man ever to face a capital charge. And the crowds weren't easing off. Every time I passed through Woodford Square to and from the court nothing but people, people, people. Endless food-selling and bookies up and down hustling. I heard a man say this case was better than going cinema plus it's free.

Chunksee, all these people here and I ain't seeing Doris. You see she?

She ain't coming.

But why? That's he wife.

They separate.

You lie? When that happened? And how you ain't say nothing?

He looked away and waved at somebody. I couldn't help myself.

I could've told your pa that marrying she was a big mistake. And I hope you're watching and learning. Don't bring home no red woman for me. You hear?

I jooked he ribs.

So what happened? Boysie do she something?

He groaned and rolled he eyes.

You can't have news like this and ain't tell your own mother.

Tookra tookra the kheesa left he mouth. Soon as they'd charged Boysie, Madame Doris ups and left she lawful wedded husband. For a policeman. How long she was horning Boysie? What get me is how she's still walking around alive. I will have to tackle one of he gang for chapter and verse.

Meanwhile in court we heard things that made my stomach turn. Bumper had been in the water a good few days. He skin turned white and like fish ate out he face. Lucky thing he had a birthmark. This is the kind of thing that does happen when you live bad.

The next set of witness had me confused. We bush lawyer explained the lawyers them were showing how everything that happened was linked up. The piece of iron tied to Bumper was a boat engine plate owned by a mister named Chanika Samaroo. But he reach in court to say that Boysie was the one in charge of the boat and the only person who could have gotten that piece of iron. I never realised you had to go through all this kind of thing. Well, pressure in Boysie's tail. Chunksee held my hand.

Ma, you need to do more puja. He can't hang.

As we were walking through Woodford Square to find a route taxi home I spotted Helmet who has worked for Boysie donkey years now. He must know about Doris and she new man.

Yes Mana Lala, girl, all of we vex too bad.

How Boysie letting that pass? I'm surprised more people ain't talking.

No, they're talking. I tell the Rajah we could take care of that. No problem. He's in jail but the rest of we free to come and go as we please.

But it's a police she have.

Funny thing. That is exactly what Boysie said. What surprised me was he wasn't surprised. All he would say is, I know, and, left she there with she policeman. He go deal with she later. I don't know what he mean by that. We could leave

he alone and just take care of she red ass but Boysie don't
want we to touch a single hair on she head.

Now that got me blue vex. The neemakharam woman getting
away free so? Boysie ain't even troubling me but if I brought
home another man it would be blows in my tail. She real have
he brains tied up.

*

Gradually the trial began to turn in Boysie's favour. I was glad
but the whole Doris thing ate away any good feelings I might
still have had for Boysie. His lawyers mashed up the witnesses
like they were grinding dhal. One of them we does call Bag of
Rice gave big talk that he saw Bumper get in the jitney with
Boysie at a certain time. The whole court was laughing when the
lawyer proved that Bag of Rice can't tell time. I could see Boysie
enjoyed watching that. Fellas like Bag of Rice used to well get a
raise from Boysie. Now look at them turning against the person
that helped them.

One witness I never wanted to see was that blasted George
Harper, who nearly caused Chunksee to dead in the sea. And
really, Boysie and Chunksee had saved he life. This is how he does
show thanks? He had a story and a half, starting with Boysie owing
him money and he went looking to get it. Boysie wasn't where he
thought so he walked home to Carenage passing Cocorite. As he
passed the Cocorite gas station, he heard the radio station signing
off making the time eleven in the night. And lucky George Harper
then saw Boysie's jitney with Loomat sitting inside. He thought
Boysie might be in he house so he went further up the road.
Nobody was home. He walked back to the jitney and that was
when he bounced up Boysie and he partners. For all that Boysie

didn't have the money to give him. And you know George Harper would not budge from that story of walking up and down in the night. I smelt a rat. Watch me, that dog must be make some kind of backhand deal with the police them. No way he came up with all that chupidness by he-self.

Worse yet, a watchman who used to be in the police took the stand. He was guarding land next to the Lepers Asylum jetty and could make out all the backwards and forwards of Boysie them. As Boysie listened, I saw him loosen then take off he tie. For the first time he looked under pressure. Chunksee elbowed me.

Ma, you ever know watchman to wake whole night? All the watchman I know does sleep hard.

Apparently not this one.

I hear the bookies giving good odds that Pa will hang. What you think?

I wished Chunksee had a different father. Should I lie or call it like it is?

They still have a chance, beta. We holding on by a piece of string but we're holding on. He ain't hang yet.

DORIS

People can talk until they're hoarse. They aren't living my life. Bumper floating up at the yacht club. Boysie on a murder charge that Harry thinks will stick. The Lord's sending a clear message: move away from all this commess. It's no big revelation we're done but I still have to tell Boysie. What I keep telling Harry is that if he was going to hurt me, it would have happened by now. Even from jail he could have ordered his partners to beat me. Or worse. I've always known that. Maybe things are so far gone he's stopped caring. But then again, Harry's working in the same police station that investigated Bumper's murder so he must take an interest. What to do? Part of me feels he deserves to hear it from me and part of me is frightened too bad. On top of that Harry's begging me to stay in the background. The island's small. Of course people will know I've moved in with him. If Boysie got off because Harry's tied up with me that go be real pressure. He will lose his work for sure for sure.

Doris, write a letter. I will make sure it reach him.

A letter? What I putting in a letter so? Dear Boysie, I've met a man ten times sweeter than you. I gone. Love, Doris.

He laughed.

This ain't no laughing matter.

Harry put his head back in the papers. No help there.

For a long time I racked my brains. What to mark down in an end-of-marriage letter? Who will take which blame? I'm not taking all. That man do me plenty wrong. Look at me without even one child to call my own. Boysie didn't care. He came with a boy child already made. And people will point their finger and call me a Jezebel. What about all the horn he was horning me with every Mary, Martha and Beulah who gave him a sweet eye? For a time it looked like we could've been the king and queen of Port of Spain. He was definitely king but he didn't want Queen Doris except for show. Well, enough is enough. To besides, he might be dead soon.

What I ended up writing was straightforward. We're done. We know we're done. I will keep out of his way and I'm grateful he's kept out of mine. The marriage has been over for some time. I didn't hear a word back. Nobody threatened me. Nobody tried to interfere with Harry. Maybe this is wire bend, story end, but with Boysie you never know for sure for sure.

*

It's as if we've always lived together. I think it's Harry's solid, calm self that means so much to me. He will be the same today as he was yesterday and will be tomorrow. With Boysie I never had a responsible and reliable man to count on. I didn't know that quiet could be so hot. Harry's Besson Street Police Station is under heavy manners these days. People are watching to see if they're playing fair in Boysie's trial. Of course Harry's straight like a rod but the station as a whole ain't got the best reputation. Once you work there you're tarred with the same suspicion. As today is the start of his weekend off I'm spoiling him little bit. Nothing Harry likes more on a Saturday than to cock up his feet, read the papers and have me bringing coffee, hot bake and saltfish buljol. Today he's getting all that plus I'm bubbling a pot of sancoche for lunch.

While he was reading I settled myself on a kitchen stool, turned on the radio, and started peeling and cutting up ground provisions from a side. If you're doing this soup you might as well do it properly. I have the works: dasheen, eddoes, green banana, sweet potato, English potato, cassava, carrots, ochro and three whole corn I've broken into small pieces, are heading for the pot. After the stress of the last month it feels good to lose my mind in something normal. During my marriage I always had help with the cooking and cleaning and didn't realise what I was missing. But then again Boysie didn't appreciate if I did things in the house.

It's soothing to be in the kitchen standing in front my big soup pot frying up onion, garlic with fresh green seasoning. Once the onions have an edge of brown in goes the pig tail I boiled early this morning, some salt beef cut up and the two cups of yellow split peas I soaked since last night. Throw a Maggi cube in the pot, water and cover. I am not a cook who can say put exactly this amount and cook for this time. I watch and taste and taste and watch. Whatever the pot asks for, I add.

Must be half-hour later I added the ground provisions, fresh coconut milk from a grated dry coconut, and checked the seasoning. My tongue wanted salt, a tups more Spanish thyme and we're good. I left it on a slow fire and went to check on Harry.

Darling, what you reading?

Only one thing in the papers. Boysie and this trial.

I picked up his empty cup.

More?

Harry held on to my arm.

Don't go nowhere. Sit down by me.

Harry, I have a pot on the stove.

It can wait, doux-doux. Give my neck a little rub down, nah.

He turned so I had no choice but to give him a massage.

Oh luss. Nice. Right there. Ouch. Feel how my shoulder knot up?

I don't feel a single knot.

That's all right. Keep doing what you doing. Yes. Nice.

I was kneading his neck and shoulders. True they were stiff but if I said anything I would be here massaging for the next hour. I never met a man who loves touching and cuddling like my Harry.

Enough. My pot will burn.

He grabbed my arms and pulled me close so I was hugging him from behind.

Turn off the stove and let we go inside.

It's broad daylight. Behave yourself, man.

What if I don't want to behave myself?

And suddenly I realised I didn't want to behave either. I whispered,

Go inside. I'm coming.

Maybe it was the unusual timing or the fact that recently Harry's been too tired for relations, but this was the best we've had in

I can't remember how long. People find him too straight. More fool them. How to put this without embarrassing myself? Harry is the first man I ever had who bows to a lady in the bedroom. Today he made up for not bowing in nearly a month.

I was still grinning like a chupidee the next day when I went to church. God is good, yes.

ROSIE

Well today I managed to beat all them pushy-lal to get inside the public gallery by carrying on just as bad. None of this lining up decent decent. That done. Soon as I saw the police looked like they were opening the public gallery I rushed and edged inside. From the square I've been seeing Boysie in the distance as he comes and goes from jail to court. He's always fenced in by police and acting like a movie star being protected from rowdy fans rather than a man who might be meeting he maker sooner rather than later. As star boy every day Boysie's sporting a different colour suit with the shirt, tie and even socks matching. Somebody should remind him that this is a murder trial not a beauty pageant.

In the public gallery my bottom had barely touched the seat when a woman rushed me.

Aye, do fast and move. That's my seat. I there since the trial start.

Well today I'm here.

Just try. I go call security for you.

Oh sorry, ma'am. I didn't know your father own this bench.

I done sized she up and it's only mouth she have but I couldn't risk being thrown out. I quickly looked around for another seat. Near Boysie's son, Chunksee, and Mana Lala who I recognised from the papers, had a space so I went for that.

Thanks.

Mana Lala shook she head.

Don't take she on. She does talk ignorant to everybody.

My heart was racing. Should I tell her I knew Boysie from before she was on the scene and he left me for she? Just then another commotion began. Boysie them were taking their places in court. He waved to the public gallery. Did he see me? He must have done. My eyes bored into him, willing him to watch me. He looked to my left and to my right and left me out. All I need is a few seconds to clear up this thing once and for all. I will park my bottom here. He's bound to look round this side sometime.

Once court started Boysie ignored the gallery. My eyes flicked constantly from the witness stand to Boysie. Giving evidence today was a man-boy named Rahamat Ali who people know as Loomat. Barely any hair on he face, Loomat turned up in short pants held up high on he waist by a thin belt and a short sleeve shirt. This pissing-tail youth was busy sexing two ole hard-back men like Bumper and Durant? Young people today growing up real fast, yes.

Give Loomat he due. He might not have the age but he sure had guts. Loud and clear, he told the court that Boysie and he gang killed Bumper exactly how the court had already heard. He witnessed every last thing. I heard Chunksee whispering to he mother,

He lying. Why they listening to that buller man?

She shook her head.

God help him.

From inside the court we could hear the roar of noise coming from Woodford Square as news spread of Loomat's testimony.

The court ain't so big that Boysie could have missed me but he never once caught my eye. That is Boysie all over. What he want from me? Is torment he like tormenting my soul?

*

For the next week I pushed my way into the public gallery. Mana Lala, always there before, gave me the seat next to her. I tried to catch Boysie's eye and every time he refused me. True that with each day my name wasn't mentioned I relaxed a tiny bit. I don't know how court does work. Until this trial's over I feel my name could still call anytime. Why wouldn't Boysie put me out of my misery? At least look at me. I'm right here next to your son and he mother.

Boysie's lawyers took their turn and tried all how to trip up Loomat. Like he'd practised in front a mirror because every time they threw a hard question the youth would turn into a parrot who only knew three words to be repeated over and over: I don't remember. I don't remember. I don't remember. The lawyers couldn't get him to say anything other than he story or I don't remember. When he finally left the stand I thought that's it. Boysie and them men heading to the gallows.

Last man for the Crown was a Police Inspector Bleasdell. Boysie's lawyers claimed this big-time inspector had coached Loomat while he was in the station teaching him to parrot, 'I don't remember.' But it was just something they threw out there without hard proof that maybe the police had harassed Loomat to give evidence against Boysie. The defence lawyers made jokes with the inspector asking if he knew what people called Besson Street Police Station.

I do not.

Well, Inspector, let me enlighten you. It is known to a certain class of society as 'the Pacific'. Would you like to know why?

The inspector didn't say a word.

It's known as 'the Pacific' because it is where they 'pacify' people.

Even the other side lawyer held back a little smile that edged out the corners of he mouth.

*

Two whole weeks have passed and this trial ain't done yet. The crowds have definitely thinned out. By less people I mean that when I walked through the square I wasn't tripping over people. Plenty people were still there. And as the days have gone on Mana Lala and I, as two Indian women sitting next to one another, have exchanged a few words. Hard to believe a decent woman like this tootoolbay for Boysie.

If people were getting tired of Boysie's trial tying up the whole of Trinidad that exhaustion clean vanished the minute Rajah himself jumped on the stand. This was it. If he didn't sell me out now then I could rest easy. I will give him this: for a man dangerously close to the gallows he was cool as a Christmas breeze. And he real knock them good coming and going. He even made a joke about the calypso that's playing on the radio steady these days. It had a line about Loomat saying he see Boysie. Skinning he teeth, he told the court,

Loomat say he see Boysie. But hear what. Boysie say he ain't see Loomat.

Well, the gallery buss out laughing. The judge threatened to put all of we outside if we didn't hush.

The Rajah made the point that plenty people say they knew him when he hardly knew them and he barely knew Loomat. Furthermore, he was here charged with Bumper's murder on 14 April. Unless he and the fellas were talking to a jumbie, Bumper was alive and well that day plus the following day. Good point and no mention of me anywhere in this story. So far. And this idea that he went to Inspector Bleasdell was upside down. The inspector came to him asking a set of questions. Whatever answers he gave Bleasdell joined up together and called it a statement. On the off chance that all he'd said hadn't convinced the jury he was an innocent man, he wanted them to know one more thing. Even if he wanted to go out in a boat on 14 April he didn't have one to use. All he fishing boats were busy working and the *Marie Louise* had engine trouble.

The final nail came when Boysie's lawyer brought up the tides for that day. The time Boysie was supposed to be bringing in a big boat to shore and then moving with all six men in it, the tide was low low. No way, no how, he could physically do what the Crown claimed. Boysie had hit them for six.

My name didn't pass once. Boysie had spared my life.

MANA LALA

I don't know if I understand this correct. The jury hear all what we hear. The judge talked to them long. Still them couldn't make a verdict one way or the other? They tell the judge that he could lock them up until thy kingdom come and they still wouldn't all agree the same answer. Before we had time to catch we-self good the judge called it a mistrial. We have to start again. All over. From the beginning. I went home, and this is not like me, but I took a good shot of rum and went in my bed. The energy it took to go to court every day. Keeping strong for Chunksee. Making sure everybody can see Boysie's family present and correct. And now to go through all of that again?

I woke and my dream was there with me. A few old ladies were sitting down chatting in a dark place. They weren't happy at all at all. I think they were talking about a man who dead already. Dream so mean something. I found Bull, the whe-whe man, and put a dollar on number two for old lady.

But Mana Lala you just tell me you dream the dead. That is what you should play. Put the dollar on four.

I couldn't tell who the dead was exactly. I just had a feeling they were talking about the dead. The part I remember is the old ladies talking.

All right. I'll put it on two. When you lose your money don't come bawling and want to give me pressure.

Bull, hush your mouth.

That was all ten o'clock. Midday the mark buss. Before Bull reached I already knew.

You bring my money?

He laughed.

Mana Lala, you dream good. Next time you dream remember me.

Bull handed over my winnings.

How Chunksee holding up?

He there. Busy.

Yes, I hear he was selling off the boats and them to pay for the court case.

Ask Chunksee about that. All I know is that lawyers does charge a pound and a crown.

He leaned in close and dropped his voice.

Don't hurt your head. If they try and say the Rajah's guilty in this retrial the boys in the club go fix up.

How you mean fix up?

He looked around to make sure nobody was listening to we business.

Don't say nothing but if they bring back the wrong answer we blowing up the jail wall and taking Rajah to the Main. We have boat and thing ready. No way them fellas going to the gallows.

I stepped back and shook my head.

And then all you will end up in jail.

Hush. It go work. Anyhow, don't say I tell you nothing or is my head go get chopped.

You know me. I don't go about spreading news.

Bull spotted somebody he knew, hailed them and left. The problem with them fellas is that they would really try something poohar if the new trial goes against Boysie. Plain poohar.

The little change I made from whe-whe called for a nice cake. Soon as I reached home I cut a big piece so I could eat and feed Subhagya Mausi same time. I went in she room, ready to lime. The old lady was sleeping sound and never going to wake again.

DORIS

Chunksee passed by me the other night. I appreciate the visits. I don't ask if his father knows. This son would never do anything to upset his pa so I have to believe Boysie doesn't mind. Harry was working so we sat down talking like old times. For a young man he's taking on too much. No meat on them bones. Poor thing, it's not easy being Boysie's only child, yes. I told him to take better care or he'll be no use to Boysie or anybody else. And what was this I heard about a girlfriend?

Tanty Doris, where you does hear all this news?

Trinidad's small. You can't hide.

Seriously, who tell you I have a girl?

I smiled.

A friend saw you in the cinema with a girl she know named Tricia. That's your lady?

He avoided my eyes. But I saw the blush.

Yeah.

Yeah what, mister?

No amount of teasing could coax him into giving me more.

All right, but you know I will find out. I have my ways.

Tanty Doris, behave nah.

So, I could ask, what's the latest with your father?

You hear Pa take in sick?

This stopped me one time.

What happen?

Everything. Fever, headaches, throat hurting, tired all the time, hair falling out, he can't eat. Everything. In and out hospital.

They know what's wrong?

Maybe the drinking all these years. I don't know.

Look, at least in jail they'll march him off to the doctor. They can't have him sick.

I suppose.

Don't worry, son.

Chunksee scratched his head.

They can't set a new trial date until he's better.

It was supposed to be next month?

They're saying maybe three months. September time.

Spin round twice and September will be here.

He cracked his knuckles.

Stop. That does make my blood crawl.

For spite he cracked another finger and laughed when I blocked my ears.

It's not like my finger's breaking.

But it sounds like it.

All right, all right, I'll stop.

But tell me something. Boysie's good in he-self or the sickness have him down?

He does be quiet quiet. Most of the time Pa reading Bible or praying. The life come out of him. I feel he's so unlucky that wet paper could cut him.

I blew on my hot tea before sipping.

I don't know if you remember when you were small. The three of us used to read Bible together.

He smiled but didn't say anything.

All nine o'clock, half past nine, my bed like to see me and it was coming up to that time. Chunksee knows he's always welcome but I still begged him not to forget me.

I know you can't say hello to Boysie for me but I want you to know he's always in my prayers.

Later I lay in the dark worrying. What if Boysie's really sick and doesn't make it? So much I should have done differently. Maybe I could've helped him choose another path.

Harry crawled in minutes to eleven. As I was still waking I went to the kitchen, made him a cup of Ovaltine and told him about Chunksee's visit.

It's good he comes to check you.

How come you never told me Boysie was sick? What if Boysie dies before the trial?

Harry sighed.

I can't take that on now. I need my bed.

All right, I know, doux-doux. You're working yourself into the ground these days. Take off the light and come sleep.

Normally he is the one who cuddles me but tonight I loved up his back. Staff shortages have my man working too many double shifts.

Sleep good, Harry. Tomorrow you don't have to get up early.

Why?

Ain't you have tomorrow off?

They might still call me in. You never know.

Hush.

He turned around.

Boysie's real sick?

I should be asking you.

I snuggled into his shoulder and hugged him tight.

Chunksee says it's bad.

Harry sighed.

Sleep now.

Instead he pushed himself up on the pillow.

The inspector didn't talk truth in court.

I bolted upright one time.

What?

Loomat.

What about Loomat?

He was in the station the whole time. They locked up the boy so he knew what to say in court.

No. That ain't right. The papers said police showed proof Loomat signed in and out of the station.

Doris, you don't think I know that? And I'm telling you he was there for days force-learning when to say, 'I don't remember.'

Have mercy. And what about that book? You know. Help me. What is the book he had to sign?

The station diary.

Yes, the station diary. Ain't everything's supposed to be marked down in there?

They hide away the real station diary and carried a copy in with the false entry for Loomat.

Jesus, Mary and Joseph. That mean both police and Loomat perjured their souls. It's straight to hell for them.

Don't say that.

Why I mustn't say that? Boldfaced liars. And under oath. A man could hang because them lying.

Oh, so you don't think Boysie lied too?

Don't try that. Police is the law. If they're willing to lie then you can't expect anybody else to tell the truth.

Harry didn't answer back.

So how long now you know about this and keeping it from me?

Silence. I got out the bed.

I can't believe this.

Where you going, Doris?

To fetch my Bible and sit down with the Lord. You sleep.

I'll get up with you.

Leave me alone, please.

Some days you wake up good good and have no clue that by the time night falls everything in your world will be upside down. Again.

ROSIE

He never once looked at me. He wants me to know that so long as he's breathing I owe him for keeping quiet. I'm not sorry that Bumper ended up in the sea. Eye for an eye. The least Etty deserved. Yes they're having a retrial when the doctors them declare Boysie's fit. I'm bracing myself because Boysie's going to do this all over again just for his sick fun. Don't be fooled by how much money he made. It was always power that man's soul loved most.

Meanwhile life was settling down. Since Etty disappeared all I've felt is rage. The trial took away some of that anger and put a sadness in my bones that I've not had before. I feel cold even when the day making hot. My snake spirit like it's coiled up hiding. Often I'm surprised to find my cheeks wet with tears I didn't know were leaking out my eyes. No rest until this new trial happens and we all draw a line under Bumper and Boysie. If talk in my shop is anything to go by it seems Trinidad can't move on either. Town wants Boysie to hang for Bumper and whoever else he might have sent down the chute to die at the bottom of the deep blue sea.

*

As the first trial was a whole month in court and no verdict I really wasn't expecting any big set of crowd for the retrial. Well, papayo, people like peas. I was early enough to get in the gallery behind Mana Lala and Chunksee. Both looked like worries take them. I said hello and made a joke about the dark bags under she eyes. For a second I thought, but wait, she's suffering over

Boysie? Turns out an old aunty she was caring for had passed not too long ago, and she was taking it hard. Chunksee's come down even smaller. It can't be easy having your father on trial for his life. And we had a newcomer. Way behind in the back was a red woman, well dressed up, that people said is Boysie's ex, Doris.

We are all waiting to see if Boysie and them have anything new to add since the first trial. In two-twos he lawyers came out fighting. They claimed the police stitched up Boysie. And they had proof. The station diary, the real station log, was not the one the big inspector had showed the court before. That was a fake. You hear that? A fake. Three police took the stand to say that the station diary the court was now seeing was the correct one.

Well, mas in the place. All Boysie's people started partying because that showed Loomat wasn't a star boy witness after all. Police had held him for three days drilling everything into he head. And all that time the police inspector was in and out of the station questioning Loomat. Me ain't take to Loomat but oh gosh, man. The threats they used on that poor boy made my snake hiss.

From Port of Spain to Cedros to Toco to Mayaro people are in shock that the police could behave so underhand. Me ain't trusting the police again. Them just like the bandits they're locking up. Of course we ain't know how Boysie's lawyers found that station diary. Who inside Besson Street station grew a conscience? Better late than never, I suppose.

Hands down, this must mean Boysie's getting off scot-free. But what is that for me? All the time I was thinking they'll hang him and that will be the end. What if the only thing he's going to die of now is old age?

*

I wasn't planning to come for the final day of the trial. The shop's been neglected and things needed fixing. The Rajah must get off after that commess with the station diary. When Boysie comes back to terrorise people it will be the police them fault because they got him off. And he'll come for my tail. Rent collection and anything else he wants.

Yet I couldn't resist going to hear the verdict for myself. Have mercy I was glad I came, yes. If anybody had told me what happened today I would have said they lied. Justice Gomes told the jury a set of dotishness then sent them to come up with a verdict. Even without an ounce of legal brains I could tell he had it in for Boysie. Hear nah, man, he passed over Loomat and loved up on the police inspector as if everybody ain't know he lied through he teeth. But what I couldn't stomach was him instructing the jury that the station diary was only in court to help the inspector refresh he memory and nothing else. To accuse the police of trying to frame Boysie for murder was beyond he imagination and he was not having it in he court. Ain't judges not supposed to take sides? Like this one was absent the day they were teaching that in judge school.

While the jury did their deliberations I stretched my legs in Woodford Square. The mood was grim. I hadn't settled myself good when we heard the jury was coming back. Somebody said they were quick because they didn't have a choice but to let Boysie go free.

They found him guilty.

Mana Lala was crying. Chunksee looked in shock. Doris was biting she lip. Justice Gomes asked all the accused if they wanted to say anything to the court before he passed what we knew would be the death sentence. Boysie shouted and carried on like he gone mad. All outside in Woodford Square they heard him say,

I am not sorry for myself but for the people of Trinidad . . . I am innocent of this act and I have been framed. Since 1925 the police force is behind me either to kill me or get me a long sentence in prison. In this case the gentlemen have brought me in guilty. Later on these gentlemen will be sorry – perhaps six months from now. These witnesses have come in this court and swear us away! Murder cannot hide! There will be somebody to reveal this murder; it will be revealed six months from now. These gentlemen wherever they pass, in any form, in any way, in their clubs, in their homes, it will be whispered in their ears that I have been framed by Bleasdell.

Port of Spain went crazy. Boysie's going to hang. People were bawling and others rejoicing. In the shop that night fellas said they saw grown men faint when they heard the verdict. Mostly though people were over happy. All the wickedness of the Rajah on land and sea was done, done, done.

As long as I live I won't forget when they put handcuffs on Boysie and led him from the court. It's over. We done. He's going to the gallows. That is the end of that. I can finally grieve my Etty.

MANA LALA

According to Chunksee the lawyers them not frightened about this guilty verdict. They done lodged an appeal. Only trouble is the men go have to sit down in jail and wait until the judge them hear the appeal and decide whatever they're going to decide. This is costing Boysie plenty plenty money. How you think them lawyers have big house and big car so? They does dig out poor people eye.

Because of the money problem I knew Boysie would send for me to visit him in the jail. My summons came through Chunksee. The bai's supposed to sell everything to pay the lawyers them. I dressed up nice, creamed my foot, put powder and went into the Port of Spain gaol. Today was my day to face Boysie and I ain't go lie. I was frightened like hell.

I'd never been inside a jail before and I'd prefer not to go again. The guards treated visitors like we were criminals too. Twice we were searched and real rough too. One woman visiting she boyfriend didn't get in because she mini dress was showing a little too much leg. A fella in a sleeveless merino went back home. The rules say your whole arm can't be exposed. As I was in my good good dress and an orhni covering my head they hardly noticed me except when I said who I came to see. Then they well looked me up, down and sideways.

Two guards carried we into a room where the prisoners were already sitting at tables. They warned us not to touch the men. Parcels had to be inspected and were given to the men after the visit. Boysie had a table away from the others giving him more privacy. I wasn't surprised. By hook or crook that man's always getting special treatment, even in jail. He would have bribed them guards long time.

Aye, Boysie. You're all right?

Mana Lala, girl, I real glad to see your face. It look like the Lord been keeping you safe.

How long we have?

Half-hour but the guards in we section does always give we more time.

I wonder why.

It's six months I'm in there and even they think that's too long for an innocent man to wait. So they cut we some slack. Thank you, Jesus.

I have to say he looked good. He'd lost a little weight. God and Bible reading helps him pass the time or so he said. Once he felt he'd softened me up he began bossing me around. Call this one, call that one, sell this from the shed. Make sure they give a fair price. The three thousand cash I have Chunksee should give the lawyer.

Hold your horses, Boysie.

I'm going too fast for you?

No, but we have a problem.

I took a deep breath.

I don't have the three thousand.

He eyes opened big, big.

What? What happen? Somebody thief you?

I took another deep breath and we eyes made four.

I gave it to Mrs Rodriguez.

Who? Me ain't know any Mrs Rodriguez. She working for the lawyer them?

This trial and the one before bring all kind of people out of the woodwork. Some of them even came by my yard. You remember what you did with Mr Rodriguez? He wife and children suffering. Over a year now he gone missing. Me and you know she ain't ever seeing he face ever again. Ain't Boysie?

I never gave anybody with that name passage. And what happen to you? Like you feel because I'm in here you can talk to me all how? I want my money.

I surprised myself for getting this far. Might as well say all I had on my mind.

Well, you remember two Chinee fellas you gave passage? It was after you dropped them off that you handed me the three thousand. A Chinee fella was in the public gallery every single day of the trials hoping something might come out in court so he could find out what happened to he father and he uncle. Nobody ain't know where they gone.

Boysie stood up and banged on the table.

Neemakharam. Where my kiss-me-ass money? Eh, bitch?

A guard came rushing over.

Cool yourself nah, Rajah. Don't talk to the lady so.

Boysie was shaking. If I wasn't sitting down I might not have been able to stand because I was shaking too. But I held on. He can't do me nothing from in jail and he can't get fellas outside to do me anything. All them men he'd had on the payroll haven't had funds for a while because the money's only paying lawyers alone. Boysie 'fraid the truth. He's done.

I gave the Chinee people money to Mrs Rodriguez. Every last dollar.

When I done with you, Mana Lala, you'll wish you were never born.

Still shaking, I got up.

Guard, I want to go now.

Where you think you going? I say you could leave? You ain't going nowhere until you tell me how you getting my money to me right now.

Guard, please.

Boysie was so quick. He gripped my neck like he was trying to snap it in two. I couldn't breathe. Guards were on him but he held me. I thought I was going to die right there. Three big officers had to hold down Boysie. I was heaving and bawling. They dragged Boysie away. He never stopped yelling that he will kill me. If it's the last thing he do in life, he will kill me.

ROSIE

I nodded to Malcolm.

All the commess looking to starting back again.

Yeah. Look so.

Papers say 10 January for Boysie's appeal.

Ain't it's only the lawyer and the judges them? Nothing for we to see.

And how long this next case lasting?

How I go know? I look like a lawyer to you?

A lady wanted me on the dry goods side so I left Malcolm.

Morning Miss Carol, how them pretty girl children you have? They good?

They there. Troublesome as usual.

Don't say that. Them is the best children in the village. I say so. And how the husband? He well? Somebody tell me they see him walking in the road the other day and they nearly ain't make him out. We go have to call him Fat Boy just now the way he come down small small.

He good. Watching the sugar. That's how he lost all that weight.

Tell him to lose some for me.

Where he gone? He was right here with me. Must be get

catch in some ole talk about whether Boysie will hang.

What you think?

Girl, I so fed up I feel I could hang him myself. He just like killing. No doubt in my mind. Even if the police didn't do things exactly by the book the Rajah's still guilty. Anyhow, enough of he. Give me a piece of saltfish, a pack of green tea and a pack of Crix.

Hold on.

I went in the box and brought out what I had.

The last two.

She pointed to the larger piece. I wrapped the saltfish in brown paper.

But Rosie, my worry is that if Boysie ain't do it then the wrong man hanging. Two wrongs don't make a right.

Like you said. He's a real badjohn. For sure he's killed plenty other people we don't even know about.

Yeah but then the police have to bring them cases. Let him hang for who he murdered.

You stay there with that fancy talk. Town fed up of that man posing as king of Port of Spain or whatever he does call heself.

Carol's husband stepped into the shop.

Morning, Rosie. My wife's talking too much?

Try shutting us up and see what go happen to you.

They strolled off looking happy happy. I think Carol's in the majority. People want Boysie and he gang to disappear and take all their madness and badness with them. But it's hardly so simple. To besides, what I hear is that the Boysie we knew and the Boysie today are two different human beings. Seems Boysie and God friending now. Apparently in jail it's one set of hymn singing, Bible reading and Boysie preaching. He won't be the first to conveniently find God when things hard then drop Our Saviour soon as he's saved from whatever misfortune was coming. I've seen that over and over. But I have to be grateful. He could have dropped me in it and he didn't. That ain't no small thing.

MANA LALA

The appeals came through for Boysie. It took three tries but he's not guilty. Chunksee's celebrating with friends. I tell myself that if it's kill he going to kill me when he come out, then that is my karma. No use hiding or living 'fraidy 'fraidy. I did what I had to do. Even Chunksee was vexed with me because he was under pressure to get money for lawyers. Thing is, he wasn't interested in hearing my side of the story. I don't blame the bai. Look how long it took me to see who Boysie really is and all what he do.

I worried for nothing. The appeal released him and same time they jailed him again for receiving stolen goods. And like the police making sure he can't form a next gang. They put Baje on a boat and sent he tail back to Barbados. Trinidad ain't seeing he face again. Firekong make a next jail. Ten years for shooting somebody. They should lock him up and throw away the key.

Chunksee believes this whole trial, retrial and appeal have changed he pa.

He come down small, Ma. Hardly eating and quiet quiet. Sometimes he will get up and read the Bible or pray. And he ain't have a cent to he name.

What you telling me that for? You expect me to take he in?

He kept quiet.

Let him go find he wife. See if she and she new man will give him a room.

You don't have to get on so.

I was going to say something but I didn't. This is my little house and Boysie ain't coming here. End of story.

ROSIE

I've been thinking how to remember Etty. It's hard that I don't have a body or know where she died. I thought of getting another pair of the earrings she was wearing and keeping those on all the time. Maybe I'll do that. I've also been making an effort with long-time lovers like Malcolm back in my bed. Since when I have to use a word like 'effort' when it comes to loving? That's how it feels these days.

We're expecting the verdict in the Boysie circus today at ten o'clock. This is the appeal of the guilty verdict. They had to appeal when the judge ignored the station diary. I just want it to end. I brought out the radio and somebody hooked up speakers. Now inside and out the rum shop people can hear clear clear. To hang or not to hang. If the decision was made in rum shops like mine up and down the island, Boysie them would've seen the gallows from that very first trial. Never mind what we know now about the crooked police. All of them do wrong and somebody must pay.

Radio Trinidad's special, extended news announced to a packed rum shop that the Court of Appeal has reversed the guilty verdict. Boysie them are free. The judges went down hard on the Crown. Loomat got a good cut-ass trophy for lying. A little child could tell Inspector Bleasdell and Loomat had lied through their teeth. Mr Justice Gomes got he own cut tail for the way he directed the jury on the station diary. If I was Gomes, man, I would be so shame that I would haul ass back to England on the next sailing.

I heard grumblings. People are worried Boysie will start back

511

the pirating up and down the Gulf of Paria. From what I hear he ain't have money for boat and gun and thing. Diggers shook he head.

Fair is fair. Them fellas lied in court and Boysie deserves to come out a free man.

He was drowned out by disagreeing voices fed up with the way Boysie had spread he badness. Loomat lied, yes. But in between had some real truth. If only people knew how much.

The one set of people who laughing plenty are Boysie's lawyers. Someone bought the *Marie Louise* and I hear that is how he managed to pay their fees. Watch me, give Boysie a year or two and he will make back that money and buy an even bigger, faster boat. He still has enough friends in low places and now he's not guilty he will make new ones. Have mercy, yes, because I don't feel he story's done yet. So long as he leaves me alone what I really care?

DORIS

I've never been busier in the church. Everything crossed I get an annulment if I can prove that I didn't have certain knowledge of Boysie's ways when we married. And the shameful truth of course is that the marriage was never properly consummated. Never. Not once. People won't believe a ram goat like Boysie never do his wife but that is exactly how it is.

I will need to face Boysie about this annulment. I'm ready. Now he's won the retrial I can see he's not coming after me. I wouldn't be surprised if he knew about me and Harry from the beginning. The scoundrel used me. Me with a policeman? Look how that worked out. He would never have gotten off if it wasn't for me. I was more use to Boysie when I was horning him than I ever was as his wife. That is a hard thing to swallow.

One of my church friends brought news that Boysie's now preaching the gospel. After all that's come out in court? Who he think he's fooling? If he truly felt the Lord's mercy that is something else. For that I deserve a little credit. Without me he would never have seen the inside of a church or read the Bible.

I know I won't bounce him up just so because he's living somewhere in San Juan near his didi. Dead broke. Chunksee went to sell the house and realised my name was on the deed. Half was mine. With all the gambling and running down woman I knew a day might come when he'd gambled away everything. So said, so done. Like most men Boysie didn't believe in women having house and land. But I got my share, thank you very much. At least I got that from Boysie.

MANA LALA

Somebody outside was calling good morning. I peeped from the side window. It looked like a beggar. I hoped the person would get fed up and go bother the neighbour. But this one wouldn't leave. Then he called my name.

Mana Lala, you're home, girl? Mana Lala?

But for the voice I would never have known it was he.

Boysie? That's you?

Yes. I there calling long time. You was in the back?

I stayed in the gallery. If he's coming for me he will have to break down the gate.

What you doing here dressed up in white and holding Bible? You can't fool me.

I ain't trying to fool nobody. God saved me and now I does spread the word.

Well, I'm glad for you.

So, you ain't even going to invite me in for a cup of water?

I looked at him steady.

I ain't reach to make any mischief. I don't do them things again. I've been a free man nearly a year now and I only want to do good for people. Please, I have something to tell you.

He looked so thin and meagre I could choke him before he

choked me. This might be a real chupid move. Slowly I walked into the yard and unlocked the gate.

Don't frighten. I ain't come to do nothing bad.

It's you I'm worried about. It look like one hard breeze and you go fall down. Like you take in sick again or what?

We sat in the gallery. For a few minutes he sipped water and recited some Bible verse. Chunksee was due any minute. He can take Boysie away.

It's nearly three years to the day since I won my appeal. Time to make my confession. I want to make it to you.

Me? No, sir. I ain't nobody pundit, priest, imam, nothing so. Don't tell me nothing. I can't believe it was that long ago.

Please. You is the only-est person in the world I want to tell. Please.

The man eyes were watering. I sighed.

All right, say what you want to say, then go.

It's about Bumper.

The court could give any verdict they want. I know you killed Bumper.

Please hear me out, nah.

Best to do that or he go be here whole morning and I have things to do.

It started a few weeks before Bumper ended up dead in the sea.

Boysie told me that he planned to rob Brooklyn Bar in Woodbrook. The crew was Bumper, Baje, Firekong and a partner named Leo. He dropped them off by the bar and was cruising around in the jitney. Bumper was lookout and the rest went inside. But like the place was harder to get in than they thought. Baje and Firekong came outside to wait for Leo to finish picking the lock. Boysie saw police heading for Brooklyn Bar so he took off with one speed to collect the men. As he was rushing he saw Bumper, Mr Look Out, walking hurry hurry away from Brooklyn Bar. By he-self.

Boysie got there just in time for Baje and Firekong to jump in the jitney and they dust it down the road. Police held Leo.

You know that loyal boy refused to say boo to them? Not a single name. He alone got charged. In fact he case was going on same time as mines. I paid for a good lawyer but the judge gave him three years.

Boysie said he knew Bumper had to be the informer and he was worried about what else Bumper would tell police because he knew plenty.

So that is why you killed him?

I didn't do it myself. The fellas did it. My bodies never float. Never.

I got up.

I hope it made you feel better to tell me but time to go, Boysie. I can't hear more. You and God make all you peace.

I'm not that man now.

I done, Boysie. Enough.

He got up, slowly walked to the gate and out into the road. If I never see he again that would suit me. He bodies don't float. That was a confession? I ain't hear sorry come out he mouth yet.

ROSIE

Don't ask me where the time's gone. To me it was just the other day but it's a five whole years since Boy Boy passed. Granny kept up a prayer meeting to mark the day. That was pressure. A young fella gone before he time and my Etty taken before we could make something together. Pearl came for the prayer meeting and spent a two days by me. We sat down in the shop together, snacked on boiled tipi tambo in season, and prattled nonstop. She quarrelled about she sisters not doing their fair share caring for their sickly ma and pa. They feel because she ain't have man, or a string band of children, she ain't entitled to a life. I cussed about a new fella I've added to the mix. Crazy man thinks he can own me and wants to tell me who I can and cannot see. I had to put him in his place. You can't know what the scene is, come in with your two big eye open, and then want to change me up to suit you. Nah, nah, nah. He getting marching orders soon. Thing is he sweet too bad. I go take a last few rounds before throwing him back in the water for a next woman to catch.

Otherwise I can't complain. Diggers reached by me with news that had me and Pearl reeling. He heard that Boysie was still making waves but now as a preacher man. That's like somebody saying snow falling in San Fernando so he went to see for he-self.

Man, Rosie, girl, I wouldn't be bringing news if I didn't hear it with my own two ears and see it with my own two eyes. Boysie turn holy. He wearing all white like he's a priest and preaching long long sermon. All three hours the man does be preaching.

You lie.

Ask Lou. I reached home in shock. Boysie humble humble. He give me a blessing and all. Tell me to follow the ways of the Lord. You ever see more? Boysie telling me that.

Pearl got in first.

Hold, hold on, pedal back lil' bit. Which church he in?

Not as such. You could say he have he own church. Apparently the Lord does direct him. Anywhere it have a place he will set up. I saw him in the empty plot next to Habib's Variety Store in Chaguanas. End of every meeting he does announce where the next one is, the date, that kind of thing.

It had people?

Yeah, oui. At least a hundred. Probably more.

I cleared the empty beer bottles off the counter.

Well, I ain't buying that holy thing. Church is business. Who want to bet the scamp doing this to make money? Taking poor people money to line he pockets. That's Boysie all over.

No girl. He didn't take up collection. People can change, you know.

People, yes. Boysie Singh? He's in a class by he-self. And don't forget how much years he harassed me for he so-called rent. So long as he give this village a miss I'm good.

Diggers' face looked constipated. I poked him in the chest.

What?

He looked at the ground.

Tell me.

Well, he was real happy to see me and said he will make sure and come by we village.

Pearl laughed.

Diggers, when people find out you invite the man they go chase you from here.

Maybe he'll forget.

Boysie's coming? The only question is when. My snake bones rattled.

I didn't have long to wait. News reached the village a few weeks later that preacher Boysie Singh had announced his next service. God spare life it will be five o'clock on Thursday, 10 April. And the best part? It will be in front Rose's Bar. I ain't see the man in years. He ain't ask my permission. Nothing's changed. If Boysie wants something he does take it and none of we get a say in the matter. End of story.

I'm bracing myself to face him. He's come down in the world. Unfortunately that doesn't mean he memory lost away too. He wasn't guilty so should the police be looking for the real murderer? Maybe he knows a woman with a grudge who stabbed Bumper in front witnesses? After preaching he might pass by the police station with that information.

On the day small groups started gathering from all four o'clock. I thought there would be more excitement, laughing and chatting like at the trials. Today felt serious, more like a funeral. And there was something else hanging in the air. It took me a while to realise what it was and then it hit me, boom.

Fear.

Boysie still frightened people, me included. As if to prove the point I heard a mother telling she child,

> Go and sit down over so and be quiet, you hear? We come to listen to a man named Boysie Singh and he don't like children making noise.

> What he will do if I make noise?

> He will carry you in a boat far far and throw you in the sea for shark to gobble you up.

Poor thing. I hope she doesn't dream a shark tonight.

Someone shouted and the crowd of about eighty people moved to the roadside. I spotted a man in all white on an old autocycle coming towards the shop. I whispered to Malcolm next to me,

> You ain't find he's looking real old. And look how he in head-to-toe white. Hat, shirt, pants, everything. Almost like a ghost.

> At least this better than when he was wearing only black.

> Boysie like to dress up. Remember them fancy suits he had on for the first trial? Thought he was king of Port of Spain.

Boysie rode up to the shop balancing what looked like a fold-up table and a bundle tied to his autocycle. The days of a jitney or a Buick with driver and he badjohn bodyguards are gone. I took in front before in front took me and went outside.

> Afternoon, Boysie.

He put down he jahaji bundle and came through the crowd to me smiling up like I was he long lost sister.

Good afternoon, Rosie. Blessings of the Lord be upon you and your house and all who dwell within.

Thanks.

You don't mind if I preach the word in front your shop? I could set up over here in the flat?

You here now. Do your thing.

The crowd parted as Boysie began setting up without seeming to notice. On the table covered with a white tablecloth he laid out a Bible, a conch shell, two coconuts, a candle and some fake red flowers. Diggers whispered I should put out two kerosene lamps because it will soon get dark and Boysie will be in the middle of preaching. I put him in charge of all that. Suddenly Boysie's voice boomed out.

Let us begin by praying and asking God for He heavenly mercy. Repeat after me. Lord have mercy.

We all replied with,

Lord have mercy.

And so it went. Someone whispered loud loud that this was what the Catholics called the Litany of the Sacred Heart of Jesus. I remembered the ex-wife Doris is a big-time Catholic. That must be where he learnt to pray.

Well I never thought I would say this but Boysie could well preach. For a good two hours the man talked like the spirit had him. He told the crowd he'd been humbled by the Lord. Judges and police had been specially sent by Satan to test him. But Jesus Christ, with love everlasting, had redeemed he soul and that's why he preached the word of the Lord. As I listened I felt he believed what he was saying. Boysie may very well have changed, yes. Nearly three hours he kept us. I elbowed Diggers.

Invite him to stay for a drink. We have things to talk.

Diggers nodded and went to Boysie while I served customers. Everyone was in awe. I caught snatches of talk.

Aye, that was something else.

Now, that is preacher.

He convinced me.

I really feel he have love for Christ.

All you notice he didn't take up collection or beg for donations?

Good over evil. The Lord spared him the gallows to spread His word.

I was so busy that it was maybe half-hour before I thought to myself that Boysie should be done packing up. I looked for Diggers.

Ain't I tell you to bring we visitor for a drink?

He said thanks but he wanted to go home and rest.

I stared at Diggers.

Boysie gone just so?

He nodded.

He didn't want to come and ole talk?

Diggers smiled.

He went hurry hurry.

I've thought about tracking down Boysie through the preaching. Other days I know it's not worth the botheration. I'm not even sure he's still preaching. They had something in the papers about police holding him for not having a licence for the old autocycle he was using. What is the truth, eh? Only Bumper can say what he did Etty. Even if I could ask Boysie that excuse of a man would never tell everything. My healing's happening fine without any of them. But I'm still struggling to know how to keep she alive other than behind my eyeballs.

MANA LALA

Well, it looks like Boysie's killed again. Chunksee's in shock. Me? I just shake my head. I knew that God thing was only going to last so long. What confused me brain is how they could hold Boysie and he partner Boland without a body. They supposedly killed some lady, Thelma Haynes. But police can't find she body nowhere. That reminded me of what Boysie had said that he bodies don't float. Still, if you're going to court I thought you have to show the dead dead. Me ain't have no education but if I go missing and people can't find me how the court could decide I was murdered? I might be liming and forget to come home for a month.

Radio put Thelma Haynes as a Guyanese. She could've been fed up with blows every Friday when she man got pay and dhakolay rum. I bet she tell she-self it's best if she go back home, yes. Guyana big. Up in that bush he would never find she. The case will get thrown out. Imagine having to live with sending them to hang and then later Thelma Haynes turned up hale and hearty wondering what all the commess is about.

ROSIE

Rosie girl, give your boy a beer let me cool myself little bit.

Teach, tell me something, you there pushing ninety and you still going strong. What's your secret? Tell me nah.

He leaned across the counter, checking left and right to see who listening.

When people ask me I does tell them ground provisions and the Lord. But let me tell you what does really work.

He whispered,

Never say no to a chooks or a small whisky every night. Done.

We well laughed.

Hopefully you have plenty years in you yet, Teach.

Anyhow Rosie, I see we friend make papers again. Is kill he like to kill so?

I ain't know, boy. A second murder charge when you get off the first one by the skin of your teeth? I never hear anything so. And just the other day he had religion. If I get this straight Boysie and a Boland somebody get charged with murdering Boland's baby mother, Thelma Haynes.

Another fella pushed in the talk.

What I want to know is where the body? You ever hear madness so?

Well that started off the whole shop. Somebody said remember who we're dealing with. If Trinidad have a man that could make a body vanish, it's Boysie Singh. I mean, we still don't really know if it's fifty or five hundred people he killed when he was pirating in the Gulf of Paria. Apart from Bumper nobody ever reach back to tell on him.

> Well, once that trial starts they might as well give the island a month holiday. Let we sit down in Woodford Square and take it in.

Teach gave me a wink.

> As long as you ain't closing for a month. A man does get thirsty.

> Don't worry. I go be right here.

*

Every morning for the past month my eyes open by three and I can't fall back to sleep. In the day my heart does be beating fast fast and I have a constant dull headache. But I couldn't stay away. This case is too familiar. Etty is Thelma and Thelma is Etty. Both vanished like ghosts and nobody can find them. Both include Boysie. Here's the thing that's really got me feeling all how. No one cared that my Etty was missing when I knew in my heart Bumper had a hand in killing she. And why? The answer sticks in my throat. Who will waste their time looking for a missing orphan whore?

Thelma they looked all over for, put it in the papers that she was missing. Now they're making history charging Boysie and Thelma's boyfriend even though they don't have she body. This woman had a baby daughter. She had a respectable job. They say she could well dance and should have gone away touring all America and Cuba. Thelma is a body the law doesn't mind touching, protecting. I wish Etty had had she day in court like this Thelma. So although I'd rather not sit down in the courthouse watching Boysie on trial for murder again, I'm doing it for Etty.

I reached early o'clock to make sure of a seat in the public gallery. Chunksee was there without Mana Lala. But the biggest shock was when they brought in Boysie. Last time I saw that man was nearly two years ago. He didn't look great then but he had stamina. Now he's like a bloated boobooloops ready to explode. I heard somebody whisper hard that Boysie's sugar was so high that he was in a coma recently and police had to rush him to Port of Spain General. And to think that this man in a tatty old shirt and pants, looking like a pauper, used to harass my soul for rent and threaten to burn down my shop. Boysie today and Boysie from the last murder trial are two completely different fellas. Them fancy suits gone. He ain't flashing gold rings and a heavy gold watch. Two different-looking men but evil same way.

Now the next man in the dock, Boland, he looked like trouble. And them popping muscles he's sporting there? One good cuff and he could lick way a woman easy easy. But what the police had to say made all of we jaw drop open. Boland went to the police and reported Thelma missing. They didn't take him on. But he kept going back like he was haunted. Then he told the police he had a dream that she dead and in Wallerfield near a bamboo patch. The police checked all round. No Thelma. They probably thought he wasn't too right in he head but still, she was missing. Police only arrested them because Boland walked into the police station and said point blank that Boysie killed

Thelma. And hear why: Boysie wanted a sacrifice to keep the spirit of some sword happy. The sword spirit got vexed, acted through Boysie and, well, it ended up killing Thelma.

During the trial a friend who Boland trusted with he problems said Boland wanted to get rid of Thelma to please the Lord. They were living in sin and he couldn't do that and get the pastor work he was eyeing up. Like everybody gone mad or what? Any halfway loving God would have preferred him living in sin to killing the lady.

DORIS

Although Harry hasn't done police work a good four, five years now he still has friends in Besson Street. It was hard to stay in the force with suspicion hanging over his head day and night. Until the station diary was put in front the court every man jack in Trinidad thought Boysie would hang. And well, as we're together, they put two and two together and made six. For a while there I even thought we would break up. But we prayed and made it work. Life's not easy, especially if you try to do the right thing. And speaking of the right thing, it took time but my annulment came through. Harry can't wait to get married. But I can. I really can. Marriage bit me hard once already.

To besides, even without all this confusion Boysie does still weigh on my mind. Not all the time but he sneaks up on me now and then. I didn't expect after all the preaching he was doing he would ever land up in court. Again. For murder. Again. Like this is a habit? He forgot they hang murderers? Harry's police partners said Boysie handed them their case on a silver salver. After arrest, he and Boland Ramkissoon were put next to one another in the cells. The Boysie I was once married to would have been cool as ever and kept his mouth shut with police everywhere. Not now. The two men were cussing and throwing blame left, right and centre loud enough for the whole station to hear. In all this Boysie told Boland Ramkissoon that once they kept their traps shut the whole Thelma Haynes thing would pass. He'd made sure they'd never find her body. To make things worse they raided Boysie's lodgings and found the missing woman's watch. That man was always dangerous. Look like now he's also become dotish.

ROSIE

I thought it could go either way but they're going to hang. Better late than never. I wonder what whe-whe numbers to play? Boysie's made history, yes. Nobody is going to forget that he was the first man in Trinidad to get tried for murder three times. Maybe the correct whe-whe number is three. And of course he made big news beyond this small island. Never before, in the whole British West Indies, have the courts said guilty of murder when them ain't actually seen the dead.

They let him say his piece in court after the jury foreman gave the verdict. My Lord, he well carried on. He said he's a land shark that does have to take the blame for any and everything bad in Trinidad. Whether he's sick in he bed or out at sea, people bound to say Boysie Singh do wrong. All I say is if you leave cocoa in the sun you better watch out for rain. He got off when he killed Bumper. Now he go hang for Thelma and we ain't know for certain she dead. I guess it evens out in the end. It's not just me will sleep easy. The whole of Trinidad fed up with he wickedness. That's the real reason he's walking to the gallows.

MANA LALA

No child should have to go through this but I had to put down my foot. Chunksee can cry how much he want. Do it at home. Don't let me see he eye watering outside. Tomorrow, 20 August 1957 once we reach the Royal Gaol two of we must be strong. Them papers waiting to pounce for a picture of we bawling. Chunksee shouldn't give them that satisfaction at all at all. I ain't have tears left for that man.

Police helped get we through the crowds. One set of macos. It's not like we can see anything from the road. But people fass with they-self, blocking traffic, carrying on like it's fete happening. I searched to see if I recognised any of Boysie's old friends. One-one here and there were paying their last respects. Madame Doris didn't show she face. My mind flashed on Popo. I hope she spirit in peace now.

Somewhere deep inside, behind them thick, high walls, Boysie Singh and Boland Ramkissoon are waiting for the hangman. I can't imagine what it must be like knowing your life's about to end. The men killed. Now the Crown's killing. Anyhow, what I know. Me ain't have no education. Them judge and big people know best.

ROSIE

As I drifted off to sleep, my mind on the hanging tomorrow, I felt my Saapin slithering into being. I was squashed into a thick skin, stretched and pulled long. My legs and arms were caught inside this tube of skin and for a moment I panicked that I couldn't move. I breathed in and out slowly and, yes, it was all right. I was steady on my stomach. Nothing to 'fraid. I was sliding along nasty cold concrete, smelling shit and pee as if it was inside my nostrils.

Boysie was sitting on a cot talking to he-self and scribbling away in a Bible and on scraps of paper. I had a good view of his swollen feet in old rubber slippers. The little toe had an open sore on it. Look how he come down. The white prison pants hem had come loose. Rice grains and gravy stains marked the front of his white prison shirt. I heard him say as he wrote,

Son, I have offended God most grievously.

So, he was writing to Chunksee. That's good. And it seems like Boysie wanted Chunksee to think he was truly sorry for all he did.

I went back and joined my hands with wicked persons. I
must be punished by God and this is my portion.

I watched for a long while as he wrote and muttered things I didn't always understand. He didn't look frightened. No trembling, no tears. If anything, I was the one feeling miserable. If I was going to dead tomorrow, how much things would I regret?

Suddenly keys were jangling and heavy doors swung open. A priest sat next to Boysie. Well, that is when the show started. I would not have believed it if I wasn't right there in the cell with the two of them. They were discussing Boysie's last wish. You know what he wanted? I bet nobody will believe me. Boysie Singh wanted to be baptised and received into the Holy Roman Catholic Church right then and there in the Port of Spain gaol. I ain't lying. Well that was a shock. So he think he could still get in the Pearly Gates? That is boldfaceness.

The priest asked him to confess he sins. My head pushed forward a little, unravelling. This skin was holding me in, pinning me down. I didn't want to miss a word. Papayo, Boysie's confession was like me checking stock in the back room. He killed, cheated, blackmailed, beat up people, thief plenty, used women and flung them away. Mana Lala's name passed in that. The priest asked for the names of those he killed. Boysie asked for an excuse like a schoolboy who didn't learn his spelling. Please, Father, he's too stressed to remember everybody. At least he admitted it was plenty.

But most importantly, he wanted the priest to know that he would hang for Thelma Haynes and he didn't kill she. Boland was another case. That was for he conscience. And this was the shock that nearly killed me. Boysie told the priest he operated with certain rules. It should never have happened but twice he'd killed a woman. One was somebody named Popo. The other name was impossible to unhear. He said it. Etty. It took all my muscles to keep in the vomit rising through to my mouth and the shit that wanted to come out the other end. In the effort to keep myself together I lost consciousness. When I came back to myself they were still talking about the women. He was saying they weren't respectable women. Just two common whores.

Dawn light was filtering through the high cell window. The priest and Boysie prayed together while I slid out of the cell looking for the gallows. So strange to move without being seen except by a few rats, and they sprinted soon as they glimpsed me coming. Keeping to the dark edges I slithered along the narrow corridors towards the low, nervous voices of prison guards. Boysie's name spiked the conversation. I spied them in a small room and almost fell into the gallows opposite the guards.

I hadn't thought about what it would look like so I shouldn't have been surprised. Maybe I thought it would be bigger and outside in full view of anybody overlooking the prison courtyard. Instead the gallows were in a small, dark room like a big latrine. A frame at one end had steps which Boysie would soon climb to sit in a chair. The hangman's rope was thrown over the top of the frame and formed a noose for Boysie's neck. This was a different necklace from the gold chains he used to wear. When they were ready a trap door would open beneath the chair and Boysie, chair, everything would fall down in the hole. He would hang there, neck broken until they were sure he was dead dead.

As I climbed up the frame to the rope, my skin burned and pinched. I had changed again. Me and the rope were now identical. I chewed and swallowed the noose as fast as I could pretending the dry fibres were sweet sugar cane. Now my body was the noose coiled into place waiting for John Boysie Singh.

They placed me around he neck and pulled me so our bodies touched. I knew I could take his weight. This was how it should happen. Suddenly the trap door sprang open and the chair fell and Boysie fell and for a second I saw him on the cot writing to Chunksee but then Etty covered my mind. I tightened my body against his weight and felt the moment he neck cracked. I pulled harder, tighter to be sure Boysie ain't ever coming back.

THE TRINIDAD MONITOR

PORT OF SPAIN, TRINIDAD
THURSDAY, 10 APRIL 1975

Death Notice

Don't you know I love you but am hopeless
at fixing the rain? But I am learning slowly . . .

so that when you emerge . . .

I would have learnt to love black days like bright ones,
the black rain, the white hills, when once
I loved only my happiness and you.

Derek Walcott ('Dark August')

DORIS SINGH (NÉE DE LEON), age 61, passed away peacefully at home on Tuesday, 8 April 1975. Funeral mass will take place on Saturday, 12 April 1975 at Holy Cross RC Church, Santa Cruz, at 10 a.m. The family thanks you for your many expressions of support and kindness.

ACKNOWLEDGEMENTS

Thank you Zoë Waldie my agent, Louisa Joyner my editor, and Luke Neima my first reader. You each pushed me to be my best writing self.

My friend Professor Kenneth Ramchand is the expert on Boysie Singh and I learnt at his feet. Teresa White's family stories about Boysie Singh were inspirational. Dr Ricky Van Kalliecharan was a huge support with the Bojpoori language references. To my village, you know who you are, thank you.

Karol, Habib, Zahra, Fia and Mara Subjally, you cheered me on through every minute of this book. Your love seeped into the cracks and made me whole again.

In remembrance of my friend and fellow writer, BC Pires, gone too firetrucking soon.